"You say
never b...

He stepped forward while she took a step back, the smallest gasp pushing past her lips as she came up against the wall behind her. "But you deserve to be." Unable to resist the pull of her, his hand found the back of her head, moving her until she was at just the right angle. "If I may?"

Nodding, she leaned toward him and her eyelids drifted shut. Desperate for the closeness she offered, he lowered his lips to hers—carefully at first, so they could grow accustomed to each other, and then with greater urgency.

Moving closer—so close that no space remained between them—he kissed her as if he were drowning and she was his lifeline, as if she were the oxygen he needed in order to breathe. He poured every painful moment of solitude he'd endured for the past five years into that one singular moment, savoring her sweetness while imparting his own everlasting affection to her.

She was like a burst of sunshine warming his heart and soul and yet there were still too many barriers between them—barriers that kept him from taking more than he'd already done . . .

By Sophie Barnes

HIS SCANDALOUS KISS

Secrets at Thorncliff Manor

SOPHIE BARNES

WITHDRAWN

AVONBOOKS

An Imprint of HarperCollins*Publishers*

Map courtesy of Sophie Barnes.

His Scandalous Kiss. Copyright © 2016 by Sophie Barnes. All rights reserved. Printed in the United States of America. No part of this book may be used or reproduced in any manner whatsoever without written permission except in the case of brief quotations embodied in critical articles and reviews. For information, address HarperCollins Publishers, 195 Broadway, New York, NY 10007.

First Avon Books mass market printing: August 2016

ISBN 978-0-06235891-2

Avon Trademark Reg. U.S. Pat. Off. and in Other Countries, Marca Registrada, Hecho en U.S.A.
Avon, Avon Books, and the Avon logo are trademarks of HarperCollins Publishers.
HarperCollins® is a registered trademark of HarperCollins Publishers.

16 17 18 19 OPM 10 9 8 7 6 5 4 3 2 1

Terror has struck the heart of France, first with the brutal execution of King Louis XVI, and now with that of his wife, Queen Marie. The helplessness I feel, knowing that many more lives will be lost, is beyond compare. My prayers go out to them and to their families with the solemn promise that my comrades and I are doing all that we can in order to end this.

The diary belonging to
the 3rd Earl of Duncaster, 1794

Chapter 1

Thorncliff Manor, 1820

A gentle breeze stirred the air, carrying with it the smooth murmur of violins as Richard gazed out over the terrace of Thorncliff Manor. The grand estate and guesthouse where his parents and siblings had chosen to spend the summer while their own home was being renovated, sat solidly at his back—a welcome retreat for those who were wealthy enough to afford it. Standing to one side, Richard watched the guests, their gemstones scattering the torchlight while feathers bowed and swayed.

Although they wore masks, he was able to recognize a few of those present. Certainly, he had seen many of them from his bedroom window since arriving at Thorncliff a few weeks earlier. But there were those whose acquaintance he'd never had the pleasure of, like the young ladies who'd made their debuts since 1815—a year he would not soon forget. In any event, it was a long time since he'd spoken to any of these people. Some, he reflected, had been friends once . . . His heart beat slowly, dulled by the lead that now flowed through his veins.

It was briefly forgotten when a gentle voice spoke at his shoulder. "Your company is much appreciated this evening, Mr. Heartly."

Turning his head, Richard glanced down at his hostess, the incomparable Lady Duncaster. "After all . . ." His words faltered—no doubt from lack of usage. Inhaling deeply, he took a moment to compose himself before trying again, more slowly this time. "After all the effort you have gone to on my behalf, it would have been rude of me to stay away." Rigidly, he glanced in her direction, his nails digging against the palms of his hands as he clenched his fists. There was more to be said. "I . . ."

"Yes?" she queried.

"Please don't use my real name, Countess. Tonight I am Signor Antonio."

"Of course." Her eyes gleamed with the mystery of a shared secret. "As to all the effort you mentioned, your presence here after so many years of absence has made it all worthwhile." A wry smile appeared beneath the edge of her over-embellished mask. "Besides, I have always wondered what it might be like to restore the masquerade ball to its former glory."

Dipping his head, Richard acknowledged her comment, the gesture encouraging her to continue.

"In my youth, my husband and I experienced a traditional one in Venice—before the Venetian Republic fell. . . . Masquerades have since become popular in other parts of Europe, though they generally lack the flamboyance that I initially fell in love with." She shook her head somewhat wistfully, then straightened herself and earnestly asked, "What do you think, *Signor*? Is it grand enough?"

In Richard's opinion the extravagance was overwhelming, but since he knew this was probably the effect Lady Duncaster was aiming for, he said, "I think you have outdone all other masquerades, my lady. *I* am certainly impressed."

Chuckling, Lady Duncaster slapped his arm playfully with her fan. "You are quite the charmer. Do you know that?"

"It is accidental, I can assure you," he told her dryly, belatedly realizing that he probably should have thanked her for the compliment.

She tsked in response. "I sincerely doubt that." Taking him by the arm, she guided him slowly along the periphery of the terrace while the orchestra on the opposite side struck up a new tune. In no time at all, the center of the terrace had been occupied by guests who wished to participate in a country dance, their theatrical garments a testament to originality rather than taste. "I know your parents, Signor, and I very much doubt that your mother would have raised a son capable of being anything but a perfect gentleman."

Richard grunted disagreement. "I have lived a solitary life these past five years," he said slowly. "My brother and secretary have been my only contacts to the outside world since my return."

"Which is why I am so honored to have the pleasure of your company. Truly, it is greatly appreciated."

"Even if I am not as polished as I once was?"

Her mouth tilted a little. "You are just a little rusty." She patted his arm with her gloved hand. "It will come back to you soon enough."

He wasn't so certain. "I feel as though I no longer belong."

"Nonsense. But if we can find your brother then perhaps you will feel more yourself. Hmm?" She looked around.

"I must confess that he is unaware of my attendance this evening." When she turned to him, eyes wide in question, he said, "I should like to keep it that way."

"May I ask why?"

Breaths came and went in slow succession before he settled on the right words. "The last thing I want is for him to get the wrong idea—to presume that I have come for the purpose of socializing or, God forbid, dancing."

Her eyebrows rose in two sharp points. "Dancing is not so bad and neither is socializing."

"I am only here because of your insistence. As Grandmamma's dearest friend, it would be difficult for me to deny you. Which is not to say that I am unhappy that I came."

"She would be proud of you, if she were still alive."

"I hope so," he muttered. "You have offered me a refreshing change, but I am afraid that dancing and socializing would serve no purpose."

"I suppose that explains why you have not asked *me* to dance," Lady Duncaster said as they moved toward a shadowy corner where a stone bench stood vacant.

"You see! My manners have completely deserted

me." He waited for Lady Duncaster to sit before lowering himself onto the empty spot beside her. "Perhaps a minuet would not be too appalling, if I can still recall the steps, mind you."

"Forgive me, but was that an invitation?" In spite of her advanced years, it was impossible to deny that she had spirit.

Richard grimaced. "Lady Duncaster, would you please do me the honor of dancing the minuet with me?" As much as he dreaded it, he owed her the courtesy of asking.

"I would be delighted to," she said, looking pleased. "See, that was not so difficult, was it? But if you step on my toes I shall slap you."

Although Richard feared that she might have to follow through on that threat, her words eased his tension. "In public? Surely not!"

"I find that the older I get, the less I care about protocol, or the opinion of others, for that matter."

"Then we are of like minds, my lady."

Lady Duncaster snorted. "My dear boy, you are entirely mistaken! If you were really as indifferent as I, then you would not feel inclined to hide away as you do. That said, however, I must compliment you on your choice of costume. The complete concealment of your face beneath your Bauta mask and tricorn does add a distinct air of mystery to you."

"I am not the only one here who has chosen to dress in traditional *Carnevale* style," he said as he watched a couple strolling in their direction. Both wore full masks with silver lips and eye-slits outlined in blue. Just like Richard, their hair and necks had been covered by tightly fitted silk hoods, revealing not an inch of skin and making it impossible to discern their identities.

"True," Lady Duncaster agreed, "but unlike everyone else here this evening, there is a certain darkness about you that I am sure the ladies will find compelling."

"I have no interest in attracting any woman's attention." The evening black had been a given. He could not imagine himself in anything else. And the mask . . . well, he had his reasons for that as well. "I am not a coward," he told her gruffly. "I am just not ready for all the attention my return to Society will likely incur." She nodded in understanding, but said nothing further. He was grateful for that.

And as silence settled between them, he allowed his gaze to sweep across the terrace in silent observation until it finally found one singular lady who stood like a beacon in the night due to her lack of embellishments. "Who is that?" Richard murmured close to Lady Duncaster's ear.

"Who is who?" she asked, searching the crowd.

"The lady standing next to the potted rose tree." She was turned sideways, offering Richard a view of only her profile as she spoke to an older woman.

"Considering the number of potted rose trees on this terrace, you will have to be more specific."

"Of course," Richard said, surprised that he hadn't noticed. "I am referring to the lady in the . . ."—he struggled for an apt description—"whitish gown with gold along the bottom." It was a very plain gown, he noted, not as puffy as the rest. It had no frills or lace, but was cut in a simple style that hugged the torso before flaring out below the hips. It reminded Richard of something that might have been worn by a medieval queen. Rebelliously, the lady had even chosen to wear her hair down, resulting in a tumbling mass of dark brown curls that almost reached her waist.

"I see what you mean," Lady Duncaster said. "There is an elegance about her that surely would be lost if her gown had been outfitted with beads, feathers, and lace."

"She would have looked just like the rest," Richard said as the lady who'd captured his interest turned to look in his direction. The upper half of her face, including the bridge of her nose, were completely concealed by a Colombina mask that matched her gown. Even so, Richard found himself helplessly drawn to the sharp look in her eyes. And her lips . . . they were the sort of lips that a man like him—a man who'd spent five years without female companionship— would be sorely tempted to kiss. Clenching his jaw, he expelled a slow and tortured breath.

"Perhaps you should ask her to dance," Lady Duncaster suggested.

Without thinking, Richard stood, then sat back down again when he recalled that a gentleman did not stand while a lady remained seated. "Perhaps not," he said, chancing another glance in the lady's direction. To dance with her would do nothing but torment him. She would never be his. It was best if he remembered that.

Lady Duncaster shrugged. "I think you may be sorry if you do not," she said. "Take it from a woman who never held back, but who always lived her life to the fullest—there is nothing worse than growing old with regret."

Squeezing his eyes shut, Richard tried not to think of all the things that could never be changed. "Unfortunately, it does not seem as though I will have much choice in that regard." It was impossible to keep the bitterness he felt from seeping into the words.

"If you say so." She was silent for a moment before saying, "You are not the only one faced with obstacles, you know. In my experience, when it comes to romance, there are plenty of things that can get in the way of that happily-ever-after, which is why it is only the most determined who ever secure a love match. That said, I do believe it is time for that minuet you promised me. Shall we proceed?"

Reluctantly, Richard nodded. "By all means."

Lady Duncaster's insightful words had thrown him slightly off balance. His expectations of ever sharing a future with a wife and children had been dashed long ago. He'd come to terms with that, even if he wasn't happy about it. In fact, he was still bloody furious and very much aware that there was little chance of altering his fate, though he still sought retribution. Indeed, he doubted that there was anything on earth that could make him stop his vendetta. It had become an obsession over the years—a living creature whose hunger he hoped to one day satisfy. He could not afford any distraction, least of all when it would serve no purpose.

And yet, in the space of only a moment, an eccentric old lady with a towering wig perched precariously on top of her head and dressed in a gown that looked more like a bouquet of flowers than something one might actually wear, had forced a tiny piece of hope upon his mind. It made him wish that he had the courage to do as Lady Duncaster suggested and seek out the mystery lady, perhaps ask her to dance. But it was a fanciful thought—a dream that he deliberately allowed to fade.

"I must say that I have thoroughly enjoyed your company, Signor," Lady Duncaster said as Richard led her away from the dance floor a short while later. "And you danced superbly, by the way."

"You are too kind." Nothing could be truer. He'd counted five missteps in total, though not on her ladyship's toes, for which he was grateful.

"Not at all. In fact, I am quite sure that you have drawn attention to yourself."

Following Lady Duncaster's line of vision, Richard spotted a group of young ladies who appeared to be whispering behind their fans while looking his way. As soon as they noted his quiet perusal, they burst into unified giggles and batted their eyes flirtatiously.

"A lesser man might take advantage," he told Lady Duncaster disapprovingly.

"Which is why I have every intention of finding their parents and having a word with them before their daughters get themselves ruined." Leaning closer to Richard, she whispered, "I may not be as strict or judgmental as most, but I will not stand for naiveté either. Will you excuse me?"

"Of course," he said, bowing low before her. He did not grant the giggling young ladies a second glance as he walked away, his eyes searching for the only lady who'd captured his interest. Perhaps she'd gone back inside? Pausing, he looked toward the French doors and the blazing light that filled the great hall beyond. It didn't tempt him in the least, and he decided therefore that he would seek refuge amidst the shadows of the garden instead.

Crossing to the stairs, he snatched a glass of champagne from a nearby footman. Tossing back the drink, he discarded the glass and descended to the graveled path below, his long cape swirling out behind him as he went. There were plenty of revelers here as well, some strolling amidst the flickering lights of torches while others were seated on blankets spread out on the lawn. Some were even enjoying boat rides on the lake while violinists along the lakeside filled the air with music matching the tune being played on the terrace.

Stepping down from the bottom step, Richard breathed in the rich scent of jasmine permeating the air. He was just about to start forward when a lady wearing a purple gown stepped in front of him, blocking his path. Dipping into a slight curtsy, she offered him a broad smile. "My lord," she said, by way of greeting.

He didn't bother to correct her error. "Please excuse me," he said instead, hoping she'd move aside and allow him to pass. Although she was older than when he'd last seen her, he'd immediately recognized her as his younger sister, Fiona. Not even her domino mask made him doubt her identity as she stood before him now, reminding him of the sprite who'd tugged at his coattails when she was little, her hands often sticky from jam as she'd done so. He allowed a sentimental smile—one that he knew she could not see.

"Will you not offer to dance with me?" she asked.

For a second, he considered it. Indeed, his heart ached for her embrace. And yet, he could not allow himself to be tempted. She'd only want more than what he was willing to offer, as would the rest of his sisters, not to mention his mother. In all likelihood, revealing himself to Fiona would only serve to reignite the crying and begging that had taken place beyond his bedroom door when he'd refused to see them after his return from France. Gradually, their voices had faded into silence, though Richard could still hear the awful sound within the confines of his mind. He did not think that he'd be able to bear having to witness their pain again, as would likely be the case if Fiona discovered his attendance this evening.

"Not at present," he murmured.

For a moment, she looked a little stunned, but then she straightened herself, pressed her lips together and stepped past him. Without another word, she disappeared quietly up the stairs. Turning, Richard watched her until she was out of sight. Again he smiled, pleased by the cut she'd given him in response to his rudeness and comforted by the knowledge that she had grown into the sort of lady who demanded respect.

Taking a moment to assess his surroundings, Richard walked toward the lake where the *Endurance*—a large frigate that confirmed Lady Duncaster's fondness for the unusual—provided tables and chairs for the supper that would take place later.

Arriving at the lakeside, he watched as a couple moved hastily toward a copse of trees on the right, disappearing completely between the shadows. He wasn't surprised. Masquerades were after all designed to cause mischief, which was why so many people disapproved of them even as they couldn't help but be intrigued.

Turning left, he approached the violinist standing furthest away, his music swirling like stardust through the air. It carried Richard forward, all thought of revenge momentarily forgotten as the notes coursed through him, soothing his soul and calming his heart.

It wasn't until he'd come within ten paces of the musician that Richard realized that he wasn't alone. Seated on a stone bench that stood slightly concealed by a neatly trimmed hedge, was the lady he'd seen earlier on the terrace. Instinctively, he froze, his progress halted by the vision she presented. Her eyes were closed behind her mask while a smile of pure pleasure graced her lovely lips. By God, she was stunning, and it was all Richard could do not to fall on his knees before her like a subservient knight to her medieval maiden.

Instead, he studied the delicate curve of her neck and the vast expanse of pale skin below. Sucking in a breath, he forced himself not to stare or to wonder what it might be like to hold her against him . . . to lay her bare and to . . . He blinked, aware that his heart was thumping loudly against his chest. It couldn't be helped. She was perfect in every way—curved in just the right places. *Christ!* His abstinence was clearly trying to knock the gentleman right out of him in favor of welcoming a scoundrel.

He glanced toward the lake, momentarily wondering if he ought to jump in it. Probably, though the idea of getting wet did not appeal. Of course, he could simply walk away. But he did neither. Instead, he ignored what he *should* do in favor of what he *wanted* to do, and took a step forward, the gravel crunching lightly beneath his feet as he did so.

The lady opened her eyes, her lips parting slightly in surprise as she ran her gaze over him. Their eyes met, and as they did so, Richard felt some invisible part of him reach out toward her. "My apologies," he said, the words tripping over each other so hastily that he had to make a deliberate effort to slow them. "I did not mean to—"

Placing her finger against her lips, she urged him into silence, and for a moment, they just stared at each other while the music swirled around them, rising and falling in easy tones. When she patted the seat beside her and gestured for him to join her, he did not hesitate for a second, but neither did he speak. Instead, he gave himself up to the pleasure of sharing this wondrous moment with a perfect stranger while moonlight spilled across the water and stars winked at them from above. Astonishingly, it did not feel awkward in any way, but rather comfortable and . . . right.

Not until the violinist ceased playing, did Richard turn toward his companion. He had no idea of how much time had passed. "Thank you for letting me join you," he said, his words sticking together like rubber. Curling his hand around the edge of the bench, he swore a silent oath. Surely he could do better than this!

She turned to look at him, her eyes meeting his once more. They were just as sharp as they'd been earlier, but he noted now that they were also vibrant and kind. "I was not expecting company, but it does please me to know that I am not the only one enjoying the music this evening. It is impossible to listen to it properly on the terrace though. That is why I came down here, so that I could pay proper attention to it."

Nodding, he tried to think of a good response. "I am sure Vivaldi would be pleased if he were still alive and present." Dipping her chin, she encouraged him to continue. "As for me, I completely understand your reasoning. Music ought to be savored and listened to rather than heard." *Much better.*

"Precisely." The word was softly spoken and contained a hint of curiosity, or perhaps even suspicion. "Is that why you came down here as well?"

"Not exactly," he said. "I simply wished to be alone."

Her eyes widened. "Then you must forgive me. I did not mean to impose." She started to rise.

"No." The word punctured the air between them, halting her just as he'd intended. "Stay," he told her softly and with a nod toward the bench. She lowered herself back down. "If anything, *I* should be the one to leave. You were here first."

"I know, but perhaps you are in greater need of this bench than I."

The way in which she spoke, with a degree of consideration he'd rarely encountered before, set her apart from any other lady he'd ever met. "Who are you?" he asked.

Her lips curved to form a partial smile. "I thought the whole idea behind a masquerade was to remain anonymous."

"Fair enough." He considered her a moment. "But I would like to ensure that you are not married, affianced, or otherwise attached. Duels can be most inconvenient, you see, which is why I do my best to avoid them at all cost."

A soft melodious laugh broke from between her lips. "You need not fear then, for I am not attached to any gentleman in any way, nor am I the sort of lady who inspires gentlemen to resort to such drastic measures."

Her self-deprecation startled him. "Why would you say that?"

With a shrug, she turned her head away, offering him her profile as she stared out across the lake while wisps of hair toyed against her cheek. "I have always favored my own company, for it allows me the peace and quiet that my soul seems to crave. I am not a social creature, Sir, and as a result, I have never made much effort to be noticed."

"You are a wallflower then?"

She scrunched her nose a little in response to that question. "Yes. I suppose I am." Meeting his gaze again, she added, "I am also quite fond of books. In case you were wondering."

He hadn't been, but was glad that she'd chosen to share the information with him nonetheless. Wanting to cheer her, he said, "Then I am the most fortunate of men."

"How so?" she asked when he hesitated.

"Well . . . not only have I noticed you before anyone else, but I am also certain that you will be able to speak with me on matters of greater consequence than most." Seeing her eyes brighten, he decided to try a bit of banter. "Unless of course your preferred reading material happens to be romance, in which case I am entirely doomed."

She laughed, just as he'd hoped. Good lord, it seemed like a lifetime since he'd last heard someone laugh. The sound spilled over him, brightening his spirit as it lifted away the darkness.

"I must confess that I have read all of Jane Austen's books."

He couldn't help but frown. "Then you have probably acquired some high expectations—expectations that no mortal man can ever hope to live up to."

"I am not so certain of that," she told him seriously.

Unconvinced, he stared out across the lake, his mood no longer as light as it had been a moment earlier. "Romance novels have nothing to do with reality."

She was silent a moment before saying, "Perhaps if you read some of these books yourself, you will find that the heroes win the heroines through virtuous acts like honesty, loyalty, common decency, and a healthy dose of insightfulness, none of which are beyond the reach of any man."

"Point taken." Shifting, he turned more fully toward her. "But you must not forget that in these novels the heroes always happen to be outrageously wealthy and . . . extremely handsome—a state of being which certainly *is* beyond the reach of *most* men."

"Aha! So you *have* read Miss Austen's books! Admit it!" She punctuated her words by jabbing him playfully in the chest with her finger.

A shock of heat darted through him. Unprepared for it, he instinctively stiffened; astounded by the effect that simple touch had had on him. What was it she had said? With difficulty, he put his muddled mind in order and, realizing that she was staring at him expectantly, said, "I suppose I might have stumbled upon a copy or two when I had nothing else with which to occupy myself."

She smiled wryly. "Then you are probably also aware that much of the romance in these books is derived from the possibility that a woman of few means can—by proving her worth—attract the attentions of a notable gentleman. In turn, he allows his heart to lead him into marriage regardless of what Society might think of the matter. The stories are clearly based on *Cendrillon*, which of course is the perfect formula for any fairy tale."

He couldn't help but be intrigued. "How so?"

She expelled a deep breath. "Because it suggests that the impossible can be attained if we are willing to fight for what we want, make the necessary sacrifices and simply believe . . ."

Her optimistic outlook was endearing, though he was not so sure that he agreed with it. "You do not consider it wrong for women—or even men—to suppose that the path to happiness is that simple? That there is a secret formula that, if followed, will result in a happily-ever-after?"

"Based on a few observations I have made, I have concluded that love matches are more possible than we allow ourselves to believe. Especially among the middle and lower classes where financial alliances are not so prevalent."

"So what you are saying is that the less wealthy someone is, the more likely they are to marry for love?"

"It should not be the case, but I daresay that it is." She fell silent for a moment as if pondering an idea. "Perhaps the greatest problem among our set is our expectation."

Determined to keep an open mind, he tried to follow this hypothesis. "You think that marriages are doomed to fail before they even begin because couples enter into them with preconceived ideas?"

"Precisely," she said, her eyes brimming with the awareness of mutual understanding. "Aristocrats are raised to believe that love is secondary to wealth, status, and a desirable title. They are taught that they will one day marry for the latter and that they will likely live separate, though comfortable, lives as a result."

Richard considered this. He could clearly see the point she was making and found himself agreeing with her view. "Perhaps if they were not so biased from the start, then they would have a greater chance of finding common interests, resulting in more time spent together, which would inevitably lead to some measure of respect and perhaps even love."

"At the very least they would probably be more happy than not."

Impulsively, Richard reached for her gloved hand and enfolded it in his own, amazed by the sizzling energy spreading from that simple point of contact. "You must give me a name—some means by which to address you properly."

A moment of silence passed between them before she said. "When I ordered my gown for this evening, I was inspired by a painting in my bedchamber. I believe it is meant to represent Eleanor of Aquitaine, so

I suppose that you can call me Lady Eleanor, if you wish."

"Then you may call me Signor Antonio," he said, supplying her with the same name he'd given Lady Duncaster.

With a secretive smile upon her lips, she said, "It is a pleasure to make your acquaintance, Signor."

Raising her hand to his masked lips, he murmured, "Indeed, the pleasure is all mine."

Chapter 2

Mary couldn't help but be charmed by her mysterious gentleman companion. Who was he? What did he look like? He gave neither away with the silver mask he was wearing, but whoever he was, he had not thought her dull when she'd told him about her fondness for solitude or about her love of reading.

She considered him now as he sat beside her, his hand still wrapped around her own. A thrill of . . . something she failed to define . . . seeped through her, producing a most unusual sensation in the pit of her stomach. It was almost as if her insides had grown unbearably ticklish.

Inhaling deeply, she decided to make an attempt at more conversation—something concrete that she could relate to with greater ease than she could to the torrent of unfamiliar emotions coursing through her. "Since you are clearly not a fan of Miss Austen, would you care to tell me which books you *do* enjoy reading?"

"You must not misunderstand me." His words were measured, as they had been throughout their conversation. There was a wariness about him—a distinct hint of uncertainty. Squeezing his hand, she hoped to reassure him. He flinched, but did not pull away. "I think Miss Austen is remarkably talented and I commend her for turning her passion into a success. Furthermore, your assurance that her books can be enjoyed without women imagining that every moment of their lives should be filled with romantic walks and grand gestures, has helped ease my concerns."

"That is not to say that romantic walks and grand gestures ought to be dismissed," Mary told him lightly. "I am sure that most women would place great value on both."

"Would *you*?" he asked her softly.

An odd little flutter captured her heart. "Since I have no intention of marrying, it does not signify."

He said nothing in response, but the look he gave her was so intense that Mary could not help but shift beneath his gaze. If only they could return to the sort of repartee they'd enjoyed earlier. It had been fun, not only in an entertaining way but in an intellectual one as well. Not at all the sort of silly conversations Mary often overheard other young ladies participating in. The superficiality with which most of them spoke had lessened her interest in trying to make friends. In fact, she could say with certainty that she only had one actual friend, and that was Lady Sarah, now Viscountess Spencer, after her recent marriage to Viscount Spencer. Through her, Mary had of course become acquainted with Lord Spencer's sisters, but Mary couldn't in good conscience call them friends yet, since she'd spoken to them on only a few occasions.

"When I was younger," Signor Antonio said, breaking the silence, "I read a lot of non-fictional books on a number of subjects."

"Did you have any favorites?" Mary asked, relieved by the change of subject.

"I liked Sun Tzu's *Art De La Guerre* very much. It is the only book that I have read more than once."

"*The Art of War*," Mary translated.

Signor Antonio nodded. "Have you read it?" he asked with interest.

"Not in its entirety. It was one of those books that I just happened to snatch off the shelf one rainy afternoon and never ended up finishing. As I recall, it was philosophical in nature."

"Yes. In my opinion it is the most impressive work on military strategy ever written."

She considered this before saying, "Some might argue that Machiavelli's book, *The Prince*, is of greater value."

"Hmmm . . . Another book that you happened to browse through on a rainy day?"

Mary couldn't help but smile, aware that she'd probably surprised him once again. *The Prince* was hardly the sort of book that most young ladies would ever bother reading. Perhaps they should, so they could enjoy more meaningful conversations with men. "Something like that," she admitted. She shrugged one shoulder. "As with the *Art of War*, I failed to complete it, but in this instance, it was mostly because I found it to be entirely too devious and self-serving for my liking."

"Deception, as advocated by Machiavelli, can be a powerful tool when used correctly."

Something about his tone—a hint of contemplative sharpness—sent a shiver down her spine. "Perhaps, but I believe that it will eventually corrupt the soul and that it is therefore a path best avoided."

His hand tightened around hers, almost painfully so, and she instinctively drew back.

Releasing her, he abruptly stood and stepped toward the lake, offering her his back while he stared out across the moonlit water. "Forgive me," he said when he faced her again after a long, drawn-out moment. "I am sorry if I frightened you just now, but our conversation . . . it prompted some unpleasant memories."

His confession surprised her. "I do not understand," she said.

"And you never will," he told her grimly, "for you have not experienced the horrors of war. Nothing encourages a man to reveal his true nature quite as well as the possibility that he will not survive to live another day."

Understanding dawned and she slowly rose to her feet. "You are a soldier," she whispered through the darkness. He hadn't read the books they'd been discussing for pleasure alone, but for a professional reason as well.

"I used to be," he quietly murmured.

Curious, she couldn't help but ask, "Did you kill anyone?" His eyes widened and she pushed out a breath before lowering her gaze to the ground. "Of course you did. I was not trying to—"

"It's all right." He waited for her to raise her head and look at him before saying, "Wars cost lives. There is no denying that. So yes, Lady Eleanor, I have killed."

"And if you had not?" The words swirled softly in the warm night air.

"Then they would have killed me." Detecting the anguish behind his words, she felt her chest tighten around her heart, squeezing it until it ached. "To this day, their faces haunt me—the terror in their eyes a constant reminder of the blood I have shed for England."

"For freedom."

He scoffed at that. "Whatever the reason, the price was too high."

She couldn't argue with that. "But surely you must have saved some lives as well." When he nodded, she reached for his hand and said, "Tell me about the people you rescued."

Dipping his head, he closed his eyes, his bearing so still that she imagined he must be looking into the past. When he eventually looked at her again, his eyes shone like drops of ink. "Perhaps some other time."

Mary knew better than to press him for more information. She could tell by the tone of his voice that it was a subject she shouldn't pursue. Still, she could not help but wonder about his experiences. Had he fought in the Peninsula War, the War of 1812, or the Battle of Waterloo? She'd forgotten to ask. Perhaps he'd even been wounded. If so, then how?

A gradual murmur of strings rising through the silence drew her attention away from these contemplations and toward the *Endurance* where guests were presently beginning to gather. "I believe it is time for supper," she found herself saying. "Will you escort me?"

He hesitated briefly before offering her his arm. "With pleasure."

A gentle tremor swept through Mary's body as she linked her arm with his, the firmness of him beneath the wool of his jacket making her exceedingly aware of the strength that he possessed. She tried to think of something to say—some inane topic with which to lighten the mood and, perhaps more importantly, to distract her from the way he made her feel. "Signor Antonio, I—"

He drew her closer, his hold on her tightening as he started leading her toward the ship. Mary inhaled sharply, her entire world tumbling toward the unknown as his scent assaulted her senses: the masculine smell of sandalwood mingling with brandy and a faint hint of tobacco. Her heart rate accelerated—more so as she felt her upper arm pressed against his.

"Perhaps after supper, you will grant me a dance?" His voice was low, a gravelly whisper that brushed the side of her neck.

Focusing on her breaths, Mary struggled to regain control. Her reaction was purely physical, she reminded herself—the thrill of winning a gentleman's favor for the very first time. And yet she knew that there was more to it than that. She'd genuinely enjoyed their conversation and sensed that he had as well. "I have promised to dance the reel with Viscount Bertram, and after that is the country dance with the Earl of Rotridge."

"I see." They walked a few more paces before he asked, "Are you free for the waltz?"

"I . . ." She felt herself grow inexplicably warmer.

"I must admit that I have never danced it before. I am not familiar with the steps."

His hold on her tightened even further. "The waltz is simpler than the other dances. I trust we can manage." The words rumbled around her as he spoke. "Besides, I do believe it is the only dance worthy of a woman like you."

"A woman like me?"

Turning his head, his eyes met hers from behind his mask. The intensity of his gaze sent a rush of heat spiraling along her limbs. "I saw you when you were listening to the music. Your eyes were closed and your expression was filled not only with pleasure, but with deep focus." Nearing the gangway leading onto the *Endurance,* they found themselves gradually surrounded by other guests who were making their way to supper. He lowered his voice and dipped his head toward hers. "It appeared as though you were listening to a story."

"Of course I was," she said as he guided her onto the gangplank and escorted her aboard. "A piece of music is not merely a collection of notes strung together with the sole purpose of pleasing the senses. There is always a story."

"One that most people are incapable of hearing unless someone tells them what it is," he said. "And even then they often lack the patience required. But you clearly heard it. This knowledge, coupled with your fondness for Miss Austen's books, suggests that you are a romantic, possessing a creative mind and a passionate nature. It therefore goes without saying that the waltz is the only dance that will move you, and consequently the only one worth dancing."

His analysis made her feel slightly dizzy. It was true that she'd never had a particular fondness for dancing, perhaps because she'd always felt that most dances were a poor expression of the music, completely lacking in any emotion. But the waltz . . . she had to admit that the waltz had always tempted because it seemed to allow for a deeper expression.

Stepping down from the gangplank and onto the deck of the ship, she held on to Signor Antonio's arm as they drifted between the round tables dotting the deck. Each had been dressed in pristine white with bouquets of bright red roses adorning the centers. Spotting Sarah, Mary tapped her companion on the arm. "I see my friend, Viscountess Spencer," she said. "Perhaps we can join her and her husband?"

Signor Antonio stiffened as he looked in the direction she indicated. "It seems rather crowded over there, does it not?"

"Not especially," Mary said, a little surprised by his obvious reluctance. "But if you would rather stay here, then—"

"No. I will not keep you from your friend, my lady." Releasing her arm, he took a step back, leaving Mary bereft. "Enjoy your supper with the Spencers, and your dances with Bertram and Rotridge. I will find you when it is time for the waltz." Reaching for her hand, he bowed over it with reverence. Then, straightening himself once more, he hesitated only a moment before turning away and striding back toward the gangplank. In an instant, it was almost as if he'd never been there at all.

Mary's chest tightened, and she deliberately took a breath to force back the feeling of loss that assailed her. She was being ridiculously silly. After all, she'd barely known him for more than one hour. And yet within that hour, she'd felt a connection blossoming between them. For the first time in her life, she'd felt both beautiful and understood.

"Who was that?" Sarah asked when Mary joined her.

"Someone with whom I seem to have a great deal in common."

Sarah smiled. "Commonality is a wonderful foundation for a lasting relationship."

"We have only just met," Mary confessed. She frowned in response to her own words. "Or at least I believe we have. I did not recognize his voice."

"You have not seen his face?" Sarah asked with a note of surprise and interest.

Mary shrugged one shoulder. "It is a masquerade. The novelty lies in the mystery." In truth, the more she'd spoken to Signor Antonio, the less she'd cared about what he might look like beneath his mask, though she'd be lying to herself if she said she wasn't curious.

"I suppose that is true to some extent," Sarah agreed. "Besides, a man may be the handsomest one in the world, but that is neither here nor there if he lacks the ability for intelligent thought and conversation."

"I completely agree," Mary said. Her eyes strayed to Lord Spencer who was too busy talking to his friend, the Earl of Chadwick, to be paying attention to the conversation that Mary was having with his wife. "But it does look as though you have managed to acquire a husband who lacks neither wits nor looks."

Smiling broadly, Sarah sighed with obvious contentment. "I know. I am the most fortunate woman there is." Lowering her voice to a whisper, she leaned a little closer to Mary and said, "Perhaps you can be too."

Mary felt her spine stiffen. "A brief encounter with a perfect stranger is hardly enough to suggest an imminent courtship."

"You never know," Sarah insisted. "It did for me."

"Yes, but your situation is entirely different. You have always wanted to get married."

"And you have not?"

The look of incomprehension in Sarah's eyes made Mary feel like a whale who'd somehow managed to get itself stuck inside a fish bowl. She shook her head. "I like my life the way it is."

"But what about your aunt? I thought she brought you here with the sole purpose of securing a good match for you."

It was true. In fact, her aunt was growing quite desperate where Mary's prospects were concerned—a difficult situation since Mary had other plans for her future. To Sarah she said, "That does not mean that I am destined to end up at the altar."

"But surely you must have considered the idea of marriage and what the benefits would be for you?"

"Of course I have," Mary said, recalling the conversation she'd had with Signor Antonio earlier. Reading Miss Austen's books had made it very difficult *not* to consider it. But what most people did not think about when they read such books, was that they only described the process of falling in love. They did not address the life that followed the early days of young romance or the restrictions forced upon women the moment they entered into the marriage itself. "After much deliberation I have come to the conclusion that the benefits will be few when compared with what I stand to lose. I value my independence too much to sacrifice it for any man."

"Independence should certainly not be dismissed, but unlike you, I do believe it is worth sacrificing for the *right* man." Glancing toward her husband, Sarah said, "Especially since the right man will not seek to restrict you without good reason."

"I shall have to take your word for that as the more experienced woman among us," Mary said, deciding not to argue.

Sarah smiled. "I know that you are not convinced and yet I cannot help but wonder if your mystery companion might tempt you to change your mind."

Deliberately, Mary rolled her eyes, diminishing the impact of Sarah's words. "When I know next to nothing about him? How absurd!"

"And yet you continue to blush whenever he is mentioned. I find that delightfully curious."

"Very well," Mary conceded. "I will admit that I thought him both charming and interesting, but to imagine that he and I might form an attachment based on that alone would be quite a stretch, would it not?"

"Oh, absolutely," Sarah said with trembling lips. "I cannot see how it can possibly work when you are so set against it."

"Now you are just mocking me," Mary muttered.

"I would not dare." But the sparkle in Sarah's eyes said otherwise, and Mary couldn't help but laugh in response.

Returning to the terrace after supper, Mary joined Lord Bertram for the reel. He was an older gentleman—perhaps fifteen years her senior—with polite manners that unfortunately failed to compensate for his lack of conversational skill or sense of humor. As the well-bred young lady that she was, Mary made a genuine effort to respond to his comments. But discussing how wonderful the evening was, the magnificence of Thorncliff, and their good fortune in regard to the weather, proved increasingly tedious. So much so that Mary was extremely relieved when the dance finally drew to an end so she could escape Lord Bertram's company.

Looking around, she sought Signor Antonio, wondering where he might be, but was quickly discouraged from doing so when Lord Rotridge stepped into her path. "Are you ready for our country dance?" he asked with a crooked smile. Dressed in evening black, he'd chosen a domino that revealed more of his face than it hid, making him easier to recognize than most.

"Certainly, my lord," Mary said with a final glance directed toward the far corner of the terrace where light disappeared into darkness. A figure stood there, silhouetted against the shadows. Mary stared, the leap of her pulse ensuring her of who it was, even as he melted away completely. Inhaling sharply, she turned away and accepted the arm that Rotridge offered, acutely aware that she was being watched.

"You look delightful this evening," Rotridge said as he guided her between the colonnade of dancers a few minutes later. "Such a lovely departure from your usual self. A man would have to be mad not to dance with you."

Mary couldn't help but frown. "Is that supposed to be a compliment, my lord?"

He chuckled slightly. "Forgive me, Lady Mary. It was not my intention to insult you but rather to praise your choice of costume. I cannot recall ever seeing you with your hair down before. It suits you."

Looking up at him, she studied the confident glow in his eyes, "I must admit that I was surprised when you asked me to dance with you this evening. You have never made the effort before."

His expression turned instantly somber as he took her by the hand and led her in a small circle at the end of the colonnade. "A mistake, on my part, for which I can only hope that you will eventually forgive me." There was a brief pause, and then, "I have known you since you were a little girl, Lady Mary. Admittedly, it has taken some time for me to realize that you have grown into a beautiful young woman."

They drew apart, joining the colonnade while other couples danced between them. Standing across from her, Rotridge regarded her with heated interest. She waited, expecting to feel something in return, but soon discovered that she felt nothing at all. Again, she chanced a look toward the far corner of the terrace, disappointment surging through her when she found only empty darkness.

"Perhaps you would care to go boating with me some time," Rotridge inquired when they stepped toward each other again and spun around the floor. "Or if you prefer a picnic, I shall be happy to make the arrangements."

"Afternoon tea on the terrace would be equally nice," Mary said. She might not be any more interested in him than she would be in a rock, but at least he was finally making an effort.

Rotridge frowned. "Is that not too mundane?"

"I do not know," Mary hedged. "I quite enjoy my afternoon tea and the terrace here is so lovely, filled as it is with the scent of roses and jasmine."

"But you can have tea on the terrace whenever you please," Rotridge protested. "It does not seem special enough and I . . ." He offered her a broad smile. "I was hoping to do something special for you—something that might convince you of my high regard."

Mary attempted a smile in return. "That is very kind of you, my lord. Perhaps you are right. A boat ride does sound like an enjoyable way in which to pass the afternoon."

"Splendid!" His eyes flashed brightly. "It will give us a chance to make up for lost time."

"I suppose so," Mary said as they stepped apart once more. Watching him, she could not deny his good looks. But ever since he'd inherited the property neighboring her grandfather's almost ten years ago, he'd done little more than greet her politely whenever their paths had happened to cross during her annual visits. True, she had been a child then while he had been a young man affected by his father's early passing, but his keen interest in her now still seemed odd.

The music faded and she dropped into a curtsy while Rotridge bowed elegantly in response. Rising, Mary accepted the arm that he offered and allowed him to lead her toward the refreshment table. "My lord, may I ask you a question?"

Glancing down at her, Rotridge raised an eyebrow. "Of course."

They reached the refreshment table where Rotridge picked up a glass of champagne and offered it to Mary. "Thank you, but I would rather have some lemonade, if it is not too much trouble."

"Lemonade?" Turning his head, he glanced down at a large glass jug, his mouth twisting into something of a grimace. Returning his attention to Mary, he said, "Only spinsters and wallflowers would ever think to drink lemonade at a ball, and you, my lady, are neither." He held the champagne toward her with greater insistence.

Mary's back went rigid. "My lord, there is nothing wrong with being a spinster or a wallflower, and there is certainly nothing wrong with drinking lemonade, not even at a ball."

For the briefest of seconds, his eyes narrowed into two dark slits, but it happened so quickly and was rapidly replaced by the most understanding expression, that she wondered if she'd imagined the anger she'd seen there. Her doubts only grew when he said, "Please forgive me. I only mean for you to enjoy the evening as much as possible. If lemonade is what you prefer, then by all means . . ." Lifting the jug, he proceeded to fill a glass for her.

"As to the question I was going to ask you before," Mary said as soon as he'd handed her the glass and she'd allowed herself a sip.

"Yes?"

"Why your sudden interest in me?"

Rotridge went completely still for a moment, his glass of champagne halting en route to his mouth.

But then it passed, he sipped his drink, and smiled benignly. "As I said, it took me a while to realize how grown up you are now, perhaps because you never seemed interested in encouraging the attentions of any gentleman. So while I have noticed your attendance at various balls, I also believed you were out of my reach—that asking you to dance would have been a wasted effort."

"Out of your reach?" The man was either mad or lying through his sparkly white teeth. "But you are an earl, my lord. I would have been a fool not to consider you if you had shown an interest."

"You say so now, but I can assure you that I have known plenty of women who wish to cling to their independence. I suppose I assumed that you shared their sentiment based on your lack of effort."

Mary's mouth dropped. "My lack of effort?"

"Until tonight of course. Tonight you have clearly proven that you are ready to consider a courtship."

"I . . ." She could scarcely speak, she was so shocked by his presumptuousness. Swallowing the anger that simmered inside her, Mary tried to concentrate on slow and steady breaths. "You are entirely mistaken, my lord, for I consider my independence to be my greatest asset. Consequently, I am no more eager to lose it through marriage now than I was yesterday."

"Your choice of gown and your long flowing hair say otherwise."

Mary shook her head. "Why would you suppose such a thing?"

Tilting his head, he grinned down at her. "Come now, my lady, there is no need for you to play games with me."

"I can assure you that I am not trying to do so."

Frowning, he studied her a moment. "Are you not aware that by wearing not only the plainest gown but the *only* gown cut in this particular style . . ." he waved his hand in her general direction, "you have made yourself the center of attention? Additionally, you are also the only lady here tonight who has chosen not to dress her hair."

"Only because doing so would not have suited my costume," Mary said as she looked around. When Lady Duncaster had announced the upcoming masquerade two weeks earlier, Mary had leapt at the opportunity to order a gown inspired by the beautiful painting of Eleanor of Aquitaine that hung in her bedroom. Not once had she considered that all the other women would choose to dress as though they belonged at Louis the Thirteenth's court. "I did not realize that there would be a theme," she said, more aware of herself than ever before.

"Lady Duncaster did mention it when she announced the ball."

Mary nodded. Her aunt had told her about the ball after Mary had missed the announcement but had neglected to mention the theme until Mary had already ordered her gown. By then, it had been too late for her to order another. "Even so," she said, determined to return to the more important matter at hand, "the fact remains that you must have gotten the wrong idea. I am not in the market for a husband at present."

"Then you are a fool," Rotridge warned as he snatched her glass right out of her hand and set it aside. Before she could manage a protest, he'd taken her by the arm and was steering her toward the dark corner of the terrace. "Independence is a novel idea, but you are a woman and since you are not an heiress, you will need a husband for the sake of security, if nothing else."

With a tug, Mary tried to break free of his hold, but Rotridge wouldn't have it. "My lord, if it is my dowry you are after, then I suggest you reconsider. It is not—"

"Dowry? Why on earth would I be interested in your dowry when I have more money than I know what to do with?"

"I cannot imagine," Mary confessed.

"If you were to marry me, I would allow you full control of your dowry. I certainly have no need of it, and if it is a modest sum, I will even be happy to add to it. I suppose, in a way, that this would give you the independence that you seek. Financially, at least."

It was the sort of bargain that would appeal to most young ladies. "Forgive me, but I understand your motivation even less if it is not driven by monetary gain."

Reaching the corner, Rotridge pulled her into the darkness, his arm circling around her waist and forcing her up against him. "Perhaps I simply want you for you."

Mary shook her head. "No. I do not believe that." She tried to pull away—to return to the light—but he only tightened his hold. "Please. Let me go."

"In a moment," he said. Raising his hand, he used his teeth to pull away his glove. Then, on a sharp inhale of breath, he ran his naked fingers through her hair, his breaths increasingly shallow as he gathered up a handful of locks and pressed them against his nose. "You smell divine," he murmured.

A tremor snaked its way through her. "I think we ought to rejoin the festivities," she whispered, her words faltering as she glanced toward the other guests. If he kissed her where everyone could see, she would have no choice but to bow to his will or accept ruination.

Rotridge pinned her with a hard stare. "In a moment," he repeated as he tightened his hold even more.

A low growl shifted the air around her. "I believe it is time for our dance," a harsh voice spoke.

Mary turned her head toward the masked figure who'd quietly materialized beside her. He was taller than Rotridge—broader too. Relief eased the tension that had quickly been building inside her.

"And who might you be?" Rotridge asked, releasing both Mary and her hair so he could face Signor Antonio properly.

"That is none of your concern," Signor Antonio said.

Rotridge stared at him a moment before returning his attention to Mary. Bowing, he said, "It has been a pleasure, my lady. I shall look forward to our boat ride with great anticipation. Will tomorrow suit?"

While instinct urged her to make an excuse, Mary knew she would not be able to avoid the earl indefinitely. "Yes, my lord, tomorrow will suit just fine."

With a curt nod, he muttered something indiscernible to Signor Antonio before striding away at a brisk pace.

"You should have said no," Signor Antonio said as he grasped her by the arm and steered her back into the flickering light of a nearby torch.

"I did not want to be rude."

"And I suppose he demanded politeness by treating you with respect, unwilling as he was to release you when you asked him to do so?"

"No . . . I . . ." What could she say?

"He took advantage of your kindness."

"Perhaps," she admitted.

He sighed audibly. "Did you tell him that you have no interest in marriage?"

"Yes."

Abruptly, he spun her around so she faced him. "Promise me that you will be careful."

"You think he might prove dangerous?"

"For you, yes."

"Because he was not deterred by my lack of interest in courtship or marriage?" Forcing herself to stand tall, she stared back into his dark eyes. "You were not deterred either, it seems."

"Perhaps not, but at least I am not pulling you into dark corners in order to smell your hair." There was a dangerous edge to his tone. "Can you honestly tell me that his actions did not disturb you?"

Slowly, she shook her head. "No."

"Then perhaps, even if you do not feel as though you know me well enough to heed my warning, you will listen to your own instinct?"

"Yes," she assured him.

A moment passed, during which neither one of them moved. Eventually, Signor Antonio nodded. "That is all I need to know. Thank you."

The relief in his voice melted her insides. With her heart beating rapidly in her chest, she accepted the arm he offered her, aware once again of the masculine strength he exuded as he guided her toward the dance floor in preparation for the waltz.

Chapter 3

When the first notes of music rose through the air, Richard pulled Lady Eleanor into his arms, just as he'd longed to do since the moment he'd first seen her. Pure pleasure rushed through him, pushing away the anger that he'd felt at seeing Rotridge with his lecherous hands on her. Christ, he'd been tempted to give the man a sound thrashing. But he'd held back, aware that he would only be allowing an elemental possessiveness that he had no right to, to guide him.

Moving along the edge of the dance floor, he hesitated only a moment before setting his hand more firmly against Lady Eleanor's back. Her eyes widened ever so slightly, which in turn made him smile. "You are managing very well, considering you've never danced this before."

"You were right to say it would be easier than the other dances, though I do believe you are holding me inappropriately close." Her words were followed by a delightful flush of pink across her chest.

Perhaps she was right. For a second, he considered adding more distance between them, but then thought better of it. The uncertainty that plagued him came from lack of practice, nothing else. It simply had to be tamed. "I disagree." He deliberately tightened his grip on her, reveling in the way her lips parted with surprise while heat tore its way through him. She glanced around, her eyes slightly anxious. "Look at me," he said. "We are only dancing. There is nothing wrong with that."

Giving him her full attention, she quietly whispered, "Then why does it feel as though I am committing a sin?"

Her words, though innocently spoken, stirred his blood like nothing else ever had. *Jesus!* For the first time in five years, he was not only speaking to a woman, but holding one in his arms—a delightful one at that. Temptation did not even come close to describing the longing that was steadily building inside him, brought on not only by her beauty but by her sensuality and intellect as well.

Forcing back all thought of potentially kissing his way down the side of her neck and over the smooth skin of her shoulder, Richard struggled to gain control. "Perhaps it is the atmosphere," he suggested. "Masquerades do have a tendency to encourage more carefree behavior."

"I suppose it must be because of the anonymity. Hidden behind masks, people have the opportunity to do things they would not otherwise dare to consider."

"Such as?"

She pursed her lips, which made her look adorably cheeky. "A shy gentleman might suddenly feel emboldened, allowing him the courage he needs to ask a lady to dance."

"I hope you are not suggesting that I might be shy,

for I can assure you that I am anything but." Not entirely true, though he preferred apprehensive.

"And yet I have no clue about your identity. In truth, you could be anyone, perhaps even a grooms-man who happened to chance upon some quality clothing."

"I see your point. But if I were a groomsman, would I be as well-read as you know me to be?" Emboldened by their light repartee, the magical touch that the evening provided, and the reminder that nobody knew who he was, Richard moved his hands to her waist and lifted her right off the ground. He heard her suck in her breath while several onlookers gasped in confounded shock. Heedless of it all, he proceeded to swing Lady Eleanor around while spinning in a wide circle.

"That was far too daring," she chastised as soon as he set her back on her feet and resumed their previous pace.

"Tell me you did not enjoy every second of it."

Setting her mouth in a firm line, she looked away from him. "Everyone is watching," she eventually said, not answering his question. "My aunt does not look the least bit pleased."

"Then it is fortunate that I care more about *your* opinion than I do about your aunt's."

The corner of her mouth twitched. "You are intolerable. What if you had dropped me?"

"A gentleman never drops a lady." Twirling her around, he led her between two other couples.

"Perhaps not, but then again, we have not yet established that you are in fact a gentleman. For all I know, you could be a scoundrel."

"I can assure you that I am no such thing." Dipping his head, he whispered close to her ear. "In time, you will learn that I value honesty and dependability. That I consider a man's honor to be paramount to his character. So I would be much obliged if you would refrain from suggesting otherwise, even if you only meant to do so in jest."

Briefly closing her eyes, she gave a little nod. "Forgive me," she whispered, regret marring her features. "I did not mean to insult you in any way."

"I know." The music gradually faded and their movements slowed until they came to a gliding halt. Stepping back, Richard offered Lady Eleanor a bow while she curtsied in return. He didn't like the tone he'd just taken with her, but it was too late for that now. "Will you join me for a walk in the garden?" he asked, stiffly offering her his arm. He was suddenly desperate to smooth away the tight expression that he'd caused.

"As lovely as that sounds, I am not so sure that it is going to be possible," she said, her eyes fixed on a spot directly behind his left shoulder.

Turning, Richard winced as he spotted an older woman bearing down on him with Lady Duncaster in pursuit. "Your aunt, I presume?"

"Yes. With Mama and Papa abroad, I am presently under her protection." She looked up at him with calmness in her eyes. "No need to worry. She is not as fierce as she looks. Just be polite."

Squaring his shoulders, Richard stood his ground as Lady Eleanor's aunt came to a halt before him. She was a slim woman with delicate features, possessing a chin that was sharper than most. Her dark brown hair was streaked with random lines of silver, and in front of her eyes, she held a lorgnette surrounded by a vast array of colorful feathers.

"Signor Antonio," Lady Duncaster said, coming up alongside her, "May I present my dear friend, Lady Foxworth?"

"It is a pleasure to make your acquaintance, Countess." Reaching for her tiny hand, Richard bowed over it while hoping that his gallantry would win him her favor.

"Thank you," she said as she peered up at him from behind her lorgnette. "You clearly have me at a disadvantage. Will you please tell me who you are? I should also like to know why you presumed to have the right to dance with my niece in such a scandalous manner."

Every muscle in Richard's body grew taught. Was it just his imagination, or was his cravat more restrictive now than it had been earlier? With rigidity, he met Lady Foxworth's assessing gaze. "I must apologize for allowing myself to get carried away during the dance. It was not my intention to offend anyone. As to my name . . . I am afraid that Signor Antonio will have to suffice."

Lady Foxworth pressed her lips together in a firm line of disapproval. Beside him, Richard sensed Lady Eleanor's surprise. Like her aunt, she'd probably expected him to reveal himself when asked to do so.

"Unfortunately that is not good enough," Lady Foxworth said. "Not when I am responsible for my niece's reputation."

"I can vouch for his character," Lady Duncaster said with a hasty look in Richard's direction. "Signor Antonio comes from a very respectable family—a family with whom an association would be a coup."

Raising her chin a notch, Lady Foxworth was silent for a moment and Richard realized that he was holding his breath in anticipation of what she might say next. "I have always trusted your judgment," Lady Foxworth eventually told Lady Duncaster, "but I am afraid that my conscience will not allow me to do so in this instance. Unless I am made aware of Signor Antonio's exact identity, then I am afraid that I cannot allow him to continue socializing with my niece."

Closing his eyes on the finality of her words, Richard expelled the breath he'd been holding. Silently, he cursed the fear that kept him from living and the hatred that fueled his vendetta. Because in spite of what Lady Eleanor had told him—that she had no desire to marry—the way in which she responded to him suggested that he might be able to change her mind if he was allowed the chance to do so.

"What if he confides in me?" Lady Eleanor asked, cultivating this idea.

Lady Foxworth regarded him shrewdly. "I do not believe that he is prepared to do so. Are you, Signor?"

Heart hammering in his chest, Richard forced himself not to look at Lady Eleanor. He didn't want to see the hope brimming in her eyes or the disappointment that would take its place when he said what had to be said. "Not yet."

As soon as the words were out, he felt as though a cavern had been carved into the ground, separating him from the woman who stood by his side. Tonight, for the first time in years, he'd felt a sliver of hope that the happy future he'd always dreamed of might one day be his—if he could only win Lady Eleanor's affection. Unwilling to give up completely, he said, "Perhaps in time—"

"No," Lady Foxworth said, her hand slicing the air between them. "You have every right to keep your secrets, Signor, but until I am made aware of what they are and have been reassured that they pose no threat to my niece's reputation or happiness, then you will stay away from her. Is that clear?"

The ultimatum was not to Richard's liking even though he understood Lady Foxworth's reasoning completely. Had he been in her shoes, he would have made the same demand. "Yes." He spoke the word with difficulty.

Lady Foxworth finally allowed a faint smile. "Thank you. I appreciate your understanding."

Clenching his jaw, Richard nodded. "If you will excuse me," he said with a curt bow directed at Lady Foxworth and Lady Duncaster. Turning toward Lady Eleanor, his heart ached at the sight of her pained expression. "It has been a pleasure."

She gave him a bleak little nod, but said nothing in response. Turning his back on her, Richard walked away without a backward glance, his pace brisk as he strode toward the French doors leading into the house. Rushing through the well-lit hallway, he marched toward the stairs, climbing them quickly in his haste to return to his bedchamber and the darkness that beckoned within.

"I am sorry," Lady Foxworth told Mary as soon as Signor Antonio was out of earshot, "but it is for the best."

"I disagree," Mary said as she watched Signor Antonio disappear amidst the crowd. "He is the only gentleman whose company I have ever enjoyed and rather than welcome his interest in me, you chose to send him away."

"You must understand my reasoning, Mary." Her aunt no longer bore the hard façade that she'd presented Signor Antonio with. Instead, she looked deeply sorry about what she'd had to do. "Secrecy has no place in any relationship, and you must admit that the secret he chooses to keep is quite significant."

"I am sure he has a good reason for it, and if Lady Duncaster is willing to vouch for him then—"

"You are not Lady Duncaster's responsibility," Lady Foxworth said. Addressing her friend, she added, "I hope you will forgive me for I mean no offense, but it is my duty to assess all potential suitors myself."

"I understand you completely," Lady Duncaster said.

"Perhaps you could share his identity with Aunt Eugenia, without making me aware of who he is," Mary suggested, addressing her hostess.

"I am sorry," Lady Duncaster said, "but I have given him my word."

"But—"

"You must accept his reasoning as well, Mary," Lady Foxworth said.

"Even if he is the only gentleman to ever spark my interest?" Mary asked. "It hardly seems fair!"

Sympathy filled Lady Foxworth's eyes. "Perhaps that is because you have chosen to keep to yourself until now. But tonight you danced with three gentlemen, which means that you have been noticed. It is only a matter of time now before others show an interest, and once they do, then I am certain that one of them will prove to be worthy of your affection."

"You are probably right," Mary found herself saying. She was suddenly eager for the conversation to be over.

"Lord Rotridge looked quite taken with you," her aunt added, sounding hopeful.

"Yes," Mary said, suppressing a shudder. "He has invited me to go boating with him tomorrow."

"Well there you are then," Lady Foxworth said. "I have every confidence that you and the earl will have a marvelous time getting better acquainted. And if you decide that he is not for you, then I am sure that we will have no issue with finding someone else who is more to your liking."

Mary nodded. She was not about to tell her aunt that she had no intention of marrying anyone or that the only man who'd ever come remotely close to potentially changing her mind about the subject had just been forbidden to speak with her. Doing so would only lead to a series of unpleasant questions that Mary was not prepared to answer.

"The Earl of Chadwick is exceedingly charming as well," Lady Foxworth added. "Such a fine young gentleman. Would you be kind enough to make the necessary introductions, Lady Duncaster?"

"Of course," Lady Duncaster said. She craned her neck and looked around. "There he is, ladies. Follow me!"

Mary cringed. "I dislike approaching him like this," she told her aunt as they walked behind Lady

Duncaster toward the opposite side of the terrace. "The idea of being forced upon a man with the expectation that he will keep me company or ask me to dance is humiliating."

"Nonsense, my dear," Lady Foxworth said. "Everyone does it. It is the way of things."

"It is not the natural way," Mary said. "And if he had ever had any interest in me, then he would have asked me to dance without being prompted to do so."

"Please stop turning this into an ordeal and just enjoy yourself," Lady Foxworth said.

Mary sighed. "Very well," she agreed, "but only because of all the effort that you have gone to on my behalf."

"Thank you." Lady Foxworth gave Mary a wide smile.

"I should probably warn you not to get too excited," Mary said. "Before Mama and Papa left for India, they told me to follow my heart, and I intend to do so."

By the time Mary returned to her bedchamber two hours later, she was exhausted. Chadwick had proven himself to be delightful company, and she'd danced with three other gentlemen after him, each with a similar result: not one of them had heated her insides or made her skin tingle in response to their touch. They did not compare to Signor Antonio—a mystery man whom Mary would never be able to forget.

"Did you have a pleasant evening, my lady?" Mary's maid, Amy, asked as she helped Mary disrobe.

"Partly," Mary told her honestly. She hesitated a moment before saying, "I met a gentleman who was very much to my liking."

If this surprised Amy, she did not show it. "What wonderful news!"

"Unfortunately, Lady Foxworth has forbidden him from ever seeing me again." Aware that this wasn't entirely true, Mary said, "Or at least until he reveals his identity."

"You do not know who he is?"

Mary shook her head, her teeth catching her lip in contemplation. "He wore a mask and a hooded cloak."

"And yet you still found him appealing?"

"Yes. I cannot seem to stop thinking about him and wishing that we would have had more time together."

Fetching Mary's nightgown, Amy proceeded to help Mary into it. "It seems to me that this is the perfect way in which to fall in love with someone. Your eyes have not yet been distracted by looks, allowing your heart to make an unbiased decision."

"I suppose so," Mary said as she thought of the time she'd spent in Signor Antonio's company. "But that is neither here nor there since I doubt I will ever see him again. He wants to remain anonymous for some reason while I . . . Even if he turned out to be a duke and made me an offer, I am still not sure that I would be able to accept."

Folding Mary's gown, Amy placed it carefully in the trunk at the foot of the bed. "Because of your work?"

"You know how important it is to me, but the

ton will never approve of what I am doing and neither will a gentleman. If I marry, my husband will demand that I give it up so as not to cause a scandal."

"If he loves you, he might help you continue as you have been doing thus far, disguised as Lucia."

"It is highly unlikely and certainly not a risk that I am willing to take without a great deal of consideration first. Not as long as I need the income." Seating herself on the low bench in front of her vanity table, Mary began removing her earrings.

"Speaking of which," Amy said, crossing to Mary's bedside table, "this letter arrived for you earlier this evening. It looks as though it is from Lord Carthright." She placed it on the vanity in front of Mary, then reached for a comb and proceeded to pull it through Mary's hair.

"I was wondering when I would hear from my brother again," Mary said as she fingered the shiny blob of wax that sealed the paper shut. Reluctantly, she tore it open, unfolded the paper and read, her stomach tying itself into knots as she did so. "He requires another five thousand pounds." Raising her gaze Mary stared into the mirror. "The investments he made, following our last correspondence, were not to his advantage."

Amy's hands stilled. A few seconds passed, and then, "I know it is not my place to say this, my lady, but I do wish that you would refuse him for once."

"There is also Carthright House to consider," Mary murmured. "I daresay that he was ill-prepared for the expense of running such a large estate. The repairs have been extensive. I saw the need for a new roof myself when I last visited."

"Even so, he is a grown man, my lady. Perhaps it would be wiser to insist that he stand on his own two feet."

"My conscience will not allow it, Amy. Not when I have the means by which to help him and especially not since my help is intended to ensure that he will eventually be capable of supporting himself in a home that is worthy of his title."

"Lord Carthright is a lucky man to have so generous a sister." Amy wove Mary's hair into a long plait.

Mary sighed. "He is my brother. If the situation were reversed, I am sure that he would do the same for me."

The look Amy gave her in the mirror disagreed. "I doubt we will ever know since such a situation is unlikely to occur. If I were you, I would still inform your parents of his situation."

"They are half a world away," Mary said. "There is little they can do."

"You are right." Reaching for a ribbon, Amy tied the end of the plait securely in place.

"I will send a letter to the bank first thing in the morning," Mary said decisively as she refolded the letter and set it aside.

Catching her eye in the mirror, Amy asked, "Does this mean that you will be giving up on your mystery man?"

Mary blinked. "What choice do I have? Lord Carthright still needs me and as long as that is the case, I do not see how I can possibly encourage any man to pursue me. Besides, I have already told you that my aunt has forbidden him from doing so."

"True. But has she placed the same restriction on you?"

"To think otherwise would be deliberately ignorant."

Amy shrugged. "If you like him as well as your blush suggests, then I think perhaps you should try to spend more time with him. He clearly has secrets of his own if he does not wish for you to know who he is. I think it may be likely that he will not only understand your situation better than most, but that he might be more accepting."

Chapter 4

"**Y**ou look terribly tired," Lady Foxworth remarked the following day at breakfast. "Did you not sleep well?"

"Not particularly," Mary replied. She'd been too busy thinking about Signor Antonio and about what Amy had said about trying to spend more time with him.

"Well, you did have a very exciting evening, so I do not blame you." Spooning some sugar into her tea, Lady Foxworth stirred the hot beverage before taking a dainty sip. Dipping her head toward Mary, she then lowered her voice to a whisper and said, "And in case you failed to notice, you are still the subject of attention."

Glancing along the length of the table, Mary caught a couple of gentlemen staring in her general direction with unfeigned interest. They nodded politely in response to her awareness, whispered a few words to each other and served her a pair of brilliant smiles. Flattered, Mary smiled back at them before turning away. "It makes no sense."

"Of course it does, my dear. You are far more beautiful than you give yourself credit for and last night, dressed in that gown you were wearing . . . well, you can see the result for yourself, surely."

Mary scrunched her nose. "I hope this does not mean that I am going to have to fight off a hoard of annoying suitors."

"I certainly hope it does," Lady Foxworth said, her teacup clattering loudly against its saucer as she set it down a touch harder than usual. "And there is no need for you to find them annoying as long as you keep an open mind."

To Mary's way of thinking, any man who would try to convince her to do something that she had no desire to do—like marry, in this case—was bound to be annoying. To her chagrin, Rotridge had even managed to make her go boating later, in spite of her protests. Signor Antonio would never have tried to force her like that. Her heart trembled a little at the thought of him and of what she intended to do.

"What are your plans for the day?" Mary asked her aunt when they were done with their meal and had exited the dining room.

"Lady Duncaster tells me that Mr. Thomas Young will be arriving today and she has very kindly offered to introduce me to him."

"That will be exciting for you," Mary said, aware of her aunt's admiration for the scientist. "I suppose you will be discussing his wave theory of light?"

"Oh yes. That, and his theory on color perception, which I find most fascinating."

"I am simply dumbfounded by all the languages he can speak. Ten, is it?"

Lady Foxworth raised her eyebrows. "Twelve," she said.

"That is incredible," Mary remarked.

"And useful too, as proven by his successful efforts in translating the demotic text of the Rosetta Stone."

"He did that as well?"

Lady Foxworth nodded. "I believe he is still working on the hieroglyphs, though I have every confidence that he will eventually decipher those too. How about you, Mary? What are your plans for the day? I know you have your boat ride with Rotridge later this afternoon."

"Yes. I received a note from him this morning, suggesting that we head down to the lake together after luncheon, which allows me some time right now in which to see to my correspondence."

"Then you have a busy day ahead of you as well, it would seem. I shall leave you to it then," Lady Foxworth said as she started to turn away. "Perhaps you can join me for tea on the terrace after your boat ride?"

"I would love to," Mary said, happy to have an excuse to extricate herself from Rotridge's company if it became necessary for her to do so.

Returning upstairs to her bedchamber, Mary seated herself at her escritoire, prepared a piece of foolscap, readied her quill, and proceeded to write two letters—one to her brother, Lord Carthright, and the other to her bank, informing them to transfer the necessary funds to her brother upon his request. Sealing the letters, she sat back in her chair, pondering the idea that had been forming in her mind since the previous evening. "Amy," she said, drawing her maid's attention from across the room.

"Yes, my lady?" She'd been mending a loose ruffle on one of Mary's chemises, but paused in her task and raised her head, giving Mary her full attention.

"I have been thinking about what you said last night—about giving my mystery man a chance." Amy said nothing, but her curiosity was clear due to her arched eyebrows. "The problem is that I do not know where to find him."

"There must be something for you to go on."

"He called himself Signor Antonio."

"Perhaps it is a clue," Amy suggested. "His real name might be Anthony. Do you know of a peer by that name?"

"A couple of gentlemen come to mind, but one is not here and the other is married, so I doubt it can be either of them. But what if . . ." Biting her lip in contemplation, Mary drummed her fingers casually against the surface of her desk. "What if I were to write to Signor Antonio and leave the letter on the silver salver in the foyer. I doubt the butler will know who to deliver it to, so he will probably ask Lady Duncaster, and then she will have no choice but to help me."

"She will be duty bound to deliver the letter," Amy said, her eyes brightening with excitement.

"Yes. And then it will be up to Signor Antonio to decide what to do with the proposition that I intend to make him."

"You will be going against Lady Foxworth's wishes," Amy pointed out.

"Are you trying to dissuade me now, after every-

thing you have said? This was practically your idea."
Shifting in her seat, Mary reached for her quill. "Besides, it is a well-known fact that a good romance has a dragon that must be slayed in order to allow for a happily-ever-after."

A choked sound escaped Amy. "I hope you are not referring to your aunt."

Pressing her lips together, Mary tried not to laugh as she set her quill to the piece of paper in front of her. "Of course not," she managed. "I am referring to the situation as a whole."

It was just after noon when Mary descended to the dining room. She'd entrusted Amy with the tasks of posting her letters and discreetly placing the note for Signor Antonio on the salver in the foyer. Entering the dining room, she was met by Rotridge who looked as though he'd been standing guard in anticipation of her arrival.

He smiled broadly and offered her his arm. "You look just as lovely today as you did last night," he said as he guided her toward a vacant spot at one end of the table.

"Perhaps we can join my aunt and Lady Duncaster," Mary suggested, noting their presence at the other end of the room. "The gentleman they are talking to is Mr. Thomas Young, the scientist. I would love to participate in their conversation."

"Perhaps we can do so later," Rotridge said, not deviating from his path. Reaching the table, he pulled out a chair for Mary and gestured for her to take a seat. Leaning close to her, he murmured, "At present,

I am too delighted by the prospect of having you all to myself."

It was the sort of pronouncement that would make most young ladies blush. Mary arched a brow, but did as she was expected to do and claimed her seat with elegant poise. As soon as Rotridge was seated beside her however, she turned to him and said, "My lord, I know that you have the very best of intentions, but if you wish to win my favor, then I would advise you to pay attention to my interests." Her heart beat rapidly in her chest as she waited for his response.

There was a brief moment of silence, but then he chuckled beside her. "You cannot honestly tell me that you would rather join *them* in favor of having a quiet tête-à-tête with me?"

Did his arrogance know no bounds? "You and I will have plenty of time to ourselves once we are out on the lake."

"True, though I daresay it will hardly be enough." His gaze drifted away from her eyes and toward the side of her head. "It is a shame that you did not choose to leave your hair down today. It looked so stunning last night, the way it tumbled over your shoulders in thick flowing curls."

His voice had dropped to a gravelly tone that made Mary feel slightly uncomfortable. It shouldn't, she supposed, since he had done nothing but compliment her. But there was something about his voice that she did not like, just as she hadn't liked the way in which he'd smelled her hair the previous evening. It had felt . . . intrusive.

Aware that she would somehow have to come to

terms with this if she was to spend the entire afternoon with the man, she decided to make an effort to
change the subject. "Do you like to read?" she asked,
hoping that they might be able to find something interesting to discuss.

"I had no choice but to do so when I attended
school and university. It was such a chore really,
which is why I have not bothered to read much of
anything since."

Mary's mouth dropped. "But surely there must
have been at least one book that you enjoyed during
your studies."

Reaching for his glass of wine, he seemed to
ponder that for a moment. He suddenly grinned, his
eyes flashing with unhindered mischief. "Now that
you mention it, there was actually one particular
book that could hold my interest for hours on end."

"Oh? What was it called?"

"I cannot possibly tell you that."

"Why on earth not?" she asked. "I am very well
read, my lord, so it is possible that I have read this
one as well and . . . What is it? Why are you looking
at me like that?"

"I think it highly unlikely that you would have
read this particular book." His voice was a low
whisper as he leaned closer to her—so close that his
shoulder brushed against hers.

Mary shook her head. A plate of food was placed
before her and she sat for a moment, just staring at it
in confusion. "Was it political in nature?"

"Hardly." He took a bite of his food.

Following suit, Mary tried to quell her annoyance,
but couldn't quite seem to manage it. "My lord, I may

be a woman, but that does not mean that I cannot discuss matters that are of interest to men."

Tilting his head, he stared into her eyes with an intensity that made her squirm. "Very well then, I shall humor you. The book was called *How to Please a Lady*."

Mary frowned. "I do not recall hearing of it before, but I must admit that I am surprised that you would find a book on etiquette so diverting."

"Etiquette?" His eyes shimmered with mirth. "My dear, you are entirely mistaken."

"How so?"

Shaking his head, he took another bite of his food. "It is becoming increasingly clear to me that no matter how educated a lady may claim to be, she has absolutely no knowledge of the only subject that truly matters."

"My lord, I cannot help but feel as though you are mocking me."

"Then you must forgive me, for that is not my intention. Indeed, you are not the one to blame for your ignorance in the one area that will determine your ability to not only find a husband, but to keep him."

"As I have said before, I have no interest in marriage."

He allowed his eyes to roam over her for a moment. Mary dropped her gaze to her plate and proceeded to study a piece of lettuce with great interest.

"Perhaps if I enlighten you, you will change your mind." There was a buoyancy to his words that made them sound more casual than Mary knew them to be.

A shiver danced across her skin, but it was not the welcoming variety that she'd felt when Signor Antonio had held her in his arms during the waltz, but rather the sort that warned her to beware. "I doubt it," she said. Finishing her meal, she reached for her wine. "Once I set my mind to something, I am not easily swayed."

"Then we are not that dissimilar, you and I." Pushing away from the table, he rose and helped her do so as well. "Shall we?"

Mary hesitated. Every fiber of her being warned her not to do as he asked. She decided to act on her instinct. "Please forgive me, but I do not feel entirely well."

He gave her a dubious look. "The fresh air will do you good. Come along." Unable to forget the look in his eyes when he'd smelled her hair, his unwillingness to let her go when she'd asked him to do so, or the strange cadence of his voice when he'd spoken of that book he liked so much, she shook her head. "I apologize, but I think you will have to go without me."

Although he did not look pleased by the change in plan, he smiled tightly and nodded in acquiescence. "I see that your aunt has departed. Would you like me to call for her to assist you?"

"No. There is no need to trouble her."

"In that case, please allow me to escort you to the stairs."

Seeing no harm in that, she agreed. In fact, his exemplary behavior right now made her wonder if she might have misjudged him. And yet . . . she could not ignore the soft tremors that shook her every time he glanced her way.

"I do hope that you will give my suggestion some serious thought," he said as they walked along the corridor that would take them through to a larger hallway beyond.

It took her a moment to recall the matter to which he was referring. "Are you aware of how unusual it is for a gentleman to voice his desire to marry a lady as hastily as you have done?"

"You think me too forward?"

"I think your interest in me is too abrupt. It defies logic."

"Then let me be clear," he told her bluntly. "My desire to marry you is based exclusively on physical attraction."

"But I am not especially pretty." Staring ahead of her, Mary focused on her destination, relieved to know that she was not alone with Lord Rotridge, but surrounded by other guests and servants. "And even if I were, a marriage based on looks alone will never be successful or happy. In time, as I grow older, you will tire of me."

He shrugged. "You are probably right, but by then you will have children with which to occupy your time. I doubt you will notice if I choose to take a mistress."

Mary turned her head toward him so abruptly that her neck hurt. She stared at him. Had he really just said that? The flint in his eyes confirmed that he had. "What you are suggesting is absurd! There would be no love or even friendship. All I would be to you is an object for you to own." She shook her head. "I do not wish to marry, my lord. I have told you this, but in case you choose not to believe me, please know that your confession right now has done nothing to change my mind—quite the contrary."

"I need an heir," he said, his jaw visibly clenching as he met her gaze.

Mary fought the urge to pull away, refusing to be cowed by him. "Then I am afraid you will have to find someone more obliging."

"I am accustomed to getting what I want, Lady Mary, and I have decided that I want you." Shards of ice spilled from his words. He drew her closer. "But if it is a courtship that you demand, then a courtship you shall have. By all means."

Jitters flurried around her belly, rising up into her chest like a swarm of bees. "It will make no difference," she told him defiantly. "You are not the sort of man whom I would wish to be bound to for the rest of my life. I am sorry."

For one frightening moment, his expression hardened and Mary feared he might actually try to harm her in some way. But then he drew a breath and loosened his hold, smiling at her as if he found humor in her comment. "Is that because you have already set your sights on someone else?"

Mary shook her head. "No. It is because you do not want me for the right reasons. Consequently, you do not tempt me to abandon the life that I have otherwise imagined for myself."

His smile tightened a little around the edges. "What about *Signor Antonio*? Does he tempt you?"

"It is too soon to tell," Mary said without thinking. "I know very little about him."

Rotridge's eyes narrowed into two dark slits, but he said nothing further, for which Mary was remarkably grateful. Instead, he led her to the foot of the stairs. "I believe an apology is in order," he said upon releasing her arm. "Directness has always served me well, but I fear I may have been too candid with you. If I have offended you in any way—"

"It is not just the candidness, my lord. It is the fact that you and I want entirely different things out of life. If we were to marry, one of us would be burdened with unhappiness, and I suspect that someone would be me."

"You would be financially independent with children to care for and a husband who would stay out of your way. I have always believed that to be most women's dream."

Allowing a smile that took some effort to produce, Mary said, "It may well be. Unfortunately, I am not like most women. My hopes and dreams are entirely different from the norm."

He did not look mollified, but seemed to accept the finality of her statement nonetheless. Bowing, he thanked her for her company before excusing himself and heading back in the direction from which they'd come. Expelling a breath, Mary started up the stairs, thankful that her brief encounter with the Earl of Rotridge had finally come to an end.

It was five o'clock in the evening when Richard woke and got out of bed. As usual, he'd slept through the day, the heavy curtains drawn tightly together in order to keep out the light. Reaching for the tinderbox on his bedside table, he struck a flint and lit an oil lamp, his thoughts returning, as they always did, to the sound of shots being fired, of screams wrought from frightened men's throats while hooves thudded upon the bloodstained ground. Next came the memory of a dimly lit room, of heavy chains wound around his limbs while fire consumed him. He could feel it even now—the fierce torment of his burning flesh.

Briefly, he closed his eyes. It wouldn't be long now before the man responsible for it would finally pay the price he deserved. As far as Richard was concerned, that day could not come soon enough.

Crossing to the washbasin, he splashed cool water on his face and reached for a towel. Deliberately, he turned his mind to happier thoughts and considered the lady he'd met the previous evening at the masquerade ball.

Following the conversation with Lady Foxworth, he'd returned to his bedchamber where he'd watched the rest of the ball from his window. He'd seen Lady Eleanor dance with Spencer's friend, Chadwick, irritated by the overwhelming sense of possessiveness that had come over him. Once the ball had ended and the guests had gone to bed, he'd stayed up, just as he'd done every night for years, trying to rid his mind of her. It had been a futile effort that not even his violin had been able to help him with.

Reaching for his shirt, he pulled the garment over his head and tied the closure shut. He put his stockings and breeches on next, not that he was planning to go anywhere, but Spencer would be stopping by with food soon and Richard felt that he owed his brother the respect of at least getting dressed before he arrived.

With this in mind, he glanced toward the door and immediately frowned. What the devil? It looked as though a letter had been pushed beneath it, which was slightly odd since Spencer usually brought him his correspondence. Striding toward it, Richard bowed down and picked the letter up, briefly studying the wax seal of a rose before flipping the letter over. His heart made a loud thud inside his chest at the sight of the neat script gracing the front. *Signor Antonio.*

Crossing to one of the armchairs, he lowered himself onto the seat. Holding the letter between both hands, he hesitated opening it, unsure of whether or not he wanted to know what it said. It had to be from her. But how had it arrived in his room? The only explanation he could think of was that Lady Duncaster must have gotten involved, but how Lady Eleanor had managed to convince her to defy Lady Foxworth's wishes, he could not fathom.

He slid his finger beneath the wax, breaking it. Considering the way in which they'd parted last night, he supposed the letter would insist upon some sort of explanation. As much as Lady Eleanor deserved one, he knew it wasn't something that he was prepared to grant. Unfolding the letter, he started to read, his heart kicking up a notch at the recognition of her voice delivered to him so clearly in the form of writing.

Signor,

> *I dearly hope this letter will somehow manage to make its way into your hands. If it does, then I would like to tell you how well I enjoyed your company last night and how saddened I was by your departure. Please understand that my*

aunt feels a great responsibility toward me, for you see, my parents have entrusted me entirely to her care. She is my sponsor—a position that she takes most seriously. And while I was honest with you when we spoke, regarding my position on marriage, I—

A soft knock at the door drew Richard's attention away from the letter. Muttering a curse, he folded it back up, got to his feet and placed it securely in the pocket of his breeches as he went to the door and unlocked it. Moving away, he went to stand by the window, drawing back the curtain so he could look out at the garden while his brother entered the room and closed the door behind him.

"It was quite a lively event last night," he said, staring toward the part of the garden where he'd first spoken with Lady Eleanor.

"I wish you could have participated," Spencer said.

Richard heard him walk over to a small table and setting something down—a tray with food, no doubt. Turning slowly away from the window, Richard offered his brother the side of his face that remained unscarred. "Such things no longer interest me."

Sighing with resignation, Spencer indicated the carafe on the side table. "Mind if I pour myself a glass?"

"Be my guest," Richard told him. Stepping toward the armchair he'd recently vacated, he asked Spencer to pour him one as well. His thoughts rested on the letter in his pocket and what the rest of it might say, but he could hardly throw Spencer out of his room in his eagerness to discover this.

"I do not understand you," Spencer said as he placed a glass of brandy in front of Richard and sat down across from him. "You are still an eligible gentleman."

Studying his brother, Richard raised his glass to his lips and took a slow sip. "You know how untrue that is. One look at me and all the young ladies will have a fit of the vapors."

"Sarah did not," Spencer reminded him. "If you recall, she told you that the scarring is not as bad as all that." Richard grunted disagreement. "And besides, the ball last night was a masquerade. You could easily have been there without anyone being the wiser."

For a fleeting second, Richard considered telling Spencer that he had been. Sharing his encounter with Lady Eleanor was especially tempting, but he resisted. If Spencer knew, he would probably become more adamant about Richard going out in public. There was also the added risk that he would mention Richard's attendance at the ball to their parents and sisters, which would only make Richard's situation more difficult. "To what avail?" he asked instead.

"I do not know," Spencer murmured with a shake of his head. "You have always loved music."

"True."

"You would also have had an opportunity to meet someone."

"I presume that you are referring to a lady?"

"Well, you are hardly going to form an attachment by remaining in your bedchamber all the time, and with a mask—"

"We have discussed this many times before," Richard said, annoyed by Spencer's insistence.

Spencer stared at him for a long moment. Picking up his glass, he drained it in one long gulp. "You cannot stay dead forever."

Richard clenched his jaw. "It is best this way."

"Best for whom?" Rising, Spencer went to the sideboard and set down his glass on the tray there. "You will not let Mama or our sisters see you, yet you expect them to carry on this farce on your behalf."

"I have never asked them to lie for me. People made their own assumptions when I failed to put in a public appearance after the war was over. It was commonly known that I was missing in action. All I asked was that nobody celebrate my return when I finally managed to make my way home."

"It is dishonest."

"To some degree perhaps, but I believe that Mama and our sisters preferred to go along with it rather than having to answer an endless amount of intrusive questions."

"They respect your decision because they love you, Richard. That is not the same as agreeing with it, and it certainly does not make it right."

Richard knew that there was a great deal of truth to this. Unfortunately, he couldn't give in. Not now when he was so close to exacting his revenge on the man who'd once betrayed him. "It has been five years. I am sure most people have forgotten about me. To make an appearance now would make no sense unless I was planning to live a normal life, but we both know that doing so will be impossible."

"Richard—"

"I look the way I do, Spencer. There is no changing that, so even if I were to meet a woman who appealed to me—one with whom I might imagine spending my future . . ." He saw Lady Eleanor's kind eyes within the confines of his mind, her pretty mouth curving as she smiled up at him. "There is very little chance that she would agree to become my wife, least of all when I am not even in possession of a title."

Spencer's left eyebrow went up a notch. "You have a fine fortune, thanks to those clever investments that you have made with your secretary's assistance."

Richard nodded. "Mr. Collister is, without a doubt, invaluable. But money will not be enough. Not when it comes to capturing a young lady's heart."

"Clearly you have forgotten the way in which Society operates." Pouring himself another glass of brandy, Spencer returned to his seat. "There are plenty of young ladies among our set who would not give a damn about what you look like as long as you are rich enough to supply them with new gowns and fripperies every Season."

Richard felt his forehead strain beneath a frown. "If you think that I would have any interest in *those* sorts of women, then you do not know me at all. I despise superficiality and greed."

A hint of a smile touched Spencer's lips. "The thing of it is, Richard, if you do happen to find a lady who is not in it for the money, chances are that she will not care about your appearance either. Such a woman—a selfless and kind woman—will want you for *you*, in which case your scars will not make any difference." Placing the rim of his glass to his lips, he took a sip, his eyes bright with the satisfaction of knowing he was right.

Needing distance, Richard rose and walked back

to the window where he looked out at the black sky. Fragments of the conversations he'd shared with Lady Eleanor spilled through his mind. She'd enjoyed his company, but she hadn't known who he was or what he looked like. "Do you suppose that if the right woman were given the chance to get to know me properly, that she might be able to develop some degree of fondness for me? Even if I did not allow her to see my face?"

"I think that you would have to let her see your face eventually." Spencer spoke carefully, as if he feared Richard's reaction. "To encourage any woman to marry you without doing so, would be very unfair."

Richard started, dropping the curtain as he turned back to face his brother. "Of course. I was not suggesting any form of trickery. I was merely wondering if a moment might arise where I could show myself to her without my appearance altering her regard."

Spencer blew out a deep breath. "I would like to think so. But unfortunately, your chance of meeting such a lady in disguise has passed. I do not believe that Lady Duncaster is planning to host another masquerade ball in the immediate future."

Richard nodded. He would not mention Lady Eleanor. She was a secret that he intended to keep close to his heart. "It is getting late," he said. "I believe you should be getting back to your wife?"

"Yes. I probably should." Spencer's footsteps tapped against the floor as he walked over to the door. "I wish you a good night, Richard."

Richard inclined his head. "Same to you. I look forward to seeing you again tomorrow evening."

As soon as he was gone, Richard reached inside his pocket and retrieved the note from Lady Eleanor.

—And while I was honest with you when we spoke, regarding my position on marriage, I cannot help but feel a certain connection with you. If there is any chance that you might feel the same way, I will be at the Greek folly beyond the west lawn tonight at midnight.

Respectfully,
Lady Eleanor

Richard felt his stomach tighten as he reread the final sentence. Clearly, the lady was suggesting a secret assignation. The thought was certainly intriguing, not to mention tempting. Glancing toward the clock on the mantelpiece, Richard noted the time, barely visible in the dimly lit room. Ten o'clock. Pensively, he reached for his violin, tucking it beneath his chin before sliding the bow slowly across the strings. The effect was a languid moan, like that of a satisfied lover.

Closing his eyes, he allowed the haunting melody to flow through him. It represented everything that he was, all that he had suffered, and the patience with which he was carrying out his vendetta. It reminded him of five long years of solitude, nights filled with equal measures of yearning and loathing, both deeply imbedded within his soul.

The tune drew to an end and Richard opened his eyes to find himself staring into the long mirror that hung on the wall. His blood pumped slightly faster through his veins as he took in the damaged flesh. To subject Lady Eleanor to such ugliness in the hope that she might be willing to accept him as a potential suitor, would be foolhardy. Worse, would be the selfishness of letting her into his life when he was so consumed by anger. He ought to dissuade her.

Still standing by the window later, he watched as the cloaked figure of a woman stepped out onto the terrace below. She didn't have to look up for him to know that it was her, her steps eager with anticipation as she walked toward disappointment. As sorry as he was for it, Richard knew that it was for the best. He waited until she was out of sight and was just about to turn away from the window when someone else exited the house. Richard peered down at the man who was presently crossing the terrace with brisk steps, the back of his neck pricking as he recognized Rotridge. And he was heading straight after Lady Eleanor. Hell and damnation!

Chapter 5

Mary's cloak swirled around her legs as she hurried across the west lawn in the direction of the folly. The night air was a little chillier than it had been the previous evening for the ball. It climbed up her legs and hugged her shoulders. Little did it help that the soles of her slippers were so thin that she might as well have been walking barefoot for all the good they did in keeping her toes warm.

Approaching a fallen column, partly overgrown by ivy, Mary glanced around, wondering if Signor Antonio might have arrived before her. Rounding the column, Mary peered through the darkness at the blurry silhouette of a Greek temple flanked by statues. Other columns lay at various angles, affording the look of a great archeological find. "Signor?" she whispered, making her presence known just in case he hadn't seen her.

No reply.

Mary crossed her arms, hugging herself against the breeze as it nipped at her from every angle. He wasn't here yet. Would he even come? The question had barely managed to form when the figure of a man emerged, his body gradually solidifying as he came closer. Mary's heart kicked up for just a fraction of a second, then froze completely at the realization that it wasn't the man whom she'd hoped for.

"What a pleasant surprise," Rotridge said as he walked up to her.

Mary took a step back. "My lord, what are you doing here?"

He came closer still. "I might ask the same of you." He looked from side to side. "Are you waiting for someone, by any chance?"

"And if I were?" Mary asked. She sounded much braver than she actually felt. Being alone like this with Rotridge was not the least bit comforting.

He shrugged, not halting his approach, though his steps grew increasingly measured. "I might offer to keep you company until he shows up."

Taking another step back, Mary found herself pressed up against the side of the temple. Swallowing, she tried to still her trembling hands. "Thank you, my lord, but you really need not trouble yourself on my account."

A chuckle made the air quiver around her. "Oh, it is no trouble at all, I can assure you." Arriving directly in front of her, he reached up, pulling a lock of her hair free from the confines of her plait. Running the silky strand through his fingers, he murmured, "Quite the contrary."

"I thought we had an understanding, my lord. Indeed, I believed you accepted my refusal to marry you when last we spoke."

A low chuckle swept over her. "You are quite mistaken, my dear. I was merely offering you a brief reprieve because you were feeling unwell. But I see now that you are fully recovered and would therefore like to take this opportunity to change your mind."

"My mind cannot be so easily swayed."

"I intend to prove otherwise."

Horrified, Mary watched as he dipped his head toward hers. "Please stop," she said, her hands coming up between them with the intention of pushing him away.

His thumb settled against her jawline. "You will be mine, my lady." A strong whiff of alcohol assailed her as he spoke. "The sooner you realize that, the better it will be between us."

Mary sucked in a breath, prepared to fight him off, just as a tall broad shadow appeared directly behind him. Before she could even manage a gasp, Rotridge had been shoved aside with such force that he stumbled to the ground a few paces away.

"What the hell?" Rotridge muttered, sounding surprised.

"I believe the lady asked you to leave her alone," Signor Antonio said. His back was turned toward Mary as he stood over Rotridge, but his voice was unmistakable. She knew it was him.

"You!" Rotridge scrambled to his feet so he could face his opponent. "How dare you involve yourself in my courtship?"

Signor Antonio grunted. "It is hardly a courtship when the lady is unwilling. If I may, I would suggest that you head on back to the house before you lose more than your pride this evening. Especially since I am the one her ladyship came to see."

"I should have known," Rotridge snarled. His eyes

flashed as he looked toward Mary. For a moment she thought he might be considering fighting Signor Antonio. But if he were, he changed his mind and bowed stiffly instead. "My apologies," he said. "I hope I have not offended you in any way, Lady Mary."

"It is nothing that cannot be forgotten," she lied, for the sake of being polite.

He nodded at that, but made no move to leave.

"If you do not mind," Signor Antonio said, "I should like to have a private word with . . ." He glanced toward her and she saw then that he was wearing the same mask that he'd worn at the ball. "Lady *Mary*."

"Forgive me, but leaving you alone with her would be highly irregular," Rotridge said. "People might think that—"

"No they will not," Signor Antonio grit out. "Not unless you happen to say something on the matter, which I would sincerely advise you against doing."

"Is that a threat?" Rotridge asked, his voice a little lower than earlier.

"Just a warning. For now."

There was a pause, and then Rotridge finally nodded again, spun on his heels and marched away with a disapproving gait.

Mary expelled a deep breath that she hadn't even realized she'd been holding. "I was beginning to think that you would not come."

He turned toward her again, offering her only the expressionless features of the mask. "I must confess that I almost decided not to."

His honesty caught her a little off guard. "Why not?" When he failed to answer, she said, "I thought you enjoyed my company as well as I did yours. Was I mistaken?"

There was a long drawn-out silence, followed by a distinct, "No."

Mary shook her head. "Then I do not understand." Easing away from the temple wall, she went toward him, her heart drumming wildly against her chest with every step she took. When he was within reach, she daringly reached out to touch his hand—bare skin against bare skin that sent a spark of energy shooting up her arm. He must have felt it too, for she heard him suck in a breath just as she did. "You know my real name now," she whispered softly. "Will you tell me yours?"

His eyes met hers, but whatever emotion she might have found there, was lost amidst the black shadows of the night. "Richard." His voice was a deep murmur filled with rich undertones.

Mary blinked, surprised by the familiarity with which he'd just introduced himself.

Warm fingers carefully curled their way around hers. "I have no title," he said, closing the distance between them. He brought his other hand up against her cheek, touching her as if it were a marvel to do so.

Mary could only gaze up at him. She'd never felt like this before—as if she were the only woman on Earth, and as if he'd spent his entire life trying to find her. The company they'd enjoyed the day before had stirred to life an awareness deep within her soul, compelling her to seek him out again. It burst through her now—a flare of heat across her skin. "Then you must be either a second son or a member of the gentry?" If he would only tell her which, then it might be easier for her to discover his true identity.

"I am certainly one of those things," he said, lowering his hand, "but I am afraid that I must disappoint you if you were hoping to discover more than that."

His secrecy ought to have made her wary. Instead, Mary found that she was all the more intrigued. "Will you tell me why?"

A moment passed during which she reveled in the comforting feel of his hand holding hers. It was so inappropriate, and yet so right. "You may rest assured that I am a gentleman and that I will treat you with the respect you deserve. You need not fear me on that account." He paused for a moment. "That being said, there are certain things that I would rather refrain from sharing with you at present. If you can accept that, then perhaps we can be friends. If not, I completely understand, as sorry as I would be to lose your company."

Mary considered this briefly before saying, "I see no reason to intrude."

He leaned back slightly. "I must confess that I am somewhat surprised to hear you say that."

She shrugged. "You are not the only one with secrets. Suffice it to say that I understand your reasoning."

A low chuckle vibrated around her. "Indeed? Now *I* am intrigued."

She smiled. "Perhaps that was my intention." Curiosity however, was a difficult beast to tame, so she couldn't help but ask, "The mask . . . do you wear it because you do not want me to know your identity, or because you do not want me to see your face?"

"Both," he answered gruffly. Stepping back, he increased the distance between them, turning slightly away in the process. "I am not . . ." His words trailed off in a blur of hopelessness.

"Not what?" she whispered, disliking the sudden change of mood.

Straightening himself, he turned back to face her. "It hardly matters. We should get back to the house before someone finds you missing, or worse, discovers you in my company." He offered her his arm.

Mary stood as if rooted to the ground. Common sense told her not to pry. She'd always respected other people's privacy, especially since she appreciated being allowed her own. But the manner in which he'd spoken told her that the words he'd left unsaid were of monumental importance. "I would like to know what you were going to say just now, before you changed your mind."

"Correct me if I am wrong, Lady Mary, but did you not just say that you saw no reason to intrude?"

Mary cringed. "You are right," she said. "I hope you can forgive my curiosity."

He inclined his head. "Of course." When he said nothing further, she stepped forward, accepting the arm he still offered. They started back toward the house at a moderate pace, neither one of them saying a word until they reached the side of the house and he turned toward her suddenly. "If you are hoping to discover a handsome gentleman beneath this mask, please stop, for I am anything but."

"I am certain that is not true," Mary said. "Your voice alone suggests—"

"Whatever romantic imaginings you may have, my lady, I encourage you to abandon them immediately. Not doing so, will only lead to severe disappointment."

The bitterness with which he spoke told her that he hadn't always felt this way. Something had changed, which could only mean that he no longer looked as he once had. A lump began to form in her throat. "Appearances are superficial. Until yesterday, nobody paid the slightest attention to me, but now that I have been noticed, several gentlemen have shown an interest. While I cannot deny that I appreciate their flattery, I would prefer it if their interest in me was based more on my character. In the end, that is what defines us. Everything else is inconsequential."

He stared down at her for a long moment. "Do you truly believe that, or are you just saying it to spare my feelings? Because if you are, there is really no need. I have had a great deal of time in which to come to terms with my circumstances."

"And yet you have not, or you would not need to wear a mask."

Richard knew that there was a great deal of truth to be found in her words, which was why he chose not to argue the point. Instead, he led her toward a narrow doorway and produced the key that Lady Duncaster had given him upon his arrival at Thorncliff. Placing it in the lock, he opened the door and ushered Lady Mary through to a small antechamber. The lantern he'd brought with him when he'd gone after Rotridge, hung from a hook on the wall, producing a warm glow that seemed to wrap itself around them as he diligently closed the door. The effort seemed to make the space smaller and more intimate somehow.

"What is this place?" Lady Mary asked. "I was not even aware that it was here."

"Few people have access to it." Reaching up, he retrieved the lantern, moving it in such a way that the light spilled over the far-right corner of the room, revealing an opening. "There is a corridor there, and at the end of it, a staircase that will take us up to the second floor. If all goes well, you should be able to return to your bedchamber unnoticed."

Tipping her head, she gazed up at him. "Thank you."

Her words were filled with appreciation, prompting him to reach up and brush his fingers along the edge of her shoulder. She said nothing as he did so, though her skin quivered gently beneath his touch and her chestnut-colored eyes, so full of warmth, held his in quiet understanding. She was perfect in every way—a true beauty, both inside and out. Was it really possible that she might not care about his appearance? Or was she just being polite when she'd claimed that character was of far greater importance. It was too soon to tell.

Struggling against the temptation their solitude offered, he lowered his hand and moved past her with the lantern. "Come along," he said, offering her his hand. "I will show you the way."

"When will I see you again?" she asked when they reached the top of the stairs. The door in front of them, once opened, would allow her to exit through a small closet located in an alcove behind a large tapestry.

"I do not know," he said, unsure of how wise it would be for either one of them to continue down this path.

"It sounds as though you are brushing me off."

"No. I . . . The truth of it is that I like you a great deal, my lady. I am just not sure that keeping each other's company on a regular basis would be such a good idea. You need to find a husband, while I—"

"You know well enough that I do not wish to marry."

He inclined his head. "So you have said. But what then? Do you really want to grow old alone? To abandon all hope of having children? Never to know what it might be like to . . ." He stopped himself, his breaths a little heavier with the realization that he'd almost alluded to something that no decent man would allude to in front of a lady. And yet, now that his thoughts had ventured in that particular direction, there was little he could do to stop the image of Lady Mary lying naked upon his bed from bursting through his mind. *Christ!*

"What it might be like to what?" she prompted.

Sucking in a breath, he turned away from her and opened the door. "You should go." His voice was too stern, but there was nothing he could do to change that. Five years of celibacy followed by the close proximity of a virginal goddess whose innocence would have him undone within seconds. If he hadn't already known that life was unfair, this proved it.

She stepped past him, but paused in the doorway. "When I asked you to meet me, it was because I needed to be certain."

"Of what?"

"That I did not imagine the effect you seem to have on me." She spoke as if in a daze. "There is something—some kind of pull that I cannot explain, except to say that I have never felt this way before."

"You do not know what you are saying." Hope, so small and fragile, began to spread against his better judgment. "It is the mystery that draws you."

She stared back at him with a great degree of pensiveness. Eventually she nodded. "You are probably right. It cannot possibly be because I enjoy spending time with you, because I have found our conversations interesting or because you saved me from Rotridge. The fact that you have shown a genuine interest in me or that you seem to care about my well-being is probably inconsequential to my opinion of you."

When she started to turn away, he caught her by the arm. "What do you want from me?"

Raising her chin, she gazed up at him with sparkling eyes. "To get to know you better, I suppose."

"For what purpose?"

A look of uncertainty crossed her face. She glanced away, and he realized then how difficult it was for her to share her thoughts. Desperate to hear them, he kept quiet, allowing her the time she needed to take courage until she eventually said, "I do not have many friends, and while it is true that I have decided not to marry, I do believe that it may be possible for the right man to change my mind."

He remained completely still, confounded by her courage. "So you wish to cultivate a friendship in the hope that it may blossom into something more?" he carefully asked.

"Yes."

"And if it does not?"

"Then I shall have had the pleasure of sharing the company of a man whom I genuinely like and admire—one who also happens to share my fondness for music."

Afraid he might pull her into his arms if he didn't release her, he dropped his hand to his side. "You are unlike any woman I have ever met."

She smiled faintly as she continued through the doorway, adding distance between them. "Thank you for meeting me tonight. I really appreciate it."

"It was my pleasure." She was gone before he spoke the last word.

Stepping back, Richard closed the door and leaned against the stone wall of the stairwell. He shouldn't want her, but by God he did. It couldn't be helped. Her scent—sweet roses in bloom—still filled the space where she'd stood only moments earlier. *When will I see you again?* Her words echoed through his mind. He was playing a dangerous game—one that would likely lead to a pair of broken hearts if he didn't retreat now.

Muttering a curse, he swung toward a passageway leading off from the small landing and headed in the direction of his own room. Hours of darkness still spanned before him, and after that, an entire day before he might see her again—against his better judgment.

"How was your walk, my lady?" Amy asked the moment Mary entered her room. "Did you see him?"

Rising from her chair in the corner, she came to help Mary with her cloak.

"You should not have waited up for me," Mary said, feeling slightly guilty. "It is very late."

"So it is, but I was too excited to hear about your meeting to get any rest."

"There is not much for me to tell," Mary said as she removed her slippers. "I still have no idea who he is."

"Really?" Neatly folding Mary's cloak, Amy set it aside before approaching her mistress.

"He wore the same mask that he wore at the ball."

"I take it that he did not give you his name either?" Amy asked as she began helping Mary undress.

"No," Mary lied. For whatever reason, Richard wanted to keep his identity secret. If she was to gain his trust, then she could not allow the risk of him discovering that she'd shared any part of their conversation with anyone.

Richard.

The informality was strange for her.

"Will you see him again?"

Blinking, Mary slowly nodded. "Probably." Because in spite of what he'd initially said, she trusted her instincts, which in this case told her that she would not be so easily forgotten by him.

Chapter 6

"**G**ood morning," Lady Duncaster said as she slid into a chair across from Mary and beside Lady Foxworth the next day at breakfast. "I trust you both slept well?" She gazed directly at Mary as she spoke, which resulted in a sudden wave of discomfort.

"Indeed we did," Lady Foxworth said, taking a sip of her tea.

Lady Duncaster's eyes remained on Mary even as she ordered a slice of cake from one of the footmen standing nearby. "Good." She seemed to relax against her seat, which in turn put Mary at greater ease. "Any plans for today?"

"Mr. Thomas Young has offered to show me one of his experiments," Lady Foxworth said. "I am supposed to meet him in the rose garden at ten o'clock."

"But, Aunt Eugenia, that is in only ten minutes," Mary said.

"Oh!" Lady Foxworth's teacup clattered against its saucer as she set it down. Pushing her chair back from the table, she rose. "If you will excuse me, I really must not keep him waiting."

Mary hid a smile as she nodded her agreement and wished her aunt a good day.

"I do believe that she is smitten," Lady Duncaster said as soon as Lady Foxworth was out of earshot. "It's very much like watching a young debutant in the middle of her first Season—all giddy and such." She stirred two lumps of sugar into her tea.

"It would be nice for her if she could find someone to make her happy," Mary murmured.

"I agree," Lady Duncaster said as her cake arrived. She dipped her spoon into it, denting the cream. "Love, marriage, courtship, and romance can be such a complicated business. In my opinion, everyone deserves a chance at happiness."

Mary kept silent, aware that Lady Duncaster was referring to the brief marriage that Lady Foxworth had entered into in her youth. It had been a love match, but sadly, her husband had died only one month after the wedding. She'd shown no interest in any man since. Until now, that was, though Mary suspected her interest in Mr. Young had more to do with the man's intellect than with his looks and that any potential relationship between the two would be based on a common interest in science more than anything else.

"How are things progressing with Lord Rotridge?" Lady Duncaster asked, her expression serene as she looked at Mary.

The unexpected question caught Mary off guard. "They are not," she said without thinking.

The edge of Lady Duncaster's mouth tilted. "Not your type?"

Scrunching her nose, Mary shook her head. "Not in the least."

The countess nodded. "It is unfortunate. After all, he is both handsome and terribly wealthy. A woman could do far worse than him."

Mary wasn't so sure about that last part. The inexplicable insistence with which Rotridge was trying to pursue her, coupled with the fascination that he seemed to have with her hair, was far too unsettling for Mary's liking. "Looks and fortune are not the most important attributes," she found herself saying.

Lady Duncaster popped a large spoonful of cake into her mouth, visibly savoring the delicacy while studying Mary closely. Too closely. "Does this opinion of yours have something to do with a certain *masked* gentleman, by any chance?"

Lowering her gaze, Mary stared down at her empty plate. "Not at all." A second passed before she chanced a look at Lady Duncaster from beneath her lashes and asked, "Why would it?"

Setting down her spoon, Lady Duncaster reached for her teacup and took a sip. "Because your interest in him has not diminished since the night of the ball. Rather, it has grown." And then, "You went against your aunt's wishes and indirectly asked me to deliver a note to him on your behalf."

Heat washed over Mary's entire body. "I am sorry, but I could think of no other way in which to contact him and"—casting a wary look at some of the other guests present, she lowered her voice to a whisper—"leaving things as they were seemed wrong."

"While I appreciate your honesty, I do not like being taken advantage of," Lady Duncaster told her crisply. "You know that your aunt is a longtime friend of mine and that it is my duty to support her wishes, yet you deliberately forced my hand."

"I needed to see him again." At least she was being honest about that.

Something in the old woman's eyes shifted. "And did you?"

Mary nodded. "But he was wearing the mask again, so I have yet to see his face."

"In other words, you are curious." Laughter from the other end of the table caught Lady Duncaster's attention. She looked away for a second, then smiled and said, "I suppose that is only natural."

Mary shook her head. The strangest need to make Lady Duncaster understand, filled her. "No," she said. "It is more than that."

Lady Duncaster tilted her head. "Go on."

"I feel a connection with him." Staring into her teacup, Mary idly thumbed its edge. "It is difficult to explain." Behind her, she could sense the footmen moving about, their precise footsteps vibrating through the floor and up the legs of the table. She watched as ripples formed in her tea, so faint they were barely visible at all.

"You do not have to," Lady Duncaster said. "I believe I know precisely how you feel."

"Really?" Surprised, Mary looked up, her hand jolting the cup and causing some of the tea to spill.

Lady Duncaster smiled warmly. "My husband had a similar effect on me when we first met. It always felt as though my stomach was turning itself inside out whenever he glanced in my direction." She chuckled lightly before turning serious. "The trouble with your situation is that too many secrets are involved and in order to keep them, too many promises have to be made." Reaching across the table, she took Mary's hand in her own. "The masked gentleman you met at the ball does not wish for his identity to be revealed. He has his reasons for that. Your aunt, on the other hand, has a responsibility toward you. It would be terribly careless of her to allow you to associate with a man who refuses to offer her even his name. How can she know that you will be safe in his company when she has no idea of who he is?"

"I understand her reasoning perfectly, but—"

Lady Duncaster snorted. "You think you know better, because you have taken a liking to him."

Mary knew how silly it sounded. "You said yourself that he comes from a highly respectable family with whom an association would prove beneficial."

"So I did, and I stand by that statement. It was, however, meant to alleviate your aunt's concerns, not prompt you into having secret meetings with the gentleman in question behind her back while making me a party to your betrayal of her trust."

Put like that, Lady Duncaster made Mary feel as though she'd just committed a terrible crime. "I am sorry," she said again. What else *could* she say? Her explanation seemed to have had little effect.

Lady Duncaster sighed. "You may not be aware, Lady Mary, especially not based on this particular conversation, but I am a big advocate of love matches. It is my fondest wish that everyone should be afforded a chance at a happily-ever-after, but in this case, I am too concerned that you might end up getting hurt."

"Because *Signor Antonio,*" she said, refraining from disclosing her knowledge of his actual name, "might look different from what I expect? Because I will likely be disappointed that he is not as handsome behind the mask he wears as I might have hoped? I am not that superficial, my lady. It is his character that draws me. Nothing else."

"And so it should be, if your feelings for him are genuine. But that is not what I am worried about."

Mary blinked, surprised that there could be any other reason. After all, Lady Duncaster knew his identity and had been willing to vouch for him the night of the ball. Something must have changed. "Then what is it?"

"I have my doubts that he is ready to form a deep attachment with anyone. If you were to fall in love with him, there is a good chance that he may break your heart. Not deliberately, of course, but . . . a man like him is bound to have other secrets as well. Until he is prepared to reveal them to you, you will only see what he wants you to see."

"You know something about him," Mary murmured. "Something that makes you think that he may be hiding more than his identity."

Lady Duncaster pressed her lips together before confessing, "All I have are a few suspicions—nothing concrete."

"So you could be wrong." When she didn't reply, Mary said, "As grateful as I am for your advice, I am inclined to follow my own instincts."

"In that case, I hope that he will be wise enough to

place his faith in you." She glanced past Mary's right shoulder and smiled. "Lady Spencer, what a lovely surprise!"

"Good morning to you both," Sarah said as she came to stand beside Mary's chair. Glancing down, she addressed Mary. "Lady Foxworth has asked my husband and me to introduce you to some of his friends."

Mary's mouth dropped open. It took a moment for her to recover and say, "Really?" Just one single mention that morning about her disinterest in Rotridge, and now this.

"Viscount Belgrave has expressed an interest in making your acquaintance," Sarah added. "If you will join me for a walk, we can meet with him and Spencer down by the lake."

"I . . ." What could she possibly say without being rude? Glancing back and forth between Lady Duncaster and Sarah, she noted their expectant faces. "I would be delighted," she said, swallowing her annoyance with her aunt as she excused herself to Lady Duncaster and left the dining room with Sarah.

As it turned out, Belgrave was not as dislikeable as she'd feared, following her experience with Rotridge, who'd thankfully refrained from approaching her that morning when they'd crossed paths in the hallway. Apparently his altercation with Richard the night before had had the desired effect. But Belgrave was nothing like Rotridge. Indeed, he was not only handsome, but courteous and well-educated as well. Of course he was not the sort of man who would ever be willing to accept Mary's scandalous career choice, but at least he proved to be good company.

"Perhaps we can ride out for a picnic tomorrow," he suggested as he, Mary, and the Spencers, enjoyed their afternoon tea together a few hours later. The terrace had seemed a little too crowded so they'd asked a couple of footmen to set up a table and chairs on the grass down by the lake.

Mary met his gaze, warm and inviting—so different from Richard's, which was genuinely dark and so much more powerful. A small shiver traced her spine at the memory of it, and for a second she hesitated, wishing that *he* would have asked her to go for a picnic instead. But he hadn't. In fact, he'd made no promise that they would ever see each other again. So she smiled back at Belgrave and said, "That would be lovely, if the weather permits."

He returned the smile and offered the use of his carriage. "I will ask Lady Duncaster to recommend a good location."

"We actually happen to know of one," Sarah said, looking at Spencer. "Remember that hill we visited a couple of weeks ago?"

"The one with the church ruin behind it where Lady Fiona lost her bonnet?" Spencer asked as he swatted away a bothersome fly.

Sarah nodded. "The very one."

Belgrave looked intrigued and when he asked Mary if she thought the place would suit, she realized that she felt the same way. There was just something adventurous about the idea of picnicking on a hilltop close to a church ruin.

"It is settled then," Belgrave announced as he emptied his teacup.

The fact that the Spencers shared a knowing look

did not escape Mary. If they would only realize that they were completely wasting their time in the match-making department.

That evening at dinner, Mary glanced from one gentleman to the next. During the course of the day, she'd concluded that Richard was not an uncommon name. In fact, from what she'd discerned, there were no fewer than six gentlemen present at the dinner table who bore that exact same name. Two were too old, however, which left four, none of whom seemed to fit the man that she imagined to be hiding behind the mask. Their faces were far too perfect.

"I need a distraction," she told Amy later when she returned to her bedchamber.

"It sounds to me as though you may have found it in the form of Lord Belgrave," Amy said as she located Mary's nightgown, laid it on the bed, and came toward Mary with the intention of helping her undress.

"No," Mary said, stepping away from her. "Lord Belgrave is kind, but he does not affect me in any way." Turning, she looked Amy straight in the eye. "I need to sing."

"I heard you sing tonight in the music room after dinner. It sounded lovely, as I am sure all the guests will agree."

"You know that is not what I mean," Mary said. "That kind of song is supposed to showcase a lady's finer qualities. It is more about me being put on display than it is about conveying any kind of emotion."

"I know." Amy sighed. "You enjoy the passion that the other kind of music provides."

"It is more than that," Mary said. It was never easy, describing the cravings of her soul, knowing that whatever she said, it would likely fall short. "When I really sing, Amy, it does not matter how many people surround me. They all fade away until it is just me and the music thrumming through me, clasping at my heart. One moment I am filled with joy, the next with great sorrow." She paused before speaking the truth that clung to her heart. "It is in these instances that I feel most alive."

Amy nodded. "You feel every nuance of emotion that the composer was trying to convey through words and music, and you impart that emotion to your audience with incredible skill."

"It means a great deal to me that you understand."

"How could I not when I have helped you practice before every concert? I know the lyrics to every song just as well as you do, which is why I know how important it is for you to continue doing what you are doing."

"It comforts my soul in a way that nothing else ever will."

"I think it also helps you clear your head," Amy noted.

"Yes," Mary agreed. She crossed to the wardrobe and pulled the door open, searching for her dark green velvet spencer. Finding it, she began slipping her arms through the sleeves while Amy helped hold it in place. "I need to sing," she repeated.

"Allow me to accompany you, my lady."

Mary shook her head. "We have been over this before. If my aunt comes looking for me, then you must be here to offer an excuse on my behalf."

"I doubt that she would do such a thing, given the late hour."

"It is not that late—only ten o'clock—and when I came upstairs, she had not yet retired."

Amy blinked. "It seems her schedule has changed since coming here." She helped Mary button up her spencer, then handed her a pair of kidskin gloves. "Nevertheless, I dislike the idea of you venturing out alone like this, in the dark, no less."

"I have done so before without issue." Since accidentally discovering a cave during her first few days at Thorncliff, Mary had practiced her singing there a couple of times already. Granted, that was before Rotridge had shown an interest in her. She'd deliberately avoided telling Amy about her encounter with him the previous evening.

Amy did not look convinced. "I tried to dissuade you then as well, and I shall continue to do so until you see reason. What if something were to happen to you? What do I tell your aunt then?"

Placing her hand against Amy's shoulder, Mary told her seriously, "If anything were to happen to me, then you must tell her the truth." She retrieved her hand. "But you must not worry. I will be perfectly fine."

Amy sighed with resignation. "If only you would enjoy needlework and poetry like other young ladies."

"I find such activities far too tedious, and besides, I am not like other young ladies."

"No, you certainly are not." Crossing her arms, Amy said, "Your aunt will have both our heads if she ever finds out."

Mary nodded. "Yes. She will."

"And yet you still insist on going through with this?" Amy shook her head. "It is unwise."

"It is necessary!" Softening her tone, Mary said, "Besides, she has not discovered what I am up to yet, and it has already been two years."

"I hope you are right," Amy said as she helped Mary put on her cloak, "because in my experience, secrets always have a way of surfacing."

Unwilling to argue the point, Mary wished her maid a pleasant evening, accepted the lantern that she offered her, and slipped out of the room and into the dimly lit hallway beyond.

Sipping a cup of coffee that Spencer had brought up to his bedchamber a short while earlier, Richard stood, surrounded by darkness, and looked out at the silhouetted shapes of the garden. He hadn't been able to sleep during the day, his mind consumed by thoughts of Lady Mary, of what she'd said about appearances and character . . . of her beauty.

Seeing Rotridge so close to her, against her will, nonetheless, had put him in a rage. Perhaps because of her innocence—the knowledge that she was untouched by any man—pure, but with great passion simmering beneath the surface. He hadn't thought twice about tossing the earl aside, barely resisting the temptation to pummel him. Discipline had helped keep him in check. That, along with the disturbing thought of allowing Lady Mary to witness such brutality.

So he hadn't slept as he usually did during the day, though not for lack of trying. Eventually he'd tossed the sheets aside and risen, allowing himself the luxury of peering out at the garden from between a thin parting in the curtains, only to see her in Belgrave's company.

Even now, the anger he felt at the memory of it was acute. More so now that he knew her true position on marriage—that the right man might stand a chance. God help him if he didn't want to be that man. For although they'd met only twice before, they had been two remarkable times. And the letter . . . *I could not help but feel a certain connection with you.* She might not have made any promises, but with that comment, she'd bound them together anyway. Surely she wouldn't say such a thing only to encourage another gentleman's favor?

He thought back. Belgrave had made her laugh. Richard felt his shoulders tense. He gritted his teeth. What the devil had Belgrave said that she'd found so amusing? Closing his eyes, he leaned forward, setting his forehead against the cool glass of the window and expelling a deep breath. He couldn't even compete for her hand on equal terms. Not looking the way he did. Not when he didn't want anyone to know that he was even at Thorncliff. In England. Alive.

Her hand . . . In marriage.

Impossible.

Leaning back, he set his coffee cup aside. He didn't know her well enough to entertain such thoughts, had not so much as kissed her yet. But he wanted to. Desperately. And the idea of forming a more permanent attachment sent a thrill through him. Perhaps because it had been so long since he'd been with a woman? No. It wasn't just that. It was her—

the kindness she emitted, the intelligence brimming in her eyes, her openness and the way in which she responded to him. There was an attraction between them that stirred his blood, tempting him to forget his plans and all that he'd worked for these past five years. If he was wise, he would keep his distance from her so he could focus on what still remained to be done.

The terrace door opened below and Richard watched as a woman stepped out, light flickering from the lantern she carried. It was her. He knew it even though she'd pulled the hood of her cloak up over her head. Mesmerized, Richard watched as she crossed the terrace to the right as if she were heading toward the same place where she'd invited him the previous evening. But she hadn't invited him tonight, which made him wonder about where she might be going and, more to the point, whom she might be planning to meet. Belgrave, perhaps? The thought rankled.

Letting the curtain slide back into place, Richard spun away from the window and grabbed his mask and cloak from the wardrobe, putting them on as he crossed to the wall-panel next to the bed. A slight nudge was all it took for it to spring open, revealing the passageway through which he always found his way in and out of the house.

Snatching the lantern that stood on his bedside table, he stepped inside the narrow passageway and closed the wall behind him. It didn't take long for him to exit into the stairwell he'd shown Lady Mary, descending at a pace that quickly led him through the small antechamber and into the garden beyond.

Taking a moment, he glanced around, hoping for a hint of Lady Mary's whereabouts. Met by nothing but darkness, he started in the direction of the Greek folly, his hasty footsteps grating against the graveled pathway until he stepped onto the lawn. Hidden behind a row of trees, this part of the garden had been divided into long walkways, interspersed by neatly trimmed grass quadrants. The folly stood to the right, but further along, to the left of it, a tiny dot of light acted like a beacon—there, then gone, then there again, according to Lady Mary's movements.

She shouldn't be out here like this, late at night and alone. It wasn't safe. He hurried after her, eager to know her purpose. If Belgrave was involved, he was not as honorable as Richard had thought him to be, but an irresponsible cad, luring her so far away from the house. Richard clenched his fists. But if he *wasn't* involved . . . some of the tension eased from Richard's body as he considered that possibility, even though he couldn't fathom what else might have prompted her to show so little regard for her own safety, let alone her reputation if someone happened to see her.

The light disappeared through between some bushes toward a part of the property that Richard had never visited before. Drawing closer, he realized that there wasn't even a proper path here, just a narrow gap that led him through to a wide slope. Glancing down, he saw the light some distance below, moving off to the right. He muttered a curse. The woman was clearly mad to risk coming here in the dark. If she were to fall and hurt herself, nobody would even hear her calling for help.

Careful of his own steps, Richard had no choice

but to move more slowly than before as he descended toward the flat ground below. His chest was tight with concern for the lady by the time he reached it. Was she not aware of the peril she placed herself in by venturing this far from Thorncliff? Having vanished from view, Richard could only continue in the general direction that he'd seen her go, his lantern casting a steady glow against the slope as it grew in height by his side. The grass upon it gradually disappeared, giving way to the jagged outlines of rocks. His heart beat faster. This was no place for any woman. He considered calling her name and letting his presence be known. If this *was* Belgrave's doing, Richard would have no qualms with letting the viscount know that he thought him an ass and an utter scoundrel for suggesting such a hazardous location for his midnight rendezvous with her.

A faint sound drifted toward him, carried upon the breeze like a boat upon a wave. Holding still, Richard listened as it hummed through him, heightening each sensation. A melodious tune that couldn't be mistaken for anything else: *Singing*. His stomach contracted with pleasure. It couldn't possibly be her, could it? And yet he knew, before he found the parting amidst the rocks, before he stepped between them, and before he rounded the corner to discover the vast cavern that awaited . . . he knew without a doubt that it was her. And so it was; her voice loud and clear, filled with light and goodness as it soared through the air—a creature released within this secret place beneath the ground where no one else would ever hear it.

Turning down the flame of his lantern, Richard

set it aside and leaned into the darkness, fearful that she might stop her song if she noticed his presence. He recognized the piece immediately. It was one of his favorites—*Porgi, Amor*, from Mozart's *Marriage of Figaro*. He'd heard it a dozen times before he'd gone to war, though never with this degree of pure talent. It was so unexpected that he practically forgot to breathe.

Turned slightly away from him as she sang, he could only see the profile of her face, partly concealed by shadows. Even so, there was no mistaking the raw emotion that she shared through her voice. It filled the cavern, wrapping itself around him as he stood there, confounded by her skill and her passion for the music. He'd noted it when they'd first met, but this . . . he had no words for it. She was like a supernatural being descended from the heavens to convey a message from God.

Responding to each and every note—to the rise and fall of the song, his soul seemed to extend beyond the confines of his own body, reaching out to share in the divinity of the moment. But then she turned, muted as she met his gaze, and he realized that in his captivated state of awe, he'd stepped away from the darkness and gone toward her, like a sailor lured by a mystical siren.

Chapter 7

Mary caught her breath, her skin prickling with tiny bursts of heat the moment she saw him. "Why are you here?" She had to say something in order to break the strange silence now hanging between them. Knowing that he'd heard her—that he'd spied a part of her soul—unnerved her in the most peculiar way. Indeed, he might as well have caught her in a state of complete undress for all the difference it made.

"I was worried about your safety," he said as he stepped further into the light. She'd placed her lantern on top of a large rock, the warm glow now casting him in yellow tones that shifted as he moved.

Swallowing, she gave a small nod, accepting his reply. "You saw me leave the house?"

"I did." He stopped his progress and glanced around. "This place is quite a surprise. How on earth did you find it?"

She shrugged one shoulder. "I discovered it one day when I was out for my morning walk."

His eyes met hers from behind his mask, their dark perusal sending a shiver down her spine. "And do you often go wandering about on your own? Without a chaperone and far away from anyone who might be able to help you in case the need should arise?"

Her breaths quickened slightly in response to his censure. "You think me foolhardy for coming here alone at night."

"Considering what happened yesterday with Rotridge, much closer to the house than this and in the open, you cannot be surprised." His tone was sharper than before.

"It is not the first time that I have come here," she said, determined to show him that she knew what she was doing. "Nobody has ever followed me before."

"Until now," he told her gruffly. "It was difficult not to notice you, Lady Mary. Anyone keeping a lookout would have done so." He dropped his tone to a softer one. "And if they had happened to be the malevolent sort, you might have found yourself in grave danger."

Her breath hitched a little as he stared back at her from across the distance, aware that a man did not necessarily have to have ill intentions for him to be a threat. She swallowed the thought even as she wished for him to come closer. "This is the only place where I can sing," she said, hoping to direct his attention away from the danger she courted by coming here.

"And considering how well you do it, I daresay that you should be allowed to continue singing, undisturbed by anyone."

"Thank you," she whispered.

He tilted his head. "Does your aunt know about this . . . hobby of yours?"

She almost laughed at the idea of her singing being considered a hobby, reminded that although he'd witnessed her performance just now, he had no idea of how vital it was to her life. "Of course not. She would think it scandalous. Anyone would, thanks to the ill repute of opera singers."

Richard grunted. "I am sure they simply do what they must in order to survive."

Mary knew that wasn't quite true. For some perhaps, but not for all. There were those whose salaries were high enough to allow for a comfortable life without lowering themselves to the same level as a demimondaine. But she chose not to argue, saying instead, "You are probably right, but that does not change the *ton*'s view on the matter."

He took a step in her direction. "Perhaps not. So I shall make a bargain with you."

"What?" Hidden away beneath her chest, her heart thrummed away at an increasingly rapid pace.

Another couple of steps brought him closer still. "I will promise to keep your secret safe on one condition."

He halted before her, just a few feet away, and she sucked in a breath. Panic struck her unawares at the realization of the power he now held over her. Was he aware of it? Squaring her shoulders, she tried to appear confident—unperturbed by his proposal—praying that it worked. "What are you suggesting?" Thankfully, her voice showed no signs of distress.

Closing the distance between them with two swift strides, he brought his hand to her cheek, tilting her head until she was staring up at him, her composure failing in response to his touch. Her heart quickened as the comforting warmth he provided flowed through her, contorting her stomach and weakening her knees. "You touched my soul with your voice." He spoke with wonder, then blinked as if the words surprised him.

The sincerity in them—the importance—filled her with undeniable pleasure. "You know my secret now." Though far from all of it. "Will you share yours with me?"

He drew away. Distance fell between them. "I doubt that either one of us is ready for that just yet." He didn't have to say that he wasn't sure they ever would be for her to know that the thought was there, at the forefront of his mind. "As to my condition for keeping yours . . ."

Apprehension made her stiffen. "Name it," she told him boldly.

He eyed her for a moment before saying, "You may come here as often as you like, but only with my escort."

The idea of keeping his company on a more regular basis, whenever she required it, sent a thrill straight through her. "I accept," she said, unable to keep from smiling. He stared at her in silence. A long drawn-out moment followed, until she had to struggle not to fidget beneath his gaze. Eventually he nodded, and she expelled a deep breath, startled not only by the fact that he was willing to accept her for who she was, but by how relieved she was by that. "Shall I sing some more?" She felt completely exposed now, as if he knew too much about her while she knew next to nothing about him. The knowledge brought a degree of awkwardness with it that she desperately wished to escape from. Singing would allow her to do precisely that.

Inclining his head, he took a step back. "Are you familiar with the Queen of the Night's second aria from *The Magic Flute*?"

"Indeed, I know it very well."

"Then that is what I should like to hear, if you would be willing to oblige me." He moved toward some large rocks protruding from the ground at the base of the cavern wall, away from the light. Taking a seat, he leaned toward the shadows, cocooning himself until he blended into the background.

Mary took a few breaths, her nerves now rioting with the knowledge of his presence. Her heart was beating furiously against her chest while her hands had long since grown clammy. For the first time ever, she felt as though she might be sick from the unease roiling around inside her stomach. Which of course was silly. It wasn't the first time that she would be singing in front of another person, though it would be the first time that she would be doing so as herself.

Clasping her hands together before her, she turned away from where he sat and where her lantern stood, and stared into the darkness. The first few notes were hesitant—too soft and tremulous for her own liking. She closed her eyes, gave herself up to the music . . . listening, as her voice grew stronger, rising and falling with flawless clarity as it resonated around her. Gradually, everything fell away, including herself, until all that remained was the song.

It wasn't until it drew to a close, dying upon her lips, that she became aware of the tears pooling behind her eyes and the ache that filled her chest—a common occurrence whenever she allowed the music to take control of her senses. A second of silence followed. She drew a breath, and then, the sound of clapping, reminding her that she wasn't alone.

"Remarkable," she heard him say from somewhere close behind her, informing her that he'd come toward her once more. What surprised her the most, however, was the sound of his voice. It was raw with emotion, as if he too had been brought to tears by the song.

She prepared to turn, to face him with the hope of somehow returning to some sense of normalcy. But before she could manage to do so, she felt the warmth of him against her back—the hard contour of his chest, just before his arm came around her, securing her in place. A gasp escaped from between her lips, and she instinctively stiffened against him.

"Shh . . ." His voice was tender against her ear. "You know that I mean you no harm."

Her body relaxed and she allowed herself to lean back against his strength. "You should not be touching me like this." And yet she wanted him to, even as she heard herself say, "It is not proper."

He chuckled—a low rumble that coiled its way around her. "Indeed, it is far from it, but I cannot seem to stop myself." He spread his fingers against her waist. "You are the light to which I am drawn."

"And you are the darkness that lets me shine," she whispered. His mask was cool against the side of her neck, but his body was all heat, cascading through her and making her want things she'd never wanted before. "I cannot seem to escape you."

"Do you wish to?"

A simple question, the answer to which she sensed

would direct their future. "No." His hold on her tightened. "I wish to know you."

Without warning, he pulled away, leaving her cold. She turned, addressing his back. "Tell me about the war, your childhood . . . anything that will allow me to form a clearer image of the man you are."

He paused, considering her request before looking back at her over his shoulder. Their eyes met, and his body immediately responded, recalling how good it had felt to hold her in his arms only moments earlier. She'd been so soft and warm, perfectly molded against his firmer contours. It occurred to him that he would have liked to remain like that forever. Lord, it seemed like a lifetime since he'd been that close to a woman.

Inhaling deeply, he tried to return to a more relaxed state of being. He blamed the song for his momentary lack of propriety—that, and the beauty she exuded. And yet he'd chosen to use it against her, threatening her with her secret while she had accepted his proposal without the slightest degree of anger or even irritation. He owed her something in return. "No man, who has ever been to war, returns the way he was before he left. It changes you . . . affects you . . . in ways you cannot possibly imagine."

A long moment of silence passed between them before she eventually asked, "Did you lose many friends?"

He turned more fully toward her. "When you witness the kind of devastation war causes, it no longer matters if they were your friends or not. All you can think of is that they were living, breathing people; fathers, brothers, sons. Their loss was unacceptable, even if I did not know them personally."

She nodded as if she understood, even though she couldn't. Not really.

"The truth is," he found himself saying, "that none of us wanted to be there, even though we all pretended otherwise. At least in the beginning, before the fighting started." The memory of what had followed pulled him back into the past, flooding his mind with images he'd rather forget.

"And then?" she prompted.

He blinked, startled by her sudden proximity. "Seeing men blown to pieces by canon fire, trampled to death by horses as they lay wounded in the mud, wandering aimlessly about with missing limbs . . . horrifying does not come close to describing the brutality of it."

"I cannot imagine what it must have been like."

"Nobody can. Not unless they were there." A memory surfaced—blonde hair tied with blue ribbons. "There was a girl, perhaps sixteen years old. She was French." He could still hear her screams. *Laissemoi! Je t'en supplie!* "Some British soldiers—my own countrymen—had captured her during an unsanctioned raiding party in Lille. They snatched her from the street and brought her back to camp with them, almost eighty miles away from her home."

"What did they want from her?"

He could tell from her voice that she dreaded the answer, so he decided to spare her the details. "Something they never got."

Her eyes widened with understanding. "You

fought your fellow soldiers in order to save a French-
woman?"

"It was the right thing to do." He shook his head.
"The war brought out the worst in those men. They
deserved the beating I gave them and the dishonorable discharge issued by Wellington after I told him of
their actions." A flash of bare limbs twisted beneath
the torn fabric of a gown shot through his mind. The
girl had been bruised and battered by the time he'd
found her, but she'd muttered an almost inaudible,
merci, when he'd set her down in front of her parents'
house the following day.

"Will you tell me how you sustained your own injuries?"

Blinking, Richard focused his mind on the present
and on the woman standing before him. He'd known
the question would come—had suspected that she
must have figured it out—and yet it still caught him
off guard. His shoulders tensed and his heart rate accelerated, as was always the case when he thought
back to the moment when his face had been taken
from him. "I was captured," he said, pushing the
words past the knot in his throat. "It was a reconnaissance mission, ordered by the Duke of Wellington. I volunteered along with a few others, but
something went wrong and . . ." He winced, sensing
the blind rage that threatened to consume as he recalled the betrayal, forcing it back so she would not
see. He took a deep breath, expelled it, aware that
his nails were digging into the palms of his hands as
he clenched his fists. Willing himself to relax, he told
her bitterly, "The French wanted information. They
decided to burn me in order to get it."

Pain captured her features, twisting them with anguish on his behalf. "I am so sorry," she whispered.

"You must not pity me!" The words whipped through the air, echoing around them.

"I do not," she told him gently. "But I cannot help but feel a tremendous amount of sadness for what you have been through. Nobody should have to experience such a thing."

Soothed by the goodness she exuded, he felt his anger dissipate. "I agree." Shifting, he took her by the hand. "Spending time with you allows me to forget. When we are together, I feel like the man I once was."

"Before the war?"

He nodded. "I used to be social. Now I choose to live alone, surrounded by no one."

"What about your family? Your friends?" Incomprehension filled her voice. "Surely you must have seen some of them since your return?"

"Only my father, my brother and my secretary," he confessed.

"Surely your friends must have called on you, to welcome you home?"

Gently, he squeezed her hand. "I was reported missing. When I returned to England, I did nothing to change that status."

"They think that you are dead." The words were but a whisper in the dim light of the cavern. "Why?"

"Because it was easier than facing them, of having to explain what happened and subjecting myself to their shocked responses to my altered appearance." There was another reason as well, of course, but he had no intention of sharing *that* with her.

"I suppose that makes sense," she said, surprising him with her level of understanding.

That spark of hope he'd felt when they'd first met, and then again last night when she'd mentioned that character was of greater importance than looks, returned. "How long have you been singing?" he asked.

"For as long as I can remember."

"And this particular style of music?"

"Just a few years," she confessed. "I visited the opera for the first time with my parents when I was fourteen and was so impressed by it that I could not help but make an attempt at that style of singing myself."

Her openness impressed him. "It is a pity that nobody else will ever hear you, because in my opinion, you are the best soprano that I have ever had the pleasure of listening to."

She smiled, clearly pleased by his praise. "Thank you. That is very kind of you."

He looked her straight in the eye, wanting her to know what he saw. "It is the truth."

She said nothing in response as she stood there staring back at him, her eyes widening with deep understanding. "This is the strangest thing," she eventually murmured as if she wasn't even talking to him but to herself.

"What is?"

Her hands moved, indicating the space between them. "You and me. I never thought that I would meet someone who would actually *see* me, but I believe that you do. Don't you?"

Richard felt the atmosphere change around him, aware that they were no longer having a casual conversation. "I can tell that singing is vital to your well-being, that it feeds your soul and that you would suffer without it. I suspect that this is the reason why you are reluctant to marry, because you fear that if you do, you will have to sacrifice your greatest passion."

"I would have no choice but to do so. No man would allow me, as his wife, to engage in such activity. Not to mention that few men would even consider marrying me if they knew."

"Then they are fools." Lord, he'd give anything to be able to listen to her every day for the rest of his life.

She tilted her head a little. "Do you not realize how scandalous it would be if anyone were to find out?"

"Why would they? If you married, then I am sure that you would be able to find a private place on your husband's estate where you might practice."

She smiled slightly in response to his suggestion. "And in London?"

He inclined his head, seeing her point. "You might have to refrain while staying in Town, but at least you would have a normal life with children to love and care for."

"I must admit that foregoing the chance to have children would be my greatest regret, but to choose a life without the freedom to sing whenever I please, seems like an unbearable sacrifice to make."

He studied her for a moment, frowning as he said, "I doubt that it would be so different from the life you are presently living. After all, finding a place in which to practice whenever you are in London must be just as difficult now as it would be if you married. At present, you have your aunt to worry about."

She started a little at his words as if he'd somehow surprised her with his reasoning. Blinking, she said, "Of course."

There was something about the way she spoke that gave him pause. For a second, he couldn't help but wonder if she might be hiding something else— another reason to avoid getting married. He couldn't seem to stop himself from being curious. "Have you ever explored the cave beyond this point?" he asked, deciding to change the subject for now.

Her expression relaxed, as did her posture. "No. I did not think that it would be wise to do so alone."

He almost laughed, stopping himself at the last moment. "I see," he said as he went to fetch his lantern. Returning with it, he passed the spot where she stood and swung the light around. "There appears to be a small decline over here that continues down toward another level deeper underground." The adventurer inside him called out and he turned back to face her. "Is there any chance that you might like to explore it with me tomorrow afternoon?"

"I would have to find a reasonable excuse to be absent from Thorncliff."

"Perhaps after dinner then? You could feign a headache." He held his breath, realizing how eager he was for her to say yes.

She nodded once. "I think I would enjoy that." Her tone held a great deal of thought to it and then her eyes lit with excitement. "Perhaps we will find something wonderful."

"Like skeletons and pirate treasure?"

She scrunched her nose in the most adorable way. "The treasure would not be so bad, but skeletons?" A visible shudder raked along her spine.

"They will not hurt you, you know."

She gave him a look of distinct displeasure. "That certainly is a comforting thought."

"You need not worry," he said as he moved toward her, bathing her in the light of his lantern. "I will be there to protect you."

"Another comforting thought," she said, her words dancing through the darkness, carrying with them a secret confession that immediately stirred his blood.

Reaching out, he trailed his thumb along her jawline, his breath escaping him as she swayed toward him, eyes closing on a sigh of pleasure. "Mary." He spoke her name with reverence, foregoing the honorific without even thinking; loving the way it curled over his tongue.

Unrest churned around his stomach, like a storm rising upon the horizon, drawing nearer with every aching beat of his heart. His thumb continued across the soft ridge of her cheekbone, toward her ear where a strand of hair had come undone. Tucking it back in place, he noted her shallow breaths and became conscious of his own. *If only* . . . There were a million ways in which he might finish that wish. "It is late," he said, dropping his hand to his side. "I should get you back to the house."

"It is unlikely that anyone will notice my absence."

"Nevertheless, I insist. We can come back tomorrow at a more reasonable hour. As we discussed." He offered her his arm, which she thankfully accepted after a brief hesitation. But when he moved to escort her out of the cave, she failed to follow, effectively halting his progress. He looked down at her. "What is it?"

"It is just . . ." She bit her lip and looked away, took a breath and tried again by saying, "Forgive me, but I am having trouble expressing myself correctly."

"Take your time." He placed his hand over her arm, hoping to offer support and courage—curious about what she might say.

Hesitantly, she met his gaze, concern and sincerity blending in her eyes like a pair of puddles flowing together. The effect was one of complete vulnerability, tightening his chest until he felt his heart squeeze. "Am I imagining it, or is there more between us than just a cordial acquaintanceship?"

He stilled, fearing the fragility of the moment. "You wish to know if I am attracted to you." His pulse leapt with anticipation the moment she nodded her response.

"Are you?"

God yes!

"I enjoy your company a great deal," he said, afraid of where his honesty might lead.

She winced. "That does not tell me much, considering how little company you have had for the past few years. I daresay any conversation would be welcome."

"You may be correct." Her face fell. "But I doubt that anyone else would be able to sing as well as you." Fear stopped him from mentioning her looks, how beautiful he found her or how desperately he wanted to kiss her.

"Is that all?" Hope clung to her voice.

"No. But it must suffice for now."

She stared back at him. "I am sorry to hear you say that."

"Why?" He could not help but ask—could not help but hope, just as he'd done from the very first moment he'd seen her—in spite of everything. The odds against them were enough to discourage the most determined of men.

A crease appeared upon her brow. "Because although we have known each other for only a brief time, I rather imagined that you were tempted to kiss me before."

Lord help him, she was brave, bold and utterly divine. Heat exploded in the pit of his stomach while his chest expanded, a rush of energy tumbling through him, filling him with want. "And?" He forced himself to take courage.

A miserable smile captured her lips. "And I found myself hoping that you might."

Richard's heart thudded against his chest, his breaths carefully measured as he stared down at her upturned face. He swallowed, unsure of what to say in response to such a forthright confession.

She averted her gaze, began to turn away. "I am sorry," she muttered, shame dripping from the voice that had been so confident barely a second before.

It was more than he could bear. "You must not be." When she tried to move away from him, he held her firmly in place, knowing that he would be the greatest ass that ever lived if he failed to meet her honesty head on. "The truth is that I *would* like to kiss you, more than anything in the world. But I cannot."

"Because you do not wish for me to see your face."

"I am afraid of what will happen between us if you do."

She frowned, her expression more serious than he'd ever seen it before. "You think that it would alter my opinion of you?"

"I am certain of it." He knew he was being harsh and that he wasn't giving her the chance she deserved to prove him wrong, but it couldn't be helped. He liked her too much to risk losing her on account of his appearance.

"I am not that shallow, Richard," she said with conviction. "Far from it."

His name upon her lips, spoken with fondness, prompted him to pull her into his arms. "I know," he whispered against the top of her head. "But I am not ready for you to see me. Not yet. Please, Mary . . ." He fought for breath as he wrapped his arms around her, holding her close. "Try to understand."

She didn't reply. Instead, she wound her arms around him too, hugging him back. Lord knew he needed this—the warmth and comfort that she provided. It wasn't until now that he realized how much he'd missed physical contact with another person. Spencer and his father had provided him with conversation, but this . . . the feeling of her heart beating steadily next to his, almost brought tears to his eyes. "Promise me that you will not look."

A brief hesitation followed, as if she wasn't sure of what he was asking of her. She finally nodded. "I promise."

Holding her against him, her cheek pressed into the black wool of his cloak, Richard raised one hand to push back the hood. Taking a breath, he then tilted back the mask and dipped his head, allowing her hair to tickle his face as he inhaled her scent. "You smell so good," he whispered, realizing belatedly how ridiculous that sounded.

Her fingertips dug against the muscles spanning his back. "Chamomile mixed with lemons. It is my favorite scent."

"Mine too," he told her gruffly, to which she chuckled gently—a sweet sound filled with promise. Spreading her fingers, she pulled him closer.

For a moment they just stood there like that, chest against chest until Richard decided to lean back a little so he could look at her. Tilting her head, he saw that her eyes were closed, just as she had promised. He was grateful for that. Exceedingly so. Staring down at her delicate neck and at the pulse that beat there, he carefully lowered his lips to the smooth skin that awaited, pressing a series of kisses against her. She gasped in response to each individual one, and it was all he could do not to press his lips more fully against hers.

Raising his head, he lowered his mask before pulling back from her embrace, adoring the befuddled expression that captured her face as her lips parted with surprise. "One step at a time," he told her softly.

With a dazed nod, she allowed him to escort her out of the cave, their lanterns lighting the path in the darkness as they made their way back to Thorncliff like a pair of specters stealing through the night.

When he returned to his bedchamber, Richard expelled a deep breath as he closed the door behind him and leaned against it. He deserved a medal for the degree of restraint he'd shown this evening. Which of course made him immediately wary. His situation was complicated—more than Lady Mary even realized. The demons that plagued him demanded retribution, blackening his heart while hers shone bright with purity. They were completely ill-fitted. There was no denying that. Nor was there any denying the fact that he would be the worst possible scoundrel if he continued to seek her company. No good could possibly come of it.

And yet . . . he still had hope that maybe . . . maybe she would still want him once she saw his face. He winced. But would she be able to accept what he was doing? Women were sensitive creatures after all. Perhaps she'd judge him harshly for it.

Glancing down, he caught sight of a crisp piece of paper, neatly folded upon the floor; a letter, slipped beneath the door while he'd been out. Picking it up, he tore open the seal and unfolded the missive. There were only a couple of lines.

> *The funds you requested are now in your possession. Please be advised that the damage they've incurred seems surprisingly slight. How do you wish to proceed?*
>
> *Collister*

Pondering the importance of the words, Richard crossed to the sideboard, poured himself a brandy and went to sit behind his desk. Retrieving a piece of pristine paper, he dipped his quill in the inkwell and wrote:

Thank you for your letter, which was well received. We will set our sights on the property now and see how well he deals with that. Also, I believe I should like to invest one thousand pounds in Sir Davy's electromagnetic research. Please make the necessary arrangements.

RH

P.S. Please gather as much information as possible on the Earl of Rotridge.

Once the letter had been folded and sealed, Richard took a sip of his brandy. He'd always considered himself the forgiving sort. Not anymore though. Rising, he went to the window and looked out, the positive mood he'd shared with Lady Mary earlier now clouded by the anger that followed him daily, like a loyal dog. He would be rid of it soon though. He would make certain of that.

Chapter 8

Early rays of sunshine warmed Mary's skin as she strolled through the garden with Viscount Belgrave the following day. She'd been planning a visit to the library, but her aunt had intervened, suggesting that spending time with his lordship would be of far greater value.

"But I shall be joining him for a picnic later," Mary had protested, to which her aunt had replied, "The more time you spend in each other's company, the more chance there is of him making an offer."

Deciding not to argue with her aunt's logic, Mary had done as she had asked.

"My lady?"

Mary blinked, startled by the insistence of Lord Belgrave's voice and realizing they'd come to a halt. Turning her head, she noticed that his eyebrows were raised in question. He was a handsome man, no doubt about that, but looks did not a love match make. More was required for that. "Yes?" she inquired.

It was his turn to blink. "You seemed very deep in thought just now. I wonder if you heard any part of what I was saying." She stared back at him until he eventually said, "About my decision to extend one of the parlors at Belgrave House and turn it into a conservatory?"

Knitting her brow, she bit her lip and shook her head. "Please forgive me, my lord. I believe I must have been woolgathering." When a perplexed expression crossed his face, indicating that he'd likely spoken on the matter at great length, she added, "Though I am sure it would be a wonderful improvement to your home."

Expelling a deep, dissatisfied breath, Belgrave resumed walking, guiding Mary toward the shade of an elm tree and a bench that stood beneath it. He waited for her to sit before allowing himself to claim the vacant spot next to her. A true gentleman in every sense of the word. More so than Richard, who'd held her shockingly close while his lips . . .

"May I ask what it is that has you so distracted?" Belgrave asked, forcing Mary's attention back to him once more. "If you are concerned about something, I would be happy to offer advice. As a friend, of course."

She smiled up at him. "That is very kind of you, but I can assure you that nothing is troubling me."

Stretching out his legs, he crossed them, drawing attention to his perfectly polished boots. "Well, whatever it is," he said with a slight tilt of his lips, "it does appear as though you are more interested in *it* . . ." he paused for a moment as if considering something, then added, "or *him* . . . than you are in me."

Shocked by his statement, Mary turned so abruptly

toward him that she almost toppled backward onto the grass behind her. Belgrave's steady hand stayed her. "I beg your pardon?" she couldn't help but ask.

He chuckled slightly. No hint of annoyance. "I see now that I am correct. Someone else is preoccupying your mind, which makes me wonder why you are not keeping his company instead of mine. After all, you are an exceedingly lovely woman, Lady Mary. A man would be mad not to have some interest."

"I . . . thank you, my lord." What was she to say without lying? "You have been exceptionally kind and I can only hope that you can forgive me for not paying greater attention to you. I fear I have been unconscionably rude."

"It is quite all right." Briefly, he gazed up at the leaves rustling overhead before looking back at her. "If I were to hazard a guess, your aunt is eager to see you married and has insisted that you become better acquainted with the gentlemen visiting Thorncliff."

"How did you know?" Mary asked, embarrassed that he'd discovered that she'd practically been pushed at him against her will.

He shrugged. "It is the way of things. People like us do not expect to make a love match. When the Spencers introduced us, I was just happy to discover that you are a beautiful person, both inside and out."

Glancing up at him, she saw his gentleness reflected in his eyes. "You give the very best compliments, my lord, but you cannot honestly claim to have known me long enough to make such an assessment of my character."

Allowing a smile, he reached for her hand, raised it to his lips and placed a tender kiss upon her knuckles. "A woman who laughs and smiles as much as you do, cannot be anything but beautiful and kind." He leaned back, allowing her to mull over his words a moment before saying, "Does this man whom you like reciprocate your sentiments?"

A flush of heat rose to Mary's cheeks. "I do believe that you are being entirely too curious about my personal affairs, Lord Belgrave."

He nodded at that. "Forgive me, but since I do enjoy a fair amount of gossip myself, I—"

Her eyes went wide. "You do?"

"Certainly."

"But you are a man!"

His mouth contorted into something ridiculously strange until he suddenly, quite unexpectedly, burst out laughing. "And what?" he asked when he'd gotten himself back under some measure of control. "Men cannot enjoy listening to news of scandalous behavior?"

"There is nothing scandalous about my behavior!" Not entirely true, she realized, once the words were out.

"I see." He turned more fully toward her and looked her straight in the eye. "Is he married?"

Her jaw dropped. "What? No! Of course not."

"Then he must be someone whom your aunt would not approve of. It is the only logical explanation for why you are not with *him* instead of me."

Mary didn't respond. It had taken him all but two conversations to figure her out, and all because she kept on getting distracted by thoughts of Richard. Lord help her, she'd barely slept a wink last night after they'd parted, continuously going over the time they'd spent together in the cave. He'd heard her sing. Had actually liked it! And then of course there was his embrace and the maddening way in which her body had responded. She'd never felt like that before, and had been completely taken unawares by the sudden need for him to touch her in the most shocking ways possible.

Her heart quickened at the memory of it and her stomach quickly tightened. "If you do not mind, I think I should like to visit the library before it is time for us to join the Spencers for the picnic." She needed to get off this bench and move—expel the restlessness that churned inside her with the anticipation of seeing Richard again. It wouldn't be long, and yet it seemed like forever.

"I would be happy to escort you, if you like," Belgrave said. "In fact, there are a couple of books that I have been meaning to take a look at myself."

She accepted his offer, happy with the feeling that their strange conversation had not made things too awkward between them. Rather, he seemed surprisingly tolerant of the fact that he had no chance of winning her hand in marriage. As if to underline this notion, he said, "I am sorry that your situation appears difficult to you. Hopefully you will find the solution that you seek, but in the meantime, if you need anything, I am happy to assist in whatever way that I can."

Linking her arm with his, she said, "And in return, I shall endeavor to find a lady who is more deserving of your favor than I will ever be."

They crossed an intersecting pathway leading past a row of trees, from which a shadow emerged, solidifying as the sun fell upon the man's face, revealing none other than Rotridge. "Lady Mary and Lord Belgrave," he addressed them dryly. "What a lovely little walk you appear to be having."

It was, until just now, Mary felt like saying. Instead she allowed Belgrave to respond.

"It is a perfect day for it," he said, seemingly unperturbed by Rotridge's scowl, though he did draw Mary a little closer to him, as if he sensed that she needed protection.

Rotridge's eyes darkened, even as he attempted a smile. "Do you enjoy masquerades, Belgrave?"

Belgrave straightened his spine, increasing his height as he stared back at Rotridge. "If you are referring to the ball the other evening, I must confess that I found it most enjoyable."

"Indeed?" Rotridge's lips drew up to form an ugly snarl.

"Indeed."

Mary's temper started to rise. "Is there a point that you would like to make, my lord?" She gave Rotridge her best glare.

His eyes turned toward her. "Only that I do not recall seeing Belgrave there."

"Perhaps because I was wearing a Bauta mask?" Belgrave suggested. "My entire face was hidden from view."

"Precisely," Rotridge said, taking a step closer.

Belgrave frowned. "Please forgive my ignorance, Rotridge, but I am having trouble understanding your implication."

"He is not the man you are looking for," Mary told Rotridge. She'd hate for him to do something rash and for Belgrave to suffer the consequence on account of a mistaken identity.

Rotridge appeared to study Belgrave for a moment before finally saying, "No, I don't suppose he is. Never mind. I will simply have to keep on trying to figure it out." He tipped his hat in the most condescending manner that Mary had ever seen. "Good day."

"He really doesn't like you, does he?" Belgrave asked as they watched Rotridge walk away.

Mary expelled a deep breath. "No," she agreed, "He does not."

Belgrave seemed to ponder that for a moment before saying, "He is also very jealous of your secret beau."

Mary's mouth tightened in a grimace. "I do not have a beau."

"No?"

"No," she said decisively.

A brief silence followed as they continued back toward the house until Belgrave said, "In any event, I would like to inform Spencer and Chadwick about Rotridge's behavior. Between the three of us, we will have a better chance of keeping an eye on him, just in case he decides to give you trouble."

"Thank you, my lord," Mary said, appreciating his concern. "Your assistance is most welcome."

They set out with a pair of curricles when the sun was at its highest. Tied securely beneath her chin, Mary's bonnet shaded her eyes as she gazed out over the bright display of wildflowers dotting the countryside.

"It is nice to escape the crowd for a while," she told Belgrave as he steered the horses along the dirt road.

"Too boisterous for you?" he asked, briefly dropping a look in her direction.

"A little perhaps. I enjoy the company of others, but there is also something to be said for peace and quiet." Thinking of Richard, she considered how odd it was that her world was so full of people while his was completely lacking.

It took a half hour drive for them to arrive at the hilltop that Sarah and Spencer had mentioned. After parking both curricles at the bottom, the party alit and gathered up their supplies before making their way to the top.

"There is quite a splendid view from up here," Mary said as she turned to look out over the countryside below. "Have you seen?"

"It is one of the reasons why I suggested coming here," Sarah said. Setting down the blanket she'd been carrying, she came to stand beside Mary. "Look, you can see Thorncliff over there in the distance."

Turning in the direction that Sarah indicated, Mary searched for the manor until she finally found it. "It looks so small from here."

Sarah chuckled. "I know. It is hard to believe that there are hundreds of people residing within its walls at present, if one considers all the servants as well."

Nodding her agreement, Mary turned away from the view and approached the spot where the men were unfolding Sarah's blanket. Offering them her own, she gave her attention to one of the baskets and, with Sarah's help, began organizing the plates and the food until everything had been laid out.

"It looks delicious," Spencer said as he dropped down onto the blanket, seating himself beside Sarah while Belgrave lowered himself next to Mary.

For the next hour, they enjoyed the food that Cook had prepared for them while discussing a subject that Mary found most uncomfortable: marriage. But since Spencer and Sarah had recently had their wedding and Spencer's sister, the former Lady Newbury, had married the Duke of Stonegate in secret, it was apparently a subject that Sarah was very much interested in.

"What say you, Belgrave?" Spencer suddenly asked. "Do you suppose you might choose to marry any time soon?"

Starting at the question, Mary looked at the gentleman seated at her side, immediately embarrassed on his behalf even though he showed no sign of concern over the question. Instead, he seemed to ponder it quite seriously before eventually saying, "Perhaps. If the right lady comes along, I see no need to delay."

"Quite right," Spencer concurred.

Sarah on the other hand offered Mary a very deliberate smile that made Mary want to shrink away into nothingness. Thank God that Belgrave knew of her disinterest in him or this would have been the most awful conversation ever.

When they were done with the food, Sarah said, "Perhaps you would like to enjoy a quiet stroll?" She gave Belgrave a pointed look that made Mary cringe.

To her relief, he merely shrugged and said, "I was actually hoping to use this time away from the masses to discuss an investment that I have in mind with your husband."

Spencer gulped, the wine he'd been drinking

almost spilling from his glass. "Of course," he said, apparently just as surprised by this statement as his wife was.

"Are you certain?" Sarah asked while Mary quietly prayed for her to stop trying to make a match where there was no match to be made.

"Quite," Belgrave said, "but if you and Lady Mary would like to go for a stroll, then by all means, do not let me keep you."

Mary required nothing further to get her on her feet. Addressing Sarah, she said, "Come. Let us leave the men to their financial discussions and take a look at that church you mentioned. I find that I am quite eager to see it."

Side by side, they wandered away from where the men were sitting. "Am I mistaken, or are you and Belgrave completely disinterested in each other?" Sarah finally asked.

Mary glanced briefly at her friend, noting her curious expression before returning her gaze to the view. "We are friends," she said, "but there is little chance of us ever being anything more."

"Why? I can hardly think of anyone more eligible than Belgrave." There was a brief pause, and then, "Does your disinterest in him have something to do with the gentleman you met at the masquerade?"

A gentle breeze toyed with the grass while Mary considered the question. "Perhaps," she said, not bothering to hide her smile.

"Then you have discovered his identity?"

Mary scrunched her nose. "No." When Sarah spoke her surprise, Mary quickly added, "but I have met with him a few times since the night of the ball."

"Without knowing who he is?"

"I do not expect you to understand," Mary said, "but there is something about him that draws me. I cannot seem to help it."

A contemplative pause followed until Sarah quietly asked, "Do you have any clue at all regarding his identity?"

"Not yet," Mary lied. She'd told her friend enough and would not risk betraying Richard's trust.

"Just be careful then," Sarah said as she linked her arm with Mary's. "I would hate for you to get hurt."

It was past ten o'clock when Richard heard her footsteps descending the stairs that would lead her toward him. A second passed, and then the glow of her lantern came into view, blending with the light of his own as she entered the small antechamber, beyond which, the gardens of Thorncliff awaited.

The slightest tremor shot through him at the sight of her. She wore her hair up in a complicated style that only a maid would have been able to produce, revealing a pair of delicate earrings that dangled from her lobes. Her gown this evening had been cut from the sheerest white muslin in multiple layers that added an air of ghostliness to her. Over it, she wore a tight spencer jacket that was meant to keep her warm. To Richard's mind, it only served to draw attention to her shapely figure.

"Are you ready?" he asked. Something had to be said before he forgot himself completely.

She nodded. "I have been looking forward to it all day."

There was something in her tone that made him want to wrap his arms around her and pull her against him. Instead, he shrugged the feeling away and turned toward the door.

Fifteen minutes later, they were back inside the cave, their lanterns casting a yellow glow that danced across the walls. Carefully, Richard headed toward the other end of the cave where the floor slanted downward. Turning up the light of his lantern, he held it out in front of him and glanced down. "It appears to be a little steep," he said. "Do you think you can manage?"

Stepping up beside him, Lady Mary paused for a moment before saying, "I am glad that I put on my walking boots after dinner."

Dropping his gaze, he spotted the leather tips of them peeking out from beneath her hemline. "I will help you, of course." Moving forward, he realized the slope wasn't nearly as challenging as it appeared, for which he was grateful. He turned when he was halfway down and offered Lady Mary his outstretched hand, a shock of heat rushing through him the moment her palm settled against his own, alerting him to the fact that she wasn't wearing gloves.

With trembling heart, he guided her toward him, then stepped back the rest of the way until they were both safe on the flat surface below. Unwilling to sever the bond between them, he failed to release her hand as he ought, waiting instead for her to do it. To his surprise, she curled her fingers more tightly around his—so tightly, that he almost forgot to breathe.

"I went for a walk with Belgrave today," she said. The softness of her voice made it sound as though she was speaking of a mundane matter like the arrangement of flowers in the garden. "Later, we enjoyed a picnic with the Spencers."

Richard stiffened. Instinct told him to retreat. Instead he held his ground, thankful that his expression would be hidden behind his mask. Allowing a moment to pass, he aimed for a neutral tone. "I trust you had an agreeable time?"

"It was pleasant enough," she said as she pursed her lips. "He knows that I have no interest in him."

"Is that true?"

Her eyes widened with surprise. "Of course it is."

His chest tightened around his heart. "I daresay that there is no 'of course' about it. After all, he is both handsome and titled. In fact, the truth of the matter is that he would make an excellent match for you." What the hell was he doing, talking up another gentleman in favor of himself?

She nodded her agreement. "He is also exceedingly kind."

Richard grit his teeth together. "I have no doubt that he is."

"In fact," she told him thoughtfully, "I do believe my life would be far less complicated if I *were* interested in him."

"But you are not?" He held his breath in anticipation of her answer.

She frowned. "I thought we had already established that I am not."

"Right." He made to turn away—to avoid asking her who she might be interested in then—knowing what her answer would be but also knowing that he really shouldn't encourage her favor. Except of course, he wouldn't be roaming around a dark cave with her in the middle of the night . . . alone, one might add . . . unless he wished to encourage her favor a great deal. Damn, what a mess he'd made. And all because he couldn't stop himself from seeking her out on the night of the ball.

"I also spoke with Rotridge."

A chill raced down Richard's spine. His shoulders tensed. "About what?"

Her eyes widened a little, no doubt in response to how angry he now sounded. "Actually, he approached Belgrave while I was in his company. Apparently Rotridge was of the opinion that Belgrave might have been you."

"I see." Thank God he'd had the foresight to inquire about the earl. If only he could find something condemning that he could hold against him, then hopefully he'd have a means by which to ensure that he would stay away from Lady Mary forever.

"You should know that Belgrave has mentioned it to Spencer and Chadwick and that the three of them have offered to keep an eye on Rotridge—to ensure that he does not try to do something foolish."

"Good." Richard knew little about Belgrave, but with Spencer and Chadwick looking out for Lady Mary, he was confident that she would be safe from Rotridge. How safe she'd be from *him*, however, was an entirely different and far more complicated question. Raising his lantern, he immediately forgot about his predicament regarding his increasing fondness for Lady Mary because of what he suddenly saw. "There are steps over here." It seemed unfathomable.

"Steps?" She sounded equally surprised. "So much for discovering unchartered territory."

He almost laughed in response to her obvious disappointment. "I see no reason why we cannot still explore it."

"I suppose you are right, especially since there is less chance of either one of us falling into a ravine as long as a proper path exists."

"Were you really worried about such a thing happening?" he asked. He'd warned her that their exploit could prove hazardous, but a ravine? "I have never heard of caves having ravines in them," he told her thoughtfully.

"A pit then?"

He blinked and murmured a drawn out, "No," before adding, "When I spoke of potential danger, I was merely considering a sprained ankle or some other minor injury. Not once did I imagine either one of us plummeting to our deaths."

She scrunched her nose again in that adorable way that he'd grown so fond of. "I am sorry. It was not my intention to be quite so dramatic about our adventure, but I have recently been reading *The Dark Secret of Mistletoe Forest*—"

"And you imagined ending up at the bottom of a pit with only a ghost for company?"

She gaped at him. "Have you read it?"

"In case you were not aware, I have had a surprising amount of time on my hands since returning from the war." He shrugged. "As it happens, I found it to be an amusing read—undoubtedly one of the most unpredictable books that I have ever encountered."

"I find it vastly entertaining myself," she said. "Especially the part where the hero descends into the pit to save the heroine by tying the harness from his horse together with his jacket, shirt, stirrups and saddle."

"A touch unrealistic, I suspect, but the fact that this amused you tells me something else about you," he said.

"And what might that be?" She gazed up at him, her eyes wide with curiosity.

"Well, some might say that *The Dark Secret of Mistletoe Forest* is one of the stupidest books in existence—a mockery of English literature. But since you do not, I can only conclude that you appreciate the satire behind it and that you also have a splendid sense of humor."

The smile that spread its way across her face, like the first rays of sunlight brightening the sky at dawn, stole his breath. She was without a doubt the most exquisite creature he'd ever encountered. "That is one of the best compliments I have ever received," she said. "Thank you."

Dipping his head in a bow, he turned back toward the stairs. "Shall we proceed?"

"Oh, indeed we shall!"

Richard counted fifteen steps before they reached another plateau. "Do you hear that?" He whispered the question.

"It sounds like water."

Moving closer to the sound, Richard noticed a series of torches, held in place by iron sconces that had been mounted into the rock wall. Taking one down, he held it to the flame of his lantern, then used it to light the rest of the torches until the cave was perfectly illuminated, allowing them both a clear view of the space they were now in—an area at least twenty paces in width. Looking up, Richard saw that a thin waterfall flowed out from between a crack in the wall. He followed the movement until it dove behind a ledge at the opposite side of the plateau, splashing against a larger body of water below.

Crossing the area, he peered down, confounded by what he saw. "It looks as though there is an underground river down there." He glanced toward the left where a gradual slope appeared to form an embankment. "I can even see a boat."

She was beside him in an instant. "I thought you were joking," she said. And then, "This is without a doubt the best adventure I have ever had. Shall we see what else we can find?"

Richard laughed, the sound so foreign to him that he startled himself with it, which resulted in something of a croak. He heard Lady Mary draw a sharp breath, and then she said, "I gather that it has been a while since you found something amusing?"

He nodded, increasingly aware of how much he enjoyed her company.

"In that case, I feel remarkably lucky to have had the good fortune of sharing this moment with you, and one day, when you are ready, I hope to not only hear your laughter, but to see you smile as well."

"I must confess that as much as I would like that, I cannot help but fear how you will react." His throat tightened around his breath until his chest ached and his heart felt uncomfortably heavy. He'd never been this honest, this open, with anyone.

"I know," she said as she reached out and took

him by the hand, her fingers wrapping around his. She looked at him with imploring eyes. "But we cannot go on like this forever. Not if we are to have a future together."

"I am aware of that."

She nodded, her gaze shifting to their hands. "Then you must face your fears at some point and trust that I will accept you for who you are." She paused a moment before saying, "And I must do the same."

He frowned at this. "What do you mean?"

A shy smile traced her lips. "You are not the only one who is afraid to show your true self. There is something about me that you may not be willing to accept."

This surprised him. Indeed, he did not believe it. Nothing about her would ever deter him from wanting her in every conceivable way. "I take it that you are not referring to your fondness for opera, for I already know about that."

She dropped her gaze. "You are right. There is something more."

He didn't like the sound of that—the not knowing what sort of stain might tarnish his view of the lady whom he'd come to hold in the highest regard. "What is it?" he managed to ask.

"I will tell you as soon as you are ready to show me your face. One truth in return for another, to test the depth of our affection and whether or not we have a chance for true happiness together."

He sucked in a breath, unprepared for her suggestion. "You drive a hard bargain, my lady."

"Perhaps," she conceded, "but I will not marry a

man who cannot appreciate me for who I am, and neither should you."

"Marry a man? God no!"

Her laughter was immediate, completely unpretentious, and filled with the sort of happiness that was only made possible when one was completely comfortable in the other person's company. He loved that he'd made her feel that way and couldn't resist pulling her toward him. Indeed, he'd been struggling not to do so the entire evening, the memory of her warm body from the day before tempting him every second that they were together.

So his arms found their way around her, hugging her close until she was flush against the length of him, her face buried against the black wool of his cloak. He could feel her chest rising and falling just as unevenly as his, her heartbeat vibrating through him until it matched the beat of his own.

Chapter 9

Mary had never doubted that she was a romantic at heart. But with the turn her life had taken in
recent years and the fact that she'd never met a man
who'd made her heart flutter before, she'd long since
realized that she would probably never marry. She
certainly wouldn't make a lifetime commitment to
someone for anything less than love. And then her
brother had gotten into financial trouble and she'd
dismissed the idea of marriage completely.

But now, wrapped in Richard's warm embrace,
there was no doubt that her heart was fluttering. As
for love . . . she was beginning to suspect that it might
not be long before that particular emotion enveloped
her completely. Which was strange, not only because
she had no notion of who Richard was or what he
looked like, but because they'd only just met three
days prior. Yet somehow, in a strange and almost
magical way, she already felt as though she'd known
him forever.

Inhaling his scent, she leaned back, forcing him to
loosen his hold. For a long moment, she gazed up at
the silver mask that concealed his features, desper-

ately wishing that he'd take it off—remove the barrier that stood between them.

"What are you thinking?" he asked, his voice soft and husky as it curled its way around her like smoke.

"Nothing." She refused to push him before he was ready.

"Now you are being dishonest." His hand caught hold of her chin as she started to look away, holding her face steady as he gazed back into her eyes. "Tell me what it is."

Swallowing, she allowed a few breaths to pass before saying, "Very well. I was thinking that I would like for you to kiss me." Heat crept up her neck and into her cheeks. Her pulse leapt at the realization of what she'd just said. "Forgive me. That was . . . too forward."

"There is nothing to forgive," he murmured, his thumb gently stroking along her jaw until she feared her knees might buckle. "I have thought of little else myself, since holding you in my arms last night."

"You kissed my neck." She sounded breathless, and indeed she was. The memory of what he'd done—the acknowledgment of it—was making it near impossible for her to function properly.

"It was not enough." His statement, the simplicity of it, the boldness, was almost more than she could bear. His thumb stilled against her cheek. "Have you ever been kissed before? Properly, that is? By a man who desires you?"

She shook her head. "No."

His eyes held hers for what seemed like an eternity before he suddenly dropped his hand and stepped away. "I think the river must lead toward the sea," he said as he headed toward the steps with his lantern.

Mary blinked as she watched him go. What on earth had just happened? Feeling somewhat unraveled, she went after him. "Did I say something wrong just now?" she asked, unable to comprehend the sudden shift in mood.

Reaching the embankment, Richard crossed to the boat and began inspecting it. "Not at all," he said without looking at her. "I think this must have been here for many years. It is in pretty bad shape—part of the wood has rotted away."

"Then why are you acting so strange?"

He ran his fingers along the edge of the boat. "I do not think that I am, all things considered. After all, we have just discovered a river and a boat beneath Thorncliff Manor. There is also a tunnel just over there, in case you failed to notice it yet. Do you not agree that what we have found demands further investigation?"

Frustrated, she almost stomped her feet. "Well yes, but that is not what I was referring to, and you know it."

He sighed then, his head dipping a little as if in surrender. "You fear being alone with Rotridge, and yet you have clearly placed your trust in me. Why is that?"

"I do not know," she said. "Perhaps because you are the one who has saved me from Rotridge's unwelcome advances twice already."

He shook his head and then grunted. "You are naïve if you think that you are safe in my company."

Her eyes widened at this, surprised by the harshness of his voice. He studied her a moment before adding, "For the last five years, I have been celibate, and then I meet you, a woman who tempts me in every possible way. You would be a fool not to fear me."

Squaring her shoulders, she held her ground. "And yet I find myself incapable of doing so."

A long pause followed, and then, "You claim that you want me to kiss you." There was a bitter undertone to his words that made her shiver. "Wait until you see my face and you will reconsider."

She shook her head. "No. I will not."

"So you say, but I can assure you that I have had good reason to stay away from Society all these years. Give me a few more days to bolster my courage and I shall show you what I mean."

"It will not change anything between us."

He winced. "I would hope not, but I also have to be realistic. As much as I like you—however dependent I seem to have become on your company in the short time that we have known each other—I cannot ignore the fact that you are beautiful while I . . . I am anything but."

"You must not say that!" He drew back, her sharp tone visibly shocking him. "Don't you dare tell me that you are less deserving just because your face happens to be scarred. In my eyes, you are the hero who went to war and fought for his country, the man who suffered torture at the hands of his enemies, the very same man who could have taken advantage of me several times over by now, but who refuses to do so because he is at heart a gentleman." She struggled against the tight knot forming in her throat while her eyes burned with emotion. "You deserve every bit of happiness in the world, including . . ."

"What?"

She shook her head, almost gasping for air. "Nothing. I . . ." She blinked. "It is nothing."

He muttered something incoherent before saying more loudly, "Considering your very impassioned speech just now, I daresay that it is not nothing. Will you tell me what you were going to say? That I deserve everything, including . . ."

She took a deep fortifying breath before diving in headfirst. "Me," she whispered, feeling ridiculously self-conscious all of a sudden. "I was going to say, me."

Silence fell between them, filled only by the soft trickling of water against the stone and the gentle splash that it made as it spilled into the river. Gradually, almost as if realizing he ought to do something, Richard stepped away from the boat and came toward her. "Winning your hand, would be the greatest honor," he said when he was finally before her once more.

"Then take courage and trust that all will be well."

With a slow nod, he took her by the hand and began leading her over to the tunnel. "I will," he assured her, "but you have to know that revealing myself to you is going to be more difficult than anything else I have ever done before in my life. Your opinion and what it will mean . . . I know what you have said and I have no doubt that you believe it to be true. Nevertheless, I must prepare myself for disappointment, and I advise you to do the same, in spite of your convictions."

She said nothing further, knowing all too well that the subject had already been pushed beyond the bounds of comfort. So she followed him instead, hoping that they might find something else of interest to distract them from the awkward atmosphere that seemed to have fallen upon them.

"Tread carefully," he said, his hand closing more firmly around hers as he slowed his progress. Descending over a slight ledge, he helped her down, shining the light to reveal a turn in the tunnel.

"Do you think Lady Duncaster knows about this?" Mary asked, her curiosity heightened at the sight of more sconces and torches inserted into the rock. "This was clearly deliberately built beneath Thorncliff's foundation and actively used."

"I have no idea, though I suppose someone in recent history must have been aware." He stopped next to one of the scones and studied it more closely. "There is no telling when the tunnels were built. In all likelihood, they were here before the Thorncliff that we know today, but the sconces and torches . . . they appear to be modern in style."

"It would have taken years to construct such a passageway." It was difficult to fathom how long exactly.

"I suppose so, but think of the mines that have been built here in England, or the tunnels located beneath Rome. Have you read about those in any of your books?"

"No," Mary confessed. They continued walking, the glow from their lanterns pushing back the darkness as they went while pebbles crunched beneath their feet.

"Apparently, Rome contains a vast structure of underground passageways dating back thousands of years to when the city was first built." He halted abruptly, almost causing Mary to stumble.

"What is—"

"Shh!"

She paused to listen, aware of a faint rustling sound, almost like leaves blowing in the wind. Except it couldn't be leaves, considering their current location, which meant that it had to be something else. The most alarming part of all was that it seemed to be growing louder. Her first thought was that it might be a swarm of flying insects, but that too seemed somehow illogical.

"Bats," Richard said. Spinning toward her, he pulled her down to the ground without warning and flung his cape over her head just as the air stirred to life around her. Mary instinctively felt like leaping to her feet and running, especially when the bats dipped low enough to brush against her back. She shuddered in response, huddling closer to Richard who knelt beside her, his arm draped securely around her waist.

"Are they all gone?" she asked when it was once again quiet.

Pulling his cloak away from her, he helped her to her feet. "I believe so." He continued forward while she followed hesitantly behind, ready to duck down again if the need to do so arose. A few more paces and she heard him suck in a breath.

"What is it?" she asked, edging closer to where he was standing.

"Something that is bound to astound you."

Curious, she hurried up alongside him and peered

through the yellow haze illuminating the space beyond the tunnel as Richard held his lantern forward. It took a moment for Mary to comprehend what she was looking at, all things considered. Eventually, she said, "This appears to be a foyer." It wasn't nearly as large as the one inside Thorncliff Manor, but it was impressive in its own right, the floor a mosaic of intertwined ropes, spiraling disks, animals and warriors, combined in the most intricate pattern that Mary had ever seen. The ceiling was flat, though beautifully painted in bright shades of blue and red. Across from where they stood, a thick pair of columns marked a doorway.

"My lady?" Richard inquired.

"It is beyond compare," Mary whispered, scarcely able to believe that she wasn't dreaming.

"Speaking of Romans, I believe that they are the ones who built this." Stepping forward, he headed in the direction of the doorway. "The architecture is reminiscent of their style."

Shaking her head in dismay, she went after him. "Under the ground like this? It makes no sense."

With a shrug, he said, "Unless they knew about the cave, built the tunnel to allow for easy access to the sea, and then constructed this room as some sort of transitional area."

"I suppose anything is possible at this point," Mary agreed. Even so, she wasn't quite prepared to discover a hallway beyond the doorway—least of all one with a sweeping staircase at the end of it. On either side of the hallway were a series of rooms, each concealed by a wooden door similar to those inside Thorncliff.

Unable to contain her curiosity, Mary reached for the handle closest to her and pushed down. The door swung open, revealing a room that was equally Roman in style, though the furnishings suggested that it had been used in more recent years. Any doubts that this might have been the case were immediately eliminated by the presence of a large painting that hung on the wall—an impressive portrait of the former king.

"It looks as though this might have been used as a study," Richard said, peering past Mary's left shoulder.

She stepped aside so he could enter the room properly, watching as he walked across to the large desk that formed the centerpiece. "Anything of interest?" she asked when he opened a drawer and pulled out a book.

He didn't answer immediately, flipping instead to the first page and taking a moment to read. Too curious to wait for Richard to offer an explanation, Mary hastened over to where he stood and looked down at the text herself. It appeared to be the title page of a personal notebook, reading simply: *The Cardinal Truths*.

Mary frowned, uncertain of what that meant. Richard turned the page, revealing an elegant script that seemed to fill the entire page. At the top was a date. *1780*. Below it, Mary read:

*Our duty, as described below, defines us.
It runs through our veins and keeps us on
a steady course, guiding us in the name of
justice. We are the defenders of the weak and*

*the protectors of the poor. Our sacred oath is
first and foremost toward God. May He give
us strength and courage in the years to come.*

"Do you recognize the handwriting by any
chance?" Mary asked.

There was a brief hesitation before he answered.
"As a matter of fact, it bears a striking resemblance
to my late grandfather's."

"Your grandfather's?"

Richard nodded absently. "He was a close friend
of Lord Duncaster's father."

"So then, Lady Duncaster knows you well?" She
hadn't realized, though it did explain the countess's
insightful words when she'd spoken of Richard.

"Yes. Or rather, she used to. Our families have
been close for as long as I can remember." Closing
the book, he placed it just as they had found it. "It is
growing late and we have been gone for longer than I
expected. We ought to return to Thorncliff."

"And abandon our search?" It felt as if he was
asking her to do the impossible. "At least take the
book with you."

He shook his head. "I feel as though it would be
wrong of me to remove it from here. We can come
back tomorrow, preferably at an earlier hour if you
can manage it." Turning toward her, he forced her
back a step. "But if your aunt discovers that you are
not in your bed where you are supposed to be—"

"I claimed a headache like you suggested and insisted upon a good night's rest," Mary said, determined to argue his point. "She will not disturb me."

"Nevertheless," he insisted, already pulling her

toward the door. "If she finds you gone, then you can forget about coming back here any time soon or of ever seeing me again."

Knowing how right he was, Mary reluctantly followed him out of the room, surprised to discover that it was almost two o'clock in the morning by the time she returned to her bedchamber. She'd spent over three hours in Richard's company, yet the time had flown by, making it feel like no time at all.

Careful not to make a sound that might wake Amy, whom Mary had insisted should go to bed, Mary snuck inside her room and closed the door gently behind her. It didn't take too long for her to undress, thanks to the gown she'd selected, which wrapped across her front and fastened at her sides. Letting down her hair, she then pulled on her nightgown, attended to her toilette and climbed into bed before retrieving the book that she'd brought up earlier in the day from the library: *Debrett's Peerage and Baronetage.*

Fluffing up her pillow, she leaned back with the book in her lap and opened it, determined to get a better idea of who Richard might be. He'd mentioned siblings, and the way in which he'd spoken of his parents suggested that they were still alive. Considering all the people she'd seen at dinner since her arrival at Thorncliff, Mary looked up each family in turn, checking to see if any of the peers had a son, or even a nephew, named Richard.

Of course, there was every possibility that he might have given her another fake name. In fact, the thought had just occurred to her by the time she reached the Earl of Oakland's family. Her index finger trailed below the fine print listing the earl's name, his date of birth, title and parentage, along with other relevant information. Next was a mention of his wife, with similar details attached, followed by their *issue*: Christopher Maxwell Heartly, Viscount Spencer, born, 1790. Below him, Mary found Spencer's sister, the Duchess of Stonegate's name, along with a mention of her previous marriage to the Earl of Newbury, and then . . . Richard Anthony Heartly.

Her breath caught and she sat up straighter, leaned forward and continued to read. Born, February 27, 1795, at Oakland Manor in Wiltshire near Swindon. Fought at the battle of Waterloo, 1815. Reported missing in action.

It had to be him. The coincidences were just too great.

Setting the book aside, Mary scooted down beneath her blankets and turned down the light. Her heart felt jittery. No wonder Lady Duncaster had been willing to vouch for him. She'd been right. Richard . . . Mr. Heartly, that was . . . did indeed come from a very good family. And if she married him . . . Good lord, she could scarcely breathe at the very thought of such a possibility.

She bit her bottom lip, not wanting to ruin her excitement with thoughts of her brother and the duty that she had toward him. Wincing, she turned on her side. Mr. Heartly worried that she would not care for his appearance, but at least his actions were commendable. She, on the other hand, was a scandal waiting to be discovered. And yet, he had approved of her singing, so perhaps he'd understand? Perhaps he might even be willing to help her deal with her brother's difficulties? It would be so much easier to share the burden with someone, but would he be open to the idea or would he judge her harshly for what she'd chosen to do?

One thing was certain: she wouldn't know until she told him the truth.

Chapter 10

Four days later

"**A**re you feeling all right, my dear?" Mary's aunt asked. The two of them were sitting in the zoological salon where wildlife murals of exotic animals and plants graced the walls.

"Perfectly so," Mary said, a little surprised by the question. "Why do you ask?"

"Because it has not escaped me that you have been rising later than usual for several days now." Lady Foxworth peered at Mary from behind her spectacles. A maid arrived with a knock at the door, bustling in with the tea tray the ladies had ordered. As soon as she was gone, Lady Foxworth said, "I fear you might be ill."

"Well, if you will recall, I have had a headache almost every evening for close to a week," Mary said, reaching for the teapot and beginning to pour. "And then of course there is my ankle to consider." Much to her annoyance, she'd sprained it three days earlier, preventing her from exploring the villa any further.

The only positive outcome had been Richard's insistence on carrying her to and from the cave so she could at least continue singing.

"My point exactly."

"But I feel much better now." Eying her aunt, Mary slid one of the teacups across the table in her direction. "I have had to socialize a great deal more than usual since coming here so the rest required by my injury was not completely unwelcome."

Sipping her tea, Lady Foxworth nodded. "Yes, it can be quite exhausting, having to speak to other people all day, though I must admit that I do enjoy the change. It is a departure from our otherwise tranquil life."

Mary didn't argue, though she did momentarily wonder how her aunt would react if she knew that Mary's life was far from tranquil. "How are things progressing with Mr. Young?" she dared ask. "Has he shown you any of his experiments?"

Lady Foxworth's eyes lit up. "Oh, indeed he has! Truthfully, he is such a kind man, Mary. I have enjoyed his company immensely these past few days and shall hope to continue doing so."

"I am pleased to hear it," Mary said, and then she added, "You should invite him to Dunholm in the fall. I am sure Vicar Brinsley would be happy to have him stay at his home for a week so that Mr. Young can call on you at Foxworth House during the day."

"I . . . I really don't know," Lady Foxworth hedged, her cheeks flaming as she dropped her gaze to her lap. "I am not so sure that we know each other well enough yet for me to suggest such a thing."

"Perhaps not yet, but I do believe that you will

by the time we leave Thorncliff." Mary paused a moment before adding, "Imagine showing him your telescope, Aunt Eugenia. I daresay he would be quite impressed!"

The smile that graced Lady Foxworth's lips belonged to that of a young girl fresh out of the schoolroom. Raising her gaze, she looked at Mary. "I think you might be right about that." She reached for a sweetmeat and turned a little more serious. "But what about you? How are you progressing with the young gentlemen here? Do you find either Rotridge or Belgrave pleasing?"

Suppressing a shudder, Mary sat up a little straighter and proceeded to tell her aunt the truth. "Belgrave has proven himself to be most agreeable—a true gentleman through and through."

Lady Foxworth inclined her head. "This sounds promising."

"Except for the fact that there is no spark."

"No spark?"

"Precisely. In fact, I fear a marriage between the two of us would be somewhat bland and . . . lacking any degree of passion."

Lady Foxworth's eyebrows rose. "Have you been reading fanciful novels recently?"

Mary shook her head. "No, but if I marry—"

"*If* you marry?" Lady Foxworth's eyes widened with horror while her voice conveyed her alarm.

Mary bit her lip. "What I meant to say was *when*." Her aunt breathed a visible sigh of relief, as did Mary. The fact that she'd seriously been considering spinsterhood until recently wasn't a conversation that she wished to endure at present. "When I marry, I would

like for it to be for love. Mama and Papa have both
allowed me to try and do so."

"And how much longer do you suppose that will
take?" Lady Foxworth raised an eyebrow. "In my estimation you are extremely fortunate to have gained
Belgrave's attention. To receive an offer from him
would be quite splendid."

Mary was aware. But her heart could not be con-
trolled by the promise of a title. Instead she found
herself increasingly drawn to a man whose face she'd
not yet seen, though she knew it to be scarred. He
didn't know that she'd discovered his true identity
and she had made no further mention of any desire
that she might have to see his face. Instead, she allowed him the time that he needed to accustom himself to the idea of her knowing him so well.

"Mary?"

She blinked, her mind abandoning the memory
of the time that she and Richard had spent in each
other's company these past few days and the pleasure that she felt when she sang for him. Instead, she
forced herself to return to the conversation that she
was having with her aunt. "You are right, Aunt Eugenia. But I need to know that I am making the right
choice before I commit to spending the rest of my life
with someone. And frankly, if I am to be honest with
myself, none of the eligible bachelors I have met since
my debut has been able to hold my interest. Not even
Belgrave."

Lady Foxworth snorted. "If you ask me, they
cannot all be lacking, Mary. Are you sure the problem does not lie with you?"

Mary sat back. "With me?"

Lady Foxworth nodded sharply. "You are too picky."

Of course she was, but she wasn't about to admit that. Instead she countered with, "I liked Signor Antonio well enough. A pity that you would not allow me to spend more time in *his* company or I might have been on my way to the altar already." A stretch perhaps, but a valid argument nonetheless. At least to Mary's way of thinking.

"You must understand why I could not allow for you to continue associating with him." Lady Foxworth paused a moment before adding, "Although, if he is a guest here, as he surely must be, then you must have crossed paths with him since the night of the masquerade. He has to be one of the gentlemen among us, which means that unless he happens to be Lord Belgrave, then he has yet to approach you without wearing his costume. The fact that he has not done so only confirms the fact that he is not deserving of you."

Mary felt her lips flatten in a tight smile. As always, her aunt's thought process was logical, even though it happened to be completely wrong in this instance. But Mary couldn't tell her that. Not without the risk of being prevented from seeing Richard again. So she simply nodded her head in agreement and said, "You are probably right." Determined to return to their initial topic, she said, "As for Rotridge, however, please don't ask me to spend more time with him."

Lady Foxworth frowned. "Has he done something to displease you?"

Mary didn't want to talk about how disturbed she was by the earl's strange advances, but she didn't want to lie any more than necessary either, so without answering the question, she said, "He has made it clear to me that he requires an heir."

"So . . . not the love match you were hoping for?" Mary shook her head. Lady Foxworth raised her chin and studied Mary closely. "It is not an uncommon reason though, for marrying someone, that is. Perhaps there is something else that I ought to know about?"

Mary's shoulders slumped. She averted her gaze. "He enjoys sniffing my hair."

A brief silence clung to the air between them. "How positively peculiar," Lady Foxworth eventually said.

"I did not enjoy it in the least," Mary admitted. "In fact, there was something horribly unnerving about it—like being forced to sit still while a large spider crawls all over you."

"An unpleasant experience indeed," Lady Foxworth murmured. "I shall have a word with Lady Duncaster, but I doubt she can ask him to leave unless there were witnesses."

"There were not," Mary said. Richard wasn't an option.

"Nevertheless, I will make every effort to ensure that he keeps his distance from you from now on. A pity since you would have ended up spending part of the year as your grandfather's neighbor. I know how fond you are of him."

It was true. Mary had always been close to her paternal grandfather—perhaps because she'd been her father's only child. "I would rather visit him a bit more often than marry Rotridge in order to become his neighbor."

Lady Foxworth nodded sadly. "And to think that I was encouraging you to spend more time with him!"

Seeing the distressed look in her aunt's eyes, Mary leaned forward and clasped her hands between her own. "Please, you must not blame yourself, Aunt. You are not at fault here."

Lady Foxworth nodded. "No, but apparently I have more work ahead of me than I had thought. Since neither Belgrave nor Rotridge will do, we must consider other gentlemen if you are to leave Thorncliff with an agreeable offer." She rose to her feet while Mary tried not to look too dissatisfied by such an idea. "Not to worry though. I asked Lady Duncaster to make a list of the most eligible gentlemen currently staying here, as well as those who plan to arrive before we depart. There are fifteen in total."

Mary's mouth dropped open as she followed her aunt out into the hallway. *Fifteen gentlemen for her to consider?* The fact that they might not be willing to consider *her* was apparently not a possibility worth mentioning. It was however a fact that was further compounded by the unexpected presence of Lord Rotridge in the hallway. He was standing a short distance away, his eyes on the parlor door as Mary and her aunt made their exit. Bowing his head toward Mary the instant their eyes met, he remained where he was while she and her aunt began heading in the opposite direction.

"Come along," Lady Foxworth said as she drifted toward the French doors leading out onto the terrace, her tone so light and airy that Mary doubted she'd noticed Rotridge's presence. "If you hurry, you ought to have enough time to take a walk with Lord Toncham before luncheon."

Knowing better than to argue, Mary bit back the immediate comment that formed on her tongue about Toncham rhyming with luncheon. She tried not to smile and surrendered herself to her aunt's incessant attempts at matchmaking instead, convinced that none of the gentlemen Lady Duncaster had suggested could possibly be worse than the man who was currently staring at her back as she hurried away, following her aunt.

"There is something different about you," Spencer said as he studied Richard. Leaning back in his chair with his legs stretched out before him, Spencer took a sip of his drink before adding, "You look suspiciously happy."

Richard raised an eyebrow. "*Suspiciously* happy? What the hell is that supposed to mean?" He knew the answer of course. The fact that he'd actually been smiling for the first time in five years, in spite of his best efforts not to, had apparently not gone unnoticed.

Spencer tilted his head to one side in a ponderous way that caused Richard to square his shoulders. "It means that I am extremely curious to know the reason behind that ridiculous grin that you have begun wearing."

"I am *not* wearing a ridiculous grin," Richard protested.

"You were, just a moment ago. Now you look as though you might like to wring my neck." Spencer frowned. "What is going on?"

Rising from his chair, Richard crossed to the sideboard and poured himself another drink—his third, that evening. "Nothing," he said with a shrug. Spencer did not respond to that, and when Richard turned with the intention of resuming his seat, he found him staring at him. His brother was clearly not convinced. Expelling a deep breath, Richard made a noncommittal gesture with his hand. "Very well. If you must know, I have been re-reading *The Dark Secret of Mistletoe Forest*." He would not, *could* not, mention Mary.

Spencer gave him an odd look. "Really?"

Richard nodded, took a swig of his brandy and said, with the most serious expression he could muster, "Really." And then, "You should give it a try yourself. It is terribly amusing."

Spencer looked increasingly uncertain. "I think I will take your word for that."

Richard shrugged, took another sip of his drink and asked, "Have you and Sarah discussed a wedding trip yet? I suspect that the two of you must be eager to get away and spend some time alone with each other." And just like that, the conversation changed course, directed away from Richard and his suspicious happiness.

When Spencer eventually left Richard's room half an hour later, Richard leaned back against the door and breathed a sigh of relief. Jesus, he had to be more careful about his facial expressions.

But it was difficult not to smile, considering how wonderful he felt. Mary was a godsend, her positive nature brightening his nights, chipping away at the melancholy and the constant anger with which he'd grown accustomed. And her voice! She'd sung for him these past few nights, and as she did, it was almost as if he could feel her reaching out and touching his heart with her very soul. That part of him beat loudly now at the thought of seeing her again soon. He glanced toward the clock on the mantel. Just another hour and they would be alone again, able to share each other's company while hope blossomed around them.

Passing the palm of his hand across his face, he considered what she'd told him a few days earlier: *take courage and trust that all will be well.* It was time, he realized as he pushed himself away from the door and went to retrieve his cloak and mask. Tonight, he would show her his face and pray that she would indeed accept him for who he was. Sarah had been surprisingly unappalled when Spencer had introduced her to him, but then again, she'd had no romantic aspirations as far as he was concerned, whereas Mary . . . He feared that she was about to be terribly disappointed—that she imagined him to be something more than what he was, and that she'd try to hide her shock as politely as possible while contemplating the number of ways in which she might escape his company.

Fastening his cape at the nape of his neck, he slid the mask into place and pulled the hood over his head. He then gave the wall panel next to his bed a gentle push and slipped out into the passageway beyond.

It was later than Mary had hoped by the time she was able to sneak out of her bedchamber and make her way to the room where Richard would be waiting. After dinner, her aunt had insisted that she join her for a game of cards—an invitation that had been difficult to turn down without raising any questions. Especially since Mary had claimed to be feeling perfectly fine earlier in the day.

The soles of her shoes tapped lightly against the stone steps as she made her way down through the hidden stairwell at the far right corner of the house, her stomach already forming a complicated knot at the thought of the man who awaited her arrival. He *would* still be there, wouldn't he? It was an hour later than they'd discussed, so she couldn't be certain. She could only hope.

With rising excitement, she hurried forward, the glow of her lantern preceding her arrival.

A deep rumble greeted her. "I was beginning to worry that you might not come."

Mary breathed an instant sigh of relief upon seeing Richard, his shoulder resting casually against the wall as he leaned up against it. He'd waited.

"I apologize for being so late," she said, her eyes following his every movement as he straightened himself and came toward her. "My aunt—"

"You need not explain." Reaching for her hand, he turned it over and pressed the inside of her bare wrist to his lips. "I am sure that you have a good reason for not arriving sooner." He released her hand, producing an inexplicable flutter in her chest. "It cannot be easy for you to get away unnoticed. At least not until your aunt has retired for the evening."

"Thank you for understanding."

"Think nothing of it." He dropped his gaze. "How is your ankle?"

"Much better. It no longer hurts me to walk, so you won't have to carry me anymore." Her words were softly strung with silken strands of regret.

Raising his gaze, the shimmer in his eyes plucked at her skin, the pull between them so achingly hard to resist. "A pity." She held her breath, her heart like a caged bird inside her chest longing to be set free. The moment stretched until he turned away, picking up a case that Mary hadn't noticed before. "I have brought my violin with me. I thought perhaps you might like some accompaniment."

"Your violin?" She looked down at the case he was holding, then returned her eyes to his. "I was not aware that you played. You never mentioned it."

He shrugged one shoulder. "I am not the sort of man who believes in pressing his achievements upon others. On the contrary, I generally disapprove of such tactics." She could only stare at him, puzzled by the fact that he'd said absolutely nothing before. Not one word even as he'd encouraged her to sing. "But I am letting you know now," he added.

"By bringing your violin with you," she murmured.

He gave a curt nod. "Precisely."

In a peculiar way, she understood. She wasn't one to tell others about her singing either. An easy moment of silence passed between them, and then she smiled and asked, "Are you any good?"

"I think I will let you be the judge of that."

His voice held a note of humor, which led her to believe that he was smiling too. A pleasant thought, that—the idea that she was able to bring some joy to a man who'd clearly lived without it for a very long time.

He offered her his arm, which she accepted, her hand slipping comfortably into place, just as it had done the evening before, and the evening before that. And as was always the case whenever they touched, Mary's stomach trembled a little while heat rose to her cheeks, her heart rate accelerating just enough to leave her feeling breathless. Of course, it didn't help that she'd decided to tell him the truth about herself, and by the time they reached the cave, her nerves had become a tangled mess.

"What is the matter?" he asked when they reached the place that amplified her voice the best. "You seem distressed."

She pulled her arm away from his, simply because she could not seem to think very clearly when he was that close. "Do you . . ."

"Do I what?" His voice was strong but gentle.

Mary focused on her breaths. Slow and steady. "Do you remember when I told you that you are not the only one with secrets? That I have mine as well?"

"Of course." Some of the softness left his voice, cooling it a fraction. "You said you would tell me what it was as soon as I was ready to show you my face—one secret in return for another."

"As well as a sign of complete devotion and trust." Stepping toward the ledge, she glanced down toward the river below, the water barely visible, like a flat piece of glass in the dim tones of gray that surrounded it. "You might not be ready to share your secret with me. Indeed, it is possible that you never will be. But I am ready to share mine with you."

"Mary, you—"

"It is important," she said, cutting him off as she

turned back to face him. "Because until the truth is out in the open, until we are each given the choice that we deserve, then we cannot possibly try to move forward."

"I know."

He did not approach her, but remained exactly where he was, for which she was grateful, because if he held her in his arms, she'd likely lose her resolve. "I do not want what we have to change, Richard, and I am terrified that it will. But you deserve to know the truth about me, for the one simple reason that I do not want you to fall in love with a lie." The words were out in a rush before she could think about what she was saying. A gasp followed, and then, "Forgive me. I did not mean to imply anything. I just—"

"You should not apologize. Not when you are right." He watched her for a long time before setting down the case he'd brought with him and snapping it open. Wordlessly, he pulled out his violin, set it against his chin, and started to play.

In that moment, it was as if Mary's world stopped spinning before gradually reversing its rotation. "You play beautifully," she said as soon as the song drew to an end. "But I did not recognize it."

"Perhaps because you have never heard it before?" When she didn't reply, he quietly confessed, "I wrote it myself. A couple of years ago."

"You are a composer?" She could scarcely believe it.

He chuckled slightly. "I would hardly call myself that."

"Why on earth not?" She shook her head, dismissing the question and asking instead, "How many pieces have you written? Is this the only one?"

"No," he admitted. "There are five in total."

"Well." She could not think of what to say, she was so surprised, except, "I should like to hear them all!"

"Some other time perhaps." He started to play again, but this time Mary knew the melody instantly. It was by Rossini, written for one of his more recent operas, *La Cenerentola*. It wasn't one that Mary had had the opportunity to sing many times, so the words came a little hesitantly at first, though with increasing strength and certainty as she gained confidence.

She realized something as she sang, listening to the sound of her voice flowing alongside the tune of the violin, like two souls engaging in an elaborate dance. The music was closing the space between them, creating unity and understanding on a level that she'd never thought possible. It was like magic, in a way.

"Perfect," Richard whispered, mirroring her thoughts as the final notes drifted off into the darkness and the song came to a close. He sounded just as awestruck as she felt—as if they'd somehow been joined together on a higher plane of existence. Carefully, he returned his instrument to its proper resting place before walking slowly toward her, his arms extending until they found their way around her in a tight embrace.

They stood like that for what seemed like forever, but it was the most wonderful version of forever that Mary could possibly imagine. "I need you to know," she began, her voice breaking the silence. He would understand. She was certain of that now. More certain than she'd ever been about anything else before. "I am not just Mary Bourneville. I am also Lucia Cavalani."

Inhaling sharply, he leaned back so he could look down at her, his eyes narrowing as he did so. "The most famous opera singer in England? That cannot be." But in spite of what he said, his words held an edge of doubt, as though he wanted to believe it, but couldn't quite figure out how it might be possible.

"Why not?"

He shook his head, his arms still holding her as he seemed to puzzle this over. "How?"

Encouraged by the fact that he hadn't let her go and that he wasn't sounding horrified, but rather curious, she said, "I developed a fondness for opera, for the passion that it embodies, after my parents invited me to watch *The Marriage of Figaro* for the first time. At first, I did not allow my voice full range because I didn't want to be found out, but then one summer, while visiting our family home in Leicestershire, I discovered a private spot in the woods where I could practice properly."

"That does not explain how you got onto the stage—an impressive feat, by the way, considering your station."

She drew away from him then, requiring freedom of movement as she told him of her greatest secret—the one that could ruin not only her own reputation, but her entire family's as well, by association. "When Mama and Papa left for India and I was sent to live with my aunt, Lady Foxworth, she made every effort to introduce me into polite Society. I was to make a splendid match, after all. But while her concern was in pairing me off with handsome dance partners, I took more interest in an older gentleman who happened to attend a dinner party hosted by the Duke and Duchess of Pinehurst, to which my aunt and I were also invited."

"Let me guess. The gentleman in question was somehow associated with the King's Theatre?"

She nodded. "His name is Mr. Taylor."

"The manager himself? What a fortunate encounter that must have been for you." He tilted his head slightly. "I assume that you requested an audition?"

"Not exactly. At first I just told him that I was interested in taking a tour of the theatre and asked if such a thing might be possible." Richard said nothing in response to that but held silent instead, allowing her the time she needed to share everything with him. "A meeting was arranged and my maid, Amy, accompanied me there."

"And while you were there you asked if he would be interested in acquiring a new talent?"

"At the time, I did not consider my voice to be very spectacular." Mary shrugged one shoulder. "What I initially hoped, was that I might be able to receive some training."

He nodded as if he understood. "And then what happened?"

Hesitating only briefly, Mary said, "Mr. Taylor was very reluctant at first and warned me of the risk to my reputation, but then he heard me sing and . . . It did not take long for him to find a solution to the problem by suggesting that I wear a disguise."

"It must have been a very convincing one indeed since no one has ever suspected a thing." His voice now conveyed a strange mixture of admiration and concern. "You . . ."

He stiffened while Mary sucked in a breath, alerted

by the crunching of pebbles, a scraping sound, and then the thud of retreating footsteps. Spinning away from her, Richard snatched up his lantern and rushed toward the entrance of the cave. "Who goes there?" Mary heard him call out into the darkness.

"Do you think whoever it was might have overheard our conversation?" she asked, coming up behind him.

"I am certain of it." Without another word, he started back toward Thorncliff at a brisk pace while Mary hurried after him, her skirts tangling around her legs now that the wind had picked up.

"So then my secret . . ." Panic began to rise inside her, tightening her chest at the thought of how reckless she'd just been. "I should have been more careful."

"And you were doing precisely that by confiding in me in a secret location," he shot back angrily. "You did not know that we were followed anymore than I did."

Biting her lip as she reached the top of the slope and pushing past the bushes before stepping out onto the damp lawn, she felt her heart pound painfully against her chest. "I am very much concerned that it might have been Rotridge."

"It is a possibility," Richard agreed, "but whoever it was, he or she is gone now, so we cannot be certain."

They continued on in silence until they reached the door to the antechamber and he ushered her inside. "What should I do?" She really had no idea. If Rotridge was aware of her secret identity, then there was every possibility that he might try to use it against her. In fact, she was confident that he would.

"For now, there is no proof that you are also Lucia," he whispered. "The best thing you can do is to refrain from returning to the cave and from practicing your singing."

Raising one hand, she started to reach for him, but changed her mind and hugged herself instead, too afraid of how he might answer her next question. "What about us?"

"What you have just told me . . ." She looked away, but he caught her by the chin and angled her face toward his own. "It changes nothing, Mary. If anything, I admire your courage." Turning his hand, his palm met her cheek, cradling it softly while his thumb caressed her skin. "Denying the world with the opportunity to hear your voice, would have been a tragic shame."

Her eyes, so honest and pure, gazed up at him with transparent hopefulness. She lifted her hand, and Richard's chest contracted with the realization of what was to come. He wasn't ready, but he was also acutely aware that he never would be.

"My secret in exchange for yours," she whispered as she carefully drew his hood back, her hands skimming over his hair with such fragile gentleness that his entire body ached. "I trust you, Richard, with my heart and with my soul. But can you trust me?" Skimming the sides of his neck, her fingers found his shoulders and then his chest. "Will you let me see your face?"

Having infiltrated enemy ranks and faced what he had believed would be death at their hands, Richard knew that the level of fear he felt now, in response to such a simple question, was out of proportion. And yet, he could not help the chill that made his skin tremble or the knot that tightened in his stomach at the thought of possibly losing her. But how could he hope to win her—*truly* win her—without reciprocating with the same level of truth that she'd just given him? He had no choice. And so, in spite of every apprehension and the sick feeling that settled over him, he nodded.

It took a moment before she responded, and when she did, it was with the utmost of care. Richard sucked in a breath as her fingers left his chest, climbing higher until they touched the edges of the mask. They hesitated there while he made every effort to stand completely still and not turn away. "Are you ready?" she asked.

"No," he said, speaking the truth. Seeing the uncertainty in her eyes, he quickly said, "But I doubt that I ever will be."

"It is the only way forward." She sounded almost regretful, which in turn pained him more than the thought of what she wanted to do.

"I know. Which is why it must be done." Raising his own hands, he placed them against hers and began lifting the mask away, her eyes holding his while he continued to wait for her to drop her gaze. She didn't. Not even once the mask had been completely removed.

Instead, she did something that both confounded and humbled him. Without a word, she rose up onto her toes, leaned closer and placed a tender kiss upon his lips.

Richard blinked, startled by the unexpectedness of it. "I . . ." He really wasn't sure of what to say, so he glanced around the small room instead, wondering if perhaps the light was too dim for her to see him properly, because surely that could be the only explanation.

"Regarding your appearance . . ."

Ah!

"You are the handsomest man that I have ever seen, and if you do decide to venture back out in public, I would be proud to be seen on your arm."

He stared at her, utterly speechless until he finally managed, "But the scars!"

"They are not as bad as your mind has convinced you that they are. And since I did not know you before and can draw no comparison, they have no influence on the way in which I see you."

Unwittingly, Richard felt the corners of his eyes begin to moisten while his throat began to close. His heart, aching with the beauty of her words, unfurled like the petals of a blooming flower, spreading joy throughout his veins. "You say that you have never been kissed." He stepped hesitantly toward her. "But you deserve to be." Unable to resist the pull of her, his hand found the back of her head, moving her until she was at just the right angle. "If I may?"

Nodding, she leaned toward him and her eyelids drifted shut. Desperate for the closeness she offered, he lowered his lips to hers—carefully at first, so they could grow accustomed to each other, and then with greater urgency. Moving closer—so close that no space remained between them—he kissed her as if he were drowning and she was his lifeline, as if she were the oxygen he needed in order to breathe. He poured every painful moment of solitude he'd endured for the past five years into that one singular moment, savoring her sweetness while imparting his own everlasting affection to her. She was like a burst of sunshine warming his heart and soul and yet there were still too many barriers between them—barriers that kept him from taking more than he'd already done.

Resisting the urge to give in to temptation, he struggled against the deep craving that she instilled in him, determined to win against it, for both their sakes. "If only we could stay like this forever," he said, trailing kisses along her cheek. "I never thought . . ." Allowing his words to drift off into the shadows, he hugged her closely against him, relishing the soft welcoming warmth of her body and her complete acceptance of him.

"These last few days with you have been the best of my life," she murmured. Her fingertips dug against the wool of his cloak, accentuating the point she was trying to make. But then she released her hold on him and drew back, her eyes meeting his. A moment later, he felt her hand upon his cheek, the smallness of it so seemingly fragile that it fairly stole his breath.

With the utmost gentility, the tips of her fingers trailed carefully over the side of his face where the skin rippled like dry sand on a stormy beach. "I can understand your reluctance to show yourself in public." A brief hesitation followed before she said, "And to me as well. But I am glad that you finally have, because hopefully, you will now understand that your scars would never be enough to frighten me away. Especially not after I have gotten to know the man that you are." Lowering her hand, she pressed it firmly against his chest, covering his heart as she spoke. "You are both noble and good, Richard. I hope you realize that."

It was difficult for him to breathe, let alone speak. So he said nothing in response to her words, his eyes struggling against the burning sensation of unshed tears. "Come," he eventually managed, his voice rough like gravel. "You must return upstairs."

She didn't argue, but when they reached the door that would lead her back out into the hallway and toward her bedchamber, she couldn't help but ask, "How do we proceed from here?"

"With difficulty, I suspect."

She would not be so easily deterred. "If I tell my aunt about you—if I confide in her your identity—then I am sure she will allow us to see each other again, just as long as the meetings are chaperoned."

"And how exactly do you plan to explain your knowledge about me? I doubt it will take her long to figure out that you have been sneaking off for secret rendezvous, and what then? If I were the sort of gentleman she would approve of, I would never have encouraged you to spend time with me against her will."

"You are not the only one to blame for that," she told him hotly. When he said nothing in response, she expelled a deep breath, feeling suddenly deflated. "You are right though. It will not be easy for me to convince her that I did the right thing after having defied her wishes."

His voice was heavy when he spoke again. "Since there is no place for us to meet in complete secrecy, besides the cave, and with the possibility of Rotridge planning an attack against you, I believe that the best course of action right now would be for us to stop seeing each other completely. At least until this situation is resolved."

Why did it feel as though her heart was being torn right out of her chest? "There has to be a way for us to continue—"

"Can you not see that it is too risky? We have been lucky so far, but until we know who it was that happened to overhear our conversation, then we have to avoid being seen together at all cost. Your reputation—"

"Hang my reputation!"

A lengthy pause followed. "You do not mean that," he eventually said, his voice barely more than a whisper. "Especially not until you are absolutely certain that you will consider marrying me."

"I—"

He held up a hand, effectively silencing her. "That was not a proposal, Mary, but a suggestion that you take some time to consider what you want. A lot has changed for you tonight. You have confided in me your secret identity, you have seen what I truly look like beneath the mask, and you are now faced with the very real possibility of being revealed for who you are." Crossing his arms, he studied her a moment before adding, "If it was Rotridge in the cave, he will undoubtedly use the information against you, and when that happens, the last thing you need is for things to be further complicated by an association with me. That said, if the need arises and you require my help, I will stand by you."

Expelling a quivering breath, she nodded. "Thank you." She made no attempt to touch him again, afraid that she'd end up back in his arms, relishing the comfort of his embrace while knowing that she would not be able to stay there forever. Not yet, at least. So she made an attempt at a smile instead, afraid that it didn't quite reach her eyes. "What if I need to reach you?"

"I shall not be far, but if there is something urgent, come back here and leave a note for me above the door. I will check for a message from you as often as I can." Placing his hand against her arm, he nudged her toward the door, saying with greater insistence, "Now go."

And so she did, even though the pain in her chest suggested that her heart was breaking.

Chapter 11

When Mary left her bedchamber the following morning, it was almost as if she'd been disconnected from her body. Returning from her meeting with Richard the previous evening, sleep had been an impossible goal for her to achieve, her thoughts consumed by every conversation they'd had with each other since the moment they'd met, until one incredible fact had become startlingly clear to her. She loved him.

Making her way to the dining room, she pondered this new revelation, asking herself if she was sure and, more importantly, how she could possibly tell? She'd known him for . . . blinking, she realized that she wasn't exactly certain. Logic told her it had only been eight days, but that couldn't possibly be right, could it? Not when it felt like so much longer.

Mentally, she began ticking off the reasons for *why* she loved him. His acceptance of her was definitely at the top of the list, but even before she'd revealed that she was also Lucia Cavalani, Mary had become increasingly fond of him.

"I cannot tell you how pleased I am to see you

again," a silky voice spoke at Mary's right shoulder, scattering her thoughts.

"Lord Rotridge," she said, her head turning instinctively toward him. He was wearing an arrogant smirk that made her insides squirm. Looking away from him, she surveyed the dining room, relief flooding her from head to toe when she spotted her aunt. "If you will forgive me, Lady Foxworth is expecting me and I would prefer not to keep her waiting."

"Of course," he said, inclining his head.

She started forward, eager to increase the distance between them, but froze at the sound of a whispered, "I know your secret."

It took every bit of self-restraint she possessed to remain calm, her expression completely inscrutable as she turned back to face him. Allowing her eyebrows to rise and her spine to straighten, she gave him the most condescending stare she could manage before saying, "I cannot imagine what you might be referring to."

It clearly wasn't the response that he'd been expecting or hoping for, because although he did open his mouth as if to speak, not a single word followed. Mary decided to use his silence as an excuse to quit his company and walked brusquely toward the end of the table where her aunt was sitting.

But as the day wore on, Mary became increasingly aware of Rotridge's gaze following her wherever she went. By the time she joined her aunt for afternoon tea, she was certain that he'd not only overheard her conversation with Richard the previous evening, but that he was plotting a means by which to use what he'd learned against her. To what avail though?

Because she'd turned down his sudden proposal? It seemed absurd.

"Mary?"

Her aunt's voice drew her attention away from her worries and back to the present. "Hmm?" They were seated in a private corner of the Greek salon, a space decorated exclusively with white marble and furnishings upholstered in creamy silks. A collection of statues had been placed throughout, some in corners and others as a means by which to divide the room into smaller, more intimate, areas.

"What on earth is on your mind? You seem completely distracted."

"Forgive me, I was just woolgathering. That is all."

Lady Foxworth pursed her lips and set her teacup aside, making Mary aware of how long her mind must have been absent from the conversation, because she didn't recall her aunt ever picking up the teacup in the first place. "I may be getting on in years, but I am not a fool, Mary. I would much prefer it if you did not treat me like one." Before Mary could argue, her aunt said, "It's that man again, isn't it? You are still thinking about him."

Mary cringed with the shame of knowing what she'd done. Her aunt had always been good to her, yet Mary had deliberately lied to her time and time again. First, by convincing her aunt that she liked to retire early in the evenings in order to read, when in fact, she was sneaking off to the opera instead. Now, she was being deceptive once more, going against her aunt's specific wishes in order to meet Richard in secret.

"It is impossible for me not to," Mary confessed, offering Lady Foxworth some small amount of truth.

Her aunt snorted. "I cannot say that I blame you, all things considered. After all, people do tend to be drawn to the mystery of the unknown, and that gentleman you keep on thinking about does seem to be something of a puzzle, though I do hope you realize that there is little point in continuing your ponderings over him." Reaching for one of the sweetmeats sitting on a plate between them, she held it delicately between her fingers, studying it as she said, "Now, I have it on good authority that the Duke of Lamont will be arriving tomorrow. Word has it that he is actively seeking a bride." The sweetmeat went straight into Lady Foxworth's mouth.

Mary slumped. "But—"

"Mary," Lady Foxworth said sternly, "I do believe I have been extremely patient with you, particularly since your parents asked me to give you the time you require to make a love match." Mary opened her mouth to speak, but her aunt held up a staying hand. "However," she added, "they also made it perfectly clear to me that they want to see you settled when they return to England, which is why I must insist that you start considering your options more seriously. Take Belgrave, for instance. By all accounts, including your own, he is an amicable gentleman—titled, no less—who possesses the means by which to offer you a comfortable life. Most young ladies would be thrilled to make such a coup."

"You are right. They would be, Aunt, but I am looking for more than wealth in a husband. I want a companion, a friend, and a confidant—someone with whom I can share every aspect of my life. But in addition to that, I want a spark. With Belgrave it simply was not there."

Lady Foxworth pressed her lips together and frowned. "Do you hear what you are saying? The sort of expectations you have? They are impossible, Mary. Nobody finds that sort of compatibility in marriage, least of all among the aristocracy where the only true purpose of a wife is to produce an heir. It is a harsh truth perhaps, but it is reality, and I daresay it is time for you to face it."

Unwilling to back down, Mary said, "*You* married for love, and so did Mama and Papa." Seeing her aunt's pained expression, Mary quietly added, "I believe they have precisely the sort of relationship that I would like for myself."

Sighing, Lady Foxworth leaned back against her seat, her eyes steady on Mary. "Perhaps you are right, but that does not change the fact that we are running out of time. You have had three Seasons already. One more and you will be on the shelf. The longer you wait to form an attachment, the harder it will be for you, not only because you lose the advantage of being a young bride, but also because everyone will start questioning why you have not been snatched up yet. They will start wondering what is wrong with you."

"Everyone knows that I barely have a dowry worth talking about. My only asset is my father's title and the possible connection that a suitor might gain by association—a connection that is of little value to a peer of higher rank than viscount." Mary picked up her teacup, took a sip, and winced. The drink was only lukewarm.

"Which makes it even more important for you to

socialize while you are here at Thorncliff. Given the chance, I have every confidence that your positive demeanor, intelligence, and wit, will achieve what your limited dowry will not."

"In other words, I must make every effort to socialize with the duke when he arrives." Mary could scarcely think of anything less appealing, not because she disliked the duke in any way, but because he wasn't the one who'd captured her heart. Trying to attract his attention and gain his favor would not only seem false, but like a betrayal of her feelings for Richard.

"I see no other option at this point. You have dismissed everyone else."

"Everyone with a title, that is," Mary said as her brain worked to find a way out of this mess. "What if I chose to encourage the attentions of an untitled gentleman? A second or third son perhaps?"

Lady Foxworth's gaze grew pensive. "I see no issue with that," she eventually said. "Not as long as he comes from a respectable family and has the means to support you." Her eyes narrowed. "Do you have someone particular in mind?"

Yes!

"Perhaps." Seeing the change in her aunt's demeanor—the flash of interest in her eyes—she quickly added, "Mostly, I am just trying to figure out what my options are at this point."

Nodding, Lady Foxworth agreed with the wisdom of that before returning Mary's attention to the subject that they'd been discussing earlier—before Mary's concentration had slipped to Richard—and continued elaborating on Charles Bonnet's conclusion regarding the relationship between the spiral arrangement of leaves on a plant and the Fibonacci sequence.

Later, as Mary ate her dinner, her apprehension over Rotridge and the comment that he'd made earlier in the day resurfaced as he continued to look at her from further down the table. She'd left a note for Richard before returning downstairs, informing him of her suspicions just in case the situation with Rotridge grew less tolerable.

"It does not seem as though his interest in you has diminished," Lord Belgrave said. Seated at Mary's left, he'd been regaling her with stories of his boyhood exploits, most of which had ended with him getting hurt in one way or other.

"Quite the contrary," she agreed, her tone grim with trepidation. Rotridge was like a predator waiting for just the right moment in which to attack.

"Spencer, Chadwick, and I have been trying to keep an eye on him, just in case you ever need us to step in, but it is difficult for us to do so at all hours of the day without his knowledge."

"And I would never expect you to ruin your holiday in such a way on my behalf," Mary said, "though I do appreciate the gesture. It is most kind."

Leaning closer, Belgrave lowered his voice to a whisper. "Has he done anything recently to upset you? Because if he has—"

"No," she said, panicked by the thought of Belgrave discovering what Rotridge clearly knew. Her hand trembled as she reached for her wineglass, raised it to her lips and took a fortifying sip. "As uncomfortable as I feel in his presence, I am sure that he is quite harmless. His pride has been hurt by my rejection. That is all."

"I hope you are right," Belgrave said as he straightened himself in his seat.

So did Mary.

It wasn't until she made her way upstairs to her bedchamber later, that she realized just how wrong she'd been to do so. Turning down the hallway that would lead her back toward her bedchamber, Mary listened to the accompanying sound of her footsteps tapping lightly against the floor. Carefully, she undid the ties on her reticule and reached inside to retrieve her key. But as she rounded a corner, a man stepped out of an alcove, blocking her path.

Rotridge.

Startled, Mary took a sharp breath and instinctively reared back. "My lord," she eventually managed, though her heartbeat refused to slow and her voice sounded quite out of breath. "I did not see you."

The edge of his mouth curved into a menacing smile. "Forgive me, my lady. It was not my intention to frighten you."

Clearly not, Mary thought as she took a few small steps away from him. He followed her though, his strides longer than hers and swiftly closing the distance between them. "What do you want?" she couldn't help but ask.

Raising an eyebrow, he studied her a moment before saying, "I do believe that I have made that quite obvious, but let me tell you again; I want *you*, Lady Mary. I want your hand in marriage, and I daresay that I now have the means by which to convince you to accept my offer."

Aiming for a blank expression that she hoped would convince him otherwise, she said, in a voice far calmer than she felt, "I have absolutely no idea about what you might be referring to, my lord."

He leaned closer, likening her to a child about to be reprimanded by an adult. "Is that so, *Lucia Cavalani*?" His voice was a sneer, filled with vehemence, and Mary knew then that getting what he wanted was the only thing that mattered to him. He was like a spoilt child throwing a tantrum over a toy that he was being denied. Except it wasn't exactly a tantrum. It was something far more dangerous than that.

"Who?" Mary asked, feigning ignorance. She could think of no other course of action than to deny his claim.

"I would caution you not to take me for a fool, Lady Mary." His hand curled tightly around her wrist, twisting her skin until it burned. "Accept defeat and we can still try to make the most out of our marriage. Fight me, and I will make certain that you hate every moment of it." With a hard yank, he pulled her into his arms, the impact forcing the air from her lungs. "Now then," he murmured, "how about a kiss?"

Try as she might, Mary couldn't escape his hold. His arms were like bands of steel around her body, holding her firmly in place. "I will never be yours," she told him fiercely. But the panic of somebody else arriving in the hallway and discovering her in such a compromising position was very acute. Terrified, she tried kicking him instead. But even though her feet made contact with his legs, her efforts seemed to have no effect on him.

Instead, he merely grinned, his eyes holding a wild gleam that sent a chill to Mary's bones. "Oh yes you will," he said, "because unless you agree to become my wife, I will tell the world that you have done something as disgraceful as sing at the opera. Everyone will know that you have been cavorting with other men's mistresses, and that will make them wonder if you are even as innocent as you are meant to be. Perhaps, in disguise, you have been tempted to do certain things . . ."

His hand moved to her breast, his mouth descended over hers, and for one frightening second, Mary knew that she was doomed. She knew without a shadow of a doubt that her life had evolved into a hellish nightmare from which there would be no chance of escape. He was simply too strong and far too determined, not to mention that they were in a public place. Other guests would be retiring soon. They would see her in a most inappropriate position with Rotridge. Her aunt would be informed, and then . . .

The hold on her suddenly lessened and, looking up, Mary saw that Rotridge's eyes had gone wide with surprise. In the next instant, he was thrust aside, completely removed from her vicinity as a cloaked figure wearing a mask bore down on him. Richard's fist flew through the air, landing squarely in Rotridge's jaw, the impact producing a loud *thwack!*

Rotridge yelped, like a puppy that had just been stepped on. But then, as if realizing what had occurred, he straightened his spine and stood his ground, glaring back at his assailant. "You are very brave, hiding behind that mask of yours. Show yourself, you coward."

"I will do so when I am ready," Richard replied. "At present, I am only interested in discussing your reluctance to stay away from Lady Mary as you were specifically told to do."

"And I might have continued doing so had I not discovered an interesting detail about her. Now that I know what she is, you no longer have the right to make demands. Either she does as I say, or I tell the world about her secret identity."

With a feral growl, Richard leapt toward Rotridge, delivering another blow to the earl's nose that resulted in an ugly crunching sound of cartilage breaking. Blood ran down over his upper lip before dripping onto his chin and from there, staining his cravat. But rather than accept defeat, Rotridge's eyes burned with increased fury. Retrieving his handkerchief, he held it to his nose as he stared defiantly back at Richard. "I will find out who you are as well, and once I do, I shall call you out. In the meantime, however, you will have to kill me in order to silence me."

"A tempting prospect," Richard murmured, his body positioned protectively between Mary and Rotridge.

"But one that you will not follow through with or I daresay you would have attempted it already." Chuckling, Rotridge executed a bow. "A pleasure as always, Lady Mary. *Signor Antonio*." Without lingering for another moment, he turned on his heels and strode away, his mad laughter echoing through the hallway as he went.

"Are you all right?" Richard asked as he turned to face Mary, concern evident in the depths of his eyes.

"I believe so," she said. Rotridge was gone, replaced by the man she loved. But despite the relief that she felt, apprehension wound itself around her so tightly that she feared she might suffocate from it. "Thank you for helping." The faint sound of voices approaching drifted toward them. "I should probably return to my bedchamber before someone sees us together."

With a nod, he stepped back and executed a perfect bow. "You must not fret over Rotridge, Mary. I will protect you from him by whatever means necessary. You have my word on that."

Attempting a smile, Mary thanked him again before hurrying toward her bedchamber. She knew that he meant what he said. The only problem was that if Rotridge did indeed follow through on his threat, Mary doubted that Richard would be able to protect her from her aunt.

Chapter 12

When Mary awoke the following morning, it took an enormous amount of effort for her to get out of bed and dress. In fact, all she wanted to do was to go back to sleep so she could avoid the nightmare that undoubtedly waited for her downstairs. To her surprise, however, her aunt appeared to be in a very pleasant mood. There was no indication at all that Rotridge might have spoken to her or revealed anything to incur her anger.

Eventually, Mary decided that her worries had been completely unfounded and focused on her breakfast instead while her aunt spoke happily about another conversation she'd had with the great Mr. Young, as she was now prone to calling him. "Oh, I completely forgot to tell you," she said after chewing on a bite of toast. "Lord Rotridge left Thorncliff this morning."

Mary jerked at the mention of the earl's name, effectively spilling her tea. "Really?"

Lady Foxworth nodded. "I thought that you would like to know since you did voice some concerns about him."

"Of course," she said, blinking. This was simply too good to be true. Surely.

"Now, I know that you and I have not spent much time together lately," Lady Foxworth continued, changing the subject as if it held no more importance than the weather, "so perhaps you would like to take a ride into the village with me today. We can have a look at the shops, perhaps visit a teahouse?"

Mary nodded. "I think that sounds like a lovely idea. But what about Mr. Young?"

Lady Foxworth waved her hand in an almost absentminded way. "You are my first priority. Shall we depart immediately after breakfast?"

Agreeing to do so, Mary returned upstairs only briefly in order to retrieve her bonnet and write a quick message to Richard. But when she entered her bedchamber, she found Amy waiting with a letter. "This just came for you, my lady," she said, handing the missive to Mary.

Recognizing her brother's penmanship, Mary sank down onto a chair with a sigh and tore open the seal, her hand flying to her mouth the moment she finished reading what it said. "Dear God, he has lost everything," she croaked, the words not sounding like her own. It was almost as if she'd stepped outside of her own body to watch a tragic play unfold.

Amy went completely still, her eyes meeting Mary's "Surely not."

"His house, the money I recently gave him . . . it is all gone."

"How is that even possible?"

Mary shook her head as fierce anger stirred to life inside her. "According to this," she said, crumpling the paper and tossing it aside, "he was taken advantage of. In fact, he claims he has no memory of how it happened but that there are witnesses who say he lost it all in a wager while he was too deep in his cups to think straight."

"Then he should be able to argue momentary irrationality or something of that nature, should he not?"

"Not when he has already signed away the deed to Carthright House," Mary gritted out. Honestly, she could murder her brother right now. How could he have allowed this to happen when he'd assured her that the money would be wisely invested? He'd been so enthusiastic about his ideas!

Staring at the letter, Mary tried to calm herself. As angry as she was with her brother right now, it did not compare with the livid fury that she felt for the people who'd swindled him. "As soon as I get back to London, I am going to find out who did this, even if it means hiring every Bow Street runner there is!" For now, however, there was little she could do other than help her brother in the only way she knew how. Heavy-hearted, she penned another letter to her bank before writing the note that was meant for Richard.

"If what you say is true," Lady Foxworth said as she and Mary trundled along in the carriage a short while later, "then there is even more incentive for you to marry quickly."

After telling her aunt about the letter she'd just received, it had taken a moment for the older lady to gather her wits in the wake of her initial shock. "My husband would not be obligated to help Andrew," Mary said. "And I would never expect him to."

"I should hope not!" Lady Foxworth's mouth pinched around the edges while her eyes bored into Mary. "That brother of yours may have won the King's favor by proving himself a hero during the war, but he clearly lacks common sense. In fact, I daresay it is a miracle that he even knew how to tell the front of a musket from the back of one and did not get himself killed instead. How he managed to save as many lives as he did, is absolutely baffling."

Mary couldn't help but frown. "I think that is a bit harsh."

Lady Foxworth responded with a snort. And then, "He has been of no help to you whatsoever, Mary. In truth, he ought to have played a greater role in your coming out. As a baron, he has connections now. King George himself loves Andrew, for heaven's sake. If he had cared, he would have introduced you to a slew of eligible young gentlemen. He would have danced with you at the balls you attended in order to draw attention to you. Why, even your dowry could have been larger if he had put the money that the king awarded him to good use."

Although Mary knew that her aunt had a point, she loved her brother and could not help but defend him. "Clearly the cost of running Carthright House was greater than Andrew anticipated, not to mention the money that has been spent on repairs and the new furnishings that were required. These were all necessary expenses, Aunt. The trouble is that he has had some bad luck recently."

"I do wish that you would stop making excuses for him, Mary. *You* may not be aware of how much it costs to run an estate the size of Carthright House, but *I* am." She gave a pert look. "And I can assure you that the £50,000 that he was awarded would have kept Carthright House in good order for at least ten years. In other words, he is either overpaying the staff or has spent the remainder of his money on something else."

"I cannot believe that," Mary said.

"What I cannot believe is that you fail to see him for the fool he truly is. He gambled away his entire estate, Mary!"

"True," Mary said, mourning her own losses. "But only because he was taken advantage of."

Lady Foxworth shook her head with a sigh. "Either way, it is clear to me that you cannot count on him for financial support. And since your parents are not as well off as one might have hoped that an earl and countess would be, your options are limited. You could of course consider becoming a governess or a companion, but if I am to be completely honest with you, Mary, I think it would be a pity for you to throw away your life like that."

Biting her lip, Mary had to agree. Especially now that she'd met Richard. Oh Lord, how on earth was she ever going to get herself out of the muddle she was presently in? Her brother was bleeding her dry, she was in love with a man whom everyone thought to be dead, and the villain who threatened her happiness had mysteriously vanished without explanation.

In addition to this, there was her future with the opera to consider. Richard had made no promises that he would allow her to continue singing in public if they eventually decided to get married. In fact, marriage had not even been properly discussed. She knew that she was probably to blame for that—that he was biding his time until she gave him some indication of being prepared to accept an eventual proposal.

"You are right," she found herself saying. "I promise you that as soon as we return to Thorncliff I will set my mind to planning my future."

"And since the Duke of Lamont will probably have arrived by then, I suggest you start by seeking him out." Lady Foxworth beamed. "Can you imagine? I can think of nothing better than telling your parents that you are going to be a duchess."

Mary could think of at least one, but refrained from mentioning him. Instead she said, "I believe we might be getting ahead of ourselves, Aunt. As it is, I have spoken to the duke on only a few occasions, and sparingly at that. Chances are that he will not even remember me."

"Then it is time for us to make him more aware of your fine attributes. You would make an excellent wife, Mary, there is no doubt about that."

Holding back a sigh, Mary leaned against the side of the carriage and looked out. She would speak with the duke if it would placate her aunt, perhaps even go for a stroll with him if he felt inclined to invite her. Later, however, while Thorncliff slept, she would seek out Richard, determined as she was to discover whether or not her future might include him, as she was increasingly inclined to believe that it would.

"There he is now," Lady Foxworth said when they returned to Thorncliff later in the day. Having just turned onto the Thorncliff driveway, her aunt's face was practically pressed up against the windowpane with the same degree of enthusiasm that a child might exhibit when passing a toy shop.

Following her line of vision, Mary's gaze fell on a tall, broad-shouldered gentleman wearing a smart navy blue jacket, brown breeches, and tasseled Hessian boots. Dismounting from one of the largest horses that Mary had ever seen, he handed the reins to an awaiting groom and stepped aside, his face turning toward Mary and Lady Foxworth as their carriage pulled up in front of him. The Duke of Lamont looked just as imposing as when Mary had last seen him, his posture bearing the rigidity of a man in possession of great wealth and power.

"How handsome he looks," Lady Foxworth murmured. Moving away from the window, she told Mary to do the same so they could be ready for when the door opened.

It did so almost immediately, pulled aside by a footman while steps were lowered, allowing the ladies to alight. Lamont stepped forward, extending his hand toward Lady Foxworth. "Allow me," he said, helping her down. As soon as she had thanked him, he turned to Mary. "A pleasure seeing you again, my lady."

She dipped her head, acknowledging his greeting. "Likewise, Your Grace."

Stiffly, he guided her down to the ground below. "I was not aware that you would be holidaying at Thorncliff. As it happens, I have just arrived here myself."

"Have you visited the estate before?" Lady Foxworth asked with interest.

He shook his head. "No. I have meant to, but

something always seemed to get in the way. This year I am determined to see what all the fuss is about."

"If you are not too tired from your journey, I am sure that Lady Mary would be happy to show you around," Lady Foxworth suggested as they started up the front steps. The door, which had been flung wide open, gave way to the towering foyer within.

"I would hate to impose upon His Grace since I am sure that—"

"Oh, it is no imposition at all," the duke declared as he looked to Mary, the solemnity of his gaze hinting at a man who was burdened by too much duty. "It is a pleasant day, so if you think you can spare the time, I would be very grateful for your company, Lady Mary."

Lady Foxworth beamed, her eyes like the fireworks Mary had once witnessed at Vauxhall Garden in London. Mary forced a smile, knowing how impossible it would be for her to escape the duke now, not only because it would be unconscionably rude of her to even attempt such a thing, but because she feared that her aunt might have a fit of the vapors if she did.

So she accepted the arm that the duke offered her, said good-bye to her aunt, and allowed Lamont to lead her forward. "The Indian Salon is just up ahead," Mary said in an effort to break the stilted silence that followed. "Would you like to see it?"

"Certainly," was his only response, save for the greetings that he offered other guests whom they passed along their way.

"Is it not marvelous?" Mary asked as they stepped inside the room, immediately transported to another world filled with intricately carved wood furniture, shimmering silk cushions in a vast array of colors, and ornate lanterns set in filigree cases.

Lamont's eyes widened slightly—the only evidence that he might be just a little bit impressed. "Lady Duncaster has done a fine job of creating an authentic space for her guests to enjoy."

"You speak as though from experience," Mary said as she watched him inspect every detail.

He looked toward her, a slight twitch stirring the edge of his firmly set mouth. "I traveled to India once, years ago, on business."

"What a wonderful experience that must have been!" He didn't elaborate on that point, but moved toward the door where she was standing and offered her his arm once more. Continuing on their way, Mary said, "My parents are there right now."

"I am aware." Slanting a look in her direction, he added, "Your father was appointed Governor General a couple of years ago. By all accounts he is doing an excellent job."

Mary's lips parted in surprise. "You are well informed." She instantly flinched in response to her foolish comment. Of course the duke would know who the Governor General of India was. Most people did. They just didn't seem to have much interest in *her*.

Turning a corner, they approached the interior courtyard, crossing paths with Spencer and Sarah who were heading in the opposite direction. "Lamont," Spencer spoke loudly by way of greeting. "I was not aware of your arrival. Good to see you though!"

"Likewise," Lamont said as he and Mary stopped walking.

"May I present my wife?" Affectionately, Spencer drew Sarah closer to his side.

Lamont inclined his head. "A pleasure, my lady. Felicitations to you both."

"We were just about to take a tour of the garden, but after that I have plans to meet Chadwick and my new brother-in-law, the Duke of Stonegate, in the smoking room for a game of cards. You are welcome to join us, if you like."

"Thank you, Spencer," Lamont said. "I should like to congratulate the duke on his new title—read all about it in the papers. But I was not aware that he had also gotten himself married. As I recall, he never seemed to have much interest in finding a bride."

Spencer nodded. "My sister, the former Countess of Newbury, made him change his mind." He looked to Mary, and then to Lamont once more. "So far, Thorncliff has proven itself to be quite an effective matchmaking destination. Don't be surprised if you leave here with a bride of your own."

Lamont did not look amused.

"I will see you later then," Spencer said as he and Sarah continued on their way. "Five o'clock?"

Reaching for his pocket watch, Lamont glanced at the time. "I will be there, Spencer. Thank you once again for the invitation." Resuming his progress, he pulled Mary along at a quiet pace until they reached the courtyard. "I am glad to see him settled," Lamont said. "Indeed, he looks happier than I have ever seen him before."

"You know him well, it seems," Mary said as they

made their way around the periphery of the court-yard while water splashed from the central fountain.

Glancing down at her, Lamont studied her a moment before saying, "We were close friends once—until his brother and I went off to war."

This brought Mary up short. "You were at Waterloo?"

"I was just a spare then," he explained. "The title came later."

He did not elaborate, and he did not have to. Mary knew the story about his father and brother all too well. Everyone did. "I am sorry," she said, unable to think of anything else—aware that the words fell flat.

"It was a long time ago," he said stiffly.

"But you knew Mr. Heartly," Mary pressed, eager to return to the subject of her own interest.

A brief pause followed, their steps tapping in concert against the stone floor. "He was extraordinarily brave. The sort of man who would risk his life for others without thinking twice about it. His death was tragic and . . . when I heard about it, I found it difficult to face Spencer and his family, acutely aware that I was alive and well while he . . ." He shook his head as if tossing the thought aside.

Thinking of Richard, Mary felt an overwhelming urge to seek him out immediately so she could hold him in her arms. Knowing how close he'd been to losing his life was the most unsettling thought in the world. "I cannot even begin to imagine how awful it must have been," she murmured.

Drawing her to a halt, Lamont released her arm and turned to face her, his expression grave. "You are a good person, Lady Mary. Your gentle nature and kindness are apparent in the way you speak, the things you say . . . the fact that you agreed to keep my company in spite of your reluctance to do so."

"I—"

"Please, do not apologize. It is entirely my fault."

She gaped at him. "Your fault?"

"I have made no effort to speak with you at greater length before, or even to dance with you when we attended the same balls. I am sorry for it, because it is clear to me now that you deserve all the attention in the world."

Uncomfortable with what he was saying and dreading the possible direction of the conversation, Mary shifted, her eyes darting toward the door. "You are very kind to say so, Your Grace."

The hint of a smile touched his lips, but it was gone again within a heartbeat. "Perhaps we can become better acquainted while we are here?"

Sucking in a breath, Mary looked up at the man before her, uncertain of how to deal with this predicament. Deciding that direct honesty would serve them both best, she gathered her courage and said, "As happy as I would be to keep your company, you ought to know that my heart is already engaged elsewhere."

The life seemed to drain out of him. "I see."

"But if you are truly interested in making a match for yourself, I am happy to make a few suggestions," Mary said, the words rushing out of her before she could even think.

Offering her his arm once more, he steered her back toward the hallway from which they'd come. "I appreciate that, but I am not in need of a matchmaker, Lady Mary. The fact of the matter is that I have taken great care in studying the qualities of all the young ladies of marriageable age and have found that only two will suit."

"I am honored that you would even consider me then. Especially since my dowry is rather insignificant."

He frowned. "I suppose there are those who would consider that objectionable. Personally, I can think of other merits that I would rather have in a life partner, but then again, I have no debts and my income is substantial."

It sounded reasonable enough, Mary supposed. "Might I ask who the other lady might be?"

Reaching the grand staircase, the duke disengaged himself from her and said, "I fear that would be too much information for me to disclose at present. Perhaps when I determine whether or not she is likely to reciprocate my high regard?"

"Of course," Mary said, sensing that she was being dismissed.

He gave a curt nod. "Perhaps we can continue our tour some other time?"

Mary doubted that such a time would ever present itself, but she dipped her head in agreement anyway and quietly said, "By all means."

Returning to her bedchamber that evening after dinner, Mary found a note waiting for her from Richard, inviting her to meet him in the usual spot. Changing out of her gown and into a more practical day dress, Mary exchanged her slippers with her walking boots and went in search of the man who'd stolen her heart. He was waiting for her in the ante-chamber, light flickering across his unmasked face, allowing her to glimpse the change in his expression the moment he saw her.

Warmth captured his eyes and the edge of his mouth drew upward into a smile of absolute appreciation. "I did not expect to see you again so soon," he said, stepping away from the wall and coming toward her. His hands captured hers, the touch evoking a flurry within the pit of her stomach. "But I understand that Rotridge has left—the threat of him no longer hanging over you."

"I can scarcely believe it," Mary confessed. Gazing up, she allowed herself to be captured by his gaze, welcoming the brief caress of his lips against hers— soft, gentle and filled with so much adoration that her heart almost burst from her chest.

"Let us take advantage of it," he said, not voicing the concerns that Mary knew he surely had. There were questions to be asked. Why had Rotridge left? Where had he gone? And would he be back? All were ignored in favor of savoring the moment. "Come with me. I have a surprise for you."

Leaving Thorncliff behind, they hurried across the lawn, hand in hand, both short of breath by the time they arrived at the cave.

"The Duke of Lamont arrived today," Mary said as she entered the cave ahead of Richard. "He invited me to walk with him."

"And did you?" His tone was cautious.

Looking over her shoulder at him, she gave him her reply. "Yes. In fact, he was very forthcoming."

"Forthcoming?" Richard's hand tightened around hers. "Are you saying that he declared an interest in you?"

Fighting her jittery heart, Mary allowed a broad smile. "Indeed he did. Much to my surprise." Turning away, she focused on the ground beneath her feet, careful not to misstep.

Behind her, Richard muttered something inaudible, then said, "Is it just my imagination or are you attracting the attention of all the eligible gentlemen these days?"

With a laugh, she shook her head. "You need not worry. I told him that he would have to look elsewhere for a bride, which is just as well since I very much doubt that he and I would suit."

"Why do you say that?"

"For starters, he is nothing like you." She spoke the words lightly, but deep in her heart she knew that he needed the reassurance—that his appearance made him more insecure than most.

"Go on," he murmured with genuine interest.

"He seems too grave for my liking. In fact, the most interesting part of our conversation was when he mentioned you." She paused momentarily before saying, "He spoke very highly of your heroism as a soldier and seemed quite shaken by the fact that you had not survived the war."

Stayed by the pull of his hand, she turned to face him. "Lamont was supposed to go on that fateful reconnaissance mission in my stead," he said, "but news of his father's and brother's death arrived just moments before he was meant to depart. He was no longer a second son, but a duke, so I told him to return to England right away and that I would handle the mission for him."

Mary scarcely knew what to say, her eyes holding his—absorbing the strain of his soul. "He blames himself for the death of a man who is still very much alive." She could not stop the words—the truth in them shifting the air around them.

Richard nodded. "It never occurred to me that he might. But now . . . I will have to seek Lamont out. He needs to know that I am still alive and that *he* is not to blame for what happened to me."

The hard tone of his voice made her wary. "You speak as though someone else might have been."

He shook his head. "It was a long time ago—an ordeal I prefer not to speak of."

"Of course," she whispered, aware of how difficult it must be for him to reflect on such painful memories. So she tugged on his hand and said, "Shall we continue our exploration?"

Nodding, he raised his lantern to light the way forward. "Watch your step," he cautioned as he helped Mary down the descending slope leading past the river and toward the tunnel. "You need not worry," he added, "The bats have gone. I made sure of that when I came down here earlier this evening."

Mary paused to look at him. "I thought you said that you would not explore the cave or the Roman villa without me."

"And I have not," he assured her as he tugged on her hand, urging her to resume walking, "but I did mention that I had a surprise for you."

Curious, Mary found herself increasing her pace, allowing Richard to lead her forward. Exiting the tunnel, they arrived in the foyer. Unlike the last time when Mary had been there, however, she was now able to see every corner clearly, thanks to the numerous candles illuminating the space in soft golden tones. A gasp was torn from between her lips. "This must have taken you forever," she murmured.

Beside her, his hand wound comfortably around hers, Richard grinned. "I will admit that it may have taken a few minutes."

"A *few*?"

His grin widened into an overjoyed smile. "Just wait until you see the rest of it."

Stepping forward, he led her through the doorway in front of them and into the hallway beyond. It too was illuminated by candles, torches and lanterns so Mary could fully appreciate the rich display of color in the mosaic floor beneath her feet. "This is incredible," she said as she released his hand and went toward the same room that she'd visited before. Here too the smothering darkness had been pushed back, accentuating the details of the architecture as well as the furnishings. Venturing inside, Mary went toward the desk, her fingertips carefully tracing the edge of it before sliding toward the notebook. It was just as they'd left it.

Raising her gaze, Mary found Richard watching her from the doorway. "As you can see, I kept my promise," he said.

"You waited for us to continue reading it together?"

With a small shrug of one shoulder, he came toward her. "It seemed like the right thing to do, and besides, I think it will be more fun unraveling the mystery behind this secret lair as a team."

"But you said yourself that you recognized your grandfather's handwriting." She couldn't imagine how difficult it must have been for him to resist the temptation that the notebook offered.

"I said that it bore a startling resemblance," he reminded her. "Whether or not it actually is his writing, is yet to be determined."

Picking up the notebook, Mary rounded the desk and offered it to Richard. "There is only one way to find out."

Accepting the book, Richard motioned toward the doorway. "There is a sitting room across the hall-way."

Mary arched her eyebrows. "I thought you said that you had not done any more investigating."

"That is true. I have not, but . . ." Reaching in front of her, he pushed open the door, affording her a view of the room beyond. "Serving tea on a desk seemed wrong. I decided that this room was far better suited."

Mary blinked, her lips parting as she took in the scene before her. "And I thought the lights were the surprise."

"They are just part of it."

Speechless, Mary just nodded as she stepped further into the room. Architecturally, it wasn't so different from the study. Marble columns guarded each corner with two supporting a beam in the center. Up under the ceiling on one side, arched alcoves had been decorated with murals.

The furniture, consisting of two armchairs, a sofa, and a low table, had been pushed apart, freeing up the space at the center of the room where what appeared to be a picnic had been set up. A green blanket was spread out there, on top of which cups and saucers had been neatly arranged. Next to them, was a plate filled with *petits fours*, each one prettily decorated with icing and marzipan flowers.

"The teapot is still in the basket, wrapped in dishtowels in order to keep it warm."

Richard's voice, so warm and soothing, carried her forward. Mary could barely believe the amount of trouble that he'd gone to in order to prepare everything. As far as romantic settings were concerned, this topped the list.

"Have a seat," Richard whispered close to her ear.

A delicious shiver raced down her spine, her heart skipping a little at the feel of his hand against her lower back. He did wondrous things to her, this man who'd been shrouded in mystery when they'd first met, and for quite some time thereafter. Knowing what he'd been through and discovering how good and kind he was . . . it was remarkable. He bore no signs of anger or resentment—just fear of acceptance. "I . . ." She stopped herself from continuing.

"You what?"

Swallowing, she shook her head and crossed to the blanket, lowering herself onto it and adding distance. She had to be completely sure of what she wanted before committing herself with words. And with her brother's predicament in mind, abandoning the opera was less of an option than ever before. So she indicated the artwork in the alcoves instead. "Those paintings were not done by Romans."

He gave her a funny look before sitting down across from her. "You are right. I suspect that there may originally have been windows there and that they were eventually sealed up before the entire villa was buried in dirt."

It seemed absurd. "Who on earth would bury something like this?"

"I have been wondering about that myself. If my suspicions are true and part of Thorncliff rests on top of this villa, then it would have had to have been done a very long time ago."

"How long exactly?" Mary asked, intrigued.

"Well, according to my brother, construction began in the twelfth century by a knight who served King Richard during the Crusades. It is possible that he chose to bury the villa in order to even out the foundation, or perhaps it was concealed by the Romans themselves when they left. It is difficult to say, but the artwork is recent. No doubt about that." Reaching inside the basket, he pulled out the teapot, unraveled it from the dishcloths and poured Mary a cup which he then handed to her.

Taking a sip, Mary savored the warmth of the liquid as it flowed down into her belly. "Perhaps the notebook will enlighten us?" Setting her teacup aside, she selected one of the *petits fours*, her toes almost curling in response to the heavenly flavor as she bit into it.

"Do you approve?"

"Do you really need to ask?"

With a low chuckle, he crossed his legs and placed the notebook in his lap. Flipping past the first couple of pages containing the text that they'd already read, he proceeded to read out loud to her.

"*Infiltrating The Electors has been no easy task.*

It has tested the moral fiber of not only myself, but of my comrades in arms as well. We have done things . . . things that I dare not mention due to the shadow of shame that it has cast upon us all. But it was necessary for us to do what we did as proof of our allegiance. It has all been for the greater good. For England." Looking up, Richard met Mary's gaze. "This sounds very conspiratorial."

"And terribly intriguing. Please . . ." She nodded toward the book. "Do continue."

Bowing his head over the text, Richard did as she bade. "*One day, in the not so distant future, nothing will remain of me, except for my family and this book. The actions described herein are my legacy. In spite of everything, I am proud of what I have accomplished—what we, The Cardinals, have accomplished together.*

"*During the past five years, this ancient villa has served as our base. From here, we waged our own war against The Electors—British peers who saw themselves as Gods. They ruled Europe from behind the scenes, their political power outranking that of any monarch, until they made the mistake of inviting The East Wind into their midst. From within their ranks, he ensured that the rest of us were asked to join as well.*"

Absorbing every single word, Mary listened with rapt attention as it became increasingly clear that unbeknownst to most, there were men among the British aristocracy who'd conspired to kill European heads of state. They had lit the fuse that had led to the French revolution, with the deliberate goal of toppling Louis XVI off his throne. Apparently, he'd been too difficult for them to influence, and since those closest to him had been as well, The Electors, had turned to the common people of France, encouraging their disapproval of the monarch with a few well-placed words.

A chill swept through Mary. It was horrifying to discover that such a thing was possible. Thank God for The Cardinals! "Do you think the Earl of Duncaster might have been The East Wind?" she asked once Richard had finished reading.

"I believe so. I am also completely certain now that this was written by my grandfather." Closing the notebook, he stared down at it for a moment before saying, "Reading it was like listening to his voice." He fell silent, and it looked as though he was pondering something. "He and Duncaster perished at sea after unexpectedly setting out together without a moment's notice. I never understood it, but now . . ."

"You think The Electors might have realized what they were up to?"

Looking up, he met her gaze and nodded. "More than that, I am beginning to suspect that their deaths were not accidental."

"I . . . I am sorry." As lame as that sounded, she could think of nothing else, except perhaps attempting to push the unwelcome melancholy aside with a question that formed at the front of her mind. "There are four Cardinals though, so if your grandfather and Lord Duncaster were two of them, then who were the two others?"

"I have no idea," Richard said. A frown creased his forehead. "It would have had to be men that they trusted—close friends of theirs, I would imagine."

"Can you think of anyone?"

He shook his head. "No. Not at the moment." He took a sip of his tea. "Shall we see what else we can find while we are here?"

Acknowledging that their time together in the villa was limited, Mary nodded. She'd looked forward to exploring their find in greater detail, and with the added light that Richard had provided, the opportunity to do so presently was one that she did not wish to pass up. So she placed her hand in his without hesitation, allowing him to help her to her feet. A buzz of energy shot through her fingers and up her arm the moment they came into contact. Her breath caught, and a light-headed dizziness overcame her.

"Are you all right?" he asked, steadying her on her feet, his hand slipping toward her elbow so he could offer her better support.

"Perfectly so," she said, even as the buzzing sensation persisted, making her insides flutter in response to his sudden closeness. Was it normal to feel both ecstatic and ill at the same time? Inhaling deeply, she caught a whiff of his scent, which in turn reminded her of what it was like to be held in his arms . . . for him to place his lips against hers . . . "I just . . ."

"I know," he said as he turned her toward him. With a slight nudge, he tilted her chin, whispering, "I feel it too," right before he lowered his mouth over hers.

The caress was sweet, infused with the rich flavor of vanilla and marzipan. Winding her arms around his neck, Mary savored every second of it as she pulled him closer, surrendering to the beauty of the moment just long enough to convey to him what was in her heart. As she lowered her arms to embrace him, she turned her cheek into his shoulder and secured herself in his strength while he in turn placed his chin against the top of her head. His hand stroked a gentle rhythm up and down her spine. It was wonderfully soothing.

"Shall we take a look at the other rooms down here and venture beyond the stairs?" Richard asked after a while.

"Mmmm," Mary murmured. If only she could have stayed like that forever. But they had to get moving if they were to take a closer look at the villa before it was time for her to return to Thorncliff. So she reluctantly pulled away and helped him gather up the remains of their picnic.

Returning to the hallway, they set the picnic-basket down and grabbed a lantern before approaching the first unexplored room to the left of the stairs. Pushing down on the door handle, Richard nudged the door open and peered inside. "It looks like a bedchamber," he said as he held up the lantern and stepped inside.

Mary followed, squinting her eyes until they adjusted to the dimmer light. There appeared to be two beds, each pushed up against opposite walls and with two bedside tables between them. The walls were completely bare, the only other furnishings a wardrobe and a chest of drawers. "It does not look as if this room was ever used very much," she said as she followed Richard over to the chest of drawers, staying close to the light. Leaning forward, she watched as he pulled open a drawer, revealing a pile of neatly folded shirts, two pairs of breeches, stockings and cravats.

"I agree. It seems as though it was only intended to be used in case of an emergency—a means by which The Cardinals could seek shelter if the need to do so arose."

"Whereas the study and the sitting room appeared to be more personal."

"Precisely." Moving toward the bedside table, Richard pulled open its drawer as well, but as he did so, a piece of paper slipped out from beneath the drawer and drifted onto the floor.

Chapter 13

Picking up the paper, Richard began to read.

"What does it say?" Mary asked from somewhere behind him.

He shook his head, reread the letter again. "This . . ." He stared down at the swirling script, so prettily penned . . . "This is from The South Wind," he said, his words floating somewhere above him as if they belonged to no one.

An extended period of silence followed, and then, "Can I see it?"

The question pulled Richard out of his reveries and back into the present. "Of course," he said, handing it to Mary.

"It is in French," she said, almost immediately.

Just one of the clues revealing the true identity of the person who'd written the letter.

"Judging from the form, I would say that it was written by a woman, and with the subject matter in mind . . . considering what we have learned from the notebook, I think it is fair to say that this letter was sent as a warning of what awaited the French aristocracy. In fact, it almost sounds like a plea for help." She paused. "But the mention of a box and the importance it seems to have in the context of the French revolution, makes little sense to me. If these people—"

"The box is of great value," Richard said. He watched as Mary glanced back down at the letter, rereading the part that mentioned the box.

A faint crease appeared upon her brow. "It is described as having the image of a meadow and a shepherdess watching her sheep, carved into it. The sides are supposedly edged with mother-of-pearl." She looked up at him, her eyes widening with surprise. "You know the box that is being referenced, perhaps even who it belongs to."

He nodded then, still stunned by what they had just discovered. "If it is the box that I am thinking of, then it was custom-made by a craftsman in Germany—a gift from my grandmother to her sister, the Duchess of Marveille."

Mary stared back at him. "Are you telling me that a French duchess . . . your great aunt . . . was working with your grandfather and the third Earl of Duncaster in an effort to save as many members of the French aristocracy as possible from The Electors?"

"I know how absurd it must sound, but—"

"On the contrary, it makes perfect sense that they would have needed someone in France to help coordinate their rescue efforts." She pointed to a spot on the paper. "It says here that she was readying a final cargo of twenty and that the box would be included. Forgive me, but I still do not understand the importance of the box."

"My grandmother used to refer to it as the only

surviving part of her family. Everyone else was killed by the guillotine, including her sister." Taking the letter from Mary, he tucked it into his jacket pocket. "According to my grandmother's diary, my grandfather received a letter from Lord Duncaster, informing him that the box had arrived at Thorncliff. He set out immediately in order to retrieve it, but never returned. Instead, he and Lord Duncaster chose to travel to France without notice, perishing, as you know."

"So, the box—"

"Contains my grandmother's family heirlooms—an estimated worth of over five hundred thousand pounds."

The shock on Mary's face was evident. Her mouth literally dropped open. A small pause followed, and then, "It must be here somewhere."

"What?"

"If it was sent to England, as this letter claims, and your grandfather was called upon to pick it up, then it must still be here at Thorncliff or perhaps even in this very villa. At any rate, we should try to find it."

Richard couldn't help but agree. It would have been illogical for his grandfather to take the box back out to sea with him, so it seemed unlikely for it to be at the bottom of the Channel. It was far more plausible that something unexpected had forced his grandfather and Lord Duncaster to flee England. Especially in light of what he now knew about them and their involvement with The Electors. "You are right. They probably knew that they did not have time to arrange for the box to be returned to my grandmother and hid it somewhere instead."

"Let us search the remaining room," Mary said, already heading for the door. But upon entering the room opposite, they found it to be no different than the one they'd just exited. "There is nothing here of significance. Just the necessary furniture and some clothes."

Agreeing that their search had come to an abrupt end and feeling somewhat discouraged in the wake of the excitement that he'd felt only moments earlier, Richard turned toward the stairs. "Shall we see where these lead?"

"We would be fools not to," Mary said, offering him an encouraging smile that immediately lifted his spirits.

Hand in hand, they started up the stone steps, following the staircase as it turned to the left, carrying them away from the brightly lit hallway and up into darkness. Richard's lantern cast a hazy glow around them as they walked. Occasionally swinging from side to side, it made the shadows dance across the walls.

Unexpectedly, it appeared as though their ascent had been stopped by a wall blocking the way in front of them. But when Richard investigated more closely, he found a narrow gap in the wall to the right—just wide enough for a person to squeeze through. This led them into a tiny vestibule that opened up to the left behind a large pillar that effectively hid the entrance to the staircase completely.

"Where are we?" Mary asked.

"The tunnels and storage rooms beneath Thorncliff," he said as he went to an arched doorway. The room in which they were standing was cold, the floor beneath their feet uneven. Mary followed closely behind. "I have been here before," he told her, happy to be able to share the experience with her for a change. "The tunnels allowed me to leave Thorncliff unnoticed so I could at least enjoy the warmth of the afternoon sun upon my face."

"I never would have imagined such a network existing beneath the ground," she said as they entered the tunnel that lay beyond the room they'd just been in and turned right.

"It was meant to supply soldiers with food and shelter, as well as easy access to the sea during times of war."

"Considering how cold it is right now during the summer, it must have been terrible having to live down here during the winter—for any duration of time."

"I am sure there must be some sort of ventilation system so they could build fires for warmth. It hardly makes sense otherwise." The pungent aroma of apples drifted toward them. "We are getting closer. The food storage is just up ahead. Next to that there is a staircase that you can use. It will take you up into Thorncliff's interior courtyard."

"You are not coming with me?" She sounded surprised, perhaps even a bit disappointed.

"I will use a more private route." Reaching the door to the staircase, he placed his hand against her elbow and turned her toward him. "This past week in your company has been incredible, Mary. I know you have your reservations about committing yourself to anyone—that you would like to retain your independence—but I would like you to know that if you were to accept the offer that I plan on making you, I will never try to prevent you from singing. Of course, doing so publically, disguised as someone else, might not be possible . . ." Seeing the sadness in her eyes, he added, "But if there is any chance of you continuing to perform as yourself, I will help you do so. More than that, I can assure you that I will proudly applaud you for it."

"You are . . ." Her voice trembled, and Richard knew that she was overcome by emotion. "Thank you," she managed, "but there is something else."

"What is it?" Whatever it was, Richard couldn't imagine it being more of an obstacle than her penchant for opera or his reluctance to be seen in public. But, with their acceptance of each other and the news he'd received last night, informing him that he'd finally managed to ruin his rival, Richard was ready to put the past behind him and start a new life with Mary at his side. If she would have him.

"I was not completely honest with you when I told you about my singing," she began. "In fact, there was a very deliberate purpose behind my performances. I did not do it for fame, for any kind of acknowledgment or even for the music alone."

He studied her closely. "Then what was your reason?"

Inhaling deeply, she confided the truth. "For the past two years I have been using my wages from the theatre to help my brother." Richard arched a brow. "He spent his own fortune on running his estate, so when he began speaking to me about making investments, I immediately offered to do what I could, hoping that he would secure an income. Unfortunately, he made some poor decisions, and as a result, the money I gave him is all gone. I know he must take responsibility and that I should not help him any further, but I fear what might happen to him without my support."

"You must not fret," he told her calmly, relieved that it wasn't anything more serious than her desire to help her family that now stood between them. "I may be a second son with no title to my name, but my investments have been extremely profitable. It goes without saying that my offer will include support of your family, albeit within reason. If your brother needs help of any kind, I will be happy to oblige."

"Truly?"

Nodding, he pulled her into his arms and tenderly kissed the top of her head. "Whatever it takes to convince you to be my wife, I will do it."

"I—"

Leaning back, he placed his finger to her lips, silencing her. "Do not say anything yet. Just think about it. I would like to make a proper proposal—one that even your aunt will not be able to protest."

"You plan to meet with her." She sounded incredulous, which he in turn found mildly amusing. Apparently it wouldn't be too difficult for him to be her knight in shining armor.

"Of course. I plan to follow every protocol in my quest to make you mine." Stepping back, he caught her hand in his and raised it to his lips, kissing her knuckles with all the reverence that he felt for her. "Until tomorrow," he said as he ushered her into the stairwell, lighting the way for her until she reached the top. From there, she blew him a kiss before disappearing into the courtyard beyond and leaving Richard feeling bereft.

When Mary awoke the following morning, she couldn't recall ever feeling so well rested before, which of course made little sense considering that she'd only slept for about five hours. It had to be Richard and all the wonderful things he'd said to her when they'd last parted ways. Her worries had been lifted from her shoulders, allowing her to hope for a future that she'd never thought would be hers. He was wonderful.

Stretching out upon the sheets while enjoying the plush feel of the pillow cradling her head, Mary allowed her dreamy thoughts of Richard to fill her mind, right until Amy entered her room with a firm knock and a brisk stride. "Good morning, my lady. Your aunt requests your immediate presence in the yellow parlor. I am to help you dress."

Dismayed by Amy's tone, Mary brushed a lock of hair from her forehead and sat up. "What is the matter?" she asked her warily.

Rifling through Mary's wardrobe, Amy sniffed a few times before saying, "I have never seen her look so angry before in my life." She turned to look at Mary, revealing the tears in her eyes. "She knows about you and . . . I am certain of it, though I assure you that I have said nothing to her that might give you away. Please. You must believe me."

"I do," Mary said as she got out of bed and plodded across the floor to where Amy was standing. She offered her a handkerchief, which she gratefully accepted. "It will be all right, Amy. I am certain of it. In fact, I daresay that by the end of today you may wish me happy."

"He plans to propose?"

Mary nodded, a bubble of laughter bursting from between her lips. She could no longer contain her happiness. "Indeed, he intends to speak with my aunt directly. Now that I know who he is, I see no obstacle in our way."

But when Mary entered the yellow parlor a short while later, her confidence wavered in response to the hard glare in her aunt's eyes which seemed to match the tight set of her mouth to perfection. Lady Foxworth looked visibly terrifying. "Good morning," Mary said, her hands clasped in front of her as she crossed to the sofa that faced the one on which her aunt was seated. A tea tray stood on a low table between them.

"Hardly," Lady Foxworth clipped while Mary lowered herself onto the sofa. "In fact, it has come to my attention that you have defied me . . . lied to me!"

Straight to the point then.

"I suppose you must be referring to Signor Antonio," Mary said in as calm a tone as she could muster.

"Of course I am!" Her aunt practically exploded, her cheeks reddening with the exertion. "How could you, Mary? I trusted you and rather than prove yourself worthy of that trust, you went behind my back and . . . and got yourself ruined. This is a disaster! Good God! What am I going to tell your poor parents? They will be devastated!"

"Not if they approve of him."

Lady Foxworth's eyes narrowed. "How can they

when he has no desire for anyone to know who he is? How can he offer you anything under such circumstances? You cannot hope to marry him, that is for certain, though I have asked Lady Duncaster to fetch him for me. I expect them to arrive at any moment."

Mary's pulse quickened with expectation. "In that case, I think that you will find yourself eating your words, Aunt Eugenia. Richard deserves your respect and—"

"Richard?" Lady Foxworth placed her hand against her chest. "How can you make such free use of his Christian name? It is not proper." She shook her head, her earrings dangling violently from side to side. "Oh dear Lord, Mary. I expected so much better from you. I—"

The door opened and Lady Duncaster entered, followed by Richard who closed the door behind them. He wasn't wearing the mask or the cape, his face completely visible in the bright daylight that filled the room. It was the first time Mary had seen him like this, his features untouched by shadows or flickering light. A swarm of butterflies batted their wings in the pit of her stomach, her heart skipping happily in response to the smile he was sending her way.

Dressed in a green, beautifully tailored, jacket, with beige-colored breeches and expensive looking boots, he was the very image of a well-bred gentleman. His hair had been neatly combed; his sparkling eyes the focal point of his face—a complete distraction from the pink skin that puckered over his left cheek and down the side of his neck. To Mary, he had never looked more handsome than at that very moment.

"Allow me to introduce myself," he said, addressing Mary's aunt as he bowed slightly from the waist. "My name is Richard Heartly. It is an absolute pleasure to make your acquaintance, Lady Foxworth."

The tension in Lady Foxworth's expression eased, replaced by something that could only be described as complete and utter surprise. "You are Lord Oakland's younger son?"

"The very one," Richard said as he stepped further into the room. Still standing, he waited for Lady Duncaster to considerately claim the seat beside Lady Foxworth so he could sit down next to Mary.

"But you are supposed to be dead!" Lady Foxworth blurted. With a jolt, her eyes widened and she immediately placed her hand over her mouth. "Forgive me, I did not mean . . . that is to say, I—"

"It is quite all right," Richard said. "I wanted it that way." He turned the left side of his face toward her. "As you can probably imagine, I was not very eager to make a public appearance. If news of my return to England had spread, I would have had to do so in order to save my family the embarrassment of having to explain my constant absence from social events."

"Because of the scars?" Lady Foxworth quietly asked. "They are not really all that bad."

"A fact that your niece has eventually convinced me of." He reached for Mary's hand, the warmth of him weaving its way through her. "Her kindness toward me and her ability to care for the person that I am without being influenced by my appearance, has given me a tremendous amount of hope for the future."

"I still find it difficult to agree with your method," Lady Foxworth said, her voice tightening a notch.

"After all, you refused to reassure me of your credentials when I asked you to do so. Furthermore, I have just received a letter this morning from the Earl of Rotridge, informing me that you and Mary have been cavorting with each other for the past two weeks. If you were a gentleman—"

"I hope you are not calling my character into question," Richard said, edging forward in his seat.

"What I am saying," Lady Foxworth continued, not the least bit deterred by the note of warning in Richard's voice, "is that you have deliberately put my niece's reputation at risk on numerous occasions, which is hardly very gentlemanly of you."

Mary held her breath while Richard stared back at her aunt. If only she could dive under the carpet, but unfortunately, that was not a possibility. She looked to Lady Duncaster instead, who in turn appeared remarkably calm—as if she knew that this situation would resolve itself to everyone's liking. Mary could only hope that this would be the case.

"Point taken," Richard eventually conceded. "But I saw no other way in which to get to know her better. As our acquaintance with each other turned into a solid friendship and something . . . more promising than that, it became increasingly impossible for me to imagine a day without Mary by my side."

Mary's heart swelled until it felt as though it might actually burst. Her eyes misted and a tight knot began forming in her throat.

"With your permission," Richard continued, "I would like to ask for her hand in marriage."

Mary knew her aunt well enough to see that she was pleased by this outcome, even if she tried not to show it, her expression as serious as ever as she met Richard's gaze. "A former soldier who has fought bravely for his country is certainly a quality that I cannot help but admire. Especially considering the price you had to pay for it." She paused a moment, seemingly considering her next words. "That said, however, I would like to know how you plan on supporting her. To be blunt, what is your financial situation like?"

Mary gasped. "Aunt! You cannot . . ." Lady Foxworth gave her a quelling look that forced Mary's words into silence.

"Commonality is all well and good when choosing your life-partner, Mary," Lady Foxworth said, "But there is the business side to it that should not be ignored."

"She is right," Richard said, briefly offering Mary a reassuring smile before returning his full attention to Lady Foxworth. "May I be equally blunt?"

"By all means," Lady Foxworth said. "I encourage you to do so."

"Very well then. As Mary is already aware, I have made some lucrative investments over the last few years. As a result, I currently have an income of ten thousand pounds per year. In addition to that, I have recently acquired an estate which I am sure will meet your expectations. All in all, I would say that my net worth at the moment is somewhere in the vicinity of one hundred and fifty thousand pounds."

Mary's jaw dropped, as did her aunt's. Lady Duncaster on the other hand looked very pleased—as if she'd known all along just how eligible Richard Heartly actually was. Which, Mary realized, she probably had.

Gathering her composure, Lady Foxworth reached for her teacup and took a sip before saying, "That sounds like a very comfortable number."

Mary almost choked. But before she could manage an apology on behalf of her aunt, the lady surprised Mary again by saying, "My only remaining question now is whether or not you love her."

Surely there had to be a window through which Mary could escape? Looking around, she saw that they were all firmly shut. But all plans of vaulting over a windowsill and running until her feet could no longer carry her, fled from her mind the moment Richard voiced his response. He gave no lengthy explanation and made no use of flowery prose. All he said was, "Of course I do."

At which point Mary promptly burst into tears, which of course was silly. After all, today had just turned into the most wonderful day of her life. "I love you too," she croaked out while dabbing at her eyes with the handkerchief that Richard offered her.

"In that case, I see no reason why the two of you should not be together," Lady Foxworth said. "If that is what you want, Mary."

"With all my heart," Mary managed.

"Well then." Lady Foxworth's voice sounded a little more raw than before. "On behalf of Mary's parents, the Earl and Countess of Harrodsburg, you have my blessing."

The moment the words were out, Richard slipped off the sofa and onto one knee. He took both of Mary's hands in his and smiled up at her with all the love that he'd just professed. "Mary Bourneville, will you do me the honor of making me the most fortunate man in the world by becoming my wife?"

Swallowing the knot in her throat, she nodded her agreement, sniffing a little until she finally managed to get the necessary words out. "Yes," she whispered. "Nothing would please me more."

Leaning forward, he placed a kiss upon her lips before catching her in his arms and pulling her to her feet so he could embrace her properly. It wasn't until Mary heard Lady Duncaster whisper something to her aunt that she remembered they weren't alone.

"We will have more time for this later," Richard murmured close to her ear before stepping back and adding a respectful amount of distance between them.

The words sent a tremor down Mary's spine, her cheeks grew warm and for a frightening moment she feared that her legs might collapse beneath her. So she sat down quickly and busied herself with pouring tea into cups and arranging sweetmeats on plates which she then offered to everyone in turn.

"Thank you," Lady Duncaster said, setting her plate aside, "but I am afraid that I must leave you now. I promised the butler that I would go over the social activities for the coming week with him. Do let me know if you would like to make a formal announcement this evening and I will ensure that enough champagne is put on ice."

As soon as she was gone, Richard returned to his seat beside Mary and addressed Lady Foxworth. "There is something else that you ought to know," he said as he reached for Mary's hand once more. Turning to Mary, he said, "You need to tell her about the opera."

Chapter 14

Mary sucked in a breath. It was as if she'd just been hurled into an abyss, arms flailing and all. Her entire body stiffened as the skin on her arms and shoulders tightened with a wash of prickly heat. "I cannot," she whispered, shaking away a shiver.

"It is the most prudent way forward," Richard told her calmly. "If Rotridge plans to use the information against you, your aunt will eventually find out. I think that it would be best if she did so from you."

Mary knew that he was right, but that didn't seem to diminish her fear in the least. She was terrified of what her aunt would think—of how she would react when she discovered that Mary had lied to her. How *much*, she had lied to her. Closing her eyes for a brief moment, she prayed for strength. When she opened them again, she focused all her attention on her aunt's curious expression and said, "You know how fond I am of reading?"

Lady Foxworth nodded. "Of course. It is one of your favorite activities. You always go to bed early so that you can have a few hours to yourself with a good book. I have nothing against it personally though it has struck me as somewhat odd that a young lady, such as yourself, would prefer reading to an evening at the theatre."

Hesitantly chewing on her lower lip, Mary squeezed Richard's hand. "To be perfectly honest, I must confess that I do not. Prefer reading to an evening at the theatre, that is."

"What do you mean?" Lady Foxworth's lips parted in a perfect O, her eyes darting from Mary to Richard and back again.

"I mean that I was not reading when you thought I was. I was singing." Sucking in a deep breath, Mary plunged forward. "And I was doing so at the opera, in full view of everyone who has ever bought a ticket to see Lucia Cavalani."

Lady Foxworth blinked, then shook her head. "I do not understand."

Leaning slightly forward, Mary met her aunt's eyes. "*I* am Lucia Cavalani, Aunt. I have been singing at the King's Theatre for two full seasons now disguised as her, with earnings of five thousand pounds per annum. And that is—"

"Good Lord," Richard breathed.

"I am speechless," Lady Foxworth exclaimed. "Positively speechless!"

"And that is without considering the additional profits that I have acquired from occasionally performing by special request or going on tour. If you recall, I did stay with my brother a few times during the off-season."

"Your brother knew about this?" Lady Foxworth sounded truly appalled now.

"I believe it was to his advantage," Richard said, "Though I must confess that I had no idea of just how much until this moment." Turning his head he looked down at Mary with a mixture of admiration and something alarmingly similar to pity. "What was your total income this last year, Mary?"

"Sixteen thousand seven hundred pounds. To be exact."

"Good grief!" Lady Foxworth curled her hand around the armrest as if to steady herself.

"And how much of that have you given your brother?" Richard asked.

"He needed my help," Mary said, aware of how the situation probably looked.

"How much?" Richard repeated.

Feeling horribly foolish all of a sudden, Mary dropped her gaze. "Twelve thousand pounds."

Silence fell upon the room for one long awful moment until Richard quietly said, "I am sorry, but I daresay that he has not been a very good brother to you."

"I could not agree more," Lady Foxworth said. "To think that he encouraged you to go behind my back, facilitating this . . . this folly! And for what? You could have been horribly ruined any number of times and in any number of ways too. The people you must have had to associate with . . . Good Lord! It does not bear thinking about, Mary. To say that I am disappointed in you would be a grave understatement. And your poor parents! Just think of—"

"That is quite enough," Richard cut in. "There is no need to add salt to the wound, Lady Foxworth.

Mary knows that what she did was risky, and yet I cannot help but admire her for it nonetheless."

"Admire her?" Lady Foxworth's tone reminded Mary of nails on a chalkboard.

"For better or worse, she tried to help her brother overcome a difficult situation when he had no one else to turn to. She did so by transforming her voice into a powerful asset—one that is worth five thousand pounds per annum! Can you imagine how difficult that must have been for her? Just coordinating everything so that nobody would learn the truth about her is a remarkable feat on its own. But if you hear her sing—"

"I *have* heard her sing, Mr. Heartly," Lady Foxworth said tightly and with an underlying note of exhaustion. Her nostrils flared. "In fact, it seems that I have had that pleasure repeatedly. At the King's Theatre."

"Then you must agree that she has an incredible talent," Richard insisted.

Lady Foxworth stared back at Mary as if she were seeing her for the very first time, which made Mary feel much like a rare specimen in a glass jar at the Hunterian. It took every ounce of restraint she possessed not to squirm.

Eventually her aunt nodded. "Indeed, there is no denying that." Mary breathed a sigh of relief, which came a moment too soon since her aunt continued with, "But . . ." She held up a pointed finger to accentuate the word. "That does not mean that I will forgive you for betraying my trust, Mary. Apparently, you are not the person I thought you to be, but someone else entirely, and that is not an easy thing for me to accept. I am sorry."

If her aunt had struck her, Mary doubted it would have hurt as much as the words that had just been spoken. They fell heavily between them, like thick snow dislodged from a rooftop.

"Nevertheless," Richard said. Releasing Mary's hand, he brought his arm around her shoulders instead—an intimate gesture of comfort that was terribly inappropriate, but much appreciated by Mary. "You are not the only one who knows about this. Rotridge does as well."

"The news just seems to be getting worse and worse," Lady Foxworth murmured.

"And since he has chosen to tell you about Mary's association with me, I believe it is only a matter of time before he uses his knowledge about Mary's career at the opera in an effort to ruin her socially."

"To what avail?" Lady Foxworth asked. "Because she does not wish to welcome his advances?"

"Partly," Mary said. "He claims that he is accustomed to getting what he wants and, not only did I tell him that he can never have me, but his efforts at forcing my hand were also repeatedly diverted. I believe he feels humiliated and that he blames me for that. Rotridge wants revenge, and he now has the perfect means by which to get it."

"Then we must aim to stop him at all cost." Righting herself on the sofa, Lady Foxworth served Richard a candid stare.

The corner of his mouth twitched. "I like the way you think."

"Do you have a plan?" Mary asked, eager to know how to proceed but also worried about what might happen.

"Nothing concrete—not until I know how Rotridge intends to act. Right now, his power over you has been somewhat diminished since you have told your aunt about Lucia Cavalani. But he might still try to convince others that you and she are one and the same." Rising. Richard paced back and forth a moment before coming to a halt. "I think the best bet is to deny everything."

"Of course it is," Lady Foxworth agreed, to Mary's amazement. "If any questions are asked, I will vouch for Mary. Indeed, I will tell everyone that she has spent her evenings at home and that I have personally seen her do so."

Mary gaped. "You would lie for me?"

"Of course I would," Lady Foxworth said as if it were the most natural thing in the world. "You are my niece, after all, and I am duty bound to protect you."

"I scarcely know what to say." Her aunt's generosity made her feel even worse, so she did the only thing that she could think of doing in order to make things right again between them, even though she knew that it wouldn't be nearly enough. Rising, Mary crossed to where her aunt was sitting, leaned down and placed a kiss upon her cheek. "Thank you."

Lady Foxworth managed a wobbly smile. Her eyes shimmered a little. "Think nothing of it," she said as she too got to her feet with a bit of a shrug and a nonchalant hand gesture. "Let's just hope that it works so that we may be rid of that pestering Rotridge for good."

Mary couldn't agree more as she accepted the arm that Richard offered and allowed him to escort her from the room.

"I cannot possibly thank you enough," Mary said as she and Richard made their way down a long hallway shortly after. "It cannot be easy for you to remove the mask and show your face after all this time."

"No, it is not," he agreed, noting the Duke of Pinehurst's startled expression as they passed him, "but it is necessary, not only if we are to save your reputation but if we are to be together. I cannot continue courting you in secret."

"Although you must admit that our midnight rendezvous have been terribly romantic."

Chuckling lightly, he tightened his hold on her arm. "There is no denying that."

A shrill squeal drew Richard's attention away from Mary, his feet almost taking a step back at the sight of a woman sprinting toward him. He recognized her instantly as his youngest sister, Fiona. "Richard!" His name was joyfully spoken as she flung her arms around his neck, detaching him from Mary who produced a stunned squeak. "I cannot believe that it is really you."

"And I cannot believe that you would so easily recognize me after all these years."

"Are you mad?" Pulling back she assessed him carefully from head to toe. "You look exactly the same as when I last saw you."

He couldn't help but frown in response to that obvious lie. "Except for this," he said.

She peered up at him, almost squinting. "If that has been your only reason for hiding away in your bedchamber, I just might throttle you." She crossed her arms. "And I am bigger now, in case you have not noticed."

At his right, he heard Mary choke back a laugh. "So you are," he agreed, pressing his lips together.

"I am serious," Fiona said. "With all the fuss about you not wanting to see us, I rather expected you to have turned into a troll or some other terrifying creature." Pouting in much the same way as she'd done when she was little and was being denied a sweet, she added, "I find that I am rather disappointed by how handsome you still are."

Richard straightened. "Now you exaggerate."

"Not at all," Fiona said.

"I agree with her," Mary said. Her lips pulled slightly at the corners, dimpling her cheeks in an almost mischievous way. "Indeed, I find you to be the most handsome of men."

Fiona frowned. She took a step back, her eyes darting between them. "Wait a moment . . ." Her head tilted and it clearly seemed as though she was trying to work out a puzzle. "How are the two of you acquainted with each other? I mean, if my brother has just chosen to venture back into public, I find it odd that he would do so with a perfect stranger by his side. Unless of course, you have known each other for some time, in which case"—she shook her head—"I do not understand this."

It was Richard's turn to laugh. There was really nothing better than catching his sisters by surprise and pulling the wool over Fiona's eyes had always been more difficult. "We met at the masquerade," he confessed, even more amused by the confusion that filled Fiona's eyes at that remark.

"The masquerade?" Richard and Mary both nodded. "But that was over a week ago!"

"Yes, it was," Richard agreed.

"I cannot believe that you attended the masquerade without letting your family know." She paused for a second before saying, "Don't tell me that Spencer and Papa were aware of your presence and failed to inform the rest of us."

"No, Fiona. I told no one, but Lady Duncaster insisted that I should participate and after much deliberation I decided that it would be a good opportunity for me to escape my solidarity for an evening." Bowing his head, he asked, "Do you recall the gentleman who refused to dance with you?"

She nodded, then gasped. "That was you?"

"I hope you can forgive my rudeness, but I knew how hard it would be for me to hold you in my arms without sharing my identity with you. At the time, I was not yet ready to return to Society." Looking briefly at Mary, he said, "But then I met a woman who would change my life forever. I am in her debt."

Fiona's eyes shimmered as she reached for Richard's hand, enclosing it in her own. "I am so happy for you." Blinking, she said, "I take it that the two of you have plans?"

Mary nodded. "Your brother has just asked me to marry him and I have accepted."

"Then you will soon be my sister." Releasing Richard's hand, Fiona stepped toward Mary, kissing her lightly on the cheek. Stepping back with the brightest smile in creation, she then said, "Just wait until I tell Mama and Papa!"

Richard stared after Fiona as she hurried away from where he and Mary were still standing. "I suspect my return to Society coupled with our unexpected engagement is about to put the entire house on edge."

"Your mother will certainly be thrilled," Mary said. "To marry off three children in less than a month is quite a feat."

Richard chuckled. "Perhaps she will be able to draw some of the attention away from us."

"Perhaps," Mary agreed as she placed her hand upon his arm and allowed him to guide her forward once more.

A feeling of great comfort settled inside his chest. It was one that he looked forward to experiencing every day for the rest of his life with Mary by his side.

"**I** must say that I am rather relieved to have you back in our midst," Chadwick said from across the table that evening at dinner, following a toast that Lady Duncaster had made in Richard's honor. "I thought you were done for. Spencer never said a word!"

"I can assure you that no one is as relieved as I." Taking a bite of his pheasant, Richard reflected on how wonderful it was to finally be back in Society with the freedom to do something as simple as share a meal with friends. He'd wasted precious time in his self-induced confinement, though it had been for a good reason. A smile touched his lips at the thought of how his foe might react upon realizing that he was not only still alive, but that he'd taken everything from him after years of meticulous planning.

Leaning slightly to his left, Richard whispered in Mary's ear. "Are you ready to make a public announcement?"

She didn't turn her head to look at him, her eyes trained on the piece of meat she was cutting, but the blush that rose up her neck and filled her cheeks spoke volumes about the effect he was having on her. "I fear that some may expire from sheer shock since they thought you dead until only half an hour ago." His return to Society had certainly been met by open-mouthed gapes and a succession of gasps. One lady had even fainted since she'd thought him a ghost. "To announce that you are to be married may be a touch too much."

"So you think we should wait until tomorrow?" Discreetly, Richard reached beneath the table and placed his hand against her thigh. A devilish grin swept through him when she almost jolted out of her seat, her cutlery clanging loudly against her plate.

"Mind your manners, sir," she hissed while several curious gazes darted toward them.

"Once our engagement is official, I shall not have to mind them quite as much," he murmured. "Much less once we are wed."

She said nothing in response to that, but reached for her wine instead and took a lengthy sip.

"Will you tell us what you and Lady Mary are discussing?" Spencer asked. Leaning forward from across the table, he said in a far more muted tone, "Chadwick is already placing bets on the subject of your interest."

"And what, pray tell, do you suspect the subject to be, Chadwick?" Richard asked.

A cheeky smile lit Chadwick's face. "Weeeell . . ." He took a sip of his wine and then returned the glass to the table. "I—"

"Will say nothing further on the matter," Lady Spencer cut in. Seated between her husband and Chadwick she'd apparently been following the conversation and had decided that it had gone too far.

"Then perhaps I ought to do so instead," Richard suggested. Turning back to Mary, he asked her plainly, "Are you ready to become the center of attention?"

"If you are," she said, offering him the loveliest smile in the world, "then so am I."

Confident that he would have the life that he had always dreamed of, Richard pushed back his chair and rose to his feet. A tremor raced through him and his stomach clenched as he reached for his glass and hit his knife against it, making it chime. The chatter that had filled the dining room just a second earlier, dwindled into silence as everyone turned toward him, giving him their full attention. Richard sucked in a breath, his hand trembling slightly as he set down his glass. He wasn't used to getting noticed. Not anymore. And the curious looks he was now receiving were setting him on edge.

Briefly, he glanced down at Mary, caught the affection that shone in her eyes, and felt suddenly lighter. "Ladies and gentlemen," he said, shifting his gaze to the rest of those present. "I know that many of you are surprised to see me here after so many years—that you thought me forever lost to the world. You may wonder why I chose not to announce my return from Belgium . . . Suffice it to say that I did not feel comfortable, venturing out into public with the wounds that I had sustained, unsure of how I would be greeted.

"The truth is that my injuries have served as something of a handicap. They have made me view myself in a different light. For a long time I thought myself unworthy—of friendship, of respect . . ." He paused briefly before adding, "And of love."

Reaching for Mary's hand, he enfolded it in his own as he looked down at her with all the fondness in his heart. "That is no longer the case." Pausing for emphasis, he said, "It is with the greatest joy that I am able to announce my engagement to Lady Mary. She is everything that I have ever dreamed of, and I cannot wait for the day when she and I are finally wed. So if you would all please rise for a toast in her honor, I would be exceedingly grateful."

It didn't take long for all of the guests to get to their feet and pick up their glasses. From across the table, Spencer gave Richard a distinct nod of approval that was mirrored by their father who'd been placed further away. "To Lady Mary," the guests spoke in unison. "And congratulations to you both," Lady Duncaster added after everyone had taken a sip of their wine.

"Hear, hear!" Cheers rose up under the ceiling where they hovered above everyone like puffy clouds on a bright summer's day.

"Richard," Lady Oakland exclaimed as soon as she had a chance to approach her son later. "I cannot begin to tell you how happy I am for you! Fiona did suggest a possible attachment between the two of you earlier, but having it confirmed is simply wonderful—the very best news I could have hoped for." Turning toward Mary, she reached for her hands and clasped them between her own as she leaned forward to kiss her on the cheek. "Welcome to the family, my dear."

Mary looked adorably befuddled as she nodded, smiled, and offered her thanks. Belatedly, as if it were an afterthought, she dipped into a curtsy, but Lady Oakland quickly stopped her from completing the gesture, insisting that adhering to such protocol would be completely unnecessary. It seemed as though Richard's world had somehow managed to find its center of gravity once more. And yet, in spite of the rightness of it all, a niggling feeling seemed to poke him in the shoulder, insisting that the joy he'd been granted was but a mirage that would soon evaporate before him like the fleeting memory of a dream.

Chapter 15

As it turned out, Mary was allowed two full days of blissful happiness before her world was turned upside down. It happened in the late afternoon while she was out enjoying a picnic with Richard and his siblings. Having decided that the clover-filled meadow beyond Thorncliff's orchard would serve as a splendid location, Fiona had spearheaded the venture by determining who would carry what and where it should all go since everyone had agreed that it would be a refreshing change not to have to impose on any footmen.

Lady Spencer was also in full accord and had gazed lovingly at her husband while the Duke and Duchess of Stonegate followed suite. As Richard's eldest sister, the duchess had adamantly insisted on helping Mary with her wedding preparations, though Mary soon discovered that the unmarried state of the remaining Heartly sisters would not deter them from voicing their own ideas and opinions. Indeed, they had all become rather fond of sharing their views on flowers, colors, food and music. It had gotten to a point where Mary could only hope that Lady Laura's idea of a wedding gown would not come to fruition since it sounded like more of a pastry than something that one might actually wish to wear.

"I am really not partial to large quantities of ribbons or lace," Mary explained for what had to be the tenth time. Seated beneath the shade of a handsome oak, she'd just selected a tuna sandwich when Lady Laura once again began suggesting the sort of dress that *she* thought fitting for a Society wedding.

"What about beads then?" Lady Laura inquired. "Crystal beads are especially pretty and since I do believe it will be a sunny day, they will catch and reflect the light, making you look like a princess right out of a magical fairy-tale story." The comment was, as had become the norm whenever Lady Laura spoke of anything remotely romantic, followed by a sigh and a distant gaze.

Mary automatically scrunched her nose before making a deliberate effort to smile. "Unfortunately I do not care overly much for beads either." She shrugged one shoulder when Lady Laura gaped at her as if she were mad. "I find that simplicity tends to serve me best."

"I could not agree more, especially since it was one of the first things about you that caught my attention," Richard said. Reaching for Mary's hand, he placed a reverent kiss upon her knuckles. "One cannot deny that a lady as pretty as you does not require further embellishment. Least of all when one considers that they will only serve to distract from your natural beauty."

If Mary could have blushed both inside and out, she was certain that she would have done so in response to such a publically spoken proclamation. Unable to help the smile that tugged at her lips, she offered Richard the most adoring look she could manage before shyly lowering her gaze to her lap. After two weeks of secret rendezvous, she'd grown accustomed to private signs of affection. To have their romance become the center of public scrutiny was making her feel as though she were an insect under a magnifying glass.

Still, she felt her stomach swirl when, moments later, as the rest of the party was otherwise distracted by Lady Emily reading out loud from the *Mayfair Chronicle,* Richard leaned in and whispered in Mary's ear, "What I would not give for another moment alone with you in the antechamber."

Not daring to respond, Mary did her best to focus on what Lady Emily was reading—something about an attempted jewelry heist from a wealthy merchant's house in London. But Richard's presence proved too great a distraction. Especially when he went on to tell her *how* he would like to make use of such a moment.

By the time the picnic was over and everyone decided to return indoors, Mary was quite certain that she had, in the space of only two hours, somehow managed to grow warmer than the surface of the sun. It didn't help that the younger Heartly sisters giggled and whispered to each other as they followed behind Mary and Richard. This, however, came to an end as they climbed the steps to the terrace and approached the French doors leading back inside the house. The eager chatter coming from small clusters of guests made everyone immediately aware that an event of some importance must have occurred during their absence.

"Mama," Spencer said, striding forward with purpose. Looking around, Mary caught sight of the countess, her smile filled with eager excitement as she came toward them. "What is all the fuss about?"

"Oh, I knew that coming here would be the very best decision in the world and Lady Duncaster has just confirmed this. She truly knows how to cater to her guests in every way." Inhaling a deep breath, Lady Oakland continued with, "Just wait until you hear of the treat that she has planned. You will scarcely be able to believe it!"

"Well? What is it?" Lady Fiona asked. She looked just as eager to discover the surprise as Lady Oakland looked at the prospect of announcing it.

With her arm still linked with Richard's, Mary leaned a little closer so as not to miss a single word. Admittedly, the buzz of voices swarming through the atrium where they were presently standing, had stirred her curiosity.

A very dramatic pause followed before Lady Oakland casually said, "Do any of you know who Mr. Taylor is?"

A slight shiver crept across Mary's shoulders. She felt Richard's arm tighten against her own as she shook her head.

"The manager of the King's Theatre?" Richard's sister, Lady Rachel, asked.

"Precisely," Lady Oakland said as she looked to Lady Rachel. "He has written to Lady Duncaster in response to some interest that he has received regarding none other than Lucia Cavalani."

Mary felt the ground sink beneath her feet.

"The opera singer?" Sarah put in. "Will she be coming here?"

"Well, that is just it," Lady Oakland said. "Apparently, Mr. Taylor wishes to know if Thorncliff's guests would like to enjoy a private concert, in which case, he has promised to ensure Miss Cavalani's imminent arrival."

"Breathe." The whispered reminder was made by Richard as he carefully disentangled himself and Mary from the group and proceeded to lead her back out onto the terrace. Without pausing for even a second, he hastened her down the steps and toward the far right of the garden where the Greek folly stood. At a reasonable distance from all others, nobody was close enough to hear what they said or see their expressions, which Mary felt was just as well since she was certain she looked quite ill.

"Rotridge." She spoke the word as if it were the missing piece she needed to complete a puzzle. "He wants to humiliate me—to destroy my reputation completely."

"He will never succeed. Of that I can assure you, Mary." The fierce determination with which Richard spoke gave Mary hope, even as she saw her downfall in vivid displays of color and detail.

"How?" was all she could ask. "How do you suppose we stop this catastrophe?"

Richard began to pace, the soles of his boots kicking up clumps of grass as he did so, due to frustration. "You can say that you are unwell. That you have a sore throat and cannot perform. Surely that will—"

"Mr. Taylor will not hear of it. Not when most of

England's elite is gathered here at Thorncliff. Good lord! Do have any idea of the sort of earnings he plans to make from my performance? Granted, I receive a large sum too, but Mr. Taylor, the theatre as a whole . . . it would likely secure the salaries for all the other employees for the duration of the coming year!"

"But if Mr. Taylor is unable to find Lucia Cavalani, then how is she to perform in the first place?"

"Therein lies the problem," Mary told him grimly. "Mr. Taylor knows exactly where to find me. It is part of the agreement that he and I have with each other." She watched as Richard stopped before her, his face drawn in tight lines as he took her hands between his own. "In fact, I suspect that there is a letter waiting for me in my bedchamber, informing me that Lucia Cavalani is expected to perform at Thorncliff Manor as soon as possible."

"And if you do not?" Richard asked, his voice grave.

She looked askance, her eyes settling on the slim branch of a tree as it bobbed up and down in the breeze. "Mr. Taylor has always been reasonable with me, but he is also a business man, so I would prefer not to take any chances."

"You think he might threaten to reveal who you really are just to make you sing?"

Stalwartly, Mary stared back at the man whom she'd come to love, increasingly aware of something dangerous simmering beneath the surface of his seemingly calm façade. His eyes shifted and it struck her then that he was furious. Not so much with her, though she wagered he might be a little angry that she had allowed herself to get into such a muddle in the first place, but rather on her behalf. "There is no telling what a man might do for money." She spoke softly but with precision. "Is there?"

"You would be a fool not to expect the worst," he murmured, mirroring her thoughts.

"Precisely."

He nodded at that and, with a quick glance around, led her to the side of the folly. The grass was slightly taller there. It tickled Mary's ankles as Richard pulled her into his arms, the palm of his hand pressing comfortably against her back as he simply held her. A long, drawn-out moment passed until she heard him whisper in her ear, "Rotridge means to unveil you."

"Yes," she whispered back.

"But what if he does not manage to unveil Lady Mary, but someone else entirely?" Stepping back a little, he nudged her chin just enough for their eyes to meet. "He would lose all credibility and probably embarrass himself in the process too."

It took a moment for Mary to figure out what Richard was plotting. Once she did, however, she knew that she'd found yet another reason to love him. "That's a brilliant idea, Richard. And I know exactly who we can turn to for help." Closing the distance between them once more, she wound her arms around his neck, her chest pressed flat against his. Settling her cheek against his shoulder, she inhaled deeply, allowing the scent of him to travel through her, invigorating her and giving her hope. Whatever happened, she had him. He knew the truth about her and he accepted it, was willing to stand by her and help her fight for it.

Slowly, she allowed one hand to trail down over the front of his jacket while he in turn traced circles along the length of her spine. His touch was gentle, feather light, and oh so very tempting. "I miss this closeness between us," she said as a hot shiver swam through her.

"Me too." His hand found her cheek, turning her head and angling it just so . . . The kiss that followed was delicious, filled with the flavor of tea and the chocolate they'd had on the picnic. A sigh of appreciation rose from Mary's throat and in the next instant she found herself pressed up hard against the cool stone of the folly with Richard standing over her, his eyes slightly hooded and his breath coming fast. For a long moment, he said nothing at all, but then, ever so slowly, he leaned back, adding distance. "Forgive me, Mary, but this is not like the stolen kisses that you and I have shared in the dark. People talk. If someone were to see us . . . Please forgive me."

It took a second for her dazed self to return to solid ground. Blinking, she looked back at him, saw the self-deprecation in the tight lines of his face and expelled a deep breath. "There is absolutely nothing to forgive. You and I are engaged to be married now and—"

"Even so, I would like to ensure that your reputation remains intact."

Forcing a smile, she nodded before accepting the arm he offered her so that he could escort her back to the house. They had almost reached the steps leading up to the terrace before he murmured, "Believe me, there is nothing that I look forward to more than our wedding night, Mary. I hope that you are aware of that."

This time, when she looked up at him, her smile was genuine. "Would it trouble you, Sir, if I were to tell you that I feel precisely the same way?"

The look he gave her was darker now and filled with something secret that Mary didn't quite understand. Yet somehow, she knew that she desperately wanted to understand. Especially when he said, "Nothing would please me more." His voice was low, rippling along her nerves and sending frissons down her spine.

Shuddering slightly, she steadied herself against him as they made their way up the steps. "I will write to Mr. Taylor as soon as I return to my bedchamber, informing him that Lucia Cavalani will be happy to perform at Thorncliff." Reaching the top of the steps, she drew Richard to a halt. "You were right to ask me to tell my aunt about this. The fact that she knows makes this ordeal a little less terrifying, no matter how disappointed she is with me for deceiving her."

"She will recover and she will forgive you for it." The smile he gave her was slightly crooked, puckering the skin on his left cheek a little more than usual. "That is what one does when one loves someone as much as she clearly loves you."

Her chest tightened with affection for him, for how good and kind and honorable he was. Continuing their progress, he led her back inside the house and toward the grand staircase. "She is Papa's only sibling. The two of them have always been very close so it was natural for her to have a large presence in my life. When Papa accepted the position in India and he and Mama began preparing for their journey, Aunt Eugenia was thrilled with the prospect of sponsoring me for my Seasons and acting as my temporary guardian."

"When do you expect your parents to return?"

"In another year, according to the most recent letter that I received from Mama." Her voice hitched a little. "I miss them very much, but the things that they have described to me in their correspondences are truly incredible. There is no doubt that their journey to such a distant location has been a memorable experience for them."

Inclining his head, he escorted her up the stairs. "I have heard that people ride elephants there."

Chuckling, Mary nodded. "It is true. Can you imagine? I daresay that must be quite a sight to behold."

"As are you," he said, releasing her hand. It cooled with the absence of his touch—a sensation she did not like in the least—but they had reached the first floor landing and she knew as well as he that it was time for them to part.

"You flatter me."

"Not nearly enough." A smile tugged at the corner of his lips. "Write your letter to Mr. Taylor, Mary, and I promise you that everything will be all right in the end."

After watching Mary disappear around a corner, Richard went in the opposite direction, returning to his own bedchamber shortly after. Once inside and with the door closed, he expelled a deep breath, hoping that he would be right in the assurance he'd given her.

His eyes dropped to the floor where another missive lay, recently delivered while he'd been out. Snatching it up, he tore it open and read the information that his secretary had sent him. As always, it was brief and to the point:

> *The Earl of Rotridge is a very wealthy man. He does not need to marry for money. Indeed, there is little that he desires. After some investigation, however, I have discovered that there is a property that he would like to acquire since it adjoins his own. The land is presently owned by the Marquess of Richmond, his son being the Earl of Harrodsburg. Curiously, however, the earl will not be inheriting this land since it is not entailed. Instead, the marquess has chosen to will it to his granddaughter, Mary Bourneville.*

Setting the letter aside, Richard crossed to the window and looked out, his jaw clenching with anger. Evidently, Rotridge didn't care about Mary, but to try and blackmail her into marriage so that he could increase the size of his property was unconscionable.

His brother's discernible knock sounded at the door. "Enter," Richard said as he crossed to the sideboard and selected two tumblers. Behind him, he heard the door open and close. "Brandy?" he asked.

"Thank you. I would appreciate that," Spencer said. His footsteps were measured as he went to take a seat in one of the armchairs. "I thought you should know that however unorthodox your courtship with Lady Mary has been, I am happy with your success, even if you did risk ruining her."

Snorting, Richard turned toward his brother with the two full tumblers in his hands. "You took a similar risk with Sarah, according to what you have told me," he said as he offered Spencer his drink.

"I will admit that she and I were alone a few times and that I was . . . tempted to take advantage of those situations. But I refrained."

Hesitating a moment, Richard lowered himself into the opposite chair. "I hope you are not implying that I have taken liberties."

Spencer studied him for a long drawn out moment while Richard stared straight back at him. If his brother knew about the kisses he'd shared with Mary a lengthy reprimand would surely follow. "You were always popular with the ladies, Richard, but you were never a scoundrel. I have no reason to believe that your conduct with Lady Mary has been anything but gentlemanly." Tilting his glass in Richard's direction, he took a sip of his drink.

Richard wouldn't go so far as to call himself a gentleman where Mary was concerned. His thoughts about her had certainly been of the more scandalous variety. Shifting, he followed his brother's example and drank. "Then let us refrain from discussing the matter any further."

"Mama is thrilled," Spencer added, ignoring Richard's remark. "So are Papa and the rest of our siblings, by the way. There is no doubt that Lady Mary will make an excellent addition to our family." He paused for a second before saying, "It must have taken a great deal of courage for you to reveal your-self to her."

Leaning his head back, Richard looked up at the ceiling while the memory of that important moment when Mary had first laid eyes on his face, passed before his eyes. "You have no idea."

"You care for her a great deal."

Lowering his gaze, Richard met Spencer's. "Of course I do."

Nodding, Spencer set his glass aside on the table that stood between them. "In that case, I would advise you to be completely honest with her."

The comment was so unexpected that Richard felt his entire body stiffen in response to it. Frowning, he leaned forward. "What are you saying?"

"That I think there may be more than one reason for your prolonged absence from Society and that your appearance is not entirely to blame."

Gritting his teeth, Richard felt his pulse rise. "Then you would be wrong, Spencer."

"And yet, it took only a couple of weeks for you to abandon five years of solitary confinement for the sake of a woman." Spencer shook his head. "I may not understand why, but I know that there must have been more to it than Lady Mary's compelling person-ality to sway such resolve."

"I love her."

"Not when you first laid eyes on her. What hap-pened, Richard? What caused you to realize that the life you have always dreamed of could finally be yours? None of my assurances in that regard seemed to have made a difference. Neither did Sarah's."

Looking askance, Richard stared into the empty

fireplace. His hand tightened around his glass. "Suffice it to say that I recently completed a business transaction that has given me some peace of mind."

Spencer grunted. "Good. You deserve some peace of mind after all that you have suffered. Still, you ought to tell Lady Mary about it."

"It is in the past now. I would like for it to remain there so that I may move forward with my life." For five long years his very existence had depended on getting revenge. He'd finally accomplished that goal and was happy to have found a more positive purpose.

A long moment of silence followed. Eventually Spencer said, "Secrets generally have a way of surfacing, Richard. Just be sure that if you choose to keep this one to yourself, that Lady Mary will not think less of you for it, or worse, be hurt by it if she happens to find out what it is. In my experience, people do eventually discover the things that you would most like to keep from them."

"Thank you, Spencer," Richard told him grimly. "I shall endeavor to keep that in mind." But it was an empty promise. Richard would never be able to tell Mary about the vengeance he'd taken on the man who'd betrayed him. She was too innocent and kind to understand. If she were to discover the truth, her opinion of him would undoubtedly be altered, and for what? What did it matter when he had every intention of being the man whom she thought him to be from now on? One thing was certain. He could not possibly risk losing her—not when she was everything that he had ever dreamed of.

Chapter 16

The Thorncliff Terrace, two days later

Seated at the edge of a long row of seats beside Richard, Mary glanced around at the crowd of assembled spectators before returning her attention to the small stage that had been set up in front of them. "Do you see Rotridge anywhere?" she asked as she nervously wafted her fan back and forth.

"Yes," Richard murmured. "He is sitting on the last row."

Sucking in a breath, Mary tried to calm her nerves while the orchestra tuned their instruments in preparation for the upcoming performance. She glanced around again. Where was her aunt? She should have been there by now. "This is not going to work," she heard herself say.

A warm hand settled over hers. "Of course it will," Richard assured her. "Look, here comes your aunt now. Are you ready?"

Mary shook her head. "No, but what choice do I have?"

She started to pull her hand away from his, but he held on fast. "Rest assured that no matter what happens this evening, I will stand by your side. You have my word on that."

Feeling a little lighter than before, Mary rose to greet her aunt. "Good evening," she said, loud enough for everyone to hear. "I was afraid that you might not make it on time."

Lady Foxworth chuckled. "And forego a performance by my favorite soprano? I think not, my dear, though I must say that the air this evening is a little bit chillier than I had expected."

"Would you like your shawl? I would be happy to fetch it for you."

"Thank you, Mary. I would appreciate that as long as Mr. Heartly has no issue with me keeping his company until you return."

Having risen as well, Richard gestured toward the seat that Mary had just vacated. "It would be an honor," he said. Winking at Mary, he mouthed the words, "Good luck," before offering Lady Foxworth his complete attention.

Starting toward the French doors that would take her back inside Thorncliff, Mary cast a glance in Rotridge's direction. He was looking straight at her with one raised eyebrow and a supremely annoying smirk upon his face. Straightening her spine, she inclined her head in greeting before continuing past him, praying that she would be the one to get the better of him this evening and not the other way around.

Returning to her bedchamber, she was met by Amy. "Are you ready, my lady?" she asked.

A nervous sound erupted from Mary's chest. "Mr. Heartly just asked me the exact same thing."

"And what did you tell him?" Retrieving a cloak from the wardrobe, Amy handed it to Mary.

"That I will never be ready for something like this."

"Consider it an adventure."

Mary snorted. "One that could ruin my reputation forever if it happens to go wrong."

Amy gave her a faint smile. "That risk has always existed, my lady—ever since you began performing as Miss Cavalani."

"I know," Mary agreed. "Shall we proceed with the performance then and let the cards fall where they may?"

Tying her cloak in place and raising the hood, Mary cracked open the door and peeked out into the hallway. "All clear," she whispered to Amy as they headed out together.

Reaching the stairwell that she'd used so often for her rendezvous with Richard, Mary descended toward the antechamber while Amy followed behind. "This way," she said as she opened the door and snuck out into the dark garden beyond. A soft breeze tugged at the hem of her gown as she and Amy made their way along the graveled path toward the terrace. From the lake came the occasional sound of frogs croaking, though it was soon drowned out by the chatter of voices rising from the many guests who'd gathered to watch Lucia Cavalani perform.

Certain that no one could see them arrive, they ascended the steps leading up onto the terrace, arriving directly behind the stage's thick velvet curtains.

A backdrop with only a narrow opening on one side boxed them in, shielding them from anyone who might happen to approach from the garden. "You look wonderful," Mary told Amy as she took in her appearance. "Thank you for helping me with this."

"After all that you have done for me, my lady, it is the least that I can do."

With that said, Amy parted the curtains just enough for her to step up onto the stage while Mary stood back, hidden from sight. A hush immediately descended over the terrace as everyone noted the arrival of the finest opera singer in England. Mary's heart beat rapidly in her chest, slowing only in response to the first fluid notes of music played by violins. Waiting for her cue, Mary sent up a silent prayer before starting to sing, her voice like a ribbon of silk floating through the night sky. There were five songs in total and as she rounded off the last one with a perfect vibrato, she felt the tension possessing her for the past two days begin to subside.

A brief second of silence passed after the final note had been sung, and then, a cacophony of applause. It was loud and vibrant—deafening even. But rather than stay and listen to it as she usually did, Mary left that task to Amy while she herself disappeared back into the garden.

"Magnificent," Lady Foxworth said over the loud clapping that filled the air after Lucia Cavalani's performance.

Richard nodded as he watched the famous singer curtsy while Lady Duncaster made her way toward the stage with a lovely bouquet of roses. Glancing over his shoulder, he looked toward the French doors leading back inside the house, and then toward the spot where Rotridge was now standing. Catching Richard's eyes, the earl narrowed his gaze before inclining his head in silent greeting. A menacing smile played upon his lips, tugging at the corners of his mouth until, with a jerk of his head, he turned away, pushing past the people who'd been sitting next to him. "Stop," he said, his voice slicing through the fading applause and demanding immediate silence.

Lady Duncaster halted and turned toward him, her eyebrows arched in question. "Yes?"

With heels clicking sharply against the stone-slab tiles, Rotridge made his way toward her. "While I was away in London, I made a wager in White's betting book." His eyes surveyed the guests as he progressed toward the spot where Lady Duncaster was standing. "It is a wager that can only be settled by Miss Cavalani herself."

"How intriguing," Lady Duncaster said as she looked toward the woman still standing on the stage. Her face was painted white, her lips a bright shade of red, and her eyes outlined with black kohl. The gown she wore was Elizabethan in style. On her head she wore an elaborate wig embellished with crystal beads.

"I could not agree more," Rotridge said, "for you see, it is a matter of Miss Cavalani's actual identity."

A murmur rose from the crowd. Richard squared his shoulders in expectation of what would undoubtedly happen next.

"Do you not find it strange that the most celebrated opera singer in England has never been seen by anyone, except for on the stage? One would think that she would have acquired a protector by now— that many young gentlemen would have made any number of desirable offers in order to claim her."

Clenching his fists, Richard forced himself not to react to Rotridge's statement. As far as everyone knew, he wasn't speaking of Mary, but of Lucia. And yet, Richard felt the insult like a punch to the stomach when Rotridge looked in his direction and said, "Welcome back into our midst, Mr. Heartly."

Tightening his jaw, Richard muttered his thanks for the sake of those present. Had he been alone with Rotridge however . . . A staying hand touched his arm. "Calm yourself," Lady Foxworth murmured. "You must not allow him to rile you."

"As for Miss Cavalani," Rotridge continued in a measured tone that seemed to capture everyone's attention with the promise of revealing a marvelous secret, "I would like to propose that she is not of Italian descent or that she is even a foreigner, for that matter. Indeed, I propose that she is not even of lowly birth, but a peeress in disguise."

The gasp that rose from the crowd was immediate. "Outrageous," some said. "Impossible," others said.

Rotridge held up his hand to silence them. "There is only one way for us to discover the truth, and that is to ask for Miss Cavalani to remove her wig and face paint."

"Have you no shame?" Lady Duncaster asked.

Rotridge inclined his head. "Unfortunately I have a great deal of money at stake, for you see, I have even gone so far as to name the lady whom I suspect

Miss Cavalani to be." Responding to the horrified look on Lucia's face, he allowed himself a victorious grin. "Let us dispense with the pretense. It is time for you to reveal yourself, *Lady Mary.*"

Murmurs snaked their way through the onlookers. Lucia took a step back and shook her head. She looked to Lady Duncaster with wide imploring eyes.

"This is preposterous," Richard said, voicing his opinion.

"Why?" Rotridge asked. "Because she happens to be your fiancée? Congratulations, by the way. I have no doubt that the two of you will be very happy together. After all, you do share a fondness for masquerades, do you not?"

"I ought to challenge you for your insolence," Richard said.

"You may do so after I have proven to everyone that the woman standing on that stage is none other than Mary Bourneville."

"You are making a grave mistake, Rotridge. One that is presently damaging both Miss Cavalani's reputation and Lady Mary's as well."

"Then perhaps you would care to explain Lady Mary's absence this evening?"

All eyes turned on Richard. He became acutely aware of his family's pained expressions but chose to ignore them. Somehow, he had to remain focused. He could not allow for anyone to suspect that Rotridge might be right. "She went to collect a shawl for her aunt."

"An hour ago?" Rotridge's voice was mocking now. "Are you really so naïve that you would think I might believe that?"

"Stop it!" The order was spoken by Lucia. All eyes turned toward the stage. "His lordship is correct in one regard. I am not a foreigner. Cavalani is a stage name."

"I knew it," Rotridge yelled.

"But I am not of noble birth," Lucia added, "and I am not Mary Bourneville."

Calculated fury seemed to seep from Rotridge's eyes. "Yes you are!" Striding past Lady Duncaster, he climbed onto the stage, his superior height dwarfing Lucia's more delicate frame. Leaning away from him she looked as though she wished to flee, but her large skirt made movement difficult and before she could go anywhere, Rotridge's fingers were in her hair, dislodging the wig until a mass of golden locks emerged.

A collective gasp filled the air as everyone stared at the woman before them.

"Are you quite finished?" Lady Duncaster asked as she too stepped onto the stage and snatched the wig away from Rotridge's hand.

"I . . ." He stared at Lucia, then at the wig, and then at Lucia once more. "I do not understand. You were supposed to be—"

"Me?" Mary asked. Having returned to the terrace only moments earlier, she was standing between Richard and her aunt. "I daresay that is absurd."

"But I overheard your conversation with Mr. Heartly," Rotridge said, his expression a muddled mixture of incomprehension and rapid thinking, "you clearly said that—"

"How much money did you risk on this calculated attempt to ruin Lady Mary's reputation?" Richard asked, deliberately cutting Rotridge off.

Swiveling his head in Richard's direction, Rotridge narrowed his eyes before stepping down from the stage and striding toward him. "*You* did this."

"I cannot imagine what you might be referring to," Richard spoke calmly, "but in my opinion, only the worst sort of scoundrel would stoop so low as to tarnish a lady's standing out of spite. You were determined to win her hand in marriage for one reason alone—so you can acquire the land that she will eventually inherit from her grandfather. But she refused. Not even your attempts at blackmail could sway her."

A low murmur snaked its way around the terrace, the blunt expression on everyone's faces conveying their disapproval.

"Is this true, Lord Rotridge?" Lady Duncaster asked.

"That land was supposed to be mine," Rotridge snapped, one second before lunging toward Richard.

Ducking, Richard managed to avoid the fist that was meant for his face, countering with a blow of his own instead. It landed solidly in Rotridge's stomach, producing a pitiful yelp from the earl as he doubled over in pain.

"Enough," Lady Duncaster said, her sharp tone breaking the men apart. Piercing blue eyes settled on Rotridge who was gasping for breath a small distance from where Richard was standing. "Your behavior this evening has been quite uncivil. Clearly you are mistaken in your hypothesis regarding Miss Cavalini's identity, but rather than take it like a man, you choose to attack one of my guests instead. Now, if I may offer a piece of advice to you, apologize to

Miss Cavalani and to Lady Mary right this second before you make matters worse."

Stiffly, Rotridge inclined his head. "Forgive me." His eyes sought Mary and then Amy.

"Good," Lady Duncaster said. "You may leave now."

"I beg your pardon?" Rotridge asked sounding confused.

"If you think that I will allow you to remain here after what you have just done, then you are mistaken. I expect to find you gone within the hour. The footmen will escort you to your room and help you pack."

Flattening his mouth into a thin line, Rotridge paused for a second before turning away and marching back inside the house without another word while two footmen followed in his wake.

"Do you think he will try to bother us again?" Mary asked Richard as she watched Lady Duncaster hand over the large bouquet of roses to Amy and congratulate her on her performance.

"No. In fact, I wager he will have quit Thorncliff by the time we return inside. I doubt he will want to face either one of us after this, or anyone else for that matter."

Deciding that he was probably right, Mary allowed herself a sigh of relief. "I hope so." A cool summer breeze whispered across her skin. "Thank you once again for discovering Rotridge's motivation. I had no idea that Grandpapa intends to leave so much land to me. He never said a word about it."

"Perhaps because he knew that it would attract men like Rotridge?"

"I suspect you might be right." Turning slightly, Mary smiled up at Richard. "Now that this is behind us, we can hopefully start focusing on all of the wedding preparations. Did I mention that I have written to my brother informing him of the good news?"

One side of Richard's mouth edged upward. "No. You did not."

"Oh. I am sorry. It must have slipped my mind." Around them, the other guests began moving off in different directions while Lady Foxworth went to speak with Lady Duncaster.

"I cannot say that I am surprised. You have had a lot to think about lately." Catching Mary by the arm, Richard guided her away from the seats and toward a darker corner of the terrace where a bench stood waiting.

"I am so relieved that it is all over now." Lowering herself onto the bench, she waited for Richard to join her, a little bothered by the distance they were forced to keep for the sake of propriety. Discreetly, she placed her hand upon the seat.

"As am I." His hand found hers, filling her with warmth and the assurance of his deep affection. "Do you think your brother will join us once he hears that we are to be wed?"

"I hope so. Family has always meant a great deal to me and with Mama and Papa so far away I would appreciate his support. Besides, I think it would be wonderful for the two of you to become acquainted with each other, especially since I think he would benefit greatly from your friendship and guidance."

"You are hoping that I might have a positive influence on him?" When she nodded, he said, "I will tell you this—your brother will never take advantage of you again once we are married."

"But you will help him somehow? Please, Richard. I cannot bear the thought of him living in poverty when I have been blessed with so much."

"I understand, and as I have told you before, I will do what I can, but he has to be willing to do his part as well. If he earns his fortune rather than relying on gratuity, then perhaps he will take better care of it."

Knowing how sound Richard's reasoning was, Mary turned over her hand beneath his so that they were palm against palm and curled her fingers around his. "Thank you." They sat in silence for a short while enjoying the quiet that was settling around them as the few remaining people on the terrace dispersed. "I think I will have to abandon my singing," she finally said.

"Why? I would never demand that you do so, Mary. You know this."

"Yes. I do. But I fear that while we may have averted disaster this evening, it will eventually find us again, and what then?"

"Then we will get through those troubling times as well. Together." He stretched out his legs and leaned back a little.

"You are the best man in the world. Do you know that?" He seemed to wince, but when he said nothing in response she chose to interpret his silence as proof of his modesty. "I love performing at the opera, but I cannot keep taking the risk. Especially not when there is no longer a reason for me to do so."

"Because your husband will be able to supply your brother with the funds he needs?"

She bit her lip. "I do not mean to sound mercenary, but yes."

His eyes left her and he looked up at the night sky instead. "Just as long as you promise always to sing for me."

"And for our children," she blurted without thinking.

His face jerked toward her, surprise bouncing in his eyes as if it were a living thing that wished to be set free. "Children?" His voice was but a slight whisper.

"Forgive me. I should not have—"

"Oh no, Mary." He dropped his gaze to her lips. "You will not retreat from me now. Not when you have just broached the one subject that I look forward to discussing with you in far greater detail."

Heat rose to Mary's cheeks while a funny unbalanced sensation took hold of her stomach. Was it possible for her to burst into flames right there on the terrace? An unsteady inhale of breath did little to calm her racing heart. "We should not discuss such things here."

"Would you rather discuss them somewhere else?" His thumb traced the edge of her hand.

Feeling dizzy, Mary shook her head. Somehow, in the space of a second, Richard had managed to make it seem as though her gown was shrinking. Her chest rose and fell against the now unbearably restrictive fabric. "I think it might be best if I were to retire for the evening." Trembling, she slid off the bench and rose to her feet.

He rose as well. "I have offended you."

"No," she whispered. She glanced toward the

doors leading back inside the house. "You are tempting me, Richard, and if you do not stop doing so, I . . ." Her courage failed her. She was a well-bred lady after all. She could not speak of such things. So instead she told him decisively, "We will be married soon enough."

He didn't look convinced but he inclined his head, submitting to her wishes. "Of course we will."

They started back toward the house, but there was something in his tone that Mary found unsettling. "What is it?" she asked.

His brow creased in a contemplative frown. "You do not trust me."

"Of course I do!" How could he even say such a thing after all the faith she'd placed in him since their very first encounter.

"I was not speaking of ruining you just now, Mary, but that is how you chose to interpret what I said."

Baffled, she drew to a halt. "How else was I meant to interpret it? The implication seemed very clear to me."

"Perhaps," he acquiesced, "but hopefully you know me well enough by now to realize that I would never try to convince you to do anything against your will. What I said . . . All I was suggesting was for us to enjoy a little privacy the way we used to before our engagement." Lowering his voice to a soft whisper, he added, "I miss kissing you."

An unexpected smile tugged at her lips. "Do you have any idea of how irritable you look right now?"

He raked his hand through his hair. "I feel frustrated. In more ways than one."

"What do you mean?"

He shook his head. "Nothing."

Puffing out a breath, Mary resumed walking. "As it stands, there are three weeks left until our wedding. I know my aunt will not approve of this idea and that your mother will likely be opposed to it as well, but what if we were to procure a special license?"

"What about all the preparations? From what I gather, just ordering your gown will take time."

"I have no issue with wearing one of the dresses that I already own. Especially since I am beginning to fear, judging from my recent conversations with your mother, that any wedding gown I order will be more to your sister's liking than it will be to mine."

He laughed at that, but grew instantly serious once more. "Are you certain? Because if you are, then we can be married in just a few days."

"In that case, I have never been more certain of anything else in my life."

Drawing her to a halt, he looked down into her eyes. "Truly?" Her nod made him smile. "I cannot believe how fortunate I am."

Alerted by the chatter of other guests approaching, they continued their progress, passing through the French doors and heading down the hallway that would lead them to the grand staircase. A moment passed until she quietly admitted, "I miss our kisses too." Gathering her courage, she then said, "Perhaps another rendezvous in the Roman villa would not be so bad."

His hold on her tightened ever so slightly as they climbed the stairs, sending a thrill straight through her. There was something wonderfully possessive about it that spoke to her feminine side. "Meet me in the stairwell next to the interior courtyard two hours from now."

Reaching the top of the landing, they parted ways, her footsteps falling softly against the floor while his louder tread faded into silence. Her nerves were a complicated tangle of foreign sensations. She loved this man, desperately so, and because of that she feared for her ability to resist the temptation he offered. And yet . . . they were to be married after all. Perhaps a few more stolen kisses would not be the worst thing in the world.

Chapter 17

The next two hours were, in Richard's estimation, the most torturous he'd ever endured. They were worse than the ones he'd spent chained to a table while glowing red iron was being pressed against his cheek. Worse still than the days it had taken for him to make his way from Brussels to Antwerp with a broken leg.

Pushing the unpleasant memory aside, he thought of Mary instead, of how bad she'd felt about deceiving her aunt and of how worried she'd been about the *ton* discovering her secret. Crossing to the window, he eased the curtain aside and peered out at the moonlit garden. Her transgressions were nothing compared to his—a mere masquerade performed with the best of intentions while he . . . all he'd wanted was another man's downfall. He had that now, and just as he'd feared, it wasn't enough to cleanse his soul of darkness. Mary, on the other hand . . . her smile alone could make him forget all else.

It was almost two o'clock in the morning by the time he made his way back downstairs, his heart lurching slightly with expectation. Before, when they'd been alone together, there had been rules to follow. This was still very much the case of course, though not so much to the same degree. He wondered if she realized that. Of course she did, which was why she'd been so concerned about being alone together. She was worried that he'd be tempted to do things . . . things that the gentleman in him would not have permitted before.

Naturally, he'd balked at the insinuation, even though she'd been right to be worried. The truth was, he was finding it bloody difficult, thinking of little else than what she might look like with decidedly fewer clothes on.

Stepping into the stairwell, Richard was greeted by the faint glow from a lantern. "I was hoping to arrive before you," he said as he closed the door softly behind him.

Illuminated in a golden haze, Mary's face reminded him of an angel in a Raphael painting. The corners of her mouth lifted, dimpling her cheeks. "My impatience got the better of me. I could not wait." Swinging her lantern around, she allowed the light to fall upon the stairs. "Shall we?"

"Allow me," he said. His fingers traced the outline of her hand as he took the lantern away from her, his heartbeat quickening in response to her sharp intake of breath.

With measured steps, he moved past her and began his descent, aware of her presence behind him—of her warmth and of her scent. His chest tightened, as did his grip on the lantern. Guiding them back through the chilly passageways beneath Thorncliff, to the next set of stairs, they descended toward the hidden villa below while darkness closed in around them.

"It seems so different from how I remember it," Mary said as she stepped down beside him. "The lack of light makes it almost gloomy."

Agreeing with her, Richard went to retrieve the nearest torch, holding it to the lantern until it was fully lit. He did the same with three more, brightening the hall in which they were standing before heading toward the room in which they'd enjoyed their picnic. Pausing in the doorway, he glanced toward the floor where he'd spread out the blanket and laid out the food. It seemed unbelievable to him that it was only a week ago since that had taken place.

"Perhaps we should continue to explore Lord Duncaster's study instead?" Mary asked. "I don't believe that we are likely to discover anything else in there."

"And I do not believe that we are likely to discover anything else at all."

The silence that followed was palpable. And then, "Maybe if we were to look—"

He spun toward her, his eyes meeting hers. "We have looked in every drawer already, leafed through every book, and we have discovered some vital information regarding not only Lord Duncaster, but my grandfather as well. You know that we were planning to share this with Lady Duncaster, but before we had a chance to do so, your aunt received that damning letter from Rotridge and then . . ." Expelling a breath, he stared back at her, acutely aware of the energy simmering between them. "We are not here because of the notebook, Mary."

A second passed, and then she nodded. "I know."

Holding her gaze, Richard reached for her hand and silently led her into the room beyond and over to the sofa. He placed the lantern on a table and then offered her his full attention. "Do you have any idea of how beautiful you are?"

His hand captured her cheek, caressing the skin there until she leaned against him, her eyelids closing on a sigh of pleasure. "I have missed this," she said, not answering his question. "I have missed you."

"So have I." Dipping his head, he pressed his lips to hers, desperate for the contact, the nearness, the all-consuming need to be with her. The softest murmur escaped her, followed by a shared breath as their mouths melded together, her arms reaching around his neck and holding him close. Richard's chest expanded. He could feel the rhythm of her heartbeat leaping rapidly against his own, the soft contour of her breast as he trailed his hand along the length of her side.

Perfection. No other word would ever suffice.

Breaking contact, he reached for her hand and pressed her knuckles to his lips. He wanted so much. *Too* much. Wincing, he took a step back, releasing her hand and adding distance.

"What is it?" she asked, her eyes wide with innocent wonder.

He shook his head. "Nothing."

"Would it offend you to know that I do not believe you?" Crossing her arms, she gave him the most defiant stare that he'd ever seen.

A smile tickled his lips. "No." A moment of silence stretched between them. "This is harder than I had expected," he eventually said.

She scrunched her nose. "What is?"

He paused a moment before saying, "When I invited you to join me here tonight, I thought it would be just as before—that we would enjoy each other's company and perhaps share a kiss or two."

"And so we are." She seemed to study his face as if she hoped to find his innermost thoughts written upon it.

"And so we are," he agreed.

"Except it is not the same as before." She took a step in his direction. "Is it?"

"No. It is not."

"We are betrothed now." She bit her lower lip, completely unaware it seemed, of the effect that she was having on him.

Shifting slightly, he coughed, hoping to mask his discomfort. "So we are." It was becoming increasingly difficult for him to think about anything else, not to mention the fact that she was here with him, alone and far away from anyone who might happen to find them in each other's company. She took a step closer still and he held up his hand, halting her progress. "I thought that I would be able to exhibit better self-control," he said by way of explanation, "but now that we are to be married . . . Forgive me, Mary, but I fear that I may do something regrettable if you come any closer." Squeezing his eyes shut for a second, he did what the gentleman in him insisted he do and reluctantly said, "Which is why I think it might be best if we return upstairs and retire."

She gave a pensive nod. "If what you say is true, then that would probably be the correct thing to do." She turned her face away, but not before he caught a glimpse of the joyless smile tracing her lips.

Unable to bear it, he caught her by the wrist and gently pulled her back toward him. "Tell me what you are thinking."

She refused to look at him. "I cannot possibly do so."

"Please?"

Silence was her only response. It stretched between them, altering his perception of time until he no longer knew how long they'd stood there. Just when he thought she would never give him an answer, she raised her chin and met his gaze, her brown eyes shimmering like a lake dressed in moonlight. "How do you do it?"

"Do what?" The words were softly spoken, just as hers had been—a mere exhalation.

Raising her hand, she drew the tips of her fingers across his cheek, her lips trembling as she quietly whispered, "One look from you, and my insides melt, the slightest touch, and I can scarcely breathe let alone think. You torture me with the most delectable kisses until my soul begins to burn." Pausing, she slid her gaze toward his mouth, quickening his pulse. "You have seduced me in every conceivable way."

"Mary." Her name was rough upon his lips, like waves breaking against the shore.

"I do not understand it. Indeed, I have never felt like this before."

"I should certainly hope not," he muttered in an effort to dampen the effect of her words. The storm of emotions raging inside him was threatening to ruin his sanity.

"Are you saying that what I am feeling is wrong?" Her eyes widened, her face flushing with uncertainty.

"No." The word drifted through the air as he drew her closer. "Between you and me, it will never be wrong."

Her lips parted ever so slightly, the wonder in her eyes compelling him to surrender. So he did, freeing his heart and his soul to accept the beauty that she offered, his mind no longer filled with concern, but with her and only her. "You are all that I have ever wanted." Pulling her into his arms, he ran his palm across her cheek, savoring the warmth of her skin as she leaned against the caress. "And now you are mine."

"I have always been yours." A hushed murmur of words that almost brought him to his knees, weakening his resolve until he was left with no other choice but to kiss her again. The pull was simply too great— too impossible to resist. So he gave up control and captured her lips until the simmering heat between them erupted like claps of thunder, tossing him head-first into the awaiting storm. It tore apart the pain, the broken dreams, and the anger, scattering them until all that remained was Mary, clinging to him as he clung to her.

He drew a shuddering breath, loving the feel of her tremulous touch against the edge of his jaw. Dear God, it was all too much. "You will stop me if I go too far," he heard himself say, aware that he needed to slow his pace before the fire in his veins consumed them both completely.

Dark lashes fluttered against her cheek. "Of course," she replied, her trusting eyes imploring him to guide her.

So he raised his hand to a stray lock of hair that

had somehow managed to escape her coiffure, savoring the silky texture as it slipped between his fingers. "Incredible." His gaze dropped to the softness of her lips and a ragged breath escaped him, torn from somewhere deep within—a rush of emotion that could not be put into words.

Relishing the moment, Richard carefully lowered his mouth over hers more slowly than before. A gentle gasp transformed into a mutual breath, allowing him to deepen the kiss and partake of the sweetness she offered.

Moments later, his hand found the curve of her back, his fingers spreading against the fragile fabric of her gown as he held her steady. Against his chest, he could feel the rapid beat of her heart, more so when he placed his lips upon her neck—a sensuous string of kisses caressing her pulse.

"Richard," his name was but a murmur—a benediction of sorts—the moment his lips touched her shoulder. Her skin was smooth like cream, glowing in the dim light. She was so inviting that he could easily imagine falling against her embrace and remaining there forever. Instead, he whispered her name, his breath ghosting across her skin until she arched against him, offering him all that she was and all that she ever would be.

Humbled by her essence, he kissed his way across her chest, tenderly conveying what was in his heart. "So lovely," he whispered as his hands moved over her, hesitantly exploring every aspect of her being while silently imparting his complete and utter adoration.

Light slipped against the shadows in a mystical

effect, just as gently as his fingers slipped against her contours. "Please." One word that seemed to set the room ablaze.

Unable to deny her, he lowered himself to the sofa and pulled her down with him. His mouth met hers, so full of love for this extraordinary woman who'd brought joy back into his life. He would give her the world if he could and he would cherish every second they'd been granted with each other. With profound reverence, he reached for the delicate curve of her ankle, the intimate touch tormenting him with its divinity. "Beauty, you tempt me beyond compare."

Saying nothing, she trailed her fingers along his arm, mirroring his touch as he worshipped all that she encompassed. A sigh of complete and utter pleasure escaped into the darkness while soft light from the lantern spilled across her face.

The temptation to lay her down on the sofa and claim her completely was greater than anything else that Richard had ever experienced. Squeezing his eyes shut, he took a fortifying breath and set his mind to less amorous thoughts, like the memory of his body on the cold hard ground in Belgium as he studied his enemy from a distance—waiting, assessing and planning his next move.

"Are you all right?" Mary's voice broke through his thoughts, returning him to the present.

Opening his eyes, he glanced down at her, noting the look of concern in her eyes and instantly hating himself for having caused it. "Of course." Leaning forward, he placed a tender kiss upon her lips. "You are everything that I have ever dreamed of, Mary. A truly magnificent woman."

"And you are . . ." She bit her lip but was unable to mask the smile that threatened.

Her expression was so adorable that Richard couldn't help but smile as well. "The luckiest man in the world," he told her sincerely.

"I was going to say extremely talented, but—"

His laughter interrupted her and then he kissed her again before easing her off his lap and helping her to her feet. "Just wait until you see what else I have in store for you," he teased.

She gave him a pert look while smoothing the skirt of her gown. "Your modesty astounds me."

Reaching out, he grabbed her by the waist and, lowering his head, he whispered in her ear, "Modesty has no place in the bedchamber, Mary."

He felt her shiver slightly in response to his bold remark, but rather than shy away, she said, "Then it is fortunate that we are not in a bedchamber, Sir."

Grinning, he pressed his face into her shoulder while holding her close in his arms. "You kill me, Mary. Do you know that?"

He felt her breaths slow a fraction. Her arms found their way around him in a close embrace. "And you undo me," she whispered, her words filled with raw emotion. They trickled through him, settling deep within his heart. Whatever he told her now, it would not be enough, and so he said nothing at all.

"Should we tell Lady Duncaster about what we have found tomorrow?" Mary asked as they made their way back upstairs a short while later.

"Yes. I think she deserves to know. Don't you agree?"

"Certainly." Arriving in the interior courtyard,

they fell silent until Mary quietly asked, "And what of the special license that you mentioned?"

"I have sent a request. If all goes well, it ought to arrive within a couple of days."

"We should probably warn your mother and my aunt."

He winced. "That will not be an easy conversation." In fact, he dreaded it already.

"No, but we will get through it together, and then—"

"Then we will be married." A wonderful prospect.

They parted ways at the top of the stairs with Richard offering Mary a swift kiss on the cheek. Returning to his bedchamber, he applauded himself for his control. It had been a struggle for him to refrain from taking more than what he had. Recalling the look of pleasure upon her face as he'd held her in his arms, he felt his pulse quicken. He needed a drink. Hell, he needed *her*! Clearly that special license could not arrive soon enough.

"**H**ere is another option for you to consider," Lady Oakland said as she handed Mary what had to be the hundredth fashion plate. "The gown will take at least two weeks to complete so it is imperative that you make your decision today so there can also be time for a fitting."

Seated to her right, Richard said nothing as he turned the page of his newspaper. He was almost completely hidden away behind it, leaving Mary with the trying task of dealing with his overexcited mother and siblings. Annoying man. Which was probably why she couldn't help herself from saying, "While I truly appreciate your suggestions, Lady Oakland, there is a very good chance that I will not be requiring a new gown."

Lady Oakland's eyes widened with apparent dismay, as did her daughters'. Beside Mary, Richard stilled. Clearly he had not been so engrossed in his paper as to miss out on the conversation. "What on earth do you mean?" Lady Oakland asked. "Of course you must have a new gown for your wedding. It is certainly not an expense that Richard would be unwilling to spend. Is it, Richard?"

"Not at all, Mama," Richard said, lowering his paper.

"Then it is settled," Lady Oakland declared.

Turning to Richard, Mary gave him a beseeching look. His mouth tightened a little around the corners but then he reached for Mary's hand and nodded before addressing his mother. "If I may make a suggestion, I think it might be wise to postpone any further wedding preparations until we are sure that there will in fact be a wedding."

Silence fell upon the room, followed by a collective, "What?" from Lady Oakland and her daughters.

Richard cleared his throat. "Three weeks seems like an eternity, Mama, so I have taken it upon myself to request a special license. We plan to marry as soon as it arrives, which will likely be long before any gown you plan on ordering for Mary could be ready."

"But . . ." Lady Oakland looked from Richard to Mary and then back again.

Eventually Fiona made her opinion on the matter known by saying, "First Chloe and now you, Richard. How utterly disappointing."

"I apologize," he said, "but one day you will understand."

"And when exactly *were* you planning on sharing this decision with us?" Emily inquired, crossing her arms in protest.

"As soon as the special license was in hand," Richard said, glancing at Mary with some disapproval.

She responded with a shrug.

"Well," Rachel said, speaking up for the first time, "One cannot fault you for your efficiency."

Biting their lips, Laura, Chloe and Emily dropped their gazes to the floor. If Mary wasn't mistaken, the sisters were doing their best to refrain from laughing. Lady Oakland, however, looked quite appalled, but rather than comment on Rachel's indelicate remark, she asked Mary, "Is your aunt aware of this decision of yours?"

"Not yet," Mary admitted, "but I do believe that her eagerness to see me settled will offset any misgivings that she may have about a hasty marriage."

"I see," Lady Oakland said. She studied Mary and Richard for a long, almost awkward moment, before finally slumping back against her seat with a sigh. "Well, I suppose it is your decision." She punctuated her statement with an elaborate wave of her hand. "Shall we ring for some more tea?"

Mary blinked. This conversation had certainly gone a lot better than she had expected and with far less resistance.

"I think I would prefer a glass of brandy," Richard said. Rising, he went to ring for a maid before making his way over to the sideboard. The order for a fresh pot of tea was placed moments later, arriving shortly after that.

"You ought to be relieved, Mama," Richard's sister, the Duchess of Stonegate, said as she reached for a sweetmeat. "To arrange one wedding is a task, but to arrange three? If you ask me, you are fortunate to have a daughter and a son who are willing to forego such planning not to mention the expense."

Lady Oakland barely had time to respond to that remark before a knock sounded at the door. The Thorncliff butler, Mr. Caine, entered the room. "Please excuse the intrusion," he said, "but a gentleman has just arrived." He looked toward Mary. "He claims to be your brother, Lady Mary. Shall I show him in?"

"Oh, by all means, please do," she said with unhindered excitement. As foolish as Andrew could be, he was still her brother after all. They had grown up together and she loved him with all her heart—even if it was clear that he had taken advantage of her kindness over the years. But all of that would change now the moment she got married. Richard would help Andrew become a better man and all would be well.

She reached for Richard's hand as she rose to her feet. He got up as well, standing solidly by her side as the door opened again and Andrew entered the room.

The moment he saw Mary, a broad smile lit up his face, his eyes sparkling with mischief just as she remembered. Releasing Richard's hand, she hurried over to her brother. "I cannot tell you how happy I am that you have come."

Taking her hands in his, he bowed his head to kiss her knuckles. "How can I stay away when you intend to wed? I cannot possibly allow you to do such a thing without making the acquaintance of the lucky man who has won your heart."

Stepping back from Andrew, Mary turned to face the Heartlys, their expressions warm and welcoming—all except for Richard's. His features were set in rigid lines, his mouth drawn tight and his eyes like two angry storm clouds bearing down on Andrew. "You," was all he said.

Looking toward Richard, Andrew dropped Mary's hands, his face as pale as new fallen snow. He shook his head. "No," he said, his eyes going wide. "You cannot be here. It is not possible."

"And why is that?" Richard asked, moving toward him like a panther out on the prowl. "Because I am supposed to be dead?"

Andrew shook his head, his mouth opening as if he meant to say something, but not a single word escaped him.

Halting his progress, Richard glared at him. "Because, if I am alive, then you can no longer claim to have acted as heroically as you allegedly did?" With cold detachment, he slowly asked, "Because I know the truth about you, Lord Carthright?"

An icy shiver trickled down Mary's spine. "What are you talking about?" It wasn't a question she wished to know the answer to, but one that had to be asked.

Richard's jaw clenched, tightening the rippling skin

that marred the left side of his face. Sharply, he turned his head in her direction, the warmth with which he'd looked at her a short while earlier completely gone. Instead, incomprehension and deep anguish filled his eyes. "I would never have considered a friendship with you, let alone something more than that, if I had known that you were related to *him*." The words cut deep, as they were no doubt meant to do.

Lady Oakland took a step forward. "Heartly—"

"How could I not have discovered this?" He shook his head. "I do not understand. You do not have the same surname!"

Swallowing the painful knot in her throat, Mary said, "My brother and I do not share the same father."

Richard grimaced, his shoulders slumping as if the entire weight of the world now rested upon them. "Of course."

"Heartly, I—"

"Not a word," Richard clipped, cutting off Andrew. His eyes remained on Mary. "Do you have any idea of what your brother has done?" She shook her head, unable to speak as Richard raised his hand to the scarred flesh marring his cheek. "This is because of him, because he was too great a coward to do his duty and because he would rather run and hide, leaving me to face the enemy alone."

It was a grave accusation, one that Mary could not quite believe. Still, she looked to Andrew, hoping he might deny it. Instead he said, "You got your vengeance though. Did you not?"

"What I took from you will never erase your actions at Waterloo. We had a plan, Carthright, but when I needed you, I found you gone." He paused for a moment before saying, "And then you took credit for what *I* had managed to accomplish before being captured. You gained a title that you did not even deserve—land too."

"Until *you* took it all away from me," Andrew practically shouted.

Unified gasps filled the room. "Dear God," Mary murmured as she pieced it all together.

"And I enjoyed every moment of it," Richard told Andrew. "Since you were foolish enough to stake it all at cards—"

"There is no honor in fleecing a foxed man," Mary said, "no matter what he may have done." The situation that was presently unfolding in the bright and sunny parlor was an absolute nightmare.

"Foxed?" Richard snorted. "You think he was foxed when he boasted at the gaming table that he would easily double his money?" He took a steady step in Mary's direction, his eyes sparking with repressed fury. "Oh no, my lady. Your brother had his wits about him when he chose to risk it all, of that there is no doubt since my sources have confirmed it. So if he has told you otherwise . . . well, all things considered, I would not be the least bit surprised."

Stepping aside, Mary distanced herself from her brother. From Richard too, since it would seem that there was a large part of him that she did not know at all. Recalling what her aunt had said, Mary couldn't help but ask Andrew, "Did you really spend your entire fortune on repairing Carthright House?"

"The repairs I spoke of were made," Andrew assured her, "and the staff has always been paid on time."

"Tell her the truth," Richard clipped.

A lengthy pause followed before Carthright spoke again. "Admittedly, the cost of running Carthright House was not as great as I wanted the world to believe."

"What he means to say," Richard grit out, "is that he made some risky wagers and that he lost."

"And the investments you spoke of?" Mary asked, preventing Andrew from responding to Richard's accusation. When Andrew shook his head, her heart fell. "You were supposed to use the money I gave you to regain control of your life . . . it was supposed to cover your expenses and help secure a stable income . . . but instead, you lied to me. You gambled it all away," she said, addressing Andrew as if he were a stranger, "and Heartly won it."

"Ironically, I had meant to gift the estate to you," Richard told Mary, "but after this, I wonder if there will even be a wedding."

She found that she could scarcely look at him, or her brother for that matter. "Were you ever going to tell me about this?" she asked Richard.

"I did not think it would be necessary," he said. His eyes had grown vacant, adding further distance between them. "In fact, I had hoped to put it behind me, but it seems that will no longer be possible."

A painful sob escaped Mary. "This cannot be happening. It simply cannot." Retreating, she moved toward the door.

"Mary," Richard said, the sound of her name reflecting the heartache that she was feeling.

She shook her head. "I need to think." She swallowed convulsively. "Your actions aside, you have said some things just now that I cannot easily forget."

"Mary," Richard repeated, taking a step in her direction.

Refusing to listen, she turned away from him and left the room. There simply wasn't enough space indoors for all of her emotions.

Chapter 18

Sunlight spilled over Mary as she stepped out onto the terrace with leaden feet. The air out here was fresh, and yet it felt as though she was suffocating. Blindly, she made her way toward the steps and down onto the path below. How could this be? How could she have been so filled with joy no more than half an hour earlier, only to find herself burdened by grief now—her heart, no longer weightless, but like a dull rock, heavy inside her chest.

Ignoring the sound of her name being called, she continued in the direction of the lake, toward a vacant spot where she could be alone. As she went, she thought of Andrew, of how dishonorable he'd been if what Richard said was true. She did not want to believe it, but Andrew had failed to deny the accusation.

Shoulders slumping beneath the weight of this discovery, she considered Richard and how happy he'd made her. Still, there was no escaping the fact that he'd kept a very large part of his life from her. In a way, she understood. He'd wanted to put the past behind him and move on—had not believed there was any chance of her ever finding out about what he'd done. But his words! Lord, how they hurt!

Pausing, she tried to look at the situation objectively. Richard had spoken in anger. She knew that. Doing her best to move past the pain in her chest, she considered an important question: had Andrew not been her brother, would she have approved of Richard's actions then? Did he not deserve some form of compensation for what he had lost and all that he had suffered?

Deep in her heart, she knew that he did—she knew that what Andrew had done was wrong, even if she did not know the specifics.

"Mary." The sound of her name was closer this time. Turning, she saw that it was Sarah, her pale blonde hair curling softly against her cheek.

"I called to you from across the lawn, but you must not have heard me," Sarah said. Frowning slightly, she moved a little closer. "Are you all right, Mary?"

Unable to speak for fear that she might start crying, Mary managed a solid nod.

"Clearly that is not the case." Sarah's eyes filled with concern. "You look as though you have just received some troubling news. Is it your parents? Are they not well?"

Shaking her head, Mary looked away, her eyes fixed on the soft surface of the water which occasionally rippled as mayflies darted across it. "As far as I know, my parents are both well." She took a quivering breath. "Do you know what it feels like to have your heart torn from your chest?"

There was a small pause, and then, "I am familiar with the sensation. Yes." The confession surprised

Mary. For a second she didn't quite know what to say. As it turned out, she didn't have to say anything at all since Sarah continued by adding, "Spencer and I had a few difficulties before we decided to marry. I kept something from him—something terribly important— and he judged me for it once he found out."

"What stopped you from telling him?"

"Fear, I suppose." Moving off toward the right side of the lake, Sarah waited for Mary to fall into step beside her before saying, "I did not think that he and I would ever be able to be together, and so I chose not to mention the one thing that could ruin his good opinion of me forever."

"But he found out anyway."

Sarah nodded. "The truth has a funny way of surfacing at the most inopportune moment."

"Perhaps you should have been honest with him from the start," Mary suggested.

"Perhaps," Sarah agreed. She was silent for a while before saying, "We all keep secrets, some greater than others. I daresay you have your own fair share of them."

The comment brought Mary up short. "What do you mean?"

Sarah shrugged. "Nothing, other than that it is rare for a young lady to be venturing about outside on her own during the early hours of the morning. If you will recall, Spencer and I crossed paths with you a couple of weeks ago when we were returning from a walk."

"I remember it well, even though I am not prepared to tell you the reason for it. I hope you can understand."

"Of course."

"But Mr. Heartly knows the truth." Mary couldn't stop her voice from rising. "I shared my secrets with him as soon as it became clear that our friendship was developing into something more."

Nodding, Sarah seemed to ponder that. "So you feel betrayed?"

"I . . . I do not know exactly what I feel, other than that I wish I would have discovered the relationship he has to my brother a lot sooner than I did."

"Mr. Heartly is a friend of his?"

A snort was all Mary could manage. "Not in the least."

"I see." Following the path to the right, they allowed it to lead them around some flowerbeds and back in the direction of the house. "That does complicate matters. I trust that you are fond of your brother?"

"Of course I am," Mary said. "He is my family!"

"That is true," Sarah agreed, "but being related by blood is not always enough. Character counts as well, and although I do not know the reason for Mr. Heartly's dislike of your brother, I am certain that it must be justified, in which case you may want to consider which of the two deserves your loyalty the most."

"I fear that Mr. Heartly will no longer wish to have anything to do with me," Mary said. "The look in his eyes when he saw my brother and the things he said . . . I believe he will want to distance himself as much from him as possible, even if that means cutting all ties with me."

"You cannot be certain of that. Talk to him, Mary—if you still wish to spend your life with

Mr. Heartly, that is. But be prepared to turn your back on your brother if need be."

"How can I possibly do that?"

"By asking yourself if he is worth sacrificing your future happiness for."

It wasn't a question that Mary wished to consider, and yet she knew that she had to. Andrew—the carefree boy she'd grown up with. He'd always been prone to laughter, always ready with a smile to cheer her up. But he was selfish. Undeniably so. And Richard had paid a great price for that. Didn't he deserve her support?

"I cannot think of what to do right now," she murmured, more to herself than to Sarah. On one hand, she wanted to run into Richard's arms, but on the other, she feared the power that he wielded over her. "He showed no consideration for my feelings at all, and in not doing so, he shattered my heart. How can I trust that he will not do so again?"

"I cannot answer that question for you, but perhaps if you speak with him—"

A distressed laugh pushed its way past Mary's lips. "There is nothing for me to say." He hated her for being Andrew's sister. She'd seen it in his eyes when he'd told her that he never would have associated with her if he'd known. "Nothing at all." Turning away from Sarah, Mary headed for the house, one foot stepping in front of the other, moving her forward until she eventually found her brother. To his credit, his expression was somber as she reentered the room from which she'd fled a short while earlier. He was the only one present now, abandoned by the Heartlys, it would seem.

"Of all the men in England," he said as he rose to greet her.

Stiffly, she came to a halt before him, anger swiftly taking hold in response to his flippancy. "I would caution you to think twice before mocking me."

He raised an eyebrow. "It was not my intention to do so. You know how grateful I am to you for your support."

"Do I?" When he gave her a curious look she said, "Upon reflection, it has become increasingly clear to me that you have been taking advantage of me for some time now."

Knitting his brow, he crossed his arms. "We are family, Mary. It is our duty to help and protect each other. Especially with Mama and Papa so far away."

"That is what I told myself as well, Andrew, which is why I wanted to help you invest when your own funds were depleted. But the truth of the matter is that you have squandered away your fortune, along with all the money I have given you, in the most irresponsible way imaginable." Studying him, she went on to say, "If I were to hazard a guess, you did not even discover the information for which you have been rewarded. Heartly did that before he was captured, didn't he?"

"Of course not. I overheard the conversation that those French soldiers were having just as well as he did." He looked away a moment before once again meeting her eye. "But they discovered our presence there and rather than try to silence them, I ran."

With slow and measured breaths, Mary walked toward her brother. Her hands curled tightly into fists at her sides. "Would you and Richard have been able to overwhelm them if you had not done so?"

A second passed between them until he finally dropped his gaze and nodded. "I believe so. Yes."

Pausing her progress, Mary swayed slightly on her feet, disgusted by her brother's actions. "You left him to die, Andrew! Dear God, how could you?"

His eyes filled with angst as he came toward her. "You were not there, Mary. You cannot possibly imagine what it was like, fighting for survival."

She shook her head, deaf to his excuses. "He was captured because of you, tortured even, yet you do not appear to be the least bit sorry for it."

"You are wrong about that. I feel terribly about what happened, but I am also angry at Heartly for what he has done to me. He has taken everything from me, Mary, and—"

"Stop," she said, unwilling to let him continue. "He has every right to seek satisfaction. If you do not see that, then you are a far greater fool than I would ever have imagined. Indeed, I am beginning to wonder if I know you at all, Andrew, for in my mind, my brother would never have done something this callous." She hesitated a moment before saying, "You could at least have gone to fetch help, but you made no attempt at that either, did you?"

He shook his head. "I was frightened."

"*Frightened*." The word whispered across her lips. "You were weak and unworthy of the uniform you wore."

For a second, he looked as though she'd just struck him, but then his eyes darkened and he said, "You have grown bolder since I saw you last. I find that I do not care for it."

"And I find that I do not care for a brother who would happily trade a man's life for a title and fortune!"

"Not happily," he clipped.

"Really?"

"What do you want me to say? To my knowledge Heartly was dead, so why shouldn't I have taken the reward when it was offered to me?"

"Because it was wrong!" The words whipped across the room leaving Mary's throat feeling sore. Tempering her voice, she met her brother's resentful glare. "What happened to you?" She could scarcely believe that the man before her had once been the boy with whom she'd played so well as a child. "You were always so kind and considerate toward others."

"I have made mistakes. I cannot deny that."

She gaped at him. "Is that supposed to make it better?"

"What can I say, Mary? Heartly suffered for what I did and I am sorry for that, truly I am, but I have suffered too. The humiliation he has forced upon me . . . You ought to know that I have challenged him to a duel. We meet tomorrow at dawn."

Staggering back, Mary steadied herself against the back of a chair while her hand covered her mouth. "You must be mad."

"Of course not," Andrew bit out, "but if you think that I will allow that man to methodically plan my ruination without demanding satisfaction for it, then you clearly do not know me at all."

"Indeed, I am beginning to see that I do not." She

shook her head. "They burned his face, Andrew, broke his leg and his arm. The fact that he was able to escape at all is a miracle in itself and yet you have the audacity to feel as though you have been wronged when you are no worse off now than before you went to war. All he has taken from you are the things that should have been his, and only because you were foolish enough to gamble them away."

"You cannot marry him, Mary. Not after what he has done to me. Promise me that you will not do so."

Pain tore through her heart. "I do not think I need to make such a promise. It is unlikely that he will still want to marry me now that he knows that I am related to you."

Andrew nodded. "You are probably correct." He tried to smile. "On a positive note, Heartly has assured me that he will return all my funds to me along with the estate if I win against him tomorrow. Wish me well and hopefully I will soon be able to repay some of the money that you have given me these past two years."

"No," Mary said as she took a step back. "I will not wish you well, Andrew. Not after all that has been revealed today."

"You would rather that Heartly wins?" he asked with dismay.

In spite of how hurt she was by Richard's words, she knew he deserved to have her on his side. "He is ten times the man that you will ever be. The fact that you may be my brother is insignificant in this instance."

"Your mind is clouded by your love for him, Mary. Clearly he has managed to influence your way of thinking, but you cannot ignore the fact that you and I have history. We have known each other for twenty years, grown up together, spent Christmases together . . ."

"And that might have meant something if you had been more honorable . . . more deserving of my high regard and admiration. As it turns out, you deserve neither. My support lies with Heartly."

"But I am your brother." The words were desperately spoken as she went to the door.

Looking over her shoulder at him, Mary shook her head with sadness. "Not anymore."

Forcing back the tears that threatened in response to the familial tie she'd just broken, Mary hurried down the hallway with only one goal in mind: to return upstairs to her bedchamber where she could be alone with her thoughts. But as she turned a corner, she found her aunt exiting one of the salons alongside Lady Duncaster, her eyes filling with concern the moment she spotted Mary. "Is everything all right?" Lady Foxworth asked. "You look a little out of sorts."

Nodding, Mary glanced toward the salon which appeared vacant. "May I have a private word with you?"

"Of course," Lady Foxworth said.

"You are welcome to join us, Lady Duncaster," Mary said as she looked to the countess. It was time she found out about the Roman villa and the cave. Mary and Richard had kept it from her long enough and with what had just happened and what might yet come, Mary didn't want to risk leaving Thorncliff without Lady Duncaster knowing about its existence.

Lady Duncaster looked a little uncertain, but rather than excusing herself, she said, "If that is what you would like."

As soon as they were all inside the salon, Mary closed the door. "Andrew is here," she said without preamble while Lady Foxworth and Lady Duncaster each claimed a seat. "Lord Carthright, that is. My brother."

"But that is excellent news," Lady Foxworth said. "It's about time that he offers you his support, and by coming here as you have asked him to do, he has clearly . . ." Her words trailed off the moment she met Mary's eyes. "What is it, my dear?"

Lowering herself into a vacant armchair, Mary took a deep breath before saying, "As it turns out, he is already acquainted with Mr. Heartly, though not in a good way."

Lady Foxworth's expression grew wary. She leaned back slowly in her seat and cast a fleeting look in Lady Duncaster's direction before asking, "What exactly do you mean?"

"It was Carthright's fault that Mr. Heartly was captured by the French and tortured." She then went on to relate what had happened since Andrew's arrival, including the conversation she'd just had with him. "I feel terrible about all of it but I cannot possibly take my brother's side in this. It simply is not right."

"Especially not when one considers how grievously he has treated you these past couple of years," Lady Foxworth muttered. She did not elaborate, aware that Mary would know what she was referring to and unwilling to let Lady Duncaster in on that little secret. Her expression was set in hard lines as she added, "Unfortunately, I can think of only one solution as far as Carthright is concerned."

"And what is that?" Mary asked.

"That depends on what Mr. Heartly plans to tell the public. If the truth is revealed, Carthright's punishment will likely be severe. After all, he lied to the king, receiving a title, land and a rather large fortune as a result."

"Do you suppose he might hang for what he has done?" As angry as Mary was with her brother, she did not like the thought of such a thing in the least.

"I do not know," Lady Foxworth confessed.

"You must also consider the shame that he has brought upon your family due to his misguided actions," Lady Duncaster said sympathetically.

"Rest assured," Lady Foxworth said, "I am aware of it. No matter the outcome of the duel tomorrow, I will deal with Carthright, though my plan will require the assurance that Mr. Heartly will be willing to refrain from mentioning this matter again."

"I cannot promise that," Mary said. "Mr. Heartly and I did not part on the best of terms. Frankly, the thought of having to face him again is not one that I relish."

Lady Foxworth opened her mouth as if to speak, but Mary turned her attention on Lady Duncaster instead and quickly said, "There is something that Mr. Heartly and I have been meaning to tell you for some time now, but one thing or another kept stopping us from doing so."

"And what is that?" Lady Duncaster asked. Tilting her head, she studied Mary with some degree of curiosity.

Knowing how mad her story would sound, Mary hesitated a moment before saying, "Are you aware that there is a cave on your property?"

Surprise filled Lady Duncaster's eyes. She shook her head. "Where?"

"To the right, beyond the far lawn. There is a slope there on the opposite side of the hedge. The entrance to the cave is right below that, partially hidden from view by some rocks."

"And you have been inside?" This question was asked by Lady Foxworth.

Mary nodded. "I have explored it quite extensively together with Mr. Heartly."

Lady Foxworth frowned. "You are aware of how scandalous that sounds?"

Mary felt her cheeks grow warm. More so when she recalled the time she'd spent there in Richard's company. The thought that she would never feel his touch again was too unbearable to contemplate. "Which is part of the reason why we have not mentioned it until now. But, I do think that you ought to be made aware of what we have found. You see it is not just a cave."

"Then what is it?" Lady Duncaster asked, her expression increasingly curious.

"You may find this hard to believe, but there is a river inside the cave. There is even a boat."

Lady Foxworth looked incredulous. "A boat?"

"Yes," Mary said with a confident nod. "Mr. Heartly and I believe it may have provided Thorncliff with convenient and secret access to the sea." She allowed this piece of information to be absorbed before saying, "But that is not all either, for there is also a tunnel."

"A tunnel?" Lady Duncaster echoed.

"It leads to something quite splendid actually," Mary told her. "To what appears to have once been a Roman villa."

Lady Duncaster's jaw dropped. "Surely not."

"It looks as though it was buried with the intention of preserving the interior because the windows have been carefully sealed. Furthermore, it is furnished in a more recent style and seems to have been used by your late husband's father."

Wide-eyed, Lady Duncaster stared at Mary in dismay. "You must have found something to convince you of this."

"A notebook," Mary said, "which according to Mr. Heartly, was written by his late grandfather."

"Dear God!" Steadying herself against the chair on which she was seated, Lady Duncaster's hand flew to her mouth. She held herself completely still for a moment. Slowly, she lowered her hand to her lap. "This may be what my husband was looking for. Have you had a chance to study the notebook?"

"To some degree," Mary admitted. "It refers, in particular, to a great deal of effort made by the third Earl of Duncaster, Mr. Heartly's grandfather, the Duchess of Marveille, and one other person, to help French aristocrats during the time of the revolution."

"Astounding." Shifting in her seat, Lady Duncaster looked toward the door. "Can you show me?"

"Of course," Mary said. "There is an entrance

to the villa via the tunnels that run beneath Thorncliff."

Lady Foxworth stared at Mary. "I daresay you are turning out to be quite the adventurous sort."

"I did not plan to be, I can assure you," Mary told her aunt.

"Though it is tremendously fortunate that you are," Lady Duncaster said, "or I might never have found out about my late father-in-law's covert operation. My husband always suspected that his father was up to something and spent the last years of his life trying to uncover what it was. He never found any evidence though and I began to doubt that there was anything to it. Uncovering this villa you speak of would certainly be a wonderful feat, though I would like to ask that you tell no one. The rumor that there is treasure to be found at Thorncliff has existed for many years and . . . I do not like the idea of all my guests beginning to hunt for it, as some would likely do if they were to hear about the villa."

"Your secret is safe with me, Lady Duncaster."

"And if you and Mr. Heartly manage to resolve your differences, perhaps the two of you can show me the villa together?"

"Perhaps," Mary said even though she doubted such a thing would come to pass. It would all depend on how willing he was to try and make things right between them. One thing was certain—even though he'd lashed out at her in anger, she still loved him and could no longer think of any other man by her side. Perhaps the most important question then was whether or not she could forgive him and whether or not he could accept her for being the sister of the man who'd once betrayed him.

Pacing the length of his bedchamber, Richard tried to forget the fact that the man he'd sworn to destroy was not only sharing the same house as him, but that he was also the brother of the woman he'd fallen in love with. *Damnation!* He clenched his fists, ignoring whatever his brother was saying—something about finding a way in which to work it all out . . . that everything would be all right eventually . . . not bloody likely!

"I have taken everything from Carthright," Richard clipped. "Ironically, a lot of the money he allegedly owned had been gifted to him by Lady Mary. She helped her brother thwart me while I continued to try and ruin him. How can you possibly suppose that such a thing will be resolved in a favorable way?"

"What I do not understand is that you never mentioned Carthright to me or to Papa." Spencer shrugged slightly. "I feel as though I ought to take issue with that."

Halting, Richard glared at him. "Don't you dare." Spencer responded by taking a sip of the brandy he'd been nursing as Richard continued, "I have enough to deal with at the moment without worrying about you as well."

"Fair enough," Spencer agreed. He kept silent a moment before saying, "I am a little surprised that Carthright would choose to challenge you though."

"He feels the need to punish me for what I did to him."

Spencer snorted. "As if you have not been punished enough already. In my opinion, he has turned the entire matter on its head."

"I appreciate your support," Richard said. Approaching the vacant armchair, he dropped onto the seat and leaned back with a sigh. "And I am sorry that I did not mention any of this to you earlier, but I was worried that you might try and stop me from doing what I felt was not only necessary, but well deserved."

"You may be right." Setting his glass aside, Spencer glanced over at Richard. "That said, I think I would have done something similar, had I been in your shoes. Carthright does not deserve to be rewarded for his betrayal. Quite the contrary."

Silence followed for a number of seconds while Richard gazed up at the ceiling. "The trouble is that I don't quite know where to go from here."

"What do you mean?"

"I am thinking of Lady Mary," Richard confessed. Indeed, he'd been sorely pressed to think of anything else. "I have effectively taken vengeance upon her brother. Even before I discovered their relationship I feared telling her about this because I worried that she would judge me harshly for it. Now . . ." He shook his head. A strong feeling of hopelessness was beginning to wear him down.

"You think she will be unable to forgive you?"

Tilting his head forward again, Richard looked at his brother. "Yes, Spencer. That is precisely what I think."

"From what I gather, she is a romantic. Perhaps she would appreciate a token from you? A poem or maybe some flowers?"

"I have already sent her a peace offering," Richard told his brother gruffly. He knew that Mary deserved an apology, but he was beginning to wonder if his attempt at one had been good enough.

"And?"

Richard glared at him. "Do you think I would be sitting here talking to you if she had forgiven me?"

"Point taken." A brief silence followed. Spencer drummed his fingers on the armrest. The clock ticked loudly on the mantel.

"What?" Richard finally asked.

Spencer tilted his head. "I noticed that she failed to put in an appearance at dinner. Give her time, Richard. If she cares for you half as much as you care for her, then she will come to you sooner or later. I am confident of that."

"Really?" Richard drew the palm of his hand across his face. "Carthright's arrival took me completely by surprise. As a result, I said some terrible things to her."

Spencer nodded. "Your concern is understandable, I suppose. But before *you* decide what Lady Mary will think of you, perhaps you ought to ask her yourself."

"She fled the room when she discovered what had happened." The stricken look upon her face . . . he would never be able to forget that. "And now I am to meet her brother at dawn."

"A tricky business, to be sure. Especially if you win."

Groaning, Richard picked up his own brandy and took a fortifying sip. "You make it sound as though losing might be an option." Shaking his head he set down his glass. "Pistols do not allow for the sort of sportsmanship one might enjoy with swords. I cannot go easy on Carthright for the simple reason that I fear he will take advantage of it."

"Just as long as you don't kill him then." The gravity of the situation was prevalent in Spencer's tone and expression.

"And what if he kills *me*?"

"Is he that good a shot?"

Richard considered the question for a second before saying, "He may not be as precise as I am, but he is certainly good enough to hit his mark, even at a distance of forty paces."

"Then you must strike him first—a shot to his leg or perhaps his shoulder."

"Naturally, I have considered that, though I doubt Lady Mary will approve."

A frown crept across Spencer's brow. "You think she would prefer it if you are the one who gets wounded?"

Richard expelled a deep breath. "I have no idea. But her loyalty toward her brother is undeniable."

"I really think you ought to ask her if that is still the case after what she has just discovered about him."

"Perhaps—"

A knock at the door cut Richard off. Eying Spencer, he got to his feet and crossed to it. He hadn't been expecting anyone. "Yes?" he inquired.

There was a brief hesitation, and then, "It is I, Mary."

A warm shiver rolled through him at the sound of her voice. He glanced toward Spencer and found that he'd risen to his feet. Pushing back the warning that Mary's reputation was at stake by her being here, he opened the door and quickly ushered her inside. Her eyes widened at the realization that they weren't alone.

"I should leave," Spencer said as he took a step forward. He tilted his head in Mary's direction. "A pleasure, my lady."

And then he was gone, leaving the two of them completely alone in Richard's bedchamber. For a long moment, they just stood there staring at each other until Richard finally collected himself and gestured toward the chair that his brother had just vacated. "Please have a seat." He waited for her to move, to dislodge the awkwardness between them before saying, "Would you care for something to drink? The sherry is quite good."

Lowering herself onto the chair, she nodded. "Thank you. I would like that."

Stiffly, he crossed to the sideboard and prepared her glass which he offered her shortly thereafter. "You are aware that you risk ruination by coming here? If someone were to discover your presence in my bedchamber—"

"I know that my brother has challenged you to a duel, which means that lives are at stake now. My reputation seems insignificant by comparison." Her eyes met his, staying with him while he took the seat across from her.

"Just so you know, I do not plan on killing him tomorrow." He spoke slowly, gauging her reaction. "Indeed, I would like to prevent such an outcome."

The statement did not seem to ease her concern.

Her expression remained stark as she reached for her sherry, sipping it before setting the glass aside and saying, "I appreciate that, but . . . I am actually more worried about you. If anything were to happen to you . . ." She looked away, her teeth puckering the soft flesh of her lip as she bit into it.

Richard felt his heart rate increase. "If anything were to happen to me?"

"It would destroy me," she whispered, her voice so fragile that it sounded as though it might break.

"What about your brother?" He held his breath, fearful of her answer.

She gave a small shrug. "He has wronged you in the most despicable way. I cannot support his actions."

The statement eased some of his concerns. Still, he needed to know that things were once again right between them—that her coming here meant that they might at least stand a chance. "So you are not angry with me anymore?"

"Of course I am!" Raising her head, she looked at him directly. "Do you have any idea how deeply your words wounded me today?"

"I was unprepared to discover that you are Carthright's sister." A ridiculous excuse. One that he knew she neither wanted nor needed, so he dropped to his knees before her and said, "I have wronged you in the worst possible way by betraying the trust that you placed in me when you gave me your heart. You are innocent, Mary, and I am sorry for what I said to you."

Her eyes seemed to strain against the onset of tears. "You should have told me what happened sooner so I would not have had to discover it like this."

He knew she was right and yet he'd had his reasons. "I feared you would not be able to accept what I was doing and that you would judge me harshly for it. Mary, I could not allow his actions to go unpunished. I hope you can understand that."

"I do."

Lowering his head, he kissed her hands before raising his gaze to hers. "Forgive me. Please, I cannot bear the thought of losing you."

A weak smile touched her lips. "The gift you sent to my room this afternoon . . . it was remarkably thoughtful—the most perfect thing in the world!"

Her voice trembled as she spoke and Richard's heart swelled with renewed hope. "It is the first song in the opera that I have begun working on, and because of the story, I thought it might be the best way of telling you how I feel."

"It is *our* story, is it not?"

Seeing the tears that clung to her lashes, he nodded. "I have drafted an outline, but I am no longer certain of how it will end."

"Perhaps you should ask yourself how you would *like* for it to end."

"Happily, I hope."

Leaning forward, she placed her hand against his cheek in a gentle caress that carried a glimpse of the future with it. "I think that would be a most excellent outcome."

Exhaling the breath he'd been holding, he rose up, capturing her lips in an aching kiss born from longing and despair. "You mean the world to me, Mary. I need you by my side."

"And I need you by mine."

He kissed her again, promising her with the loving caress of his lips that he would never again be careless with her heart. "I cannot believe that Carthright is your brother," he told her moments later as he placed his forehead against hers, reveling in the closeness. "What are the chances?"

"I have no idea. Perhaps the more important question is whether or not you are able to accept it." Sadness filled her eyes once more and for a moment it looked as though she was finding it painful to breathe.

"The alternative would be impossible for me to live with, so if you can forgive me, Mary, then I can definitely come to terms with who your brother is."

Relief flooded her features. "This must be terribly difficult for you."

He stared at her in amazement. "Difficult for *me?*" Even now, with disaster threatening to ruin their lives, her kindness and consideration for others shone through. "Andrew is *your* brother, Mary."

"By blood only." A lonely tear trickled down her cheek. "I cannot in good conscience approve of his actions. My support lies entirely with you, Richard. I have told him as much."

Overwhelmed by her love for him, he pressed her to his chest. "Oh, sweetheart"—the words tore at his throat—"I honestly thought I had lost you."

A choked sob escaped her. "The choice became increasingly clear to me after listening to Andrew's account of what happened. He was inconceivably selfish and cowardly. The fact that he did not give an accurate report of what happened but left you to die, is unforgiveable."

Leaning back a little, Richard tilted her face so he

could meet her troubled gaze. "I love you." Nothing else remained to be said as he lowered his mouth over hers once more, kissing away the remainder of her pain.

Slowly, she brought her arms around his neck, pulling him closer until he hovered over her. "You should leave," he murmured against the corner of her mouth.

The sweetest sigh escaped her parted lips. "And if I stay?"

His fingers trembled ever so slightly as he brushed them against her cheek. "If you stay . . ." Jesus, what a thought! Closing his eyes, he tried to control the tension building inside his chest. Lord, how he wanted her to do so. But it would be wrong. "I fear there will be consequences."

He heard her breathe; soft inhalations that seemed to trap them in time. "And what if this is our only chance?"

Opening his eyes, he gazed into the dark pools of emotion staring back at him. "You are worried that I will not survive the duel?"

She turned her head away. "I have to acknowledge the possibility." Her voice broke, fragmenting the words. "Considering what I now know of my brother, I fear that he will not act honorably and that you will pay for it with your life. I . . ." She shook her head, unable to speak.

"It will not come to that, Mary. I have seen your brother shoot before and while he is capable of handling his firearms, he is not nearly as accomplished a shot as I."

Shifting, she met his gaze while unshed tears

welled against her lashes. "So you believe that he will miss his mark?"

"I cannot say for sure, though I do believe that even if he does manage to shoot me, the shot will not be fatal."

Gulping, she quietly said, "But nothing is certain, which is why I find it impossible to leave your side right now. Please don't make me go."

Her voice was so imploring, so fragile, that he found his discipline wavering. "You will be ruined if anyone finds out."

"I would gladly risk ruination for a chance to spend the night with you."

He shook his head and drew back. "You say so now, but what if the duel tomorrow does not go according to plan? What if you find yourself with child and without a husband by your side? Think of what that would do not only to you, but to our son or daughter."

Her eyelids drooped with hopelessness. "They would be shunned by Society. As would I."

Rising, he drew her to her feet so he could pull her into his arms, her head nestled firmly against his chest. "We cannot allow this situation to divest us of our common sense," he whispered against the top of her head. "No matter how tempting it is to do so."

"I just want . . ."

"So do I, my love." Sweeping his hand up and down her back in long soothing strokes, he whispered again, "So do I."

Chapter 19

Dewdrops lay like shimmering glass upon the ground the following morning as Mary made her way across the lawn. She hadn't slept since returning to her bedchamber the night before, afraid that she would miss the duel that would soon take place between her brother and the man she meant to marry.

Drawing her cloak tightly around her shoulders, she fought the chill that threatened to sink into her bones. Gray tones surrounded her in a haze as light began to soften the darkness. The field was beyond the trees, and with no one else in sight, Mary quickened her pace, afraid that they might begin before she managed to arrive.

But this fear was soon brought to rest as, after following a short path, she arrived to find several people gathered together in discussion. They included Richard, Andrew, Spencer, Lady Foxworth, Lady Duncaster and a few footmen.

"What are you doing here?" Andrew asked, spotting her first.

"I came to watch the duel," she said, approaching the group.

Richard gave her an uneasy smile as he stepped away from the others and came toward her. "You should not have come. Dueling grounds are not appropriate places for young ladies to visit."

"He is right," Lady Foxworth said. "You ought to return upstairs to your bedchamber. The event that is about to take place is scandalous enough without your involvement."

"I do not plan to get involved," Mary replied, annoyed that they were trying to send her away. "I merely wish to watch."

"And whose side will you be on, exactly?" The question was bitterly spoken by Andrew.

"I believe you know the answer to that already," she replied, "but to be perfectly clear, I am in favor or Mr. Heartly winning."

"Traitor," her brother spat. "You denounce your own flesh and blood."

His sharp tone caught her off guard. She blinked. "Can you not see that you are in the wrong? That your actions are reprehensible?"

Shaking his head, Andrew turned his back on her.

"I am sorry," Richard said. He caught her by the elbow and drew her away with him at a stroll. "The terms have already been laid out, so we will begin shortly."

"Please don't ask me to leave." Leaning into him, she savored the strength in his arm and the warmth of his touch. The possibility that she might never feel it again brought a painful knot to her throat.

"Very well," he agreed. Halting, he turned her toward him so he could look her in the eye. "No matter what happens next, please know that I love you with all that I am." Taking her hands in his, he raised both of them to his lips for a kiss.

"As I love you," she whispered, fighting the tears that threatened.

"Which makes me the most fortunate man in the world." Tenderness seeped from the depths of his eyes. "To have known you and to have won your heart—"

"You must not talk like that." She could barely get the words out. "You will survive this, Richard. You have to!"

Nodding, his expression turned serious. "I will aim for your brother's arm in an effort to disarm him."

"So he will survive?"

"I see no reason why he should not."

"Considering what you told me last night about his skill, or lack thereof, I daresay that you will as well." Andrew had said that he did not plan on killing Richard, and with his inferior aim taken into account, there was a good chance that he wouldn't manage to hit him at all. As they walked back toward the others, Mary prayed that this would be the case.

"Well?" Andrew asked, glaring at her.

"I will watch the duel from a reasonable distance," Mary said.

"Mary . . ." Lady Foxworth began.

Mary crossed her arms. "You cannot force me to leave."

"She is correct in that regard," Lady Duncaster said. And then, "Shall we proceed? I believe the sun will rise within the next quarter of an hour."

As if summoned by her words, one of the footmen stepped forward with a case bearing two ornately designed dueling pistols. "Mr. Heartly, please select your weapon."

Dropping his gaze to the box, Richard picked up the pistol closest to him, leaving the other for Andrew. When both men had one in hand, Spencer outlined the rules once more. "Gentlemen, you will stand back to back with each other. As soon as Lady Duncaster begins the count, you will step forward until you have each traveled a distance of twenty paces. Once this has been achieved, you will await the signal before turning and firing your shots. Are you both in accord?"

Andrew and Richard nodded. "We are," they spoke in unison.

Looking at each of them in turn, Spencer then said, "Before we proceed, it is my duty to inquire if either one of you would like to prevent the events that will take place shortly by offering an apology instead."

"No," Andrew clipped, to which Richard said, "I fear I cannot do so."

Mary's heart crumpled. She'd known they wouldn't agree to such a thing—that their pride would not allow it—but she had still hoped.

"Very well then," Spencer stated. "Let us begin."

Removing herself to the side with her aunt and Lady Duncaster, Mary watched as Andrew and Richard took up their positions.

"Have courage," Lady Duncaster whispered at Mary's side before she started counting.

Mary felt her heartbeat quicken as the men strode

stiffly in opposite directions, the faint glow from the rising sun illuminating the sky as birds began to chirp from the treetops—an abundance of life so foreign from the bleak atmosphere on the field.

At the count of twenty, the men halted. "Face your opponent," Lady Duncaster called out.

Each began to turn, but before they'd made a full rotation, a shot cracked like thunder, rustling the treetops and scattering the birds. Mary blinked, not entirely certain of what had just happened, the confusion distracting her from the slight ache in her side.

"That foolish boy," Lady Foxworth muttered. "He cannot even conduct a duel according to protocol."

That was when Mary noticed the confused look on Andrew's face and the odd angle of his pistol. In his nervousness, he must have fired too early. Elation shot up inside her. She looked to Richard who seemed just as surprised as everyone else. As if in a daze, he lowered his pistol to his side.

Unable to resist, Mary started in his direction. He'd won thanks to Andrew's blunder, with neither man getting hurt. It was the best possible outcome! But as she hurried toward him, a fierce fire ignited inside her, slowing her pace. Blinking, she tried to understand, her hand pressing against the pain and feeling the wetness there as Richard turned toward her. The smile he gave her immediately dropped from his face, confirming that something wasn't quite as it should be.

"Mary." Discarding his pistol he ran toward her.

Stumbling, she started to fall, her legs refusing to carry her weight.

"Mary!"

The ground tilted, plunging her into darkness.

Richard's heart erupted with fear. "No!" Reaching Mary, he gathered her up in his arms, barely breaking his stride as he did so.

"What happened?" Lady Foxworth asked as he hurried past her.

"She has been shot." The words fell heavily around them. Hell, just getting them past the thick knot in his throat was an ordeal. "We have to get her back to the house." He heard Lady Foxworth sob as she conveyed the news to Lady Duncaster. Carthright on the other hand . . . Richard tightened his hold on Mary. He would deal with her brother later, as soon as he was certain that her life was not in danger. But if she died . . . He dared not think of such an outcome even as dark rage clawed at his chest.

Vaguely, he was aware of footsteps following him at a brisk pace. If someone spoke to him however, he was oblivious of the fact. All he knew was that he needed to get Mary back to her bedchamber so he could issue instructions for a physician to be summoned. A hand caught him by the arm and he instinctively spun on his heel. "What?"

The angry question was met by a very calm looking Lady Duncaster. "Doctor Florian is a guest here, Mr. Heartly. I will ask him to meet us in Lady Mary's bedchamber."

With a curt nod, he strode away, arriving in the aforementioned room only moments later where he was greeted by Mary's maid, whose face twisted at the sight of her mistress.

"We need to undress her," he said, focusing on whatever they could do to help improve the situation.

"You cannot possibly—"

"Get out of my way," he bit out.

Amy didn't argue any further. Instead, she stepped aside, closed the door and followed him to the bed where he carefully set Mary down.

"Oh no," Amy murmured as the wound came into view, visible as a large patch of blood against the left side of Mary's gown.

Richard ignored her. Aware of how efficient Lady Duncaster could be, he did not doubt that the doctor would arrive shortly. They should prepare Mary for when he did, which meant that they would have to get her out of her clothes so the doctor could access the wound properly. To this end, Richard reached down and began undoing the fastenings on Mary's gown.

"What are you doing?" Amy asked with a hint of horror to her voice.

"What is necessary," he explained as he pushed the sleeves over Mary's shoulders and began pulling her gown down over her waist. She groaned slightly, which gave him hope.

"This is highly irregular, sir. Her modesty—"

"Damn her modesty," he fairly exploded. Amy fell silent and Richard clenched his jaw. He hadn't meant to be quite that harsh, but by God, he was at his wits-end. This should have been him, not her . . . anyone but her.

With quivering fingers he turned her sideways so he could unfasten her stays.

"Allow me," Amy said, her tone holding a comforting degree of determination.

Stepping back, Richard watched her work as helplessness drove its way to his core. *I cannot lose her.* The unspoken words sent a shudder through him. An ache clutched at his heart, tightening his chest and making it difficult for him to breathe.

A knock sounded at the door and then it opened, giving way to Lady Duncaster and an older gentleman whom Richard had not yet met. He nodded in Richard's direction but did not bother with introducing himself or with making any other attempt at conversation. Richard found that he appreciated that—the fact that treating Mary was of greater importance to him than protocol.

"Please pull the covers up over her legs and then raise her chemise so I can get a proper look," he said to Amy.

The maid complied without arguing while Richard stood at Lady Duncaster's side, unsure of how he could be of assistance. Seeing the blood smeared across Mary's abdomen, he went to fetch the wash-basin that stood on a small table to one side, grabbed a clean linen towel lying next to it and presented both items to the doctor.

"Thank you," Florian remarked as he wet the towel and began to wipe away the blood, revealing a dark wound surrounded by bright pink flesh.

"Will she be all right?" Richard asked as the doctor began to feel his way around the wound. It looked as if he was searching for something. Groaning, Mary shifted against the touch. "Only time will tell." Turning her onto her side, the doctor studied her back and then muttered a curse.

"What is it?" Amy asked in a small voice that seemed close to breaking.

Richard winced. He knew what the doctor's concern was now. "There is no exit wound. The lead ball will have to be extracted if she is to survive this."

"Fetch some brandy," Lady Duncaster said, "and I will inform Lady Foxworth of the news." Suffering from shock, Mary's aunt had been escorted to her own bedchamber and offered a small amount of laudanum in order to calm her nerves.

"We will need a bit of strength soon," Florian said without looking up, "so if you can find another gentleman willing to help, I suggest you bring him with you when you return."

Relieved that he'd been given a task, Richard glanced at Mary's pale face before quitting the room and going in search of the brandy and Spencer. He felt as though his heart had been torn from his chest. What had happened . . . his steps were heavy upon the floor, carrying him forward only because he knew that Mary now depended on him to help her through this.

Coming from the opposite end of the hallway, Richard saw the man who was to blame for it all—the man who might very well have killed the most good-natured person in the world. Balling his hands into two tight fists, Richard gritted his teeth as he moved toward him. "Carthright!" The name sounded like bone crushing against bone.

"How is she?" Carthright asked, coming to a halt

at a reasonable distance. His eyes bore a haunted expression that made him look old and tired.

"Struggling for her life, thanks to you."

Dropping his gaze, Carthright muttered, "I am sorry."

The apology reminded Richard of stale bread. "Sorry?" He was incredulous. "You are *sorry?*"

"Of course!"

Marching forward, Richard raised his fist. "She might die because of you, you bloody idiot!" His knuckles made contact with Carthright's jawbone, producing a loud cracking sound and pushing Carthright back. "Why?" His voice wavered. "You were supposed to shoot *me!*"

Dropping to his knees, Carthright raised his arms to cover his face in anticipation of another hit, but Richard made no effort to attack. Instead, he hovered over him, waiting for an answer to his question.

"I was nervous," Carthright stammered. "I know that you are a far better shot and expected you to fire first, so I . . . I pulled the trigger too early."

Richard felt his anger rise. "The same reason why you abandoned me in France—because you are a coward." When Carthright didn't respond, Richard stepped past him. He didn't have time for this right now. Not when Mary needed his help.

Returning to her bedchamber a few minutes later together with Spencer, Richard poured the brandy into a large glass so the doctor could dip his tools in it. "How is she?" he asked, his gaze falling on Mary's twisted features.

"She continues to fall in and out of consciousness." Arranging some linen towels so they would be easily accessible, the doctor took a seat. "Her pain is severe, as is the wound, but I will do my best to save her. I give you my word on that." He looked at Richard and Spencer in turn. "If you are ready, I would like to proceed. The quicker we get that lead ball out of her, the better."

A heavy hand touched Richard's arm and he turned to meet his brother's gaze, the concern there so raw that it threatened to shatter Richard's tightly reined control. Turning away, Richard nodded. "Yes," he told the doctor as he moved closer to the bed, aware that Mary's pain was about to get a whole lot worse.

Holding her firmly by her shoulders while Spencer pushed down on her legs, the brothers struggled to keep her as still as possible while the doctor worked. Her anguished groans were difficult to listen to, even though Richard knew that it was for the best. But to watch the tools being driven into her, was almost more than he could bear.

Blood was swiftly wiped away by Lady Duncaster who'd proven most efficient in regards to this matter. The doctor retracted his pincers, pulling out a fragment of Lady Mary's gown, "Excellent," he murmured. "Most infections are caused by bits of foreign material getting pushed inside the wound upon impact, so I am happy to have recovered this."

Not long after, the doctor declared making contact with the lead ball itself. Richard's hands tightened against Mary, even though her body had gone limp after losing consciousness again. Still, he could not risk her waking up and disturbing the doctor's delicate work. Slowly, the shot was dragged out of her torso and dropped into a bowl. "That ought to do it," the doctor said as he leaned back with a sigh. He placed his hand against her forehead. "She feels cool to the touch, so I would suggest keeping a blanket over her for warmth."

"Do you think she will be all right?" Lady Duncaster asked, giving voice to Richard's own concern.

"Only time will tell, I suppose." Reaching for his needle and thread, the doctor proceeded to stitch up the hole.

Richard knew what he meant, even though he'd hoped that the doctor might have offered more of an assurance. But having been to war and witnessing the effect such wounds could have on seemingly healthy and strong men, he was also aware that the worst might still be to come. "I will watch over her," he said decisively.

The statement was met by hushed silence until Spencer quietly said, "I do not think that doing so would be an appropriate course of action. You are not her husband, after all."

"I will be soon enough. Once she recovers." And she would recover. She simply *had* to. The alternative wasn't an option.

"Even so, you must consider her reputation," Lady Duncaster said. "People will talk once they notice your presence here."

Grinding his teeth, Richard stared at each of them in turn, not liking the extent of their sound judgment. "Then what would you suggest I do? Because I can assure you that doing nothing is out of the question."

"Perhaps you could sit by the door while Lady Foxworth and I take turns in the room with her."

"By the door?" he muttered, feeling as though he'd just been banished to a corner.

"You will still be close enough for us to keep you apprised of her condition and you would also be of great help if we need to call for the doctor to return. Considering how invested you are in her recovery, I daresay you would fetch him faster than any of my servants."

"You can be certain of it," Richard said.

"Then it is settled?" The pitch of Lady Duncaster's voice suggested a question even though Richard was wise enough to know that it was anything but.

He nodded, because although he would have preferred to sit by Mary's bedside, he knew such a thing would not be possible. Instead, he found himself occupying a comfortable armchair only minutes later. A footman had even brought him that day's paper so he would have something with which to pass the time. As if he was able to concentrate on politics or gossip—trivialities, in truth, when considering the fact that Mary's life was still very much at stake.

Instead, he focused on his breaths, aware of how tight his chest felt against his lungs. He turned the pages of the paper, but failed to comprehend a single word that was printed thereon. It was all a massive blur, distorted by the most bizarre feeling that the only thing he cared about was in the room beyond, and that he just might lose it.

The thought stuck, disturbing him to the point of restlessness. For years he'd been motivated solely by the need for revenge. He'd achieved his goal. Victory was his. But at what cost? A shudder went through him. Carthright had definitely wronged him. Of that there was no doubt. And he might not deserve his title, his property or his fortune, but if Richard hadn't striven to take them all from him, then perhaps . . .

He shook his head, unwilling to torture himself with what-ifs. One thing was certain however, and that was the fact that he would gladly repeat the past five years of misery for a chance at a different outcome—one in which Mary would not get shot.

The door opened beside him and he was on his feet in an instant. "How is she?" he asked upon seeing Lady Duncaster.

"She is still sleeping."

"Have you touched her forehead, ensured that she does not feel feverish?" Lord how he hated the helplessness.

She nodded. "Of course."

Expelling a breath, he thanked her for letting him know, resuming his seat as she returned to the room, closing the door behind her.

Two hours later, Lady Foxworth arrived to switch places with Lady Duncaster. "Mr. Heartly," she said, her hollow eyes sparking a little upon seeing him there. "I did not expect to find you here, though I suppose I should have done. What happened today—"

"She will recover," he said with certainty.

Her only response was a tremulous smile, and then she was gone, ushered into a room that he was still denied entry to. Lady Duncaster exited soon after. "I will send a tray up with some food for you. Is there anything else you would like?"

"Perhaps a clock? I did not think to bring my

pocket watch with me when I left my room this morning and I would like to keep track of the time."

"Of course," Lady Duncaster said. "I will ask a footman to bring one up for you right away."

As it turned out, the footman brought a notebook and pencil as well, which was wonderfully thoughtful since it allowed him to jot down Mary's status every half hour. Even though there was little to say, it gave him something more meaningful to do than reading the paper.

"Would you care to join me for a drink?" Spencer asked at half past eleven when he returned carrying a brandy bottle and two glasses.

"I certainly would not mind the company." Richard began gesturing for the footman to bring another chair but Spencer stopped him, lowering himself to the floor instead with his legs stretched out before him.

"Any news?" Spencer asked as he poured the brandy and handed one of the glasses to Richard.

"She sleeps," Richard said with a shrug.

"I suppose that is a good thing. From my experience, sleep is the fastest way to recovery. That and some good food!"

Richard couldn't disagree with that. Leaning forward, he clinked his glass against his brother's and took a sip, grateful for the drink's soothing effect. "I just wish that she would wake up and let us know how she is feeling."

"She will," Spencer assured him. And then, "I bet you must be pretty angry with Carthright."

Stiffening, Richard allowed a slow nod. "Angry does not begin to describe how I feel about him. Whatever he did toward me, this is so much worse."

"Perhaps I should warn you against punishing the fellow any more than you already have done?"

"That will not be necessary. I realized this evening that it was my blind path to revenge that has led to this very moment. Without it, Mary might not have gotten shot since Carthright would not have had a reason to challenge me. Christ, Spencer! Pistols were *my* choice!"

Spencer snorted. "If you start thinking like that, you will never stop. The point I was trying to make is that I spoke to Lady Foxworth earlier. Rest assured that she will not allow Carthright to go unpunished."

"What can she possibly do to justify his actions? He is not even her son."

"Do not underestimate the lady, Richard. I find that women have a tendency to achieve their goals in the most extraordinary ways."

The door to Mary's bedchamber opened and both men got to their feet as the lady in question appeared. Her anxious expression was not the least bit comforting. "She is developing a fever."

Richard tried to look past Lady Foxworth but she blocked his line of vision. "How bad is it?"

"I think you ought to fetch the doctor."

Richard didn't question her for a second. He just handed his glass to Spencer and left at a brisk pace, returning with the doctor just a few minutes later. But when he tried to follow the doctor into Mary's room, Lady Foxworth stopped him. "She is not decent, Mr. Heartly. Please try to understand."

The door closed in Richard's face and for a long drawn out moment, he just stood there staring at it, unable to comprehend that he was being kept away from the woman he loved while her life hung in the balance. "Damn Society and its ridiculous rules!"

"Hear, hear," Spencer muttered. Leaning against the wall, he'd waited for Richard to return.

Casting a look over his shoulder, Richard said, "I ought to break this bloody door down."

"I can help you, if you like."

A tempting idea, though one that would probably not be well received by anyone else. So he waited, glanced toward the clock. Almost an hour ticked by at a murderously slow pace before the doctor himself re-emerged. From behind him, Richard could hear Lady Foxworth bustling about in an agitated way that only served to heighten Richard's concern. "It does not look good," the doctor pronounced. His apologetic manner grated.

"What the hell is that supposed to mean?" Richard asked.

"The wound does not look infected, but her fever is steadily rising. If we fail to stop it, then there is no telling what might happen as a result."

"In other words, she might die," Richard said, speaking almost mechanically.

"That has always been a possibility," the doctor said, "but now . . . perhaps a more likely outcome unless we can manage to bring her temperature down." Lowering his voice he whispered, "Her aunt believes that she should be kept warm—that the fever is a good thing and that we should allow it to grow, which of course is a misconception. In my experience, the best results are achieved when the fever is reduced, but Lady Foxworth is in a state of panic and refuses to listen to reason."

"Then what would you suggest?" Spencer asked with the sort of calm that had long since departed from Richard.

The doctor hesitated briefly before saying, "She must be cooled, so perhaps if a bathtub can be brought up, then—"

"No," Richard said. "That will take too long."

"I agree," the doctor said, "but what else . . ."

He wasn't given a chance to complete his question as Richard pushed past him, entering Mary's room in a few short strides.

"Mr. Heartly," Lady Foxworth gasped. "You should not be in here. It is not proper!"

His eyes fell on Mary, on the sheen of perspiration veiling her forehead, her flushed cheeks and the agitated state she appeared to be in as she threw her head from side to side, groaning in between. "To hell with propriety. This is about saving her life."

"We are doing all that we can," Lady Foxworth said, her voice filled with despair as she tucked the blankets around Mary and wiped her brow with a cloth.

"No. She needs to be cooled, not heated." Richard moved toward the bed, his hands reaching for Mary's blankets.

Lady Foxworth caught him by the wrist. "Please," she implored with a shake of her head. "I cannot bear the thought of losing her."

He understood her grief. "Neither can I, which is why I can assure you that I intend to make her better by whatever means necessary. You may disagree with my method, but consider her progress this past hour while you have been trying to keep her warm beneath these blankets. Has her condition improved or worsened?"

A few seconds passed and then, choking back a sob, Lady Foxworth drew back and nodded, her expression one of utter defeat. "Very well. Do what you think best."

He didn't wait another second, tossing aside the blankets so that only the sheet remained. Leaning forward, Richard tucked it around Mary as he scooped her up in his arms and headed for the door, her head resting firmly against his chest.

"Where are you taking her?" Lady Foxworth asked from somewhere behind him, but Richard didn't stop to give her an answer, nor did he deign the doctor or his brother with an explanation as he passed them both on the way out of Mary's room. Instead, he practically ran as fast as his feet could carry him, careful not to stumble on the stairs.

A few guests who were making their way up to bed stopped to look at him, their eyes widening when they saw that he was carrying Mary. Some even asked what was wrong, but Richard ignored them all as he hurried toward his destination, exiting onto the terrace and crossing the lawn. With a leap, he plunged into the lake until they were shoulder deep in the icy water.

Air rushed from Mary's lungs and he instinctively hugged her closer. "Relax," he whispered against her cheek. "This is good for you. It will make you better."

She said nothing, responding only with a deep murmur as she pressed herself against him, the sheet and her chemise floating around them, bright against the enfolding darkness. As the water settled, Richard could hear the frogs croaking from the embankment. Fully clothed, the weight of the water made standing upright a chore, his feet constantly slipping against the pliable mud beneath him.

With no way in which to tell the time, he had no idea how long he'd been standing there until Lady Foxworth called to him from the embankment, inquiring about Mary's welfare. Turning, Richard saw that Lady Duncaster was with her, both ladies cast in tones of gray while light from the lantern they'd brought flooded the ground at their feet.

"I believe this is helping," he said, his teeth chattering slightly as he spoke.

"You are putting your own health at risk," Lady Duncaster remarked.

"I would risk a great deal more than that if it means that she will live," he replied, clutching Mary closer. Her heartbeat, so faint against his chest, assured him that she was still alive even when she seemed so lifeless in his arms. "Do you know what time it is?"

"One o'clock," Lady Duncaster said. "Would you like me to leave the lantern here?"

When he nodded, she set the lantern down on a nearby bench before taking her leave along with Lady Foxworth. Alone again, Richard lowered his lips to Mary's forehead. She was still hot, though not as much as earlier. Kissing her cheek, he began to straighten himself when she suddenly squirmed, struggling against him and splashing at the water.

Her eyes flew open, startled no doubt by the cold wetness surrounding her.

"Mary!" Her name was tightly spoken as he tried his best to remain upright—a difficult task when she started kicking her feet. "I have you, Mary. You are safe. Stop fighting me!"

With a sob, she clawed at his shoulders as if holding on for dear life. "What happened?" The words were barely audible, ending on a groan of anguish.

"You were shot," he said as he shifted her to a more comfortable position. "It was an accident."

Her eyes closed and she leaned her head back against his arm, her breaths more rapid than before. "Who?" was all she managed to ask.

"Your brother."

When she said nothing in response, Richard thought she'd lost consciousness again until he saw the tears rolling down her cheeks and realized she was crying. "You developed a fever," he explained, knowing how confused she must be, "that is why I brought you here. We have to try and cool you down." Swallowing his concerns he asked, "How are you feeling?"

"It hurts like the devil," she said. "Much more so than when I ran toward you and . . . I cannot remember what happened next."

"You collapsed." When she just nodded, he added, "We should stay here a while longer, I think—at least until your fever has dissipated." She didn't reply to that, though she pressed her cheek to his chest as if trying to snuggle closer. Dipping his mouth to the top of her head, he began humming a low tune, soothing her with the sound of his voice.

They remained like that for what seemed like forever until she suddenly shifted again. "I think I would like to return to my bedchamber," she said, her body shivering as she spoke.

Richard expelled a deep breath. If she was feeling cold, then perhaps . . . Pressing his lips to her forehead once more, he found her feeling cool to the touch. "Very well," he managed against the tightness in his throat, his voice breaking as he turned and started back toward the embankment.

"I love you," she whispered as soon as they reached solid ground. "Thank you for saving my life."

His eyes misted in response to her words and for a second he found it impossible to speak at all. Swallowing the fear that he'd felt for the past few hours, he carried her back toward the house. "I love you too," he murmured, his boots sloshing heavily against the tiles on the terrace and then through the hallways of Thorncliff. The maids would not be pleased but there was nothing he could do to change that. Instead, he decided to focus on the wonderful fact that Mary would soon recover from her injury. "I feared I might lose you."

"Just tell me that we will soon be married."

Dropping his gaze to hers as they made their way back upstairs, Richard said, "I have the special license, so as soon as you are well enough, I intend to make you mine."

A small smile graced her lips. "And all this time, I thought that I would be the one laying claim to you."

Quickening his pace, he said, "If that is what you wish, then there is not a moment to lose."

Her smile broadened. "Apparently you were correct when you said that duels can be a terrible inconvenience. This one has ruined my entire week!"

He couldn't help but laugh, pleased by her ability to spar with him after all that she had been through. Confident that all would soon be back to normal, he returned her to her bedchamber and the continued care of the doctor and Lady Foxworth.

When Mary returned downstairs a couple of days later, she was met by her aunt who'd left her side the previous evening at Mary's insistence.

"You are looking increasingly well," Lady Foxworth said. "How are you feeling today?"

"A little sore," Mary told her as they strolled through one of the hallways together, "but I suppose that is to be expected." Taking her aunt by the arm she added, "Thank you for all that you did for me after . . . You took very good care of me."

"Not good enough, it would seem. Had it not been for Mr. Heartly, things might have gone differently. He was right to take you down to the lake when I wanted to keep you in bed. Honestly, I cannot recall seeing a man more terrified than he was that night when he thought he might lose you." Placing her hand over Mary's she said, "He loves you a great deal."

"As I love him." They continued for a moment in silence before Mary decided to bring up a more difficult subject. "About Andrew—"

"You need not concern yourself about him."

"Of course I do! What he did to Mr. Heartly during the war is difficult to forgive, not to mention that he almost killed me." Frankly, she couldn't recall ever being so furious with someone before.

"He committed fraud," Lady Foxworth murmured, her eyes darting in every direction to ensure that nobody heard her, "against the king of all people. It would be impossible for us to keep such a secret without becoming partial to his crime, and once the truth got out, the scandal would be overwhelming. Which is why I have asked him to leave the country."

Mary's footsteps came to a halt. "Did he agree?"

Lady Foxworth nodded. "He left for Portsmouth no more than an hour ago with the intention of starting a new life for himself in America."

"Good." She was glad that Richard would finally be rid of the man who'd plagued his life for so long. "What about funds though? He will need money—some sort of income."

"Mr. Heartly has assured me that he will have enough money with which to get by until he finds employment."

Mary blinked. "Employment? I do not believe that Andrew has ever worked a day in his life."

"Then perhaps it is time he started doing so rather than relying on others for support." They resumed walking while Lady Foxworth dropped her voice to a low whisper so she could say, "Andrew has disgraced our family, Mary. Your parents will not fault me for making this decision. Especially not since Andrew was in agreement. He seemed genuinely remorseful when he left."

"I think you made the right decision. In fact, I am relieved to know that Andrew will no longer be close enough to hurt those that I care about."

"Or you," Lady Foxworth stated. "He almost killed you, Mary!"

"Believe me, I am aware. His recklessness is unparalleled by anyone else I have ever known. To think that he almost robbed me of my life when it is only just beginning . . . I doubt I will ever be able to forgive him for that." Blinking back the tears that threatened, she quietly said, "But in spite of my anger, I fear that I will one day regret not saying good-bye to him. I suppose I just wish that I would have had the chance to do so. After all, he is my brother and if he is leaving for America, I doubt that I will ever see him again."

"That is probably true, but when I mentioned saying good-bye to you, he said that he would rather write." Lady Foxworth sighed. "If you must know, I believe he was too ashamed to face you after everything that has happened."

"I suppose so," Mary muttered feeling raw inside. Neither of them chose to mention that even now Andrew was taking the cowardly way out.

"You have been a good sister to him, Mary. Indeed, you risked your reputation in order to help him." Lady Foxworth pressed her lips together. "I do wish that you would have come to me for help though."

"In retrospect, that would probably have been a wise decision."

"One that would have stopped you from seeking out the stage."

A smile flickered across Mary's lips. "The truth is, I quite enjoyed performing at the opera. It gave me a feeling of accomplishment."

"I suppose that makes sense," Lady Foxworth said. Looking at Mary, she added, "You are aware that you will have to stop performing now?"

Mary shrugged one shoulder. "Of course. In fact, I doubt I will miss it very much since I am to marry Mr. Heartly. I certainly will not require the extra funds. Besides, Mr. Heartly says that he will happily lend an ear whenever I feel like singing, which I daresay will be just as rewarding. You see, it was never the fame that I sought, but rather the freedom to do what I loved."

"And you feared that I would judge you if I found out."

"I knew that you would."

Lady Foxworth sniffed slightly. "You are probably correct. That said, I would have helped Andrew to the best of my ability. Within reason, of course."

"Which is what Mr. Heartly seems to have done."

"And what might that be?" A masculine voice asked from directly behind Mary's right shoulder. Turning, she found Richard gazing down at her with a warm glow in his eyes. Her stomach instantly flipped itself inside out.

"I—"

"If you will forgive me," Lady Foxworth said, interrupting Mary, "I believe I see Mr. Thomas Young over there. Please excuse me."

"It looks as though your aunt is embarking on a romance of her own," Richard said as soon as Lady Foxworth was out of earshot.

"I believe she is quite smitten," Mary agreed, accepting the arm that Richard was offering her. "I hope it works out." They continued toward the French doors and out into the garden. "My aunt tells me that you have given my brother financial support so that he may start a new life for himself in America. Honestly, I cannot begin to tell you how grateful I am for that, especially after all the damage he has caused."

"Think nothing of it," he said, raising her hands

to his lips for a kiss. "Instead, let us consider this chapter involving your brother closed." Lowering her hands, he told her candidly, "I have spoken with Lamont and have asked for his forgiveness. As expected, he was not very pleased to discover that the guilt he has felt for the past five years was unfounded, though he did seem to understand my reasoning."

She breathed a sigh of relief. "Does this mean that the past is finally behind us?"

"I believe so. In fact, I would like nothing better than to start discussing our future in greater detail." A soft tremor whispered down Mary's spine. More so as he leaned closer and murmured in her ear, "In case you were wondering, I find that I am looking forward to our wedding night with great anticipation."

Heat rose to her cheeks and she instinctively dropped her gaze. Even so, she could not help but be completely honest with him and say, "So am I."

"Then perhaps it is time for me to call the vicar so we can say our vows?"

Looking up, her heart almost burst with love for him. "I think that would be a most excellent idea."

His response was immediate, his arms reaching around her and pulling her off her feet. Swinging her in a wide arc, his mouth drew into a roguish grin. "Whoever would have thought that you and I would end up like this?"

Laughing, she did not care that several guests had stopped to stare at them, no doubt appalled by their behavior. "I had my suspicions."

"You did not," he countered.

"Very well," she agreed as they started back

toward the house, "but I am glad that you chose to attend the masquerade that evening *and* that you asked me to dance. Had you not, this story of ours might have turned out very differently."

"And that would have been a terrible shame," he told her seriously though his eyes conveyed a great deal of humor.

She could not disagree with him. Indeed, she had never been happier, because she knew now that she had found the perfect man with whom to spend the rest of her life, and it was the most wonderful and extraordinary feeling in the world.

The service, which was lovely in its simplicity, took place the next day at the Thorncliff chapel. It was followed by a small breakfast, shared only with immediate family and close friends and culminating with a delicious strawberry cake served with champagne.

"Shall we go for a stroll before readying ourselves for tonight's ball?" Fiona asked with that bouncy tone of excitement that seemed to define her.

Mary looked to her husband. "That would be—"

"A lovely suggestion, to be sure," Richard said, cutting Mary off as he placed his hand against her elbow, "but Mrs. Heartly should probably get some rest first. You must not forget that she has endured a great deal lately."

Mary simply nodded, aware that her husband was deliberately trying to get her alone. The thought sent a rush of heat straight through her.

"Of course," Fiona said, looking instantly apologetic.

Lady Duncaster on the other hand merely snorted and said, "Some rest indeed!" Which of course made Mary's cheeks burn.

"Come," Richard said, pulling Mary away from the others. "Nobody will fault us for wanting to enjoy a little privacy."

Arriving upstairs only minutes later, they headed toward the suite that Lady Duncaster had allocated them now that they were married. "Oh," Mary said as she stepped inside. "This is . . . perfect!" The door closed with a quiet click behind her.

"I have to agree with you," Richard murmured, his voice conveying all that she desired as it rolled through her: comfort, acceptance, love.

Glancing in his direction, the sensation expanded, tightening her skin with awareness as the warmth of his gaze slid over her. "Will you always flatter me?" The words were softly spoken—a silver thread of emotion extending between them.

He took a moment, appearing to consider the question before saying, "I think I might."

Chuckling, she spun toward the window and pulled the translucent curtain aside so she could look out. "You are incorrigible."

She listened to his footsteps against the carpet, her breath hitching a fraction as he stepped up behind her, encasing her in his strength. Placing his chin against the top of her head, he pulled her closer—so close that she could feel the rise and fall of his chest against her back. "Would you prefer me not to be?"

"No. I would never want you to be anything other than who you are."

A moment of silence followed before he quietly asked, "How are you feeling?"

"Better," she said, her voice a little more timid than before. It couldn't be helped. Not when his fingers were playing softly against her arm. The effect was almost dizzying.

"Well enough for this?" he asked. Gently, as if he feared he might break her, he touched his lips to her temple, scorching a path down over her cheek.

Surrendering with a sigh of pleasure, she leaned further into his embrace.

"How about for this?"

His lips touched the curve where her neck met her shoulder and she immediately shivered. "Yes." The word misted across the windowpane. Releasing the curtain, she allowed it to slip between her fingers and fall back into place before turning in her husband's arms.

His hands glided over her, a delicate touch reminding her of sunbeams dancing across a field of wildflowers. Skimming her fingertips across the front of his jacket, she drew a shuddering breath before winding her arms around his neck. Her eyes met his. They were dark like the night, but filled with profound wonder. "I love you." His honesty brought her lips to his—a precious kiss wrought from the knowledge that their hopes and dreams had been fulfilled. They had each other now, their hearts in perfect harmony, beating in time to the concert that now encompassed their lives.

"I love you too," she whispered, her breath caressing the edge of his jaw. The words brought movement to his fingers, their touch like dewdrops upon the ground as they unfastened the buttons at the back of her gown.

Heat licked the length of her spine the moment his hands touched her shoulders, hovering briefly before nudging away the sleeves. Her gown, so light and airy, floated to the floor where it was met by her shift and stays.

"Exquisite." The raw emotion with which he spoke drove away the anxiety that came from being so utterly exposed. Instead, she savored the feel of his hands sliding over her, caressing her and loving her with all that he was.

When he kissed her again, she welcomed it, conveying with every fiber of her being the longing that was in her heart, and as their breaths merged into one, he gathered her carefully in his arms and carried her to the bed, lowering her against the pristine white pillows.

Heat bloomed in her cheeks as she watched him undress, her curious gaze absorbing his strength and vitality, her brow puckering at the sight of the scars that continued down the side of his neck and over his chest. Registering his awareness of her regard, she held out her hand, willing him to come closer. He did so swiftly, his bare feet padding across the hardwood floor until he arrived at her side, his fingers touching hers as though they held the secret to everlasting life. "I am sorry for what happened to you," she said as she drew him closer, "but the scars are a part of you now—a part of the man who can make me forget all else. They do not alter my feelings for you."

His eyes—those dark, dark eyes—shimmered like a starlit sky. "You are a Godsend, Mary. I swear to you that I will always do everything in my power to make you happy."

The mattress dipped beneath his weight as he sat down beside her, his closeness producing a delicious swirl of emotion in the pit of her belly. "I have no idea of what to do," she hesitantly confessed.

Leaning over her, he placed a tender kiss to her forehead. "Yes, you do. You are just not aware of it yet."

"But what if I do something wrong?"

His eyes widened a fraction, his expression bordering on incredulity. Slowly, he shook his head, conveying without words how impossible that would be. "Just love me as I intend to love you, and all will be well, Mary. I promise you."

Nodding, she accepted his reasoning, her arms coming around his neck and drawing him closer. Tentatively, he ran his hand along the length of her in long easy strokes, caressing her until glowing embers sparked against her skin. Running his mouth down over her, he kissed her with reverence until she sighed with pleasure, her fingers mapping him in irresistible exploration.

As soon as she was ready, he lowered himself over her and drew her to him, uniting them both in the simplest way possible while golden rays of sunshine shimmered across the walls in a mystical movement of light. It was gradual, and it was attentive, their fingers weaving together while words of endearment whispered between them.

"I am yours."

"Until the end of time."

Chapter 20

Later that evening, dressed in a daring red gown that Richard had purchased for her as a wedding gift, Mary arrived in the Thorncliff ballroom, escorted there by her husband who was looking very dashing in his evening black. At his request, she had declined the use of feathers and dressed her hair in a simple style with a mother-of-pearl comb as the only adornment.

"You are without a doubt the loveliest lady in the room, Mrs. Heartly," Richard spoke close to her ear, the sound of his voice tickling her insides.

"In my opinion, I am the luckiest." She smiled up at him while he guided her forward. "No other lady here can claim to have a husband as handsome as you. Indeed, I am sure that all the young debutantes here must be quite envious of me."

Chuckling, he snatched a glass of champagne from a passing tray and handed it to her. "Perhaps I should invite one of them to dance?"

"Perhaps," she agreed, taking a sip of the bubbly liquid and enjoying the fizz skipping along her tongue. "But before you do, I must insist that you partner with me for the cotillion."

He didn't look thrilled with the idea. "We will have to switch partners during, which is why I would much prefer the waltz."

"There is no reason why we cannot dance both," she said. "We are married now so we may dance with each other as many times as we like during the course of one evening."

A smile followed. "Mrs. Heartly, I do believe I like the way you think." Taking her glass from her, he took a sip as well before handing it to a nearby footman. "Shall we?"

Three other couples joined them, exchanging partners as they weaved in and out, joining hands, stepping back and moving in a wide circle. When the dance was almost at an end, Richard reached for Mary and pulled her unpredictably close. One second, her feet were firmly on the floor, the next, she was being swung through the air as he spun her around, eyes bright with love for her while everyone clapped in response.

She couldn't help but laugh, her heart so full of light that it could scarcely contain it. Lowering her face toward his, her hands placed firmly upon his shoulders, she captured his lips to a cascading roar of "hurrahs!"

"I think the *ton* approves of our match," Richard grinned. Slowly, he returned Mary to a standing position, his arm wrapped loosely around her waist.

They stood like that for a moment until the claps and cheers faded and the orchestra struck up a new tune to signal the next dance. Moving aside, they were met by Sarah and Spencer. "Congratulations once again," Spencer said. A smile lit his face, but nothing conveyed how happy he was on his brother's behalf as the sheer joy shining in his eyes. Addressing Mary, he said, "I do hope that there is room on your dance card for me."

"Of course there is," she said, handing him the card and pencil so he could jot down his name.

"Just as long as you do not claim the waltz," Richard cut in.

Straightening himself, Spencer arched an eyebrow and handed the dance card back to Mary. "No need to concern yourself about that." Reaching for Sarah, he pulled her closer to his side. "If you recall, I am also recently married and intend on partnering with my viscountess for that particular dance."

"Not to intrude," Lady Duncaster said as she joined the group, "but I would like to have a private word with all of you later this evening. After supper perhaps? We can adjourn to the music room."

"Certainly," Sarah said. Leaning slightly forward, she softly inquired, "Will you tell us what this is about?"

Lady Duncaster's assessing gaze roamed over each of them. "I prefer not to speak of it here. You will discover the subject soon enough. If you will excuse me now, it is time for me to dance the quadrille with his grace, the Duke of Pinehurst."

Mary watched her drift across the floor in search of her partner. Dressed in a frothy blue gown trimmed with white lace, Lady Duncaster looked as though she'd just stepped out of the sea. Heavy bracelets encased her gloved wrists while a sapphire and diamond necklace paired with matching earrings and hairpins sent light scattering in her wake. It was difficult to imagine that she had won the archery contest during the games day four weeks earlier. A smile touched Mary's lips at the thought of what it must have been like to have known the countess in her youth.

"What do you suppose that was about?" Spencer asked, breaking the silence that had fallen over them as they'd each considered the meaning behind Lady Duncaster's request.

Richard looked to Mary. "Do you think it might have something to do with what we found?"

Uncertain of how much she ought to divulge, Mary hesitated a moment before saying, "Perhaps. But if it is, then Lady Duncaster is right to caution us about speaking of it here."

"I agree," Sarah said. "We must respect her wishes."

When Spencer opened his mouth as if to comment, Sarah stopped him with a quelling look. Instead he frowned, as did Richard. But this quickly changed with the arrival of Lady Fiona and Chadwick who were grinning as if they'd just been sharing a private joke. "What is it?" Spencer asked after eyeing them a moment.

Pressing her lips together, her eyes shimmering with mirth, Lady Fiona allowed Chadwick to answer. "I was just doing my impression of Lord Byron," he said.

"The one where he discusses poetry with Prime Minister Jenkinson?" Spencer asked.

"The very one," Chadwick said as he straightened

his spine and brushed a piece of invisible lint from his jacket.

"You do both parts?" Richard asked.

Spencer nodded. "It is one of his best jokes, though I would caution you, Chadwick, not to do it in public since I'm not entirely certain that Jenkinson would approve of being laughed at."

"It's all in good sport," Lady Fiona said. Having gathered her wits, she'd apparently decided to defend Chadwick even though he didn't look the least bit concerned about Spencer's comment.

"I would certainly like to hear it sometime," Sarah said.

"As would I," Mary agreed.

"Perhaps tomorrow when there are fewer people about?" Richard suggested.

Chadwick's expression grew wary. "It's more of an impromptu thing that I do on occasion when it feels right. I cannot promise that it will be equally good when planned. Especially not since your expectations at this point will probably exceed the performance."

"If your delivery remains unchanged, then there is no doubt in my mind that they will find it equally amusing," Lady Fiona said. She nudged Chadwick with her elbow, reminding everyone else that she was still a novice when it came to ballroom protocol.

Edging slightly away from her, Chadwick looked to Mary. "I was wondering if I might have the honor of dancing with the bride."

She couldn't help but chuckle in response to his flamboyant tone. "Spencer has just secured the cotillion and the waltz belongs to my husband, but perhaps a country dance?"

"Splendid!" Chadwick announced, accepting the dance card that Mary handed to him so he could scribble his name.

"It looks as though it is time for that cotillion you just mentioned," Spencer said with a nod toward the dance floor. Stepping away from Sarah, he offered Mary his arm. Exchanging a loving gaze with Richard, she accepted and allowed her brother-in-law to lead her forward.

Richard watched her go, unable to resist smiling at the thought of the secret they shared. To think that Lucia Cavalani was presently dancing with his brother . . . The idea was too preposterous for words. Shaking his head, he didn't even realize that Chadwick had secured the same dance with Sarah, leaving him alone with Fiona who was studying him with great interest.

"What is it?" she asked. "You look as though you are about to start laughing at any moment."

"I'm just happy," he said, hoping to leave it at that. "Knowing that I am married to the most wonderful woman in the world fills me with such joy, Fiona."

She tilted her head slightly and looked toward Mary who was now laughing in response to something Chadwick had said. "I think you have chosen very well, Richard. She makes a fine addition to this family. Everyone agrees."

"Everyone?"

"The rest of our sisters and Mama and Papa too. They are so thrilled for you, not to mention happy to have you back in our midst. Mama suffered greatly because of your self-imposed isolation."

"I know," he said, his heart a little heavier than before, "but it was unavoidable. I was desperately unhappy when I returned to England—furious too, as you can no doubt understand. It took a miracle for me to move past all of that."

"In other words, it took Mary," Fiona said. Her eyes danced with amusement as she looked up, meeting his gaze.

He gave her a concrete nod. "Precisely."

A small pause followed while they watched the dancers. "I wonder who will be next to get married," Fiona then said. "If this pattern continues, Rachel, Emily, and Laura will leave Thorncliff with husbands of their own."

Richard slanted a look in Fiona's direction. She was not standing still, as a young lady ought to. Instead, her foot was impatiently tapping the beat of the music. At eighteen years of age, it was clear that she had not yet let go of her childhood completely. And yet, her figure was undeniably that of a young woman. In fact, now that he really looked at her without being distracted by the silliness that often defined her character, there was no denying that she would soon turn the heads of countless gentlemen. With this in mind, he couldn't help but ask, "What about you?"

With a dismissive snort she gave him a look of complete incredulity. "I have only just had my first Season so there is no rush as far as I am concerned. Besides, I can think of no man whom I would be able to tolerate for an indefinite amount of time and no man capable of tolerating me. Perhaps when I am older I will think differently about it?"

"Especially if the right man comes along," Richard agreed.

Her gaze returned to the dance floor. "Do you know, I have always thought that Chadwick and Laura would be very well suited for each other."

It took a second for Richard to process this idea. He looked toward his brother's closest friend—the man who'd been part of the Heartly family for so long. "Chadwick and Laura?" Was Fiona really that clueless? "I was not aware that they favored each other's company."

"Perhaps I ought to do something about that," Fiona murmured.

Raising an eyebrow, Richard turned to her. "Fiona, I have always liked Chadwick—ever since Spencer first brought him home with him from Eaton for the holidays—but having had no contact with him in recent years, I am curious to know what your opinion of him might be." Hesitating briefly, he chose his next words carefully. "Now that you are older, you might be more aware of his character. In fact, it has not escaped my notice that you seem to enjoy his company quite a bit."

She laughed at that. "Chadwick is hilarious, Richard. He has the ability to make everyone laugh, which when you think about it, is quite a rare talent. As for my opinion of him, I like him very well indeed and have always considered him a brother."

Richard said nothing further. He simply wondered how long it would take for Fiona to realize that the relationship she had with Chadwick was very dif-

ferent from what she thought it to be. Indeed, the
look in Chadwick's eye when she'd nudged him and
the way in which he'd added distance between them,
was telling. Making a mental note to mention it to
Spencer, Richard waited for his wife to return from
the dance floor, her eyes sparking with emotion the
moment they met his.

Later, after supper had been eaten and the waltz
had been danced, Richard escorted Mary over to the
music room where they were joined by Sarah, Spencer, Chloe, Stonegate and Lady Duncaster. Having
taken their seats, they waited expectantly for their
hostess to tell them why she'd asked them to join her.

"Since your arrival," Lady Duncaster began, her
gaze traveling to each of them in turn, "you have
discovered something relating to the past. I think it
might be time for you to share these discoveries with
each other if there is to be any hope of ever finding
the box that the late Earl of Oakland came here to
retrieve."

Spencer leaned forward. "The one my grandmother wrote of in her diary? You have proof that
it is here?"

Lady Duncaster looked to Richard and nodded for
him to continue. He turned to his brother. "Before
we were married, my wife and I discovered an underground villa that can be accessed from the tunnels
beneath Thorncliff."

"An underground villa?" Chloe looked thoroughly
intrigued.

"It appears to have been built by Romans originally, but seems to have been used in more recent years by The Cardinals as some sort of base." Realizing he was jumping ahead, Richard closed his eyes for a moment before explaining, "The Third Earl of Duncaster, our late grandfather, and Grand Mama's sister, the Duchess of Marveille, were working against an evil organization known as The Electors during the time of the French Revolution."

"The same organization that Stonegate and I were recently trying to uncover," Chloe muttered.

Frowning, Richard looked to Spencer and then to Stonegate. "I was not aware."

For the next half hour, Chloe and Stonegate took turns informing Richard and Mary of the events that had taken place only two weeks earlier. "Hainsworth's betrayal has been difficult to accept," Stonegate said in reference to the man who'd raised him, "but at least there is some comfort to be had in knowing that The Electors have finally been brought to justice."

"What astounds me," Lady Duncaster said, "is the amount of control The Electors seem to have wielded and this new discovery that my father-in-law was waging a covert war against them. I have seen the villa that Heartly and his wife have found. It is unfathomable to think that it has not been discovered sooner. However . . ." She looked to each of them in turn. "The information the villa provides will hopefully enable us to put together the pieces of a puzzle that we have all been hoping to unravel for some time."

"A few weeks ago," Spencer said, "Sarah and I found an earring in one of the tunnels. Lady Duncaster insists that it belonged to the Duchess of

Marveille, offering further proof that the box of heirlooms our grandmother was meant to receive did indeed arrive here. With your recent findings in mind, Heartly, I would suggest that we start conducting a more thorough search."

The door to the salon swung open at that moment, revealing a rather befuddled looking Earl of Montsmouth. "I . . . ah . . . forgive me for intruding. I was not aware that the room was occupied." Stepping back, he shut the door as quickly as he had opened it, his arrival and departure so hasty that it was as if he'd never been there at all.

"That was odd," Sarah commented after a moment of silence.

"I have always found him to be a bit of a strange fellow," Spencer said. "Pleasant enough, but definitely one of my more peculiar acquaintances."

"Regarding the box," Chloe said, bringing everyone's attention back to the subject at hand, "I would like to try and find it before we leave Thorncliff."

"Agreed," Richard stated. "As long as Lady Duncaster approves, that is."

Lady Duncaster gave an elaborate shrug. "None of you seemed to require my permission before when you decided to go sneaking around secret passageways, looking through the attic or going through my late husband's and father-in-law's personal belongings." She held up a hand, silencing their attempts to explain. "The point is that I will allow you to continue your quest on one condition—that you also do your best to find out who the fourth member of The Cardinals was and how my father-in-law and your grandfather died."

"We know that their ship capsized," Spencer said.

Lady Duncaster shook her head. "A mere detail, I can assure you." When nobody spoke, she added, "With Mr. and Mrs. Heartly's recent discoveries in mind, I suspect that the shipwreck was not an accident at all, but that my father-in-law and your grandfather were both murdered."

Although she knew that Richard had suspected this too, Mary couldn't help but notice how rigid he'd gone when Lady Duncaster had made this final pronouncement. Reaching for his hand, she leaned slightly closer to him and whispered, "We will figure this out together."

He relaxed with a deep exhalation. "We will certainly try."

Glancing up, she caught the sparkle in his eyes and instinctively squeezed his hand. "Sounds like another adventure."

The edge of his mouth twitched. "Perhaps this time there will be a ghost at the bottom of a pit."

She shuddered at the thought of it even as she smiled. "Will you rescue me if there is?"

"Of course," he murmured, his gaze holding hers as the rest of the world shrank away. "I will always do so, Mary, my angel of the night."

Epilogue

London, 1821

Seated on a plush velvet seat in the Oakland box at the King's Theatre, Mary stared down at the stage on which she'd stood so many times before. It almost seemed like a distant memory now with all that had happened since her last performance. Leaning back, she turned toward her husband, his expression somewhat anxious as he gazed out over the crowd. "Don't be nervous," she whispered as she reached for his hand and laced her fingers through his. "There is no reason for it."

He nodded tightly, paused for a second, and then dipped his head toward hers. "Muzio Clementi is here." Jerking his chin a little, he indicated the spot where the Italian composer was seated.

"I would consider that a compliment if I were you," she said, raising her opera glasses for a closer look.

"He has played with Mozart," Richard stated. "Indeed, it is a well-known fact that Mozart borrowed Clementi's B-flat major sonata for the overture of *The Magic Flute*!"

Slanting a look in Richard's direction, Mary couldn't help but smile. "From what I hear, Mozart was not the least bit impressed by Clementi." She brushed her thumb against the top of his hand in an effort to reassure him. "You are ready for this, Richard. The pieces you have written are absolutely marvelous, and if Clementi fails to realize this, then I daresay there must be something wrong with his hearing."

He laughed at that. "In truth, the only opinion that matters to me is yours."

"And I adore your music," she said. "So does Katharine, by the way. Your playing never fails to soothe her."

He smiled lovingly at the mention of his daughter's name. "Perhaps we should start considering a brother for her." His hand closed warmly around Mary's, the look in his eyes more mischievous than before.

She couldn't help the blush that followed or the jittery feeling in the pit of her belly as she gazed back up at him. The effect he had on her was really quite scandalous. If only they didn't have to wait three full hours until they could be alone again.

Beneath them, the orchestra finally started to play, notes swirling through the air until they soared high above them, dancing beneath the ceiling. A woman appeared on the stage, her voice accompanying the song just as Mary's had done so many times before.

"She is very good," Mary whispered, aware of the audience's rapt attention. It filled her heart with pride and happiness, because experience told her that this was going to be one of those performances that people would speak of for years after—Mr. Heartly's first showing of *The Masquerade*.

"Perhaps," he murmured with a shrug. "But she is not you, and in my eyes, nobody else can possibly compare."

"You spoil me with your flattery." She spoke with laughter in her voice.

Raising her hand to his lips he placed a tender kiss upon her knuckles. "Would you rather I stop doing so?"

"Only if you wish to divest me of my vanity."

His eyes darkened a fraction. "I can think of a number of things that I would like to divest you of, my lady, but your vanity is not one of them." His voice was low, rippling through her and heightening her awareness. "No one is more modest than you, Mary. You are perfection in every conceivable way."

"As are you," she whispered back, "which makes us very fortunate indeed to have found one another. Can you imagine the alternative?"

Chuckling lightly, he shook his head. "Indeed I cannot."

Neither could Mary. The way in which they had met and the events that had happened since, seemed to have been orchestrated with the sole purpose of leading them both to this exact moment in time. It was miraculous, in a way, given the odds initially stacked against them.

With her hand placed comfortably in her husband's, Mary closed her eyes and allowed the music to guide her back to Thorncliff, to the night of the masquerade and to when they'd first met. He'd been a stranger then, asking to share her company. Now, little more than a year later, he had become the most constant part of her life—the father of her child and the only man she would ever love, until her dying day.

Author's Note

I'm always surprised by some of the incredible information that I come across during the course of writing a book. When I began work on this one, I knew that I wanted my heroine to be a covert opera singer, but in order for the plot to work and for her to be able to support her brother financially, her income had to be substantial. So I began digging until I came across Angelica Catalani on whom I've based my heroine.

Unlike Mary, Angelica was not of noble birth but the daughter of a tradesman. She debuted at the opera in Venice at the age of sixteen—the beginning of a career that would span for almost thirty years and with a voice so full, powerful and clear that Angelica was capable of executing even the most difficult songs with a natural charm that has rarely been equaled since.

As her fame grew, Angelica traveled throughout Europe, oftentimes by royal request. She arrived in England in 1806 where she signed her first engagement with the King's Theatre in Haymarket at a salary of £2,000 for her first season, equivalent to almost $178,000 today. Now, I know that Mary mentions much higher earnings (£5,000 per annum with a total profit of £16,700 after including additional revenue received from tours). These numbers are actually an accurate reflection of Angelica Catalani's earnings for the year 1807, an astounding $1,483,893.89 today and an exorbitant sum for any single artist to receive during that period.

Other references to historical figures in the book include Mr. Taylor who managed the King's Theatre from 1793 until 1821 and Mr. Thomas Young whom I took the liberty of including as Lady Foxworth's potential love interest. He was an incredible scientist during the Regency period, a polyglot who established the wave theory of light and provided the translation of the Rosetta stone that made it possible to decipher the ancient Egyptian hieroglyphs. Additionally, he described the characteristics of elasticity, developed a formula for determining the drug dosage for children and has even been called the founder of physiological optics.

Personally, I'm fascinated by these real-life stories and simply love incorporating them into my books, not only because I want to share my findings with my readers, but also because I feel as though these factual tidbits help in the portrayal of the time period in which I'm writing.

I hope that you agree.

Acknowledgments

Writing is a continuous learning experience—a journey of the imagination—and because of this, there are moments when I find myself stumbling, overthinking an issue, or simply coming to a complete standstill. Thankfully, I work with an extraordinary group of people who always help me get back on my feet, point me in the right direction, or give me that extra push that I need. Each and every one of them deserves my deepest thanks and gratitude, because when all is said and done, a book isn't the work of just one person, but of many.

I'd like to thank my wonderful editor, Erika Tsang and her assistant, Chelsey Emmelhainz, for being so incredibly helpful and easy to talk to—working with both of you is an absolute pleasure!

Together with the rest of the Avon team which includes (but is far from limited to) copyeditor, Nan Reinhardt, publicists, Katie Steinberg, Emily Homonoff, Caroline Perny, Pam Spengler-Jaffee and Jessie Edwards, and senior director of marketing, Shawn Nicholls, they have offered guidance and support whenever it was needed. My sincerest thanks to all of you for being so wonderful!

Another person who must be acknowledged for his talent is artist James Griffin, who has created the stunning cover for this book, capturing not only the feel of the story but also the way in which I envisioned the characters looking—you've done such a beautiful job!

To my fabulous beta readers, Dee Foster, Kathy Nye, Doris Henderson, Cerian Halford and Marla Golladay, whose insight has been tremendously helpful in strengthening the story, thank you so much!

I would also like to thank Nancy Mayer for her assistance. Whenever I was faced with a question regarding the Regency era that I couldn't answer on my own, I turned to Nancy for advice. Her help has been invaluable.

My family and friends deserve my thanks as well, especially for reminding me to take a break occasionally, to step away from the computer and just unwind—I would be lost without you.

And to you, dear reader—thank you so much for taking the time to read this story. Your support is, as always, hugely appreciated!